Praise for Robin W. Pearson

"With her distinctive voice and gorgeous insights, wordsmith Robin W. Pearson takes a brave and deep journey through the tall weeds of a family's old pain, nagging fears, and challenging choices—painting a portrait of the path any willing family can take to finally walk into the promise of courageous, new life. Her invitation is beautiful, offered to our broken world at just the right time."

PATRICIA RAYBON, award-winning author of *All That Is Secret* and *I Told the Mountain to Move: Learning to Pray So Things Change*, on *Walking in Tall Weeds*

"There's a special kind of musicality to Southern fiction that delights my mind, and Robin W. Pearson's novels never fail to sing directly to my heart. . . . She's given us another gift in her newest, *Walking in Tall Weeds*. . . . Pearson invites us—a large family from different backgrounds, skin tones, experiences—to tune our ears to the song of unity and forgiveness that is only possible through the power of Christ. Robin W. Pearson's voice is strong and powerful. Listen up! You don't want to miss a note!"

SUSIE FINKBEINER, author of *The Nature of Small Birds* and *Stories That Bind Us*

"In her latest novel, *Walking in Tall Weeds*, Pearson weaves together a rich tapestry of Southern charm while exposing issues often hidden behind polite dialect. Where families will finally see the importance of looking at their past through a lens of awareness in order to do better, instead of allowing the past to rob them of the joy of the here and now."

T. I. LOWE, bestselling author of *Under the Magnolias*

"When I read Robin W. Pearson's latest, I saw my own heart. She mixes life's pain with Duke's mayonnaise and smoked sausages and drop biscuits. And in the tapestry she weaves with words, I find what I hold on to, what I need to set free, and the striving in between."

CHRIS FABRY, bestselling author of *A Piece of the Moon*, on *Walking in Tall Weeds*

"Robin W. Pearson has a gift for capturing the complexity and nuances of family relationships. She brings a remarkable tenderness and compassion to the struggle we all face to know and be known in a family. Prepare yourself for a rich and satisfying read!"

SARAH LOUDIN THOMAS, award-winning author of *The Right Kind of Fool,* on *Walking in Tall Weeds*

"Pearson delivers a satisfying tale of one woman's secrets returning to haunt her. . . . Pearson's excellent characters and plotting capture the complexity and beauty of family, the difficulty of rectifying mistakes, and the healing that comes from honesty. Pearson rises to another level with this excellent story."

Publishers Weekly on *'Til I Want No More*

"With help from her community, Maxine learns that by confronting her tangled past, she can face her future and discover her true self. Uplifting faith-based messages are included throughout, and the story's easy pace allows time to take in each lesson."

BookPage on *'Til I Want No More*

"This novel's slow pace allows readers to gain valuable insight into Maxine as she braves a great deal of soul-searching. A heartfelt tale about faith and family, readers can walk toward the altar with Maxine Owens as she tends to her past wounds."

Deep South magazine on *'Til I Want No More*

"*'Til I Want No More* feels like an extended afternoon at a family reunion barbecue, complete with mouthwatering food, spilled family secrets, and voices of faith that never lose hope. This brilliantly written story reminds us that God is bigger than the struggles that all families face, yet as a woman of color, I love that Robin's courageous characters look and sound like me."

BARB ROOSE, speaker and author of *Surrendered: Letting Go and Living like Jesus* and *Joshua: Winning the Worry Battle*

"Robin W. Pearson has done it again—she truly knows how to captivate her readers and have them eagerly turning each page, anticipating what is going to happen next. *'Til I Want No More* is no exception. Maxine's journey of love, longing, and finding her identity and worth is relatable to so many women, all of whom will be able to resonate with the many emotions of this bride-to-be as she seeks to find the joy and sense of belonging she's been missing."

ANGELIA WHITE STONE, CEO and editor of *Hope for Women* magazine

"Pearson writes strong characters who wrap their arms around you and pull you into the family circle, a hubbub of loyalty, secrets, faith, and yes, forgiveness. Nobody's perfect—but maybe that's the best theme woven through this book."

BETH K. VOGT, award-winning author of the Thatcher Sisters series, on *'Til I Want No More*

"Pearson's excellent debut explores forgiveness and the burden of secrets. . . . Pearson's saga is enjoyable and uncomfortable, but also funny and persistent in the way that only family can be."

Publishers Weekly, starred review of *A Long Time Comin'*

"Pearson delivers a poignant debut that explores the faith of one African American family. . . . The writing is strong, and the story is engaging, and readers will be pleased to discover a new voice in Southern inspirational fiction."

Booklist on *A Long Time Comin'*

"Robin W. Pearson's debut novel is a contemporary fiction master-piece. . . . Set in North Carolina, readers will feel the heat, smell the food, and hear the bees buzzing in the background. . . . Pearson has created a story that makes you feel like you're in the same room as the characters. Do not miss this one."

CHRISTIAN FICTION ADVISOR on *A Long Time Comin'*

"Readers will cry, laugh, sigh wistfully, and even rage a little at this moving story. *A Long Time Comin'* is a wonderful tale of love, family, secrets, relationships, and forgiveness that will teach us all how to live well in the midst of real life."

The Banner magazine

"Robin W. Pearson delivers a fresh new voice for Southern fiction, treating readers to an inspiring journey through the complex matters of the heart."

JULIE CANTRELL, *New York Times* and *USA Today* bestselling author

"Robin W. Pearson's authentic faith and abundant talent shine through in this wholehearted novel. Bee and Evelyn will stir your heart and stay with you long after the last page of *A Long Time Comin'* is turned."

MARYBETH MAYHEW WHALEN, author of *Only Ever Her*

"Robin W. Pearson's singular style and fully realized cast of characters ring proudly throughout this novel. Her masterful voice is a welcome addition to the genre of family sagas rooted in hope and faith."

LIZ JOHNSON, bestselling author of *The Red Door Inn*, on *A Long Time Comin'*

"*A Long Time Comin'* is a tender and sweet story of a cantankerous grandmother and her dear family members. . . . Her characters are charming, endearing, and flawed. I hope we have many years to come of reading Pearson's work."

KATARA PATTON, author

Walking in Tall Weeds

Walking in Tall Weeds

Robin W. Pearson

Tyndale House Publishers
Carol Stream, Illinois

Visit Tyndale online at tyndale.com.

Visit Robin W. Pearson's website at robinwpearson.com.

Tyndale and Tyndale's quill logo are registered trademarks of Tyndale House Ministries.

Walking in Tall Weeds

Designed by Lindsey Bergsma

Edited by Kathryn S. Olson

Published in association with the literary agency of Books & Such Literary Management, 52 Mission Circle, Suite 122, PMB 170, Santa Rosa, CA 95409.

Walking in Tall Weeds is a work of fiction. Where real people, events, establishments, organizations, or locales appear, they are used fictitiously. All other elements of the novel are drawn from the author's imagination.

For information about special discounts for bulk purchases, please contact Tyndale House Publishers at csresponse@tyndale.com or call 1-855-277-9400.

Library of Congress Cataloging-in-Publication Data

A catalog record for this book is available from the Library of Congress.

ISBN 978-1-4964-5371-6 (HC)

ISBN 978-1-4964-5372-3 (SC)

Printed in the United States of America

28	27	26	25	24	23	22
7	6	5	4	3	2	1

To the one true God,

who knows my heart,

and my one and only Eddie,

who makes it beat faster.

"Behold, You desire truth in the inward parts,

And in the hidden part

You will make me to know wisdom."

PSALM 51:6

Chapter One

When Paulette was six years old, her daddy tried to explain how a half-baked plan was as bad as no plan at all. Worse even.

"Those teachers should've known better than to send the children out willy-nilly. Pure foolishness." Harold Burdell stood there outside Greater Hope, one hand clasping her shoulder, the other fisted on his right hip. Around them, the ocean of grass undulated in the spring breeze, wrapping around the churchyard and the sprinkle of broken-down headstones that poked like alabaster-colored mushrooms through the earth.

Paulette paid him about two cents' worth of attention as she watched all the Easter eggs get snatched up by the older Sunday school students. Her breath hitched, making her head rock back in a mournful rhythm. She rubbed the spot in the middle of her chest where another rambunctious child's elbow had poked her.

Her daddy tipped back the brim of his tan bowler and he knelt, one leg hovering over the springy fescue, just shy of a stain. "What's the good in cryin' over some dyed eggs? The whole church knows Sister Franklin don't have enough sense to tuck any extra under that fancy Easter bonnet of hers."

Briny drops coursed over the rough thumb he brushed across Paulette's cheek. "Now, dry those tears, and let this day be a lesson to you about the importance of layin' out your steps and followin' 'em. It makes it harder to fall. That's a powerful lesson I wish somebody had taught me when I was your age. It would've saved you and me both a heck of a lot more heartache in life than cryin' over some hard-boiled eggs."

Paulette had promptly dumped out most of her daddy's advice along with the artificial dirt and grass in her berib-boned, empty Easter basket. What had tried to take root in her mind, she'd plucked like a weed. Sticking to a plan never became her forte. Yet she had learned not to cry when her world didn't look the way she wanted it to.

Now, nearly fifty-four years later, as she squinted at the stack of electric-pink sticky notes in her hand, she could hear her daddy's *tsk, tsk,* chiding Paulette for lacking the foresight to retrieve her reading glasses before electing to work outside. It made no never mind, she decided, shaking off the rebuke. She had a clear understanding of what she was writing even if she had to squint to see it.

1. Work.

2. The flight.

3. Ask about Kerry . . . Kristy . . . Katina? His girlfr—

Whirrrrr. Paulette's hand froze. A hummingbird with a shimmering, deep-purple throat hovered barely five feet away, just above the boxwood shrub flanking the brick patio attached to the house. Its head jerked one way, then the other, its charcoal bead of an eye taking stock of Paulette. After a few seconds, without visiting either of the orange feeders dangling from wire on the left and right of her, the palm-size bird vanished in the canopy of hickory, maple, pine, and oak trees enfolding the house.

Paulette finished writing *-iend*. But something about that compound word didn't sit right with her. She studied it for a heartbeat or two before drawing a bold X through the first syllable and underlining the *friend* that remained. Then she sat back and soaked in the quiet of the morning, much as the thirsty blades of grass drank up the dew, and tapped the pen against the glass table.

The gentle, far-off calls of the larks, swallows, and warblers contributed to the hush surrounding Paulette. A grateful interloper, she eyed the hazy gray-blue of the sky framing the North Carolina side of the not-too-distant Blue Ridge Mountains before jotting down a few more thoughts that she pressed to the table one by one.

4. His flying lessons! Did he start those?
5. The plants—

"Ahh!" A firm squeeze on both shoulders sent Paulette's pen clattering to the brick pavers. She leaped to her feet, a paper square adhered to her index and middle fingers, and faced a pair of deep-set brown eyes she always felt could swallow her whole. "Frederick Baldwin, you liked to scared me to death!"

Her husband raised a brow; two lines creased the otherwise-smooth milk chocolate of his forehead. "'Liked to'? I must have, because you sound like the old Paulette who grew up in eastern North Carolina."

"That's because the new Paulette livin' in Hickory Grove nearly fainted dead away. You know I hate surprises. Shame on you, Fred." She wondered if he could hear the pop her knees made as she squatted to retrieve the pen.

"I didn't realize you were swimming around in those thoughts of yours. What's all this?" Fred peeled a note from the glass.

Paulette grunted as she extended her arm under the chair. Her fingers brushed the silver clip on the cap before she finally hooked it with a nail. She leaned into the hand that cupped her elbow and stood. As she moved away, Fred draped an arm around her and pulled her closer, causing her nose to bump his shoulder.

"Good morning, by the way." He seemed to hesitate before dipping his head toward her.

Paulette relaxed into him but her kiss was merely a sprinkling of fairy dust on his lips. She lifted the square from his fingers and stacked them all in numbered order. "Mornin'. I see you're up and at 'em, but don't you start rushin' me. I know how you get when you have to wait." She stepped away to lift the black wrought iron chair and set it under the table. Then she faced her husband again and noted his raised arm, hanging with nothing to do, no one to comfort. She squared her shoulders to help her bear the cumbersome weight of his steady gaze. "What?"

Fred's lips contorted, nearly forming a smile before they flattened into a line under his thick mustache. He lowered his orphaned appendage and hid his hand in his pocket. "Nothing. Just admiring you." When he cleared his throat, it erased any glimmerings of thoughts from his face. "When did you start making lists?"

"I didn't. Well, not really." She fluffed up the layers of her dark-brown shoulder-length hair, wishing she could've squeezed in a trip to the salon between piano students or canceled the afternoon's lessons altogether. But no, that was nowhere near the truth. Some of those children never even thought of the piano between lessons, let alone touched one. And eight-year-old Lucy, that child's ear for music made up for her intractability. Why rearrange the afternoon to flat iron and color some nappy roots that McKinley would never notice?

His mail! I need to make sure I give him his—

"I can see your mind churning like the wings on that hummingbird over there." Fred inched back his wide white cuff to reveal his watch. The sun glinted off its crystal face. "But whatever thought you just picked up, set it down again and let it rest. We have a long drive ahead of us. You can elucidate your honey dos on the way." He hooked an index finger under the strap of her green crocheted satchel and let the bag swing gently to and fro. "That's all I was coming to do: collect my worker bee and get a move on."

"Just layin' out my steps, not makin' work for you. I thought I'd plan some talkin' points with McKinley so I don't forget what I want to say." She stuffed the notes into a leather book that still had a price tag on its cover. Then she lifted the bag from his finger and stowed everything inside.

Fred shook his head. "I wouldn't resurrect your daddy's list making, Etta."

"You don't have to worry about that. I'm only followin' what he said, not what he did. These are more like . . . ideas. Reminders. You know you and I don't have the best track record for stayin' out the weeds, Fred."

There was no give in the lists of dos and don'ts Harold Burdell had raised his daughter by, just take. Her daddy's timekeeping didn't set riverbanks that kept Paulette's life from overflowing with too much; his planning erected stultifying, narrow walls. There was always a right thing to do, which meant there was a wrong, too. Paulette had never been able to see the maybes or what-ifs that life offered every now and again because her daddy and his infernal lists blocked her view. Considering life's possibilities hadn't done him much good, and he'd tried to keep his only child from coming to the same tragic end.

Hence, her sticky notes and her new journal . . . and Fred. This was the closest she'd ever come to planning ahead. She'd do what was within her power not to mess up this time with her son.

"I know we haven't seen McKinley since he tore outta here after Christmas last year, but he'll be here long enough. You'll have plenty of time to say everything you need to say but not enough to say the things you shouldn't. By the time you get through with him, he probably won't mind a little quiet." Her husband led the way to the French door opening into the sunroom.

Suddenly Paulette grasped his hand and held it between both of hers, drawing him up short. "McKinley . . . he's finally coming home!" She flung her arms around his shoulders, pressing her curves against him, and planted a kiss on Fred's obviously shocked lips.

After a second, he recovered and gave both his arms and lips a home, however briefly.

· ᥱꙄ ·

Fred whipped into the spot nearest the section delineated as American Airlines arrivals, grateful that the airport outside

Greensboro allowed them to park close enough to see him the second he emerged through the automatic doors. It had been too long since he'd seen his boy—Frederick McKinley Baldwin Jr. His only son. His namesake. When Paulette had announced her pregnancy after years of trying, Fred had imagined himself the progenitor of a passel of Baldwins; this child's, one of many sets of hands and feet to crawl across their hardwood floors. But a post-birth emergency had inserted an exclamation point after his son, not a comma. Thank God he hadn't had to arm wrestle Paulette for that privilege to append "Junior" to his baby's name, for he was to be the only, not the first.

To think his wife needed conversation starters! Those two typically communicated whole sentences with a wink or a shrug. He glanced at Paulette, whose pen was poised over another daggone pink square stuck inside that book, tapping out little polka dots around the paper. Fred's heart tilted in her direction, and he considered leaning over and placing his lips on a spot her periwinkle sundress had left bare. Maybe they could talk about some of those "conversation starters." He probably could use a refresher course himself in the art of conversing with Junior, what he'd call his son in front of God and everybody if Paulette wouldn't have such a fit about it. In her mind, McKinley was to be a junior in name only.

He gave himself a brisk mental shake and turned away from Paulette's sun-kissed shoulder. This visit had rattled him as much as her. Instead, he combed the flow of rumbling metal carts and chattering, snatch-their-children-back-in-line, loaded-down humanity pouring from the bowels of Piedmont Triad International Airport.

Wait. Is it . . . ? Fred shifted and leaned forward in his seat as a tall, broad-shouldered figure emerged through a set of automatic sliding doors at the next bay marked for Delta, right behind a family leading a stocky, raspberry-vested dog with a smushed face. *Yes, Junior!* Paulette must have tripped up somewhere about the airline. Seeing the familiar clean-shaven jawline, Fred swallowed a suspicious tickle in the back of his nose and a grin that attempted to wrench control of his face. No need to get emotional, make the boy run for the hills.

He leaned across the console to Paulette—so engrossed in each darn tree she couldn't see the forest—and pointed out her window. Then he quickly opened the door and climbed from the car as the *ding-ding-ding* reminded him to extract the key from the ignition. Fred raised his hand to draw Junior's attention their way, across the two lanes of stop-and-go traffic between the metered lot and the sidewalk. His hand hovered at his shoulder for a second before dropping to his side. What was Junior doing—the funky chicken?

From Fred's perspective, his son was dancing in place as other travelers converged around him and his suitcase, but not before they gave him the stink eye. Two squares of side-walk in front of Junior, a white couple pulled a set of luggage, performing an odd side-to-side jiggle of their own. All the boy had to do was step off the curb to his right or jag to his left, and the man and woman could pass undeterred. Fred stood straight, lifted his chin, and reared back his shoulders, readying himself to take a direct hit in the gut for his son, if only he could.

"You'd better not put a toe off that sidewalk, Son. Not one toe." Frederick was barely aware of his lips moving as he watched the scene, of his own voice that was a decibel louder than a thought.

"Fred . . . ? What are you talking about? Who are you talking *to*?" Paulette had finally put down that infernal pen and stepped out. She braced her fingertips on the car's roof, creating a bridge for the shadows of the birds overhead to flit under. "What's set you off this time?"

He nodded in their son's direction, his eyes pinned on him. "Just thinking about how my grandfather had to dip his head and move aside when men like Clinton George walked by. Papa said he used to act like he owned the whole street, that he was entitled to be first just because God made his skin a few shades lighter or his eyes blue. Papa would squeeze my hand nice and tight, which was his way of telling me, 'Don't worry about the man. Hold on just a little while longer. God will make everything right . . .' I used to wonder if God might need a little help. He sure seemed to be taking His time."

The man. His grandfather's name for white folks in authority—particularly the George family, long-standing citizens of Hickory Grove. Papa had passed down this designation through the generations to land squarely on Frederick, who held on to the past with one hand and pulled himself up the ladder with the other. Sometimes, like his papa, he dunked the words into a reservoir of bitterness when a cup of sugar-laced coffee relaxed his tongue or a memory whispered his name. It didn't matter if Fred was sitting cross-legged on their front porch or witnessing a chance encounter like this one; the experience tasted the same. He blew air into his right cheek, chewing on the recollection like he'd sneaked a plug of Papa's Red Man tobacco and stuffed his jaw with it.

Fred's low voice seemed to speak to his own heart as much as from it. "Raise those eyes, Junior. Stand tall. Keep walkin'. Do it for Papa. Do it for me."

Paulette turned in the direction of her husband's glare. "Frederick . . ."

"I don't care how slowly you say my name, Paulette, and don't come telling me I need to love the Georges and everybody who looks like them. You know I do, even if they don't all love me. Papa didn't step off those sidewalks because he was weak; he did it because he was strong enough to take care of me. I just hope I've taught my son in such a way that he knows the time to step aside is long gone, Etta. I see the world as it is, not the way I want it to be."

And maybe just a little like the way it was. It didn't take much effort to squash that whisper of his conscience, but it wasn't so easy to turn a deaf ear to his wife.

"Your vision is clouded by memories, Frederick, and not just your own but all the ones you inherited. Only the Lord sees who we really are and what controls us. He knows what we need to hold on to and what we should set free. Down deep, where we feel the most hurt. The way you talk makes me wonder what you see and feel when you look at me."

His chest muscles constricted as he disregarded the entreaty plainly written on her face to aim an unspoken appeal of another kind in his son's direction.

Just then, a pearl Yukon XL, its finish so clean and shimmery it reflected their image, drove up and braked, blocking the Baldwins, the elder set from the younger. By the time its passengers unloaded and the truck pulled away, Junior's dancing partners had left him behind in the thinning crowd, his head bowed toward feet embedded in the concrete.

Fred expelled his breath, wondering if someway, somehow, the boy's mind had overcome his heart. For a change.

"Goodness gracious!"

Fred's hand clenched. "What is it, Paulette?"

She stood there, her fingers no longer a bridge but a muffler over her mouth. "What in the devil did he do to his hair?"

· ✃ ·

Honk!

"McKinley! Mac-*KIN*-ley!"

That couldn't be anything but his mama's voice—the sonorous alarm that used to drag him from bed on Sunday mornings when he was squeezing his eyes shut for a few extra minutes, the bugle call that had announced mealtimes, the persistent contralto that wasn't content to let him while away

Saturday afternoons on a video game. McKinley cast a final glance at the retreating matching blond heads of the couple who had unwittingly caused beads of sweat to form on the bridge of his wide nose.

As the two had approached, McKinley's right heel had caught on the wheel of his suitcase. He suspected his leg had buckled under the weight of his decision. Or rather, his indecision.

It was simple, really: step off the curb so the couple could pass, unimpeded, or train his eyes on some distant spot between and beyond them and keep his two left feet moving. Granted, they were walking on the wrong side. And technically he'd claimed this path before they'd emerged from the back seat of the black Lincoln Continental, slammed the door, and stepped onto the sidewalk. But the strangers could have been his parents—of similar age; shoulders grazing each other, though their hands were intertwined; "Frederick" sporting a gray seersucker suit, "Paulette" resplendent in a flowing, knee-length striped dress. How could he render asunder his mom and dad, for goodness' sake?

After an awkward three or four seconds the man had smiled, nodded, and tugged his companion closer until she was plastered to his hip, more intimately than the real Paulette and Fred would ever naturally choose. Conjoined, they'd glided around McKinley on his right side in a heady, perfumed wave, blending with the traffic flowing in the opposite direction—the *right* direction—away from him. And suddenly, as they strolled off, engaged in some conversation about someone who'd "served Limburger cheese and white wine," he'd felt in the wrong, like he'd turned a cold shoulder to all his mama's gentle teaching on kindness and attacked his father's sense of honor.

"McKinley!"

Again the call, the one that surely came from Paulette Baldwin. Neither the placating tone convincing him to do something he didn't want to do nor the authoritative voice denying him something he did. The sound of his name on her tongue had softened over the years—the time ticking off his life, not hers—in deference to his manhood, reflecting the change in their relationship from mama and child to mother and son who had grown too soon, at least by her estimation.

So McKinley turned toward the person waving both her hands—as if he could overlook his mother, one of the reasons he'd booked a two o'clock flight back to North Carolina—and he spied the second reason, the reason he'd fled to Pennsylvania in the first place: Frederick Baldwin Sr., squinting at him from the far side of his parked, smoky-blue Mercedes sedan. He stood tall with one arm draped across the roof of his car and his other hand propping open the driver's door.

McKinley knew his father was anything but relaxed, and the sun was nowhere near his eyes under the shady overhang of the metered lot, despite what his stance might imply to passersby. Over the years, Dad had taught him that *wait* was a four-letter word of the most obscene kind. When it was time to go, it was time, no ifs, ands, or buts. Yet out of respect for the woman whose passive, yet intrinsic lifelong aims were to resist the pressures of the clock-loving world and impress upon her husband the meaning of long-suffering, his father had learned to camouflage his impatience with narrowed eyes and perfect posture. The way McKinley imagined a panther stretched out under a banyan tree watched an impala stroll by.

McKinley sucked in thick, exhaust-tinged, Carolina-blue air through his nostrils and polluted his chest with it. Then he smoothed his blazer, the one his mama "suggested" he wear so he looked the part, not that it had earned him more than a pack of Goldfish and a miniature Coke on the short flight. He suspected his ripped, formfitting jeans would cause her all manner of stress, but the independent, mature artist within reared up at completely yielding to the part of him that ever tried and failed to simultaneously please these two, the elder Baldwins.

And yet . . . seeing them unglued McKinley's sneaker-clad feet. It also accelerated his heart rate just a touch as he strode across the road, ducking between cars blocking the white hash lines of the pedestrian crossing and travelers looking for their rides. Conflicted though he was about his trip home, he couldn't restrain the smile that stretched closer and closer to his earlobes so that, by the time he released his grip on the handle of his Samsonite case and wrapped his long arms around his mother's waist, nearly all his even, white teeth must have been showing.

Muscle memory made his knees bend just enough for

her to fit her head in the crook of his neck and her arms to encircle his shoulders, for he knew better than to form a ninety-degree angle to hug her. The first time his sixteen-year-old self had tried that, Paulette swatted his head and warned, "Boy, I'm still your mama!" McKinley closed his eyes. The past nine months looked smaller and faded faster in the rearview mirror, but gracious, they'd felt too long.

But all he murmured was "M-o-m-m-m . . . hey." Then he stepped back so she could cup his face, what she did whether it had been nine hours or nine months, and lock her clear hazel eyes with his deep-brown ones. The crinkles in the corners of her lids testified to what was always itching for a starring role on her face but what she tended to suppress, sharing her joy in teaspoonfuls rather than with a ladle. Today, though, they both grinned like they'd discovered the secret to long life and wanted the whole world to know it. Mother and son turned as one when a shadow beside them shifted and eclipsed their own.

Paulette's clenched fingers only allowed McKinley to slip his right hand free in order to clasp his father's. The elbows of the two men locked, keeping them at arm's length. McKinley nodded. "Sir."

Frederick Sr. covered their fingers with his free hand, his platinum wedding band bumping McKinley's bare knuckle. His smile was warm but emitted a lower wattage than Paulette's. "Son. You look good."

"Yes, you do, but whatcha got goin' on up here?" Dainty

fingers pulled his hair. She seemed to enjoy extending each coil and watching it spring back into place.

McKinley ducked away. "I'm growing it out, Mom . . . Kelsey twisted it for me." He dangled the name as a distraction to quell the criticism battling with curiosity for purchase in her face.

His words were the mechanism to make his mother release his hand. Her eyes widened as she pressed her flattened lips against her teeth as if trapping her words.

Clap. His father rubbed his hands together. "Why don't we get loaded and catch up in the car?"

"Speaking of . . . *Nice!*" McKinley's hand hovered just over the shiny finish of his father's latest toy. "I think this one is my favorite, by far."

"You know your daddy. If nothing else, he'll splurge on an automobile."

"It's not a splurge. Just making up for all that walking I had to do." Fred tucked his hands in his pockets, jingling the ever-present change he carried.

His father's childhood poverty, something else that was never far from him. He cradled that status like it was newly born, not a decades-old, fully grown memory. McKinley's burgeoning admiration of the car withered and died. "Hey, when was the last time you had to walk somewhere? Not counting the trip from the den to the kitchen." Though mocking, his tone was swathed in respect.

"I do know it's a long walk home, Son." Dad sounded dry despite the humidity. His words harkened back to an old joke between father and son, but the humor in the admonition had long since worn thin.

"And on that note . . ." Paulette opened the passenger door and reached down to adjust her seat.

"Yes, your mama has some surprises up her sleeve, so we'd better get moving. There's sure to be traffic on the way back to Hickory Grove. Not the kind you're used to in Philadelphia, but enough to slow us down quite a bit." He pressed a button on his key fob and stepped toward the trunk.

"Oh, and I should tell you I've decided to extend the visit through next weekend . . . at least. I purchased a one-way ticket, and I've rented a car to drive back." McKinley trailed his father, thinking of his own pocketful of secrets. He carefully set his bag beside the ever-present emergency kit his mother had put together years ago and the striped blanket in the otherwise-pristine compartment. His mother made sure none of their cars ever left home without those supplies. When he straightened, he addressed the unspoken question taking up space between them. "I know I'll have more to take back than I brought with me. I hope that's okay."

"Of course. That goes without saying."

Yet it did need to be said. Dad's furrowed brow cooled the warmth in his welcome by a degree or two. McKinley wondered if his father remembered the last time he was home. *Are you thinking I want the flexibility to cut and run again when I feel like it?*

"Well, that's an unexpected blessing! Now you can pack a cooler. I'll buy you some of those smoked sausages you love since you can't find them up there and maybe some Duke's mayonnaise. Oh, and there're some things I found in the attic you might want for your new place. I can't believe you might be buyin' a house! Even more to talk about on the way home. Right, Fred?" Paulette's voice carried a smile as the trunk closed.

"Even more . . . ?" McKinley's eyes ricocheted between his parents.

"For one, your mama has taken up list making. That's what, item thirteen?" Ironically, his father's impassive face relayed what he really thought.

"Lists? You, Mom? Does this have something to do with the surprises Dad mentioned?" As if they needed another pothole, speed bump, or detour on what looked like a portentous drive to Hickory Grove.

"More like takin' notes. I thought I'd try it on for size. See if there's room for improvement. And as far as surprises go—" Paulette winked at the men—"it's not every day a woman gets to plan her send-off to prison. We might as well make a day of it!"

Chapter Two

"SO WHEN DOES your sentence commence, Mom?"

She averted her face. Her exhalation left a tiny circle of moisture on the window. "Next Tuesday."

"Tuesday?" That left him five days. McKinley massaged his forehead with the heel of his hand. "For how long?"

"Through the following weekend." The diameter of the circle widened.

"So they'll be here for your birthday."

His mama cleared the condensation with her thumb, leaving a smudged print. "And now it looks like you might be here, too, is that right? It's turnin' into quite the shindig, what started out a simple dinner for two. If you'd told us about your change of plans, we might not have committed to their visit."

"You might be right, since I'm the one who's surprised. I thought, since I was coming down so close to your big day, I could stay a little longer, and we could celebrate it together. I guess we all will now."

"All? It's just my aunt and uncle coming, not the entire Baldwin cavalry." Dad snapped his buckle into place. His eyes connected with McKinley's as he adjusted his rearview mirror, but in a blink, his attention returned to the road that led from the airport lot. "I don't know why y'all persist in calling it 'prison' every time Aunt Juju and Uncle Lawrence come to town."

"Because Julia persists in tellin' me how I should think and feel. I can't be comfortable . . . around my own kitchen table, no less." Mama's soft voice bounced off the glass.

"Not that you're ever comfortable in the kitchen," Dad murmured, his voice barely discernible.

McKinley shifted his position on the soft leather seat as if parrying his father's low blow. When he peeked at his mother's reflection, he didn't linger long on her high cheekbones, narrow nose, or skin the color of chai tea with heavy cream. What claimed his attention was her cloaked expression. It peered inward rather than at the people they were leaving behind. Though her eyes tended to duck and hide when she was feeling some kind of way, they declared her emotions the way a herald announced the arrival of the king. Right now, they blared to those who would listen, *"When those people are around, my own skin doesn't fit me."*

Yet McKinley knew uttering those words didn't fit his mother either. And his father had stopped up his ears long ago.

He pressed his forehead to the cool glass and imagined scribbling *HELP ME* with his index finger. Wherever the folks out there were headed had to be better than serving time in the armed camp the Baldwins' house became when his great-aunt rolled into town, his great-uncle in tow. Even now, he could hear the click of pistols loading.

"Paulette . . ."

"'I don't care how slowly you say my name . . .' Sound familiar?" She lightly tapped his dad's arm as she spun in her seat, and then she propped her back against her door. After draping her left arm across her headrest, she peeked around it. "So, my boy, how was the flight?"

McKinley repositioned his bottom and rotated his shoulders as his mother resumed her mantle of wife and mother and shed the one with *in-law* stitched across its hood. He took a beat to pivot and redirect his own emotions, to adjust to the abrupt temperature change in the car.

Fred glanced in the rearview mirror. "It took less than two hours, right?"

Mama murmured, "Not everything operates on a deadline or a time limit."

In other words, *Hold your horses, and let the boy speak,* a warning McKinley had heard her issue before. After homeschooling him for twelve years, she was used to the way her son seemed to parse his spoken words as much as his written ones. It drove his father up one wall and down another. McKinley rotated his ankles, remembering how his feet had felt like they were wedged in the concrete: trapped.

The leather squeaked when he moved to another spot on the seat. "Now that I think about it, Dad's right. A little over an hour. I waited longer at the airport in Philly than it took to fly here. I refused to pay more for an aisle seat, so I felt like my knees were propping up my chin the whole time. And I learned more about the woman sitting next to me than I cared to. By the way, did you know senior citizens don't get free coffee or subs at Wawa? My seatmate, Mrs. Wright, thinks it's an outrage. Also, her neighbor's lawn is entirely too high and he should cut it more regularly." McKinley hoped his words would tamp down his mother's irritation much as her own had tethered his father's earlier impatience.

Mom's nostrils could've inhaled the three-by-three-inch square, they were so close to the paper. "Well, speaking as a future senior citizen, I wouldn't turn up my nose to free food, especially one of Wawa's apple fritters. I don't care if that place is a glorified gas station."

McKinley winced at her description, thinking of all the toes his mother had unknowingly trampled in the mid-Atlantic swath of the country. She was engrossed in her own thoughts, not soothed by his. Seeing his dad tap her knee, he reclined his head against the back of his seat.

• ❧ •

Paulette took a deep breath, sure she'd heard, *Take it easy* when Fred patted her. He was one to talk—or not to. He used to touch her because he wanted to, not because he thought she needed him to. She extended her leg below the dashboard and rearranged her sticky notes. It made more sense to circle back around to the first one later. Inhaling again, relieved that her efforts were bearing fruit, she closed her strained eyes. If only she'd noted, *Put glasses in your purse.*

The silence widened and deepened and seemed to swallow all their words whole. Paulette pulled down her mirror, ostensibly to inspect what remained of the lipstick she hadn't nibbled off. Really, however, she had to check out her son, who'd uttered nary a peep for ten minutes.

What do his clients think of his hair? And those torn-up jeans! Does he wear them to appointments? Is this the new look for architects? But there's something else about him, other than his hairstyle, his . . . twists. The style complemented that swagger of his that had settled on him sometime in the past nine months. He seemed set on distancing himself from his father, including his haircut, a style Fred had adopted more than a score ago.

Is it because of Kerry . . . no, Kelly? Kelsey. Yes, Kelsey, who's done more than twist his hair. She's turned that boy's head, that's for sure. Something they'd avoided during his teenage years. But then, McKinley wasn't a boy anymore, was he? He'd be thirty years old in a few years. And they'd never met this woman. *How serious is this relationship anyway?* He hadn't said more than two words about it, but something was surely going on that she hadn't dared make mention of on her sticky notes.

"You look like you're working on all kinds of thoughts up there, Mom. More lists?"

Though she nearly choked on her spit, McKinley's question put a stop to Paulette's wearisome cogitation. With a snap of the mirror's cover, she slapped the visor against the roof of the car, ignoring her husband's startled glance, and spluttered, "Cuh-cuh . . . *ahem*. I already told you I'm not making lists, just takin' notes."

"Why?"

"Why not? Do I have to have a reason? What do you mean by askin'? And, Fred, no need to add your two cents."

Fred's head moved to the *whah-whah-whah* of the tires eating the ridges in the concrete.

"I mean exactly what you think I mean." McKinley didn't bother to hold back his own chuckle, deep in his throat but audible in the confines of the car.

Paulette rose up on her knee to peer over the headrest.

McKinley met her eyes and raised his brows in return, as if silently wagering she wouldn't answer—or daring her to.

She humphed, turned her back on the man-child behind her, and raged at the road. Yes, the child most definitely was acting grownish.

· ᥱᏗ ·

Fred's eyes waltzed from the asphalt to the side mirrors to the rearview. His wife was alternately staring out her passenger window and inhaling ink, probably working out how to "naturally" broach number three—or was it number two? What made that woman think she needed talking points to converse with her own son? He chalked up his earlier thought as a momentary lapse; it made about as much sense as these daggone stop signs on the on-ramps to I-85.

From the even breathing in the back, Fred gathered the boy was either worn-out or feigning sleep. McKinley had been that way since he'd filled up the tank at the BP station in Jamestown. Fred figured he'd wait until they parked before rousing him. But his wife? Paulette, he needed to bother.

"Hey," he whispered, "which is first, the furniture stores or the chair? You have about forty-five seconds to decide before I take the exit."

Business, or "green" I-85 was an odd combination of country road and four-lane highway. The few travelers who hadn't opted for the newer interstate known as "Blue 85" puttered along in broken-down, patched-up cars too modern to be considered classics, raced by in vehicles whose altered or missing mufflers sputtered their coming and going, or moseyed across the roadway, taking languid left turns in front of oncoming traffic.

Fred had chosen the far-right lane, less traveled by, so he could cruise at a more moderate speed, sedate even, so actually Paulette had at least two minutes before they reached the off-ramp leading to Thomasville's downtown area. More than enough time to consult the various squares of paper adhered to his dashboard. This business of getting organized had thrown her for a loop. Him, too, for that matter. Fred wondered if she'd ever get the hang of not just knowing her next move, but promising to carry it through in that fine-tip Sharpie she was meticulously planning her steps with. *Gracious.*

In his periphery, he watched her nibble on the cap of her pen, obviously tripped up somewhere along the day's agenda. She'd nearly burned up the entire two minutes, and the exit was coming up—not exactly fast, but at a nice clip of sixty-one miles per hour. He leaned close enough to taste the fresh citrus notes of perfume she liked to dab behind her ears and other pulse points and asked softly, "Etta, chair first?"

When she nodded, fixated on peeling, sticking, and rearranging, Fred signaled he was taking the right-hand exit. He edged off the highway just as an 18-wheeler rumbled by with empty cages dotted with chicken feathers fluttering from the steel frames.

"And you're sure this is what you want to do?"

Paulette pressed together her small stack. She glanced over the seat, then responded in a low voice. "Of course. This is our family's thing. At least it used to be. And what better time? You can be darn sure he won't be comin' home again before Christmas. All our friends and family get a kick out of it."

"You mean, it's *your* thing, Paulette. I'm not so sure about you-know-who." Her scent already a memory, an exasperated Fred slowed as they approached a red stoplight. He squinted at the ramshackle building squatting fifty feet from the road that was using its gravel lot as a furniture showroom. A sprinkling of shoppers picked their way through unmatched kitchen chairs, leather sofas, rocking horses, shellacked end tables, brass floor lamps, and ceramic farm animals parked there. He released the brake as the light changed to green and eased through the intersection behind a pickup carrying chopped wood. A tiny red flag extended from a wire on one of the longer pieces, flapping a warning at Fred to keep his distance.

Paulette waggled a similar warning with her Sharpie while the fingers of her right hand drummed on her door. "Well, I disagree. Isn't this the type of thing his generation is always takin' pictures of and sharin' on social media? You-know-who will probably find this more fun than oohin' and aahin' over the wood grain in the latest desks and kitchen tables."

"You-know-who had better not mind *examining* desks and kitchen tables. He didn't just come home for a birthday party." Paulette poked at the tender spots of Fred's ego with an expert finger, and he struggled to modulate his tone. After thirty-five years, she knew good and well furniture design was more than his job; it was his life's work. *Their* livelihood. Fred could invest an hour studying the ball-and-claw of an occasional table or three weeks sketching the curve of a settee's arm. He'd hoped McKinley would follow in his footsteps "smellin' upholstered wood chips," as his wife liked to put it, but Fred had finally accepted that McKinley's career in architecture would have to be . . . well, not good, but enough.

"Don't get all worked up, Fred. We'll have plenty of time for you two to salivate over all the feet, legs, and arms to your heart's content at the furniture market." Tens of thousands of dealers, merchants, designers, media, and members of the industry flocked from all over to High Point, North Carolina, what many called the furniture capital of the United States. The market transformed the city into the world's largest showroom each spring and fall. Each year, there seemed to be fewer American-based furniture manufacturers, which was part of the reason Fred was planning to renovate George & Company.

"I just want to take a picture of you-know-who with the big chair like we did when he was little. These opportunities are too few and far between to waste them when they're sittin' in my lap."

"Forget the 'opportunities.' You-know-who isn't sitting in your lap anymore." Fred hooked his thumbs around the steering wheel and extended his fingers, easing the tension in them.

"I know tha—"

"You-know-me is awake now, by the way." McKinley's voice sounded like it was stretching with him as he yawned.

Fred scooted back until his bottom touched the seat, and he sat tall so that his head nearly brushed the roof of the car. "*Ahem.* Good. I hope that nap did the trick. We'll be there in a minute." He used the mirror to take stock of his son.

McKinley leaned forward and gazed out the window. "Since this looks nothing like downtown High Point, I take it by *there* you mean the chair?"

Paulette tucked her paper inside a leather journal and snapped the band over it. "You make it sound like there's an electric current runnin' through it."

"Maybe I'm picturing it with Christmas lights," McKinley muttered. "Next thing you know, you'll have me pretend to fold clothes in front of the chest of drawers sculpture in High Point."

Paulette's eyes widened as she whirled toward her son. "You don't mind, do you?"

Hearing the nearly audible click of a light bulb turning on in her brain, Fred looked askance at his wife as if to shield his eyes from its revealing glare. But then the car jostled the three of them as it lumbered across the railroad tracks bisecting the town of Thomasville, and he let Paulette's question dangle, unattended. As they approached the thirty-foot-tall concrete-and-steel chair sprouting from the middle of the square, Fred pondered how they'd manage to get McKinley up onto—or was it *into?*—its granite platform for this all-important photograph, to capture a moment that would get stuffed inside trash cans with the used Christmas wrapping.

Fred turned left on the second of two roads designated West Main Street and parallel parked in one of the empty spaces. He switched off the car, extracted the keys from the ignition, and angled toward the back seat . . . in time to see McKinley thrust open the back door and heave himself from the car. Fred arched a brow at his wife when the Mercedes shook with the force of the slam. "Looks like you're not the only one serving a life sentence."

Chapter Three

⎯⎯⎯⎯❦⎯⎯⎯⎯

PAULETTE HUNG BACK, admiring the fine figures her men cut as they roved the furniture showroom, stroking the carved curve of this headboard and the smooth finish of that side table. They reminded her of two planets orbiting in the same galaxy, yet millions of miles apart.

From her vantage point, she watched three women holding brochures stroll past other visitors and approach her husband first, then McKinley. When they moved on, they glanced back a few times, whispering. Paulette wanted to shout, *"Keep your eyes on the merchandise!"* but opted for a shrug when their eyes met hers as the women passed in the aisle.

They are cute, aren't they? She smiled to herself, knowing they hadn't guessed she was with the men. Paulette's sandals clip-clopped on the hardwood floor as she increased her pace to lay claim on a manly arm.

McKinley raised a brow at her when she touched him. "Dad is inspecting that credenza over there. Anything snag your attention?"

"One or two." Paulette squeezed her son's forearm. "What about you? What's caught your eye?"

"Everything and everybody, for the most part. Did you see those three women approach us?"

Like Paulette, McKinley was a people watcher. He noticed more than their clothes and hairstyles. He also studied their movements and reactions and expressions. When he was younger, their mother-son trips to the grocery store led to conversations about what and who they'd seen and heard. She glanced at Fred, so intent on his own thoughts and personal mission; in this state, he rarely widened his focus to include the world spinning directly around him. God love him. *And this one, too.*

"Yes, they didn't know I was watching them admire you as they walked away." Paulette giggled. "I wonder what they said to your father."

"Huh, is that what you're calling it? Admiration? I don't know what they said to Dad, but the one in red wearing the three-inch heels asked me to check with my 'manager' about the price of moving a dresser. They thought I worked here. Guess I shouldn't have left the blazer in the car." He grimaced.

Paulette's shoulders sagged as she rested her head on his shoulder for a moment. *Why, Lord?* More ammunition for Fred, though his aim seemed dead-on today. They walked in silence for a moment to put some space between them and their frustration with the world and its assumptions.

After a few minutes, she peeled her reluctant fingers from his arm. Her heart was stuffed with excitement and joy over his return, and she'd have to be careful not to let her ebullience overflow and spill onto him. Good gracious, she'd clearly pushed the envelope with that Christmas picture. As it was, she'd had to restrain herself from offering McKinley, her six-foot-one-inch former soccer player, a boost onto the chair's platform.

No, this visit had to seem natural, even if it killed her. Like she considered it an everyday occurrence to stroll through the High Point furniture market with her only son. It seemed she just had to attach that adjective every time. *He is an only of two onlies,* her inner Paulette stubbornly insisted.

So Paulette slipped on an air of nonchalance that felt as comfortable as a new pair of high-heeled Sunday shoes and searched for an appropriate response to McKinley. When she spoke, it sounded like she was talking to some of her piano students, the ones who couldn't find middle C with both thumbs. "He's excited you're home. In case you didn't notice."

McKinley smirked as if laughing at his own joke. "Oh, I did. I also noticed he's got something more on his mind than that credenza. And by the way, what's the difference between a credenza and a buffet?"

"A credenza typically doesn't have legs, but newer styles might. Just not as long as the legs on a buffet. They serve the same purpose though." Paulette scanned the room, then pointed to a four-legged cabinet with a set of china displayed on top. "See the difference?"

He nodded.

As they meandered through the maze of furniture, they alternated between examining various designs and checking the room to put their eyes on Fred, who seemed enraptured by a rolltop desk with a deep, high-gloss finish. He'd squatted and was tracing the carved scrollwork on one of its bowed front legs.

Paulette shook her head. You'd think her husband was buying a rare Arabian stallion. "This project with George & Company is consumin' him. It's starting to eat us up, too. I should warn you: you might not see very much of him outside the office. You're lucky he considered this trip to the market as pertinent to the business at hand. Otherwise, I don't know if he would've met you at the airport. As it is, he's probably going to work late into the night or leave early in the mornin'."

"What about Saturdays? Does he work on the weekend, too? He hasn't talked to you about why he's stepped so far from the creative side? You should ask him why he won't stick to his part of the drafting table and let Mr. George do his part running the company."

"Because I don't really need to ask him. Knox and Sarah might know what pretty furniture looks like, but they surely don't know the first thing about sellin' it." Paulette sidled over to an étagère and gave McKinley a minute to chew on her answer. She plucked a ceramic vase decorated with tiny sprays of purple violets from its top shelf and turned it over, both McKinley's questions and the glassware that was too delicate to hold anything more than its painted flowers.

Knox and Sarah George owned George & Company, a business that had been passed around their family like a plate of biscuits at the dinner table. Twenty-five years ago, Knox had uprooted his wife and baby boy from their home outside of Clemson, South Carolina, in an effort to save the company their distant cousin, Clinton George, had started generations earlier.

Folks in Hickory Grove still whispered about Clinton's nose for smelling out a good chunk of wood and his gift for making change out of rubbing two pennies together. More than a hundred years ago, Clinton combined his proclivities for woodworking and moneymaking to form a furniture company, where he proceeded to lie, cheat, and steal to eat up the forestland around him and spit out practical home furnishings such as headboards, chests of drawers, kitchen tables, and chairs.

Paulette made sure McKinley was listening before she returned to studying the vase. "We've told you before how old man George was heard to say, 'Won't no n—'" She swallowed the rest of the word her daddy never let her repeat. "'Won't no Black man ever gon' step a foot inside George Furniture Store.' Folks took him at his word, too, not that his deeds didn't bear him out; they did. Plenty of Black people found work on his forestland, includin' all that property he snookered from your dad's people, but nary a one spent a dollar in his store." Paulette felt McKinley step closer.

"But then Clinton's son ran out of land?" Although his father had shared most of these stories, every retelling held another layer of meaning to scrape off and sift through.

"Not exactly. Basically, the Georges got too big for their britches. The demand for their furniture started to outstrip their resources of raw material and the costs of manufacturing, and nobody knew how to fix it. Not at first. Then they started buyin' their wood from mills farther north, and those companies used the rail lines to ship their lumber here."

"And later, G&C used those same lines to deliver their furniture to places all across North Carolina. Then Virginia, Maryland, et cetera, et cetera."

Paulette nodded. "But nobody seemed to have the same head for doin' business, at least not the right way. G&C couldn't keep up with competition or the growing costs of fewer resources. They were simply tryin' to do too much."

"So Knox and Sarah saved the day?" McKinley sounded skeptical.

"Kind of. They worked to resurrect the business, to maintain quality, not just quantity. They focused on producing specialty furniture, not producin' what the company needed to make it."

"And the rest is . . . history. We hope the kind that doesn't repeat itself." McKinley put his palms together as if in prayer.

Paulette could tell McKinley felt some kind of way about the company's checkered past. "We can only hope and pray with Knox and Sarah at the helm. As far as we can discern, they do seem to keep company with Jesus, which doesn't leave much room for Clinton George's legacy of bigotry. On the other hand, they don't have his same head for business . . ." She shrugged. "But they have made some smart—though expensive—changes. He and Sarah amended the name to add 'Fine' to the 'Furniture' in the company logo, started replanting the trees the senior Georges had hewed down—

"And stolen?"

"And stolen." She nodded. "Then they incorporated design to appeal to people who could afford to spend money customizin' and personalizin' their furniture, specifically kitchen cabinetry." Paulette set down the knickknack and fiddled with the other pottery on the stand.

"And that's where Dad came in." McKinley reached out and moved around the vases and figurines.

"Yes, my *only* husband and his drawin' table." Paulette admired McKinley's new arrangement. Ever the designer, like Frederick, just in a different pair of shoes. In her mind's eye, Paulette could see her husband at twenty-seven years old, striding right through the very door Clinton George's family had barred the Baldwins' ancestors from using. "Two years ago, in large part because of your father's drive to get investors to help them both expand and streamline, they went from George's Fine Furnishings to George *& Company* Fine Furnishings."

"Yes, I know all about those special investors. I think the only color Mr. and Mrs. George worry about is the green on the money he brings in. That's the way it seems to me."

"And maybe the black-and-white on his design renderings," Paulette laughed.

McKinley nodded without a hint of a smile. "It's not like you and Dad had a problem with Monroe, Lacey, and Emmeline. Not one I ever saw."

"Of course not! We love their children. I'd be the last person to feel that way. They made the house full . . ." Paulette's voice trailed off as she superimposed Fred's copper-colored skin on the faces of the three younger Georges and exchanged their honey-tinged curls for her head of thick, nearly black hair. What if McKinley had had a brother instead of a best friend sitting beside him at her dinner table?

She shrugged off the thought. God had different plans, and part of them was putting the Georges in her life, just as surely as He'd planted the trees on the gentle slopes of the foothills they called home. Paulette loved them and treated those children like they were her own. Even though they ran through their own house, she spared no words telling them they'd best walk through hers. Glory to God, the Baldwin-George relationship had stood the test of time and the rise and fall of furniture prices. In fact, McKinley and Monroe were such a familiar handful, most of the company's employees called the duo "M and M."

But not Fred, she sighed. Never her husband, who yet struggled to call his son McKinley and not Fred Jr. Funny how he thought she didn't hear his tongue get tied up from time to time. That was all right though. She could understand that, his need to preserve his line. And not merely preserve it but paint it a rich, deep ebony, like the mahogany desktop he was caressing over there. A color that connected his living legacies to all the people who had worked to make possible their free and prosperous life. The parts she didn't understand, the good Lord knew all about.

Paulette squinted at her husband, such a good-looking man. She yearned to see past the strong nose and slightly receding hairline and know what pounded in that heart under his crisp, ice-blue, collared shirt. She desperately wanted to understand the Fred who was so fiercely protective of his aunt and uncle and their family heritage. Her life's partner who could sit across the dinner table and laugh with Knox, the man he didn't trust as far as he could throw him. The father who both nurtured and resented McKinley's friendship with Monroe. Fred's own faith prevented the familiarity with the Georges from breeding contempt, but he didn't let it conquer the mistrust and pridefulness that kept him walking ramrod straight through a doorway his own grandfather couldn't have crawled through.

A brisk shift in the air in front of her face caused Paulette's eyelids to blink rapidly. She focused on McKinley's hand, waving right at the tip of her nose.

"Mom? Anybody home?"

Paulette swallowed and gathered her smile the way she held the folds of her skirt. She pinched the corners of her lips and forced them up. The whole while, she trained her eyes on her husband, who was looking at a brochure and, in all likelihood, marking out their next stop. Turning her back to Fred, she set down a glass cherub that was blowing a trumpet from now until kingdom come—or until some careless market attendee jostled the étagère and sent the figurine tumbling to the floor. She was careful not to disturb McKinley's layout.

Her son touched her shoulder. "Either you're mulling over your answer, or you're dumbfounded that a member of the Baldwin family still doesn't know what a credenza is."

Paulette chuckled. "Just don't tell your daddy. About the credenza, I mean. I'm *home*, no worries. As far as why he's working so hard . . . You know how he is, McKinley. He took it to heart, the fact he was named for an inventor and pioneer. That was the best thing his mama gave him since she didn't give him much of herself or anything else—a sad fact that attracted us to each other.

"He and Frederick McKinley Jones were both self-taught and masters of their trade. Creators and designers. Leaders. His grandfather did better than right by him, but Fred never quite overcame growin' up without his father. He's bound and determined to make sure you both live up to his own name." Her voice overflowed with admiration and love—and confusion—for the man of her dreams. Paulette didn't know exactly what to do with the man in the flesh.

"Is that why he hired me for this project, to make sure I live up to that illustrious name? What does Mr. George think of this?"

"Now, why should I care what Knox thinks about that or anything else?" Fred growled behind them.

· ᘒ ·

He was plumb worn-out. He knew he'd kept them probably one showroom too long, but he was determined to walk off his irritation . . . with himself, mainly. He hadn't wanted to spoil the boy's first day back. Junior had already been gone too long as it was. Between Etta's fawning over him and his own reaction to a simple question about Knox George, he might not come home for another two years instead of nine months. Fred's eyes lingered on his wife, her head jostling against the passenger window. His fingers had a mind of their own and they itched to caress her cheek.

"What are you thinking about, Dad?"

That your mama might never get another Christmas picture. The thought disappeared in a blink as his eyes met McKinley's in the rearview mirror. "You've been quiet back there."

McKinley's seat belt made a zipping noise as he leaned toward the front seat. "Are you trying to change the subject?"

Etta was right. Fred had noticed the looks she'd given McKinley when she thought nobody was paying attention. As if she was studying a specimen under a microscope. There was a boldness that wasn't there the last time he was home. Maybe it had something to do with how he left, as if he'd been flung pell-mell from a tornado. Fred wasn't sure he liked this new, confident manner of his, but he had a feeling Junior—*McKinleyMcKinleyMcKinley*—didn't much care how his father felt about it.

Fred cleared his throat and decided to take the same forthright path as his son. "You caught me. I'm not sure how to answer."

Paulette yawned and scooted around in her seat in Frederick's direction.

Uh-oh. He'd thought they'd lost her somewhere around Love Valley.

"Are you thinkin' about what McKinley asked you back in High Point?"

They were about thirty miles from Hickory Grove, and Fred had hoped they'd make it home without bringing up that subject. With those hopes smashed on his car mat, he took a deep breath and opened his mouth.

Paulette squeezed his shoulder and shushed him. "Because I was thinkin' about it, too. And I think it's because you want to prove yourself."

Fred clamped his mouth closed so hard, his teeth clicked.

"What would Dad have to prove to Mr. George?"

Mr. George. Fred clenched his jaw. He knew McKinley was like most respectful products of the South who'd been taught to call their elders Mr. and Mrs., but he wanted to force his son to say, "Knox." His grandfather had used that formal address because he had to, and Papa made sure his children and his children's children did the same, something

44

Paulette didn't experience as a child. *Papa, I wish I could've told you what they call me at George & Company.*

Without thinking, Fred murmured, "Mr. Baldwin."

"What did you say, Frederick?" Paulette edged even closer toward him in her bucket seat.

He gripped the steering wheel. In his periphery, he watched the light leapfrog across the shadows in her face. "I was just thinking about what you said, Etta, about proving something to *Mr.* George." A flicker of light showed him she'd heard his unspoken thoughts loud and clear.

"Monroe still calls us Mr. and Mrs. Baldwin, too. Doesn't he, McKinley?"

"Yes, ma'am, as far as I know. And his sisters, too." His son's voice was low.

Paulette peered around the headrest. "Showin' respect never goes out of style. You don't grow out of being raised well. And your dad isn't tryin' to prove anything to Knox. He's provin' something to himself. Am I right, Fred?"

He had no idea what that woman was talking about. He had nothing to prove. To anybody, including her. "Etta, what's rattling around in that head of yours?"

"You're renovatin' yourself as much as you are the company. Bringin' on these new designers to redirect the business . . . You're stretchin' yourself. And of course, you want to have the best people working with you to make sure it's successful. That's why you enlisted McKinley's help. The pressure you feel is your drive for success, that sense of history in the makin'. That's a lot of pressure."

Pressure! He wasn't the one feeling the pressure. "Well . . ." McKinley relaxed against the leather as if the matter had been put to bed.

"Something like that," Fred managed. He kept his eyes on the red taillights of the cars ahead and tried to work out the kinks in his aching cheeks. Beside him, Paulette fiddled for something in her bag. He sighed.

Of course. She was at it again with that pen and those blasted notes.

· ᴇᴦ ·

Paulette shot Fred a warning look. He'd better not say one word, especially after she'd bailed him out a few minutes ago. Not one itty-bitty, mumbling word. Maybe he wanted to pretend he didn't have something to prove, but that wasn't the way he'd behaved, looking like some two-year-old over there with his lips poked out. To acknowledge any insecurity to his son would show weakness, at least in his own mind. It made him human in her eyes, brought him down to an altitude his son could touch, even if he had to stand on his tippy-toes.

"So, McKinley, how are the flying lessons goin'?" She hoped neither man could hear the fine nib of her pen scratch out number four on her square of paper.

"*Flying* lessons?" McKinley inched forward again.

She looked up at his strange emphasis on that word, now more intent on the content of the conversation than merely making it. "Yes. When we FaceTimed last month, you mentioned that you were startin' to take lessons flying planes."

McKinley's confusion was nearly audible, even in the dark. Paulette tried to see his face so she could confirm the question mark plainly etched on the lines of his brow. "Don't you remember? Lessons . . . flying . . . planes?"

His forehead smoothed for all of two seconds, but new creases formed as McKinley's eyes widened. Then he squeezed them shut and threw back his head, his hand against his lips.

Did he just snort? Paulette's mouth opened wide. Confusion she could handle; his laughter she couldn't stand. She would not be the punch line of a joke, whatever it was. Her barely parted teeth nearly chewed the four-letter word to tiny bits before she spit it out. "What?"

"I'm sorry, Mom. I'm not really laughing."

"Oh? It sounds like it. Then what *are* you doin'?"

McKinley gulped and sniffled. "*Ahem* . . . well. I'm not laughing at you, just at the misunderstanding."

"Misunderstandin'?"

"Paulette, let the boy get in a word." Fred patted her knee once before returning his hand to the wheel.

I know you're not telling me not to rush him. She squeezed her pen and faced the highway. Her chest rose and fell once as her eyes consumed the darkness.

"Mom, from what I remember about our conversation that day, I think I said, 'I'm taking some lessons on the fly about planes.'"

Paulette twirled the pen, clicking it on and off. *Isn't that what I said?*

"Planes, as they relate to architectural design. Today's workspaces are changing, so I decided I'd better study up on spaces defined by planes of walls that seemed to be floating or less fixed. Since I didn't have time to sign up for the class, I spent a weekend working with one of the designers at a local firm. The better to help Dad with, my dear."

Paulette could tell he was trying to lighten her mood.

After a pause he said quietly, "I can see how you got confused."

Lessons on the fly about planes. She cut her eyes at Fred as the lights of a passing flatbed truck illuminated his face. Yes, he was trying not to smile. She blew out a breath through her nose. It was time to concede and lose the attitude. "No, I just made a big leap. Right off a cliff, obviously."

"Not at all. Thanks for remembering. That means a lot you were following up."

"You're welcome . . . I suppose." Paulette's voice sounded as stiff as Fred's new car seats, even to her own ears. She told herself not to take personally the laughter McKinley was still trying to stifle, his joy at her expense, and directed her energies toward deciphering her chicken scratch. She moved one square to the back of her pile, wishing she could hold it up to the passing light without drawing attention to her notes. She clipped her pen to the stack and decided to lean on her history with McKinley as a crutch.

"Did you see that woman goin' into the flower shop on Main when we were in Thomasville? She looked a bit like our neighbor, you know the one across the street who has those beautiful azaleas? Something about her haircut. Oh, that reminds me, who's waterin' your plants while you're here—Kelsey?"

Silence gobbled up her innocent assumption. That was what happened when she went off topic and didn't consult her notes: she dove too deeply into McKinley's business when she intended to wade in the shallow end. Contrary to what her husband was thinking, her note-taking wasn't about getting organized. She was doing her darndest to adjust to the boundaries the adult McKinley silently erected with his shuttered eyes and terse, overly polite responses, but it was taking some getting used to. Just like Harold Burdell, Paulette had erected walls when she'd meant to place stepping-stones.

What now, Daddy? What happens when you plan your steps and you still stumble and fall?

· ↭ ·

How he hated Thomasville.

Not Thomasville, specifically. What could he hate about a small town who honored its people with Everybody's Day, North Carolina's oldest festival? Whose name was engraved on the back of headboards, under kitchen tables, and inside cabinets all over the world? Who once fed its community heartier fare than IHOP through the eleven furniture factories that employed nearly ten thousand people? When Thomasville Furniture shuttered its doors, folks feared it would take the town with it.

No, McKinley didn't hate Thomasville, North Carolina. He directed all his resentment at the thirty-foot-tall chair erected to commemorate its legacy. Because nothing stopped the Baldwins' annual Christmas photos. Not the closure of the factories, the strangers who gawked at his family, the sweaty effort of hefting him onto the platform, nor the extra benches the city provided to encourage visitors not to do this very thing. According to Baldwin family legend, the grateful new father had obliged Paulette's whimsy to prop their baby boy on the chair's base. The next year, she considered it "their idea" when Dad had acceded, though less enthusiastically; she deemed it "their tradition" year three and swept them all up into it. Mom determined to measure his growth by this yearly photo, and that she would do, regardless of her husband's commitment, which had gone from complaisant to lackluster to downright reluctant.

It didn't help matters much that McKinley lowered his head and scrunched together his shoulders a little more each year, just to frustrate his mother's need to document every inch, each curl, any missing teeth. He grew wider, hairier, and stronger but not much taller, or so attested this Christmas photograph. When all else failed, McKinley fled the state altogether. There was no big chair in Philadelphia.

And neither was there a set of bunk beds, nor a room memorializing his childhood—a 5,923-piece LEGO set of the Taj Mahal; mounted plaster replicas of his one-, five-, and ten-year-old hands; nine of the Diary of a Wimpy Kid books because Monroe never returned the rest and the entire

Gregor the Overlander series; oodles of plastic spiders, ants, katydids, and grasshoppers crammed inside plastic buckets; his trunk splattered with decals denoting his college road trip; and twenty-six Christmas cards tacked to the inside of his closet door, documenting his 9,490-plus days of journeying from infant to man. He figured he'd take the twenty-seventh with him, the photograph his mother had snapped earlier that afternoon before driving to High Point to spy out the competition at the fall furniture market. And if that didn't beat all, his father had winked as he coasted by the huge chest of drawers High Point must have erected years ago to one day torment his son.

"Of course, she brought the Nikon she'd used to capture that original moment so we could all feel nostalgic. It only reminds me of all those pictures that testify to the fact that I'll never design, build, or sell home furnishings like Frederick McKinley Baldwin Sr." McKinley gulped down the lump in his throat and masked the huskiness with a cough. He wasn't ready to share that part yet, not even with himself. With his right hand he lobbed a tennis ball off the twelve-year-old plank over his desk, mounted to the scarred, light-green walls for this very purpose, and gripped his iPhone with his left. He listened to the silence on the other end of the line.

A response wasn't a long time coming. "There are enough people who do that so you don't have to, Mac. Why don't you simply tell her, 'Mom, I hate that chair. Let's take a family photo in reindeer antlers'? Or buy forty-five Hallmark cards with a tree on the cover and mail only thirty of them like the rest of the world?"

McKinley sighed as he rubbed his forehead with the back of his arm, surprised it wasn't raw by now. "Baby, you know about our family dynamics, what all we got goin' on here. She'd tell me, 'Well, we're not like the rest of the world, are we?' or something like that." *The Lord knows that's the truth.*

"'Something like that' indeed. Because only the Baldwins can take a family picture without the whole family in it."

Soft in his ear, his girlfriend's bluntly spoken words pierced him. For a moment, all he heard was his own throbbing heartbeat, a *whoosh-whoosh* in his ears. Then he murmured, more to himself than for the benefit of her ears, "As far as she's concerned, I'm the only part of the family that matters."

"I'm sorry, Mac. I shouldn't have said that. I'm familiar with your family dynamics, but this is a big deal to you. And you're a big deal to *me*."

"And we're all a big deal to my mother." *Ka-thunk* went the ball before it ricocheted against a bucket, sending insects flying about the room. "She already suspects I'm keeping a relationship under wraps. She wanted to know who's watering my plants."

She sniffed. "All I know is I'd better be the only one watering your plants. This being kept under wraps thing has become way old."

If it were possible, McKinley pressed the phone even harder against his ear, as if he could pull her closer and snuggle with her voice. "Don't I know it. That's really why I accepted this offer and why I'm staying here longer. As soon as you give me the signal, all gloves are off. Agreed?"

"Agreed."

"You love me, don't you?"

"Yes," she sighed. "Still. Forever. Yes."

McKinley retrieved the ball and expelled a deep breath, unaware he'd been holding it.

Chapter Four

"What the devil?" Paulette grimaced at the cream-colored glop in the plastic bowl. The recipe had instructed, *Add more milk as needed*, but how much was "more"? By the looks of things, what she needed was less . . . *something*. Less Paulette, in all likelihood. She used her ring finger—the cleanest digit on her right hand—to tap out numbers on the orange antique-looking phone that Ma Bell herself could have mounted above the counter. Abruptly she replaced the receiver. After wasting thirty or so precious seconds, she lifted it again and redialed. Paulette wedged the phone between her shoulder and cheek and listened to it ring. *Finally!* she nearly shouted, hearing the "Hello" on the other end.

"Fred? Do you have time for a cookin' question?"

Papers ruffled on his side of the line. Paulette pictured her husband sitting at his drafting table in his George & Company office. He'd probably switched on the floor lamp to the right of it, virtually spitting in the face of the bright morning sunlight streaming through his large picture windows.

"What is it this time, Etta—temperature, texture, or taste?" His voice was dry.

Unlike my biscuits. Paulette scowled. Leave it to Fred to cut to the chase. The kitchen was not her milieu, and she'd been peppering him with questions all morning: What was the water-to-grits ratio, and how fast did "quick grits" cook? Should she use buttermilk or whole milk? Was a cast-iron skillet better than a cookie sheet, like the recipe suggested? But it couldn't be helped, though she was loath to bother him again. She didn't have time to hunt down the answers she needed, not when she had a perfectly good husband-cum-chef who should be home anyway, spending time with his son. What good was running things if he let the business run him?

Paulette cast her eyes toward the second floor. A creak outside McKinley's room had ratted him out in its usual fashion: he was up and at 'em. "Texture. I'm tryin' to make drop biscuits—"

"*Drop* biscuits? If I recall correctly, 'No self-respectin' Southern woman drops her biscuits. She uses a glass to cut

56

perfect circles in the dough and places them *this close* together in a pan so they'll rise nice and fluffy.' At least that's what you told me when I suggested this very thing last night. What did you do with that industrial-size rolling pin you ordered for this grand occasion?"

Paulette had neither the time nor the energy to be lectured or teased by Frederick Baldwin. She hit the Speaker button and set down the handset. "I put it in the drawer where it belongs, and it's keepin' the other one company. Maybe they'll start a family and adopt the pastry cutter. As far as I'm concerned, no self-respectin' Southern woman sends herself kitchen gadgets for a birthday gift, yet I insisted. Who else does that?" She did have to chuckle at herself as she used her free hands to rotate the bowl. No, the batter still looked off.

"Cooks like my grandmama and me, that's who. Now, what's wrong with your *drop biscuits*?"

"They're not droppin', for one. Because for two, I think the batter's too wet." Paulette jiggled the large spoon in the stainless steel bowl. If only Fred were standing in this kitchen, holding the spoon. He could prepare a meal with the same grace and aplomb he designed the table they set their dishes on, even if he was a bit too generous with the criticism. But she could compose and teach music—shouldn't that count somehow in cooking? Measures, measurements . . . close enough.

"You've had fifty-nine years to learn how to roll out some dough."

"Well, Bett didn't stick around long enough to teach me, and my husband is too busy."

"Most people don't associate cooking with neglect, Etta." His voice was soft. "I'm sorry."

His unexpected gentleness rattled Paulette, and she didn't know what to do with herself, let alone her dough. "Fred, I need you to tell me if this mess is salvageable. And make it quick because I want to slide these biscuits in the oven before McKinley comes down. I'm-a shock him out of his shoes." Paulette cocked an ear as the one-hundred-year-old floorboards above her tracked McKinley from his bedroom to the bathroom across the hall. Too late.

"Junior's just waking up?" His shock reverberated off their ten-foot ceilings.

Paulette bit her tongue. Far be it from her to correct or shush her husband when she so desperately needed his expertise. She was well aware that when Fred's people inherited nicknames, they bore them for life, growing into them but never out of them, like a wide forehead or oversize flat feet. Since her husband's roots stretched far beneath the Baldwin family tree, she was grateful her son hadn't been dubbed Peahead as a child like Fred's distant relative down in Waxhaw. Deep down, she knew that both that third cousin and her own "Fred Jr." had come into their names through no fault of their own.

So she sighed a prayer over her would-be biscuits and resisted toggling the spoon. Again. "Yes, McKinley's probably tired from all that travelin' yesterday. I'd send you a picture so you can see what the dough looks like, but I can't find my cell phone."

"Greensboro was quite a piece from us, wasn't it? Flying into Charlotte would definitely have been closer. He wouldn't be so worn-out."

"Good point, but then we wouldn't have been able to drive through Thomasville and over to the furniture market on the way home."

"You worked that all out, didn't you? Telling him to fly into Piedmont Triad International," he laughed. "Mmm-hmmm. I saw you eyeing that mahogany sofa with the velvety fabric, high, curved back, and smooth, dark finish. Did it remind you of somebody? You used to look at me that same way . . ."

"What in the world, Frederick!" Paulette gasped, wondering if he'd gotten overheated in his office, between the sun and his desk lamp. It had been so long, she couldn't determine whether or not he was flirting. Just in case, she dropped her voice several octaves. "I remembered what you told me: 'We're here to look with our eyes, not with our hands.' Now, about the biscuits—"

"That's right. Look but don't touch. Which is why you still brought home the catalog, from my recollection. I'm glad the market only happens twice a year. I couldn't afford you."

"How does the song go—'it's cheaper to keep her'? That's some good advice right there." Paulette giggled. She was starting to feel like her ancient, newly married self—a woman who didn't have more in common with the son who lived over six hundred miles away. Who desired to cuddle up and talk to her husband without benefit of cue cards.

Something clunked in his office and another male voice that Paulette couldn't discern uttered something in a drawl thick and slow as Grandma's Molasses. When he returned to their conversation, his voice sounded less playful, more formal. All Frederick.

"Try that spoon now, Etta."

She moved the bowl closer to her prepared cast-iron skillet. When a small mound of batter plopped from her spoon into it, she crowed, "Praise the Lord! Thank you!"

"It just needed a little rest. Like you, probably. What do y'all have planned after this feast you're preparing, or are you going to play it by ear?"

Paulette smiled before answering, satisfied by the circle of white pillows huddled close together in the skillet. "Well, I imagine he's headed over to you later. We both know his visit is mostly business, part pleasure."

Just like this conversation! groused Paulette Burdell, her inner "old man" she fought to keep under the heel of her shoe. But the "new man" somehow won the battle and asked through tight lips, "Have y'all talked about a schedule or any design ideas?

His phone rattled and clattered and the distance between Fred and Paulette grew. "Excuse me, I had to put you on speaker. Did you say schedule? No, he's more your son than mine, at least in that respect. You know Junior keeps things close."

"Well, you've told him what you thought, that you want your furniture to seem more . . . fun, though that's not quite the word. Hmm."

"I think the phrase you're going for is 'on trend.'"

"Yes, that's how Fred Ju—uh, McKinley put it. Hold on a minute." Paulette opened the heavy oven door on the 1950s-era range and lowered it. Then she hoisted the black skillet with both hands and shoved it across the oven rack. She closed the door and reassured herself that the temperature was set at 350 degrees before resuming the conversation.

"Okay," she huffed. "As I was sayin', he knows you brought on board two fresh, newly graduated designers, and now you want to spruce up the G&C offices to appeal to younger, up-and-comin' consumers. How did you put it? 'When buyers come in to meet with the design staff, they should feel both at home and in style.'"

"Yes, that's how I put it. Glad you were listening. Let's see how *he* puts it."

Paulette bristled at his skepticism. "He's exactly what G&C needs—an architect who thinks like a designer. McKinley grew up around the business, so he's good and familiar with how his daddy and the Georges think, with your personalities, your work habits, and what you're lookin' for. He's exactly what the company needs. And I'm always listenin', by the way."

"Sounds like you've convinced yourself, saying it twice like that. And if I'm thinking what you're thinking, it's exactly what I need, too." Papers rustled as he murmured, almost to himself, "It'll be a family business before you know it."

"Hold on there, Fred. George & Company is already a family business—just not ours." Paulette braced a hip against the countertop and glanced toward the gleaming banister curving toward the second floor. Squashing a whisper of recrimination—*Daddy wouldn't have lost his cell*—she picked up the receiver and pressed the button to take the phone off speaker. Then she wedged it between her ear and her shoulder and lowered her voice. "We have more important family matters to concern ourselves with, don't you think?"

"When did you take up counseling?"

"Isn't every wife and mother a full-time counselor too?"

An ocean-deep silence seemed to rebut her theory. Then Fred cleared his throat. "Well, I'm sure your mind is churning a mile a minute with Junior home and your in-laws on the way. I should let you get back to it."

The brusqueness of his tone rebuffed Paulette; he felt farther away than the five-mile drive to the office. "At this moment, my hands need to be churnin' at the stove. *McKinley* will be down any second, and I have a ton to do still. You know I'm no good in the kitchen."

"That's because you don't want to be."

The breath she expelled could've ruffled the papers on his desk. "Bye, Fred."

· ☙ ·

McKinley stepped over the wide plank at the top of the stairs, something he'd learned about a week after they moved into the house. If only he could've found a way to avoid all the other missteps in their household.

He paused before reaching the turn at the landing. Yes, his mother had ended her phone call with Dad—about five minutes later than she should have, from what he could ascertain. At one point, their voices had dipped and twirled in a coordinated fashion, dancing instead of sparring. They'd actually sounded like a married couple and not merely two people who'd raised a child together.

But he'd have to let them work that out. Today, he had more on his mind, like how he simultaneously yearned to see his girlfriend and dreaded seeing her. And why he felt so at home in this place that smelled like Jimmy Dean sausage and so out of place with the people who knew him first. But didn't know him best. He was weary from the constant push and pull, and today was only Friday, his first full day.

Cre-e-ak!

"McKinley?" His mother's voice sought him out.

Nearly drunk from inhaling the warm, greasy welcome, he'd forgotten about another noisy board just below the turn of the stairs. It always alerted his folks to his imminent arrival. Over time, the press of feet worked free one of the nails from the end of the plank, and he'd have to tamp it down to keep it from tearing a hole in his sock. Good thing he was wearing shoes.

"Need the hammer?" called Mom, well aware of the eccentricities of their one-hundred-year-old Victorian home.

McKinley released his grip on the rail and trod down the remaining steps. He rounded the corner to the kitchen. "Nahh. I'll fix it goin' up. Whatcha got goin' on in here?"

He winced, hearing himself. His words had begun dressing themselves in familiar Southern clothing, making themselves comfortable in North Carolina soil. He was dropping *g*'s left and right and elongating monosyllabic words so they took longer to say than to think of them. The more time he spent in Hickory Grove, the farther away Philadelphia not only felt but sounded, especially to his own ears. The other architects in his firm claimed they could always tell when he was talking to his mother.

He forced a cough to clear his throat.

"You're not comin' down with something, are you, Son?" She set down the silicone spatula she was using to stir the bubbling contents in the pot and strode over to him, her hands outstretched.

McKinley stepped back. *Was she about to bring his head down and press her cheek to his—? Yes, yes, she was.* He bent at the waist and allowed her to take his temperature the way she'd always done it, skin to skin. "Mama, I'm all right. You're the one with the pink cheeks."

"Mine come from workin'. Your forehead doesn't feel warm though. Probably readjustin' to all these trees and North Carolina air. Whenever I visited home during college, I used to break out—"

"In hives, I know. You started eating the honey produced by native bees, and after a month or so, it cleared up." McKinley recited the story his mother first shared during his freshman year of college when he'd come back for Thanksgiving and repeated whenever he returned from any extended time away. Mom acted like she was waiting for his skin to react to an alien environment, confirming her fear that neither his body nor his spirit considered her home his home, too.

Suddenly feeling this urgent need to scratch the back of his neck, McKinley hooked a hand in the waistline of his jeans and pointed to the oven with the other. "You didn't say. What're you doing?" He purposely used a hard *g* at the end of the word as if to say, *You're right, Mama. I'm just passing through.*

"Well, what does it look like I'm doin'?" His mother plucked measuring cups, a spoon, and a large fork off the counter and dropped them with a clatter into a red mixing bowl in the stainless steel sink.

To him, it looked like Frederick McKinley Sr. had left a mess behind him before leaving for work. "Um . . . stirring something with a spatula instead of a spoon? Why didn't Dad clean up?"

She lifted the lid from the pot. Her outrage sailed over her shoulder. "Can you really not tell that I'm doin' the cookin' in here?" She replaced the top with a clank and faced him again, pointing to the sink and the residue on the countertop. "That's some type of batter in the bowl. Measurin' spoons . . . flour. This pot of grits. Sausage patties. Don't tell me you forgot what cookin' looks like."

He watched her as she snatched up the milk by its handle and strode toward him, his wide shoulders barricading the refrigerator. He barely had time to step out of her way as she flung open the right door and shoved the jug onto the top shelf, nearly toppling the bottle of orange juice.

"No, I haven't forgotten. I'm just shocked that you're the one hard at work in here. I should have known it would've been strange for Dad to leave all this behind for you to merely watch over. But isn't it kinda late for breakfast?" McKinley sidled over to the square kitchen table and, feeling slightly peckish, eyed the fruit in the ceramic bowl. No, sausage would taste way better than an apple. When he headed in the direction of the meat draining on a paper towel, he ran smack into his mother's disbelieving gaze.

He froze. "What?"

His mother fisted a hand on each hip, her elbows nearly forming right angles with her body. "Well, if you like, I could call it brunch since it's nearly noon. It'll be twelve thirty before we sit down at the table. I hope you feel rested."

McKinley resisted the urge to check the time ticking away on the wall beside the refrigerator. That merciless second hand on the large clock hanging there used to mind him as he bent over his books at his makeshift desk, their kitchen table; it once held more books than plates on any given weekday. As soon as he gobbled down his sausage biscuit or bowl of Cinnamon Toast Crunch, he'd pull out that middle chair on the left side and do his best not to move until that clock told him he could.

Homeschooling, the only thing Paulette Baldwin allowed to construct a fence around their life. She actually kept to a schedule, outlined by the clock and the black leather-bound teacher planner that was still wedged beside the Bible on their bookshelf. She insisted he use one of those No. 2 pencils, the kind he had to sharpen every couple minutes because he pressed too hard on the tip. And heaven forbid he "decorated his paper" with what his mother deemed doodling, all the houses and trees and funny characters McKinley drew in the margins of his work.

Yet it was his "doodling" that had uprooted him from his own well-timed life in Philadelphia and plopped him back at his mother's table. His father needed his help with work. McKinley avoided making eye contact with his archenemy, refusing to show that clock any respect by acknowledging its presence. Not that it was hard to ignore it. His mother, fussing under her breath, had taken firm hold of his attention.

"I know he didn't walk in here and tell me I can't cook. After all that trouble I went to, makin' biscuits . . ." She stalked to the sink, rinsed out a dishcloth, and commenced to scrubbing the counter.

"Mom, I didn't mean to hurt your feelings. I'm just not used to seeing you standing in front of anything but the dry-erase board or the piano, definitely not the stove." He walked to the left side of the kitchen, where the cabinets and countertops met in a corner. After bracing his hands on the counter and hoisting himself up, he rested his back on the doors behind him.

"You've been away for nearly a year. There are a lot of things you're not used to seein' around here, I bet. However,

I see you didn't forget one of your favorite spots." Paulette turned the faucet to hot and squeezed dish soap into the sink.

"You're telling me you started baking and cooking while I was gone? Must be that fancy vintage stove."

Paulette followed McKinley's gaze to the cream-colored range. "Remember, you're not the only designer in the family. Your dad felt the old one was 'too utilitarian.' His word, not mine. He says this one fits the style of our Victorian better. Plus, it has a double oven."

McKinley laughed. "In other words, it wasn't pretty or expensive enough."

She shrugged.

"First, you greet me at the airport with a handful of 'notes' that look a lot like lists, and now this. Where's my mama? What have you done with her?"

"I put her between a biscuit and ate her," Paulette quipped with a wink. She'd turned down the flame under her temper. "Your dad is already at the office, by the way, just like I warned you yesterday. He's expectin' you to meet him there after you eat. Fred didn't think you'd sleep this late, but I guess our nine to two thirty school days are long gone. You set your own time now." Her fingers dripping, Paulette wrapped one arm around the tin of flour and her other fingers pinched the lid on the can of Crisco.

He should've known better. Most of his life, he was pulling and she was pushing, but in the same direction. McKinley had been away for so long, he'd forgotten. Or maybe he was imagining distance where there was none so he'd feel better about all that he hadn't shared with her.

Yet, he reminded himself and silently promised his mother as he hopped down and gently wrested the containers from her. "Mama, I got it. If these slip out of your hands, we'll have a mess. And then we won't be able to enjoy—"

"The biscuits!"

He caught the shortening and the flour as she turned toward the oven and flung open its door. Sniffing, he peeked over her shoulder. Golden and fluffy. But was that only the savory aroma of hope that Mom had indeed embraced her inner Bett Burdell, whose pigs' feet could tempt a five-star chef? Snuggling his armful, he backed up as his mother slid the skillet from the oven rack and plopped it on a trivet by the stovetop. Using the tip of his sneaker, McKinley closed the oven behind her. "Is everything okay?"

Mom leaned over the pan and touched a biscuit with the tip of a finger. It sprang back. She shrugged at him. "I think so. How are the grits? Has the cheese melted?"

McKinley stowed the flour and the Crisco tin on the shelf of the pantry where his dad used to place them. That might have changed, too, for all he knew. Then he stirred the grits. No lumps, fluid as the waves in the ocean, without being runny. He grinned at her. Hope springs eternal. "They look good to me."

His mother waggled her brows and tightened the scrunchie encircling her low ponytail. "Not bad for a white woman."

Chapter Five

FRED KICKED OFF HIS SHOES and stretched his legs under his drafting table. He propped his chin in his hands and allowed his eyes to drift about his large corner office. A water spot in the top left edge. Chipped paint on the molding. Dusty shelves. Crooked sofa pillows. His neglected computer on a small desk in the far right. Oh, and that begonia! From all the leaves it was dripping near the window, the time to water it had come and gone.

Etta had gotten it into her head one afternoon last fall to take a cutting from the one growing outside by their patio. He should have banned her years ago from touching anything with a root to it. For a month or so, it clung to life in their sunroom; "Willy" even seemed to rally and actually grow an inch or so, either to spite Fred or because Paulette had gone and given the begonia a name. Then she got the notion to repot the poor thing. But Fred figured setting the old plant, basket and all, inside a bigger planter and sticking it near a window in his office didn't count. He shook his head at the crispy, burnt-looking leaves that had once felt like velvet and gleamed like jade.

"That woman needs to keep her brown thumb to herself and leave these unsuspecting plants alone," he muttered as he padded to the break room up the hall.

Not that his wife's thumbs were actually brown, something his beloved aunt Juju had reminded him day in and day out. He'd given Paulette a hard time in the car yesterday, but he could understand why his wife resisted her in-laws' visits. It wasn't her way to suggest, "Hey, Fred, maybe Julia and Lawrence should come another time because I'm feeling this, that, and the other." Hers was a stacking-sandbags-against-the-door, staging-a-sit-in, storming-the-gates-of-heaven quiet yet firm type of resistance. Paulette's love suffered long.

Fred retrieved a pitcher, filled it, and headed back down the carpeted hallway to his office. Kneeling before the planter, he looked through the wall of windows facing the southwest corner of their office park, where a grove of trees at the edge of his building cast long evening shadows on a patch of tall grass. George & Company had cleared that area for those few employees who persisted in lighting up every couple of hours.

Knox called his employees "family," and like a benign father, he didn't play favorites, not even "if somebody got a mind to kill himself with one of them cigarettes." His words had moseyed from his mouth around his ever-present tooth-pick. The former South Carolina native considered himself too mannerly to force anybody to drive off the property to take a puff.

Fred was still grumbling about it, for he believed that such good intentions left a myriad of potholes on their way to a bad end. He had argued that management should take the high, narrow road and protect "the family" by designating the entire office park a smoke-free zone. In response, Knox strode right down the middle of the road as always, regardless of traffic from either direction. He cleared the space of trees, but he didn't add the benches smoking employees had requested.

After setting down the pitcher on the cherry file cabinet, he returned to the project glaring up at him. He'd been at this design since early this morning, before everyone else arrived. And here he was still at it, after they'd all skedaddled. He couldn't see how to make the arm of the chair seem comfortable, inviting. Like it belonged in someone's living room even though it was intended for the kitchen. Fred flicked his pencil, leaving a mark on the otherwise-clean sheet that crowed over his lack of creativity. Knox just might have to reassign this task.

Then Fred raised his chin. "No," he murmured. "*I'll* reassign it if I need to." But he knew he wouldn't need to. After a second or two of huffing and puffing, he picked up his pencil and erased the errant dark-gray mark.

He folded his legs around his chair that Paulette had bought him for his fifty-fifth birthday. At the time, he'd considered the gift a sign of aging—*an ergonomic chair for your birthday?*—and he was about as excited as she was for her rolling pin. But two weeks later, he was ready to post Paulette for President signs in his front yard. He stroked the deep-red fabric on the cushioned seat. "That woman."

But then his hand stilled. *That woman. What would she have him do?*

Again, Fred abandoned his drafting table and retreated to the vista on the other side of the glass. He braced his forehead against the sunbaked pane and peered over the parking lot and into the grove, searching. As the sole person toiling away in this side of the business this late on a Friday, he found only the swaying shadows of the oaks, pines, and maples that successive Georges had replanted over the years. Not even one car, let alone an answer, lurked there. He cupped his hand over his mustache and stroked the bristles on his cheeks and chin that had sprouted since his early morning shave.

"What should I do, Lord? Tell my family not to come?" Fred's words bounced off the glass. He wondered if they also ricocheted off the windows of heaven because at the moment, God's silence felt as palpable as his wife's. "Should I tell Aunt Juju she'll ruin my wife's birthday weekend if she and Uncle Lawrence show up?"

"Yes, that's exactly what you should do, Dad."

"Whuh—!" He spun toward his open door. There stood Fred Jr., one hand encircling the doorknob, the other pressed against the frame.

"Don't you think so? Based on my conversation with Mom over . . . let's see, I think we decided to call it brunch . . . you need to pick up that phone and give Aunt Juju a call and reschedule. I'm assuming canceling altogether is out of the question."

Look at Junior standing there, man enough to say something about his great-aunt, stirring those dreams Fred had long since put to bed of seeing his son at George & Company. "I've listened so long to hear your footsteps following after mine, I can hardly believe we'll be walking side by side for a little while. That'll take some getting used to."

Though Fred had resolved to keep his voice even, a slight tremor must have betrayed him. McKinley seemed to take a moment and swallow what appeared to be his shock before he spoke. "What was it Mom taught me? God's ways are higher and better. Better late than never, I suppose."

Fred gathered himself in the awkward silence that settled between the men, like cloud cover on a mountaintop.

"Did you give any thought to what I said a moment ago? Turning sixty is going to be momentous enough for her without dealing with Aunt Juju on top of it. You could always have them come down the following weekend, right after I leave. Then we can talk, and your time with them will feel more like a simple visit. What do you think?"

"You almost persuade me . . ." Frederick couldn't help but shake his head as part of a Scripture from Acts 26 popped into his head. Junior sure had a way with words when he was determined to use them. *Bold, like Papa,* he thought. *Always looks like he has something to say, like Aunt Juju, but rarely says it . . . like Etta.*

Most people would agree Junior had done what a son was supposed to do: he'd taken after his father. That was good and right. He had his father's hairline that tended toward a widow's peak if the barber didn't edge it up every two weeks. When he wasn't getting his hair twisted, Junior would brush it back from the same broad forehead he'd inherited. The boy had wide nostrils that flared when he was thinking— every bit a Baldwin trait. But his complexion was more his mother's.

Or should I say his grandmother's? Fred asked himself. That reddish undertone somewhere between hers and his that easily revealed his passionate temperament, another gift from Paulette, along with the way he took his time thinking about something. Those strong hands, Fred's. Their grace and artistry? That came from the piano-playing side of the family. *He's tall like me though,* Fred boasted to himself, and he puffed out his chest a bit and pulled himself to his full height to prove it, if only to the young man he was talking to.

"What is it, Dad? It feels like you're measuring me for the undertaker." Junior shifted from one foot to another, looking slightly uncomfortable in the center of his father's attention. He slowly entered, stopping in the middle of the room.

Fred met his son at the edge of his drafting table and extended his hand to bring Junior in close to clap him on the back. "I'm looking at you the way I want to look at you, taking stock of my genetic investment. You have something against that?" He wrapped a smile around the asperity in the question.

Junior blinked and nodded slowly, as if tasting the amount of salt in his dad's words. "I suppose that's your right," he murmured, and he stepped back.

Fred felt Junior let it go—his father's hand and the effort to argue. For the life of him, Fred didn't know why he was itching for a fight, to knock his son down a peg. It was all well and good for his son to walk into his manhood, but folks needed to acknowledge who was still in charge, at least in his own house. And by all rights, this George & Company office was where he lived and breathed.

· ୧୨ ·

A few days after his twelfth birthday, McKinley started hunting down his father. Anytime he saw Dad standing still, he'd hurry to his side, to see if he'd grown one more inch overnight. McKinley tried to inconspicuously run his hand from the top of his own head to his father's when he wasn't looking. Sometimes, McKinley would stand with his back to his dad's and raise his eyebrow at his mom. She would either shake her head or give him a thumbs up, probably wondering where all this growth came from that somehow didn't translate to her Christmas card. Every year the incline from

McKinley's brow to his father's decreased. When McKinley crossed the threshold from boy- to manhood, the difference in their heights was negligible.

Today in his father's office, McKinley looked at Frederick Baldwin dead in his eye, no longer caring that the two now stood shoulder to shoulder. Deep down his dad didn't believe he'd ever measure up anyway, not in the way it counted. He thought McKinley too soft, that he'd had too easy a life—the life he himself had worked so hard to provide. In all his getting, his son didn't get an understanding after all about how the world really worked. *But isn't that why you went through what you did, Dad? So I could live the life I wanted and not the life others—including you—meted out to me?*

While McKinley was busy ducking and dodging the tumbleweeds blowing about his mind, Dad had walked toward the door. "Well, what? Are you ready to take a look around the showroom floor, go see what you're up against? It's a big project, this remodeling job. I hope you're ready."

It didn't sound like that was what he hoped. McKinley heard just the opposite: his father believed the size of the task would overwhelm his son's ability, his vision. But he hadn't flown home with a bag of beans in his pocket and no cow to speak of. Even if McKinley had to lean on somebody, it surely wouldn't be his father, as much as he respected him.

So like his mother, to wield the strings behind the curtain, and exactly like his dad to expect—or precipitate—the worst. It was part of the reason McKinley had been all fired up and in a hurry to move to Philadelphia after he graduated from college. Partly why he'd left North Carolina the day after Christmas nine months ago, though not the main reason why he'd come back.

Apparently thinking McKinley's answer was too long in coming, Dad put a hand on a shoulder that now bumped against his own to turn his son in the direction of the hallway, but McKinley pulled back. He hadn't trekked over here to tour the rambling rooms and hallways he had grown up running through. He knew where all the secrets tended to hide themselves in George & Company, and he wasn't planning to spend a Friday evening seeking them out. Twenty-seven years was more than long enough to let his dad lead him by the hand. It was time to find his own way even if it meant stumbling around in the dark.

"Dad, before we go on this tour, I think we should talk about my last visit."

His father's hand dropped from McKinley's shoulder.

"Remember when you caught me in your office the last time I was home—?"

"Let's not go there, not today."

McKinley took a deep breath, recognizing the dismissive tone. "Okay, but what about calling Aunt Juju and Uncle Lawrence?"

"Call and say what exactly? 'Aunt Julia, I know you're my oldest living relative, and we love that you want to come, but y'all aren't welcome.'"

"I didn't say set fire to the welcome mat and give them a bowlful of ashes. It's her attitude that isn't welcome, and she just won't leave it at home. Don't you think that since it's Mom's birthday, she has a right to say how she wants to celebrate it?"

His father marched back to his drafting table and picked up his thin black pencil. He started scribbling on a large sheet of paper attached to it with clips. "You have quite a bit to say about your mom's guest list, considering not two minutes ago, you hadn't planned to attend this auspicious occasion yourself."

McKinley listened to the scratching noises the pencil made as a figure began to take shape beneath his dad's long, slim fingers. He knew the man didn't expect a response. Typically Fred preached, and McKinley nodded a silent *amen*.

Too bad. McKinley wasn't feeling "typical" these days. "True, but I'm all in now." He watched his father add curved arms to the chair, then erase them. "Why does Juju give Mama such a hard time?"

His father pursed his lips and blew away the bits of eraser from the page. "Because she feels it's her right to give everybody a hard time. She's your only great-aunt. She takes the title of family matriarch seriously."

"But it's more than that. She has this special in for Mama in particular. I know you see it."

His father looked up. He slowly brushed off his paper. "Oh, you do, do you? Any in my aunt might have is her business. It don't have nuthin' to do with me. Or you, matter of fact." Dad slipped into the familiar, relaxed vernacular he used to make his point when nobody else was around. Something happened when he talked about his family. McKinley clearly heard the memories and emotions it conjured up in his father, just like his own coworkers in Philly heard it when he spoke.

McKinley swallowed. "It has everything to do with me. Why does Mom's skin matter so much to my great-aunt? Didn't you raise me to think that color shouldn't be a barrier? It's a part of me but not the biggest by far."

"Go on with your bad self and all this 'color doesn't matter' business. You and I both know it very well does to some people. It can help you or hurt you. Everybody might act like they're down with Black folks, but let you or me pack up and move to the wrong upscale neighborhood or step into the wrong store on the right side of town . . ."

Dad moved his head side to side as if to shake off the image or in disbelief at his son's naiveté. "Talkin' about your color not definin' you. Come next week, when folks are back at work, I want you to look around you and count the number of Black people employed by G&C. Then you tell me that color doesn't matter."

McKinley huffed and shrugged. This wasn't an argument he could win, though he'd come home to take a stab at it. He was willing to return to Philly with a few knocks on his head, to get a little battered and bruised, but he hoped to leave a few marks on his opponent—not his father but the devil who tempted his father when the issue of race reared its misshapen head.

"Mmm-hmm. I thought so. That would be five, Son. Five

Black people—four of them in manufacturing who call me, the fifth, 'Mr. Baldwin.' And one of those four I recently hired. Do you know how I feel when I hear them call me— *me*—Mr. Baldwin? Like we live and work on some kind of plantation, and they're in the field and I'm in the house. But I'm not the right color to work in the house." He held out his hand, the warm hue of a slice of carrot cake, courtesy of his Black and West Indian ancestry.

"But Mama is. At least that's the way Aunt Juju tells it when she comes." McKinley didn't waste time searching for the right words. He was tired of sifting them and seeing which ones remained on his tongue. Those he spoke; the rest he tossed out. This time, he said them all.

"Maybe so. But that's grown folks business."

"Last I checked, I'm grown folks." McKinley met his dad's eyes, not insolently, but with intention. He wouldn't look down, away, elsewhere, or even up to his father. Not this time. Despite the heavy hand his father used to press down on his head, McKinley had finally caught up to the man he'd been chasing for over a decade.

Dad lowered his eyes to his table. He'd been tapping the page with the lead tip that had left minuscule dots all across his design. Dropping his pencil, he tore off the large sheet of paper, crunched it into a large ball, and dropped it into the large wastebasket under his desk.

McKinley sighed and looked past him through the large wall of windows. Treetops swayed in the strengthening breeze. A storm was brewing, partly man-made, partly natural.

· ↭ ·

The clouds broke open about nine thirty that night and divested themselves of all the rain and wind they'd been collecting since early afternoon. The storm shook the house with such a ferocity, Paulette ran to the front door and peeked through the sidelights. It was late September, seemingly too late in one season for a summer storm and too early in another to bring snow. "You're just as discombobulated as I am," she murmured to the dark sky.

What a day! The lumpy grits, rock-hard biscuits, and sage sausage links that were pink in the middle mocked her, for everything sure looked pretty on the plate. The day continued to throw up false fronts at choir rehearsal. Voices of Faith, her heinie . . . Those teenagers might have looked heavenly after getting fitted in their burgundy choir robes with cream stoles, but God only knew how they'd sound at church come Sunday morning after their lackluster, discordant rehearsal. Less than angelic was her guess. Paulette could just see those young people strolling—not marching—through the front doors and down the aisle, clutching their phones instead of hymnbooks, and forgetting the words to "Goin' Up Yonder." How dare she call herself a praise-and-worship leader!

And now this. This torrent. She cared little about the battle between warm updrafts and upper-level icy temperatures, nor the resultant dime-size hail that was pelting the grass and pinging against the windows. The downpour on the other side of the door might have given the semblance of peace and quiet within, but after her menfolk had filed into the house, their mouths straight lines, Paulette had felt anything but warm and cozy. They'd retreated to their opposing corners—McKinley to his bedroom and Fred to the den—and now Paulette resisted brushing off imaginary frost clinging to her bare arms.

She backed away from the door, toying with the idea of barging in on McKinley and asking, "What happened this time?" Before she could, however, a traitorous creak tattled on him. But was he headed down . . . or out for good?

"Shoot!" a deep voice hissed from the back stairs.

Hoping he wasn't bringing down his bags, Paulette hurried through the dining room into the kitchen. There, she found McKinley gripping his ankle and staring down a hole in the bottom of his sock. No shoes, which meant no luggage.

He looked up, grimacing. "Hey . . . I guess I should have listened to you this morning when you told me to get the hammer."

She shrugged. "I didn't exactly tell you. I merely asked . . . strongly. Are you okay?" Paulette was talking about something other than his sock. Plying a needle and thread was never her thing because she'd rather replace than repair.

He set down his foot. His eyes moved in her general direction but didn't land squarely on her. After a moment, his head slowly bobbed up and down. When he could barely reach her hip, that was a sign that tears were imminent.

"Boy, you're all right," his dad would intone while she would squat to gather McKinley close to console him. Something inside whispered that the day would come when he wouldn't fit inside her arms. She just never expected he wouldn't want to.

Paulette watched her son check himself for wounds and determine that indeed, he was all right; he would live. That had been his way since he was a teen. Stoic, "hard-pressed but not crushed." Every once in a while, she wished he would tell her where it hurt and allow her to apply a little salve on the wound. She yearned for the days of Neosporin, colorful adhesive bandages, and Mommy's kisses to make everything better. *When did you get so tall? So handsome? So . . . able?* Paulette failed to restrain her smile.

"What? Why are we smiling?"

"No reason. Can't a mama smile when her son comes home from the war? It's not the same without you here." Immediately she wished she could pluck the words from the air and plop them back into her mouth. But McKinley didn't get skittish. He didn't find a reason to go or look somewhere—anywhere—else. This time, the joy of motherhood didn't seem to come bearing weight or responsibility.

"Not enough fireworks?" He extended his fingers to simulate an explosion.

Maybe not. It had been more than an hour since she'd heard McKinley's firm, deliberate footsteps on the stairs and the heated snap of his bedroom door that had reverberated in the frigid house.

"Remember when you were fifteen, and Dad would let you man the wheel while he sat in the passenger seat? When y'all got home, you'd fling open the garage door, stomp into the house, and toss your learner's permit into the basket meant for our keys. More than once, I had to threaten, 'Boy, you'd better act like you know. Do I look like one of those mamas on teen Disney?'" She chuckled at the memory.

"And I had the sense not to answer that."

Paulette knew he had plenty of sense now and the license to prove it, yet she couldn't help wrapping one arm around his broad shoulders, something she had to raise on her toes a bit to do. Working with his father was supposed to build bridges, not dismantle them. "Are you okay?"

He returned her one-armed embrace. "Mm-hmm, a little frustrated. You know Dad."

"Yes, that's the devil I know," Paulette laughed, surprised that he'd actually responded to the question. "But what's the devil I don't? Did something happen today I need to hear about? That you want to tell me about, I mean." To give him breathing room, Paulette walked to the refrigerator and opened the door. She scanned the shelves and, relieved to find something she might actually eat, withdrew a container of cilantro and garlic shrimp she'd picked up from Costco along with a tub of whipped butter.

"Basically, he's not ready for me to drive." McKinley ran his hand lightly over his twists. "I tried to talk to him about Aunt Juju's visit."

"Y'all still walkin' in those tall weeds? That's how you get ticks." Paulette took down two small plates and set them on the counter beside the shrimp. "Care for some?"

"Sure, thanks." McKinley was quiet for a moment as his mother doled out two heaping spoonfuls for him and a smaller scoop for herself. "Yeah, and he wasn't havin' it. I get we don't want to offend Aunt Juju and Uncle Lawrence, but—"

"But what?" Paulette snapped on the plastic lid and returned the container to the refrigerator. She untwisted the tie on a bag of pita points.

"You know 'what.' It's worth discussing, don't you think?"

"Worth discussin' maybe, but not worth bangin' your head against a brick wall. That's why I pray."

"And stew. Don't tell me you don't stew over it." McKinley took his plate to the table.

Paulette trailed him with the warmed bread and sat to his right, in the spot Fred usually occupied at the head of the table. She handed him a few slices and took the time she spent chewing and swallowing to consider how to pick her way carefully to avoid any mines that could blow up in her face. "So—"

"Do *you* know why Aunt Juju mentions your complexion every time she visits?" McKinley's fork clinked onto his plate. He crossed his arms and propped his elbows on the table.

Her ears, sensitized by motherhood, heard a door opening. His stance showed that it hadn't been thrown wide, but Paulette would be able to wedge in her foot to hold it open so more conversation could squeeze through. She rested the tines of her fork on the edge of her plate. "Baby, you might be paintin' with a broad brush."

"I don't think so." McKinley squinted and contorted his lips into an upside-down U. He thrust back his shoulders and raised his chin. 'Nephew, that boy would do well to spend summers with some of his own color. Learn some Black history. No offense, to *you*, Etta.' 'Now, Etta, you wouldn't know 'bout this, would she, Frederick?' 'Shouldn't that son of yours go to school to see folks who look like him? Frederick, homeschooling with *her* kind is not enough.' 'Should've known Etta wouldn't season this food to our people's taste.'"

All McKinley needed was reddish, chin-length hair and magenta matte lipstick, and Paulette would've sworn she was sitting across from Fred's aunt. But she wasn't. *Girl, don't forget you have an example to set. You're the mama in the room.*

She cleared the plates from the table and set them down in the sink. As she ran water over them, she chided, "McKinley, show some respect. That's your family."

"You're my family, too. Despite what Aunt Juju tries to say. It's not what your skin looks like; it's the blood running under it that connects us."

She sat down. "And the blood Jesus shed for us that saves. That's the only color I care about. You know that." Paulette sighed and stepped off her pulpit. She'd be standing on that Sunday, directing her sorry choir. "You know your great-aunt is eighty-three years old; your uncle, eighty-five."

"Okay, I'm nearly twenty-eight. And you're—"

"Let's not go there. I'll be blowing out birthday candles soon enough. Next Saturday is right around the corner." Her self-deprecating laugh lived but a moment before dying. "But your aunt and uncle, and even your father, have been through things you haven't. *I* haven't." Paulette propped her chin on her fist. What was clear as day to her seemed but clouds and fog to McKinley.

"Why not? You're Black, aren't you?"

She winked at her son, loving his outrage, his defense of her. At least half of her. "My mama might take umbrage with that."

Chapter Six

―――――――❦―――――――

Tuesday Taylor was waiting for Paulette under the Christmas tree the year she turned fifteen years old. She was well past the age most girls played with dolls, but Daddy's girlfriend didn't know or care how old she was. When she was much younger, Paulette had lugged around that Sears Christmas catalog for a month, but Daddy was too busy flirting to pay attention to the big red circles she'd drawn around the Barbie Dreamhouse and its proud, plastic eleven-inch-high home-owners on the left-hand side of the page.

Her daddy used to tell her that Saint Nick had to ride in a limousine because December rarely brought snow to the sandhills of North Carolina. Paulette realized the truth the year her mama sent her that piano from California. If there was such a thing as Santa, he would've brought her mama back, not some instrument she couldn't even play at the time. So by the time she finally got the wrong doll, Paulette had long stopped believing, period—in Santa Claus, in wishing on stars and dreaming over toy catalogs, in the hope that there was such a thing as a love that lasted forever.

Neither Daddy nor his latest lady friend realized that Tuesday Taylor's feet were as big as the feet on the Ken doll sitting under somebody else's Christmas tree. They thought she'd like the child's toy that could turn brown in the sun and whose hair could change from blonde to brunette. Staring down at the grinning occupant of the cellophane-covered box, Paulette figured she'd never squeeze those painted toes into tiny high heels.

Right after Christmas, her father lost his job at the textile mill and they moved in with another one of his lady friends. Though each woman's skin was more chocolaty than the last, Daddy's heart and mind never did get straight after Bett left him. And somehow, they moved that piano with them. Paulette would sit on the bench in somebody else's house, twisting Tuesday's scalp and propping the doll in the sun so she'd turn browner than Paulette's too-pale skin. From morning to evening, villain to hero.

Almost the way Paulette changed her appearance, more than forty years later, simply by manipulating her cinnamon-colored lips before turning away from the three-story Victorian replica sitting on her husband's desk and the memories it conjured up. By widening her eyes just so, the way she practiced in her cheval mirror mounted in her bathroom, she could hold at bay the tears that threatened and seem surprised instead of horrified. *What in the world, Fred!*

"What were you *think*in'? What led you to do this?" As she drew out the *-is*, gracing her last word with a bonus syllable, Paulette's right hand gathered the front of her denim shirt dress. That second button just wouldn't stay closed. She braved another look back at the three-foot-high tower of wood shingles behind her. This time, her eyes widened of their own accord.

"Do you like it? I've been working on it for months out here so I could surprise you with it for your birthday. You just need to tell me your paint colors. I know you always wanted a dollhouse."

That way, somebody would have a real, honest-to-goodness home, even if it wasn't me. But she didn't remind him of that unfulfilled, childhood hope. Paulette couldn't pour ice water on his unabashed joys of creating and giving, even if she wasn't the real beneficiary. She swallowed, and the sigh that would have made her chest heave only produced a tremor. Real tears cut a trail through the rouge on her cheek and she took a halting step toward Frederick to embrace the man she couldn't talk to about anything that really mattered. Just like her daddy.

"Yes, I have. Thank you. So thoughtful. I'm sorry I spoiled your surprise by showing up here. I know you had the best intentions, and I appreciate this." She walked over to the model and peeked into the windows. "If Tuesday Taylor could see it, she wouldn't know what to do with herself. Who needs a Dreamhouse when I have you?"

Nothing but sweetness dripped from her words. It pooled on his lips when she worked up the energy to plant a kiss there.

· ⁊ ·

Shoot. She didn't like it. He could tell by the way she stretched her eyes like that. He thought he'd had it right this time, the perfect gift, despite the seeds of doubt Uncle Lawrence had planted when he'd mentioned it to him on the phone.

"Nephew," the older man had said after a moment, "she's already got a house and a couple of real-live baby dolls sleepin' in it. What's a grown woman gon' do with one that's make-believe?"

Fred hadn't known how to respond to his question. This was what he wanted to do, and nobody was going to change his mind about it. Especially Paulette.

"Is this gift *for* you or *from* you?"

"Uncle Lawrence, you know who this gift is for. My wife. Of course I don't picture her playing with it, but I'm clearing out a place in the front room where she can set it up. It'll remind her of how far she's come, from the little girl wanting a Barbie Dreamhouse to a wife and mother finally livin' the dream!"

"Whose dream, Nephew? Sounds to me she's still not gettin' what she wants." And that was all he'd said on the matter.

Brief yet effective. Trust Uncle Lawrence. Fred flicked at the delicate miniature eave over the side porch, what he'd always wanted to add to his own house. Maybe she'd be more excited once he had the chance to finish the roof and furnish it. It wasn't like he'd planned to unveil his surprise until Saturday, after he'd had the chance to paint it and let everything dry. Etta would fully appreciate it then, his vision. *But it still won't hold a Barbie doll,* Fred had to admit.

"You've been busy. And here I thought you were working on some project for Knox."

"*We've* got some designs in development, but that's not all I do out here in my home office." The way Etta was eyeing the room, she could've been an early pioneer, exploring the western territory for the first time. Her visits to his home office had petered out over the past few years, so he'd felt safe building her such an elaborate birthday gift right under her nose.

Paulette picked up several of the large balls of paper scattered around the room. She started to flatten one out on the battered table her husband used for a desk. "I know, I know. Don't get defensive. But we both know you finished this space to assuage your guilt from puttin' so much time into George & Company. You can pretend you're actually accessible."

When Junior was in middle school, Fred had enlisted his son's help converting the unfinished room over the detached garage. Good father-son time, working on that project. That was how it had started out. But then the office space drew him further and further away from home even though it was less than fifty feet from their back door. Etta stopped popping over for lunch when he worked there on the weekends, quit dropping off cups of coffee after dinner. Now he saw her less and worked from home more.

"Etta, what are you talking about? And here, let me have that." Fred snatched the paper from her hands and reached for the rest.

"Wha—!" She wrestled with him over them at first, but then her button popped free and she gave up. She shook her head in disbelief. "Is there something you don't want me to see?"

"You know I don't like to share my designs until I'm finished. Besides, I might need them." He redistributed the crumpled paper under the large, rectangular table in the middle of the room. "What about the house?" Fred wished he'd listened to his uncle in the first place. This wasn't turning out anything like he'd planned.

Paulette hung her head and sighed, as if his sense of defeat was catching. "What would you give up, if it meant savin' your family?"

"Wh-what?" Fred spluttered, feeling like somebody had pushed him into the deep end and he'd swallowed water. "What kind of question is that, Etta?"

"I mean it. Would you walk away from G&C for McKinley? For me?"

Fred stared at his wife's back. He couldn't believe what she was asking him. She didn't even know what she was asking. "All this because I built you a dollhouse for your birthday? Did you want something else instead? If so, don't worry. I can take it to my office or . . . I don't know, save it for those grandchildren McKinley doesn't appear interested in producing." But there was no distracting her. He could tell she was holding on to that pot of stew with both hands and she'd keep stirring it.

"I mean it, Fred. Let it go—"

"Let *what* go? I don't understand what this, this—" he waved at the Victorian replica—"has to do with me, with my work." Fred had motored past confused and was rounding on frustrated. Angry even. How did her lack of gratitude relegate him to the penalty box?

"Everything you do is about makin' up for what you didn't have, what your family lost. And you assume that's what I'm doin', too. You spend each waking minute thinkin' about how to prove your worth at that company, a company that once rejected your grandfather—"

"You mean that stole from my grandfather." If she was going to accuse him of something, she best get the story right.

"See what I mean? I only want you to hold on to us, not the wrongs that've been done to you, real and imagined. Workin' there does nothing but drive a wedge between us, all of us, and within yourself. You can't enjoy your life's work the way you keep holdin' on to the past. But what about our future? Your son's future?"

"The future? I don't know what you're rantin' and ravin' about. Our money is tied up in George & Company!"

"You call this rantin' and ravin', my concern for you and our marriage? And what do you mean, 'our money is tied up'?"

"I mean . . ." His mouth seemed to work on a mouthful before spitting out, "Well, maybe that was the wrong choice of words. But how are we supposed to have a future if I give up my salary and my retirement?"

"When God said He had a future and a hope, I don't think this is what He had in mind. Sinkin' your life into carryin' out a vendetta. Not even your grandfather could've envisioned this."

Fred's jaws clenched and he looked away from his wife. "Trust me. Papa probably never envisioned I'd be married to someone like you either."

Chapter Seven

FROM HIS VANTAGE POINT at the corner of his bedroom window, McKinley watched his mother slowly traverse the driveway toward the house. He wondered what had gone down in Dad's office. Nothing good, by the looks of things. Maybe his father had finally told her what he'd been up to all these months. If he didn't soon, McKinley would; part of the reason he'd come home was to tell his father that very thing.

He heard the back door shut firmly. Mom never slammed it. Too much Jesus in her for that. He slipped on his Nikes. This farmers' market she'd invited him to had better not be dusty or dirty or he might be the one slamming doors around here. These weren't *those* kind of sneakers.

Downstairs, he had to hunt for his mother and eventually heard her knocking about in the guest room on the other side of the house. His great-aunt claimed that the view from the bay window reminded her of the hillside on her daddy's property. McKinley tapped on the doorframe. "Hey, are you ready to go?"

Mom fluffed the queen-size pillow and arranged it with the other three before she smiled at him. "Let me change into something that can stand a little more grunge. You know I'm new to this whole gardening thing." She plucked an infinitesimal thread from the bed and scrutinized the rest of the room.

"Stop fussing, Mom. Aunt Juju's going to find something wrong no matter how hard you scrub and polish, and Uncle Lawrence will gladly welcome anything you do for him. Same as always. You might as well enjoy the rest of your day."

She frowned. "Somehow that doesn't make me feel better."

"Neither does the idea of scuffing up my kicks, but I'm going anyway." McKinley extended his leg and twisted his foot this way and that so she could admire his white-on-white Air Force One low-tops.

"Oh . . . okay." Her vacant expression told on her: she had no idea what she was looking at.

"Where y'all going?" a deep voice asked over his shoulder.

McKinley turned his head ninety degrees and found his dad standing there, holding a coffee cup. "Hey. Taking a work break?" From the sounds to his right, his mother was still at it, moving this and that around in her efforts to perfect their guest suite for the coming onslaught.

"Yep. Pretty sure I did enough damage this morning to call it a day. Y'all going somewhere?" The "y'all" his father expected to answer obviously wasn't McKinley. He was looking past his son.

McKinley's eyes narrowed. He couldn't decide whether to pursue the meaning of his father's elliptical statement about "damage" or answer the question anyway. Before he figured it out, his mother rendered him speechless by taking care of both birds with one smoothly delivered, yet sharply pointed stone.

"Maybe you can make up for it by comin' with us to the farmers' market. The one I thought about is outside of Asheville." She set a stack of towels on the end of the bed and joined them in the doorway.

His father sipped his coffee, his eyes unreadable over the lip of the porcelain cup. McKinley thought he was searching for a way to turn her down.

"Are you sure you want me to come? I get the sense this was a mother-son date. You didn't mention the farmers' market when we were talking in my office." He and McKinley pressed their backs against the wall to let her pass.

She traipsed down the hallway toward the family room, leaving a trail of words for her husband and son to follow. "Instead of startin' completely from seeds, the man at the Home Depot suggested I check out some full-grown plants at the market to supplement what's growin' in my garden. The prices are better and they're healthier there. McKinley came up with the idea of goin' to relive our old field-trip days."

That wasn't exactly how McKinley remembered it, but he didn't say anything. Of course, those field trips didn't typically include his father, but that was then and this was now. Before McKinley could change his sneakers or count to ten, they were loading up. A little more than an hour later his father was trudging uphill behind them toward the large tents along with the rest of the Saturday crowd. At the entrance Dad asked, "So where to first? Think they have any furniture I can look at?"

Maybe he was thinking about all his wife's note-taking Thursday, but a schedule was still anathema to her. Sure enough, Mom gazed at all the booths teeming with activity as if she was wondering how she came to be there towing McKinley's old red Radio Flyer wagon.

"What plants did you have in mind?" Apparently Dad was dead set on wringing a plan of some sort out of her.

She scowled at him. "Fred, if you don't . . ."

He looked befuddled. "What?"

Something behind him caught her eye. "Wait a minute." Mom hurried off but was back in a flash with a multicolored woven basket. She thrust it at her husband. "Here. You and McKinley shop for . . . whatever . . . and I'll meet you back here in an hour and a half."

"But . . ." Dad watched her walk off, the wagon rattling behind her. "Didn't we come to keep her company?"

McKinley laughed. "That's what the drive up and back is for. Maybe you started asking too many questions." He shrugged and reached for the basket. "We can fill this while we talk." He walked toward bins of cucumbers, tomatoes, and green peppers, but his father hung back, looking like he wanted to be anywhere but there. With his son.

McKinley juggled a pepper. "Is it my breath?"

Dad moved beside him. He touched one tomato after another. He gave three to the vendor. "These are firm enough."

McKinley selected a few peppers and handed them over. They purchased the vegetables and moved along the wide path past pumpkin patches, stacks of different varieties of squash, and bunches of collard greens. "When I saw Mom this morning, she was looking a little upset. Is it something you said?"

"What's that supposed to mean?" His father lagged behind McKinley to let a couple and three children pass. The toddler licked a striped lollipop as round as her face.

McKinley shrugged, not prepared to get into it now, when he could barely hear his own thoughts, let alone his father's. He knew that crowd was nothing compared to the number of lookie-loos who would flock to the Blue Ridge Mountains next month to view the fall's peak season. Right now, the leaves on the hillside were a mixed palette of shadowy gray, blue, and green as they geared up for October's extravaganza.

"Junior." Dad pointed.

McKinley applauded when he saw the words *Food Court* painted on a cloth hanging between the white pickets of a fenced-in area. He strolled with him toward the group of vendors selling smoked turkey legs, chopped barbecue and pulled pork, roasted corn, fried fruit pies, apple cider donuts, and other baked goods. Without discussing it, they both joined the queue for the sandwiches. It wasn't until they held their white paper-wrapped barbecue topped with coleslaw and Texas Pete hot sauce that McKinley spoke.

But "Is that okay?" was all he mumbled before ambling over to an empty picnic table.

Fred straddled the faded, weather-pummeled length of wood and sat, looking like he was riding a horse. He said a quick prayer, unwrapped his sandwich, and took a bite.

McKinley looped first one leg, then the other over the bench and faced the table. The paper crinkled as he fiddled with its folded edges and tried to settle his thoughts. He used to struggle with his dad's brand of quiet. It didn't feel like his mother's, who could communicate just as well without words as she did with a mouth full of them. She employed smiles, raised eyebrows, and a touch as easily as she wielded nouns, verbs, and adjectives. Her silence was more an interlude; it allowed her to process what had been said, anticipate whatever was coming, or savor the present moment.

Dad's quiet, on the other hand, conveyed his disapproval or withdrawal, almost like he was biding his time. It had taken years for McKinley to learn to wait, to avoid filling these moments with useless babble. So he sat there observing the comings and goings of the shoppers and diners and inhaling the aromas of the food while surreptitiously studying his father under his long lashes, a gift his mama had said was wasted on her son. They certainly came in handy today.

When his father was about halfway through his sandwich,

he checked his watch. "I wonder where your mother is right now."

McKinley made a show of stretching tall and peering over the heads of the people around him. He nodded at two men wearing scuffed boots and plaid shirts draped over their jeans. They plopped down their plates of fried apple pie and apple cider donuts before sitting at the other end of the table. "Your guess is as good as mine. Why did she take up gardening?"

"Your guess is as . . . To fill the time, I suppose. She's seemed out of sorts lately. At loose ends. She keeps saying all kinds of things that don't make sense." Dad took another bite and chewed slowly, his eyes on everything but the company across from him.

"Like what?"

"Like . . ." He swallowed, playing with the shreds of barbecue and coleslaw that had dripped from his hamburger. A piece of meat lodged itself in his mustache.

It wasn't like Dad to search for his words once he started speaking. He either said something or he didn't. McKinley wondered if guilt had him all choked up; it had a way of doing that. "Have you told her? Is that the problem?"

Dad crumpled up the paper around the last quarter of his sandwich and leaned over the table toward McKinley. He brushed off the hair over his lip. "That's between me and your mother, Junior. Don't start smellin' yourself. I told you that last Christmas—"

"I know what you told me, Dad." McKinley saw the men

at the other end shoot curious glances their way before turning their attention back to their food. He forced himself to
speak more calmly. "I didn't like it then, and I still don't.
Especially now that some things have changed."

"I don't right much care how you feel about it, Junior, and
nothing has changed on my side of the table. It's still not your
business." Dad rose and lifted his leg over the seat. He picked
up his trash and turned away.

"Oh, so now you're the one who's running away?" McKinley
didn't bother to lower his voice this time.

His father glared at him. "Nobody's running anywhere.
I'm just choosing to leave this conversation open-ended, like
that plane ticket you bought."

· ↷ ·

Fred let his foot off the gas and coasted down the mountain.
Any faster, he'd have to use one of the truck escape ramps
made of gravel and sand on the side of the parkway. That
boy had gotten under his skin. A quick glance in the rearview
mirror told him Junior was steaming, too.

"Everything all right?"

He heard Paulette's question but took a breath before he
answered. He was afraid his voice would shake, he was so
rattled. *Anger,* he told himself, *good old righteous anger.* Fred
refused to give credence to his son's opinions on the matter.
He knew how to handle his own—

"Fred, if you grip that steerin' wheel any tighter, your

fingers are gonna snap off. What happened?" Paulette looked around the seat at McKinley.

She always cared about what that boy was doing. Fred's eyes followed hers, but Junior had the nerve to pretend he was asleep. The nerve or the wisdom. "Nothing happened, Etta. I'm just tired, and I'm thinking about this design that has me stumped. I'm not sure why it's giving me so much trouble."

He felt rather than saw her roll her eyes. She loved him too much to do it in his line of sight. Knowing her, she was praying for patience and understanding over there. "Not to bring up work or anything else that might come between us." Fred tried and failed to strip the fine layer of sarcasm that coated his words.

"Fred . . ."

"I'm sorry, Etta." And he was. God knew how much he loved her. Oh, how much. The fingers on his right hand hurt when he unfurled them from the wheel. Slowly he lowered his hand to the seat and rested it on the console between him and Paulette. He hoped she sensed how he wanted to wrap his fingers around her thigh, left bare by the rise of her shorts.

Paulette shifted in her seat and moved closer to her right. She rested her arm on the door and propped the side of her face in her palm. Her eyes seemed glued to the miles of treetops stretching into the distance on the other side of the guardrail.

Fred's shoulders sank and he returned his hand to the wheel.

Chapter Eight

SUNDAY

"Y'all comin'?"

"Now, Dad, you know we're coming. Does nothing ever change around here? You've been asking that question more than twenty years, every Sunday morning," McKinley mumbled, safe in his room, up and away from his father's ears. McKinley perched on the end of his bed and slipped on his black dress shoes, glad he never untied them, and wriggled his toes in the soft leather.

"McKinley!" A higher voice shot up the stairs.

Uh-oh. That was too close to the back door. If his mama had neared the garage, Dad had a right to sound the way he did. McKinley *was* late. He opened his door just in time to hear his father's grumblings.

"I tell you, nothing ever changes. We're still running to church after all these years. I'm glad Jesus is comin' back for us because otherwise, we'd miss the bus."

"I see we agree on something," McKinley told himself, so low he barely heard himself. Feeling like he was sixteen again, he hurried down and jumped over the last three stairs.

With nary a how-de-do, Frederick retrieved his keys from the hook behind the open back door and enclosed them within his fist. He never tossed his set into the basket with the others. Years ago, Paulette had grabbed his set by mistake, and he'd been unable to unlock G&C's doors. That had only happened once.

But the Baldwins had reenacted this Sunday morning tableau year after year, from the time when McKinley was young enough to try to sneak Hot Wheels cars into church. He'd squeeze every last bit of sleep he could out of his pillow and jump out of bed at the last possible minute. His mother would complete a million and one chores before getting dressed, then lose the purse or the shoes she wanted to use. Dad would cook a full breakfast, study his Sunday school lesson, finish his coffee, and still have time to tap his foot for twenty minutes by the garage door. During the eleven-minute drive to Mount Olive Church, his father muttered about schedules, missing Communion cups, the church budget, the next meeting of the usher board, and the myriad other duties senior deacons oversaw.

His mama always led them in prayer.

That morning, as soon as they uttered a hasty *amen*, Fred swung into the reserved spot that embraced his Mercedes each week, between Reverend Maiden's Ford Explorer and Sister Jackson's Honda Pilot, lobbed a smile over his shoulder but didn't wait for his family to catch it, and quick-stepped toward the Family Life Center.

Paulette twisted around and stretched an arm over her seat. "Here, take this. It was on the shelf right under your bucket of bugs."

McKinley's arm was heavy as lead as he slowly lifted his hand to take the Bible she offered him. The name and date etched in the bottom right corner had nearly been scraped off, but he could make out *F d ri k M Kinl Ba win Jr.*

"Believe it or not, I thought about packin' up your things and cleanin' out your room last month. I mean, it's not like you're comin' back to stay. I walked over to your bookshelf and there it was. The pages still look crisp despite the worn-off name, don't they?"

He proved its mint condition by leafing through Genesis, Exodus, and Numbers—he always skipped Leviticus. His eighteenth birthday gift. When he would follow God as a man, a legal adult, not as a child. Only a few corners were bent, but from want of use, not lack of care.

McKinley ran his hand over the embossed cover, the weight of the Bible light in his lap. He picked it up every time he returned to Hickory Grove, along with his accent. A part of him wanted to reassure his mother he took his

Bible to church when he was in Philadelphia; it just traveled in the form of his Bible app. The stronger, stubborn part only let him offer, "Thanks for making sure I didn't forget it."

"That's what I'm here for. Ready for Sunday school?" She reached for the handle on her door.

McKinley stared out the window. His fingers traced the *H-O-L-Y* on the leather cover. "Remember how y'all had to force me go to vacation Bible school instead of soccer camp? Not that I was cut out for soccer then. I was about this big." McKinley held up his pinkie finger. "But man, I hated VBS and all the crafts, the games in the parking lot, having to do those hand motions to the music. The kids I didn't know and who didn't know me."

"You just liked stayin' home then."

"I still do. I just spell home a different way these days." He smiled to soften the sharp edges of the truth of his statement. He watched another car pull into the lot. "Remember the time you took me to the vacation Bible school at the Georges' church? Now that was fun."

Paulette frowned. "Oh, are they still at Valley Grace? From what I remember, somebody pushed you down. You came home with your T-shirt all torn and a bloody bandage on your elbow. I had to keep your father from goin' back and tearin' down that building, brick by brick, for lettin' somebody mess with a Baldwin!"

"But that's where I got to know Monroe. I was really no match for the other boy who pushed me down. He told me

I should go back to my own church, that I wasn't welcome there—"

"That's right! I'd forgotten all about that. I suppose your dad had a right to be good and mad. Then, at least." His mother's eyes narrowed, as if she was studying the events as they played out in her mind, frame by frame.

McKinley seemed to watch the same old movie as his mother, playing in the distance. "And Monroe punched him for it. Hard. Then he helped me up and told his dad on him. Mr. George took care of it. Afterwards, when we got to talkin', we realized who our parents were."

"And you've been buddies ever since," Mama murmured.

"Yep, and I hope things don't change and that Mr. George will always stick up for me like he did that day. I hate I never got to go back to his church. Dad wouldn't let me bring him with me to Mount Olive even though everybody else got to invite all their friends. I definitely would've enjoyed our VBS more if I could have asked Monroe."

"But would he have been comfortable? He might have felt out of place, like that piece of lint on your black jeans."

McKinley brushed away the fuzz clinging to his thigh.

"It's not like Knox ever volunteered to drive him over here, and we would've welcomed him."

He huffed. "Mmm-hmmm, I can just picture Dad rolling out the red carpet and handing him a church visitor card. I don't think so. Sunday mornings are notoriously the most segregated day of the week on a lot of pews, not just here in Hickory Grove."

Paulette reached between the headrests and used her index finger to tap the Bible resting on McKinley's legs. "'Then Peter replied, "I see very clearly that God shows no favoritism. In every nation he accepts those who fear him and do what is right."' Jesus welcomes everybody. Don't worry about how the rest of us feels about it."

"'Us' meaning Dad?" McKinley didn't bother hiding his skepticism.

"'Us' meaning us." She drew a big circle in the air. "And that includes the two people in this car who should've been inside the church ten minutes ago." His mother turned around and gathered her materials from the floor by her feet.

"How about we wait here a little while longer? We're already late." McKinley peered through his window at a family of four rushing up the steps leading to the front doors. Maybe this was the right moment to have a real good talk with her, since she was all prayed up from the drive over.

Mama scooted back in his direction.

Tension radiated from her like sound waves. McKinley sensed her desire to attend to whatever need her baby boy had and the pressure from managing her ministerial duties. Her faith or her family? McKinley read her burdened expression and decided to free her from having to choose what to sacrifice on the altar. "Never mind. Let's go in. I'm only trying to cut class." He waggled his eyebrows.

Paulette reached over the seat again and swatted his hand. "Boy . . ." Then she opened her door. "Comin' or . . . ?" It seemed she left the door ajar to see if he'd walk through.

Oh yeah, that's right. I'm grown. Something he didn't have to say to make it so. Unlike his dad, his mama had renounced her right to dam up the river to redirect its course; she searched for a high ground to cross it. Sure, she wanted his butt planted where it used to be, in the third row on the right side of Mount Olive. Yet she wouldn't presume to see him there or use any of her motherly wiles to put him there.

McKinley waggled his Bible in the air. "Of course I'm comin' . . . um, coming. I might not make it to Sunday school, but I'll be sitting in church before the praise-and-worship service starts. I heard the choir director keeps the church poppin'." He winked at her.

When he moved toward his door, he nearly missed her smile. The look that transported him back to the day when he was seven years old, and his mama had discovered him in one of the classrooms in the back of the church, rolling two of his favorite Hot Wheels cars up and over the back of one of the scarred pews they'd moved out of the sanctuary. How did she know he wasn't sitting where he was supposed to, with his too-short legs swinging to and fro under the seat, while she nodded and murmured, "Go 'head, Preacher!" from her spot at the piano? He never knew. She never felt the need to share those pertinent details with him.

That day, Mama had simply reached out her hand for his, wearing that same expression on her face that she wore right now, seemingly in no hurry. He could hear people in the sanctuary clapping and Miss Maybelle moaning the way she did every week as she waved her fan in her front-row seat—the sign that Pastor Maiden was reaching the peak of his sermon and would soon be wrapping up that Sunday's preaching. What his mama described as a *denouement* in English class. At any minute, the minister would stomp his right foot to signal the "come-to-Jesus music," how McKinley and his friends described it behind his mama's back. But the choir director wouldn't be there because she was busy handling things with her son in the back of the church.

The boy McKinley had read all that in her patient and unhurried, I'm-going-to-let-you-make-the-right-decision expression. So he'd stood and stumbled to her, clutching his die-cast electric-blue Lamborghini and canary 1955 Corvette. Without mumbling a word, McKinley had dropped his treasures into the trash can at the door of the classroom—something his mother hadn't told him or asked him to do. Not outright. He'd *chosen* to do it, and then he'd wrapped his fingers around hers. And McKinley hadn't seen those toys since.

McKinley watched his mama exit the car, her Bible nestled in her armpit and her stack of sheet music in her hands, confident that her son was minutes behind her. He was, a few steps even. Maybe Paulette Baldwin didn't control the twists and turns of the rivers, but obviously she was on good terms with the Man who did.

· ✆ ·

Frederick spotted Junior's head through the diamond-shaped pane in the double doors. He scooted over so his son could have the corner. His seat, where he could rest his arm during the service and wedge his backside when the service had gone ten minutes over time, but the choir had one more verse. Even the ushers knew to preserve that end of the pew while Fred was seeing to the Sunday school offering and laying hands on the pastor with the other deacons to ensure that the preacher and the Holy Spirit were on speaking terms.

Fred did his best not to draw undue attention to himself as he glanced around the sanctuary as Junior made his way down the aisle. He didn't want to preen, but his son sure cut a fine figure, even wearing those jeans of his. *These must be his dress pair since they don't have holes.*

Yesterday's brouhaha all but forgotten for the moment, Fred reveled in the way folks' heads turned as Junior passed by. Even Sarah Lou's daughter, who thought way too highly of that long hair she kept brushed back in that high, tight ponytail couldn't help but take a second look. Her forehead was a bit large, as far as he was concerned, but she came from good people. Now that he thought about it, that young lady might be just the motivation for Junior to move back to Hickory Grove, since he and Etta obviously weren't enough. He'd point her out after the service. Perhaps the girl could even distract Junior from bringing up unmentionable topics while he was home this week.

Fred nodded at Junior as he reached the pew. "Where've you been? You're all out of breath like you've been praise dancing in the hallway." He knew there was little chance of that.

"I walked across the parking lot to the FLC so I could take a phone call," Junior whispered back, his breath smelling like spearmint gum.

But before he could ask about who his son was calling, Fred heard murmurings. They rolled up from the back of the church, like a tsunami-size wave gathering strength as it approached the shore. He felt Junior shift, and when he turned to look over his shoulder, Fred ran right into the deeply set ocean-blue eyes of Monroe George.

"Hey, Mr. Baldwin. Didn't mean to scare you." Monroe reached over Junior and proffered his outstretched hand to greet the older man.

"Uh, hello there." Frederick enveloped the paler hand in his own brown one and squeezed. Firmly. The boy needed to cut his nails. Fred looked back up the aisle toward the doors of the church.

"It's just me, the bad penny," Monroe laughed, obviously reading the question written on the lines above Fred's eyes. He flipped back his hair and tucked his hands into the back pockets of his carpenter pants. "Hey, bro."

Junior shook his head. "*Bruh*, Monroe, not bro. How many times do I have to tell you? You sound like a white guy." He nodded toward the colorful Marvel insignia emblazoned on Monroe's wrinkled T-shirt. "I see you went all out for the occasion."

"Well, what you see is what you get." Monroe shrugged casually, grin still firmly planted—and growing—on his tanned face. He seemed oblivious to the congregants dressed to the nines, streaming into the church and finding their seats around them. Unlike Monroe, they knew the start of the praise-and-worship part of the service was but minutes away.

Fred felt the heat of dozens of eyes on them, and he no longer reveled in the attention Junior garnered. He and Paulette had always stressed the importance of showing respect for the HOUSE OF THE LORD—that's the way they pronounced it, like it was written in all caps. They assumed the proper mien at all times. They'd taught their son never to run in church, step onto the pulpit unless he was giving the sermon, show off, or raise his voice, "except for shoutin' out the Lord's name." Of course, they'd raised him to wear proper clothes, too, but maybe the folks in Philly or over at Valley Grace considered jeans, T-shirts, and sandals their Sunday-go-to-meetin' best.

"Uh, Dad, can you make space for one more?" Junior eyed the velvety red cushion stretching to his father's right.

Fred followed his son's look and waved at the couple perched at the opposite end of their row. He didn't inform his son that when Sister Johnson showed up at her customary ten minutes after the call to worship, she wouldn't take up but a seat and a half. He inched over and then still more when Junior's hip bumped his own. Monroe plopped down and crossed a sandaled foot over his knee, making himself comfortable in his corner of the pew. *In my corner,* Fred grumbled deep within himself and cocked an ear as Junior unfolded the program and explained the order of service to his guest.

Shoot, Fred nearly said out loud. He had planned to take his son on a personal tour of the Family Life Center after church, but more than likely Monroe's arrival had spoiled those plans. Still, Fred's chest expanded and his lips twitched under his mustache and he tapped Junior's shoulder.

Junior faced him, still laughing at something Monroe must have said.

Fred's mouth nearly touched his son's ear. "I bet you don't know what an accomplishment that FLC was. We passed a special collection plate for three years to establish that building fund. Then it took me months to get the deacon board to accept the plans."

"Is it because they thought the glass and brick didn't go with the wood of the church?" McKinley whispered. Then he leaned over to listen to Monroe.

What is he talking about? Fred pulled on McKinley's shirt and said, "You know, the banquet hall, kitchen, and meeting and activity rooms more than double the square footage of the church proper."

"That's cool, Dad. And I like the smaller chapel in the FLC, too. Good idea."

Actually, that was Etta's suggestion to set aside space for private prayer. *Should've thought of that myself.* Fred let Monroe maintain his claim on Junior's attention.

Now, that Family Life Center would've been something for McKinley to sink his baby teeth into—that was, if he'd kept his butt home instead of jaunting off to Philadelphia to work for some upstart architectural firm. There was nothing wrong with Hickory Grove, plenty of opportunities for work despite the size of the town. What a big fish Junior could've been. Why his son had felt the need to swim so far away to make rooms look pretty . . .

Junior's shoulder bumped Frederick's, and he slanted an eye over at the two younger men, chatting softly about Monroe's sisters and something or other. And Fred had thought *Junior's* attire was casual! He resisted the urge to bury his face in his hands. Junior had always grumped about having to wear "fancy clothes," as he used to put it. One day, Frederick had put his foot down about all the complaining. He figured if the sixth grader was old enough to wear man-size shoes, he could dress like one, too.

"Didn't God tell me 'come as you are'? That's what they said in Sunday school last week." At that very moment, Fred Jr. was exchanging his lime-green T-shirt and shorts for pin-striped suit pants and a light-blue button-down shirt.

"But you should want to wear your best for Jesus." Fred squatted down to buff his son's black leather shoes. "You can wear those clothes any old time. When I was your age, I had to get dressed up, too, not that I had nice things like yours. My church pants just had fewer patches than the other pairs. What would God think, seein' you stroll into church looking like you're going to dig ditches? Now, not another word about it; I don't want to hear what you don't like. When you run your own house, then you can do as you say. Until then . . ."

Fred fought to keep a straight face. Based on yesterday's conflict at the farmers' market, *then* had become *now*. Junior was running his own house and trying his best to run his father's.

"Dad." His breath warmed his father's neck.

Frederick's "Mmm-hmmm?" was low enough to properly honor the Lord.

"What's up with the foyer in the FLC?"

Junior couldn't be talking about the furniture. Fred had handpicked some of George & Company's best pieces to donate to Mount Olive. "What do you mean? Does it need more plants?"

He shook his head. "There wouldn't be space for them. That's the problem, the size. I'm surprised it wasn't a code violation. If you needed to exit during an emergency, people could get crushed trying to get through that one main door. I was planning to take Monroe over to see it after—"

Fred held up a hand. "Let's talk about it later. I see Deacon Fulton, and I should speak to him." He trampled four sets of toes to his left and his own rule about staying put once he found a seat. But he just couldn't believe McKinley had the nerve to criticize when he'd been an architect for barely a minute—and to mention it to Monroe George!

If that didn't beat all. Fred's little finger had accomplished more years of designing than the number of times those two had traveled around the sun. He threaded the buttons in the top two holes of his suit coat and went to see the deacon about some fans.

Chapter Nine

"PREACH IT!" Paulette called out unnecessarily. The minister was already dabbing at his temple with the effort he was exerting to deliver the message. But her shout was not merely exhortation. Her joy at hearing the Word had no place else to go but out of her mouth and up to heaven. She followed it up with a G-major chord progression and a two-octave run. Behind her, several people around the church clapped and shouted, "Amen!" One man even leaped to his feet. The Spirit was indeed high in the sanctuary.

Pale sunlight streamed through the reds, greens, and golds in the twelve stained-glass windows, six on each side of the church. They captured the life of eleven of the disciples.

The Babcock family had balked at donating money to commemorate the betrayer, so in the twelfth Jesus' open arms
welcomed the weary and heavy-laden. Paulette didn't find
much rest for her soul on that piano bench, but she could
see the entire sanctuary while perched on it.

Her seat was the only place where Paulette allowed her
emotion to take hold and overflow. Her daddy's people called
it "feelin' the Spirit," something he himself couldn't attest to
since he refused to let his well-sewn emotions get frayed, not
even at the edges. Daddy never stepped foot in a church after
Bett left them. No way would Harold Burdell ever loosen his
top button and trust the Lord to have His way. He'd learned
where loving with his whole heart could lead.

Paulette noted the ushers moving back to their posts at
the doors, so she transitioned into a softer song that entreated
people to "come to Jesus right now." From her vantage point
on the baby grand piano at the corner of the dais, she scanned
the sanctuary. She squinted at the fidgety hands and feet in
the choir loft—those folks never could keep still, whether it
was the high school seniors who should know better or the
boys in the sixth grade sitting in the front row whose attention spanned a whole two minutes.

Her eyes sought and found Fred and McKinley, sitting
stiffly with more than a little daylight between them. Paulette
smiled, grateful to see the visitor perched next to McKinley,
swaying side to side to the music. After the greeter had read
the announcements, she'd asked, "Is there anyone new to
Mount Olive?" Monroe had popped up from his seat, given

his name and church affiliation, and grinned like a ten-year-old at a Christmas party at the hearty "Welcome, Monroe!" the church offered in return. It looked like someone had dripped a splotch of Elmer's glue on Fred's flat mouth. Those lips wouldn't open even a millimeter.

Well, this next song should cause all my folks' shoulders to bump together and make some lips open up, she determined as Reverend Maiden let down his arms, looking slightly disappointed at the empty altar. Paulette caught the eyes of the electric guitar player and nodded as she launched into a faster beat. He stood and strapped on his instrument and began playing a bass line. She raised her right hand and motioned for the choir to stand and start rocking while simultaneously plying the keys with her left.

Some of the baritones in the back weren't paying attention and were nearly knocked over as the others stepped to the side. Paulette scowled at them—*I'm goin' to talk to their mamas. They should know better*—but nodded her head to the tenors, who sang, "'In the eye of the storm . . .'"

After two measures, Paulette nodded at the altos, then the sopranos, and finally the three boys in the back who fancied they sang bass. She rose slightly from the bench and raised her hand in a fist to cut the musical accompaniment just as the entire choir harmonized, "'You alone are the anchor.'" They kept their eyes locked on Mrs. Baldwin, their minister of music, as the musical accompaniment dropped in and they started clapping to the beat.

She had a gift for sensing the mood of the church—when

to play and when not to play. The pastor would wave his fingers or intone a certain word or Scripture, and Paulette knew whether to go with what they'd rehearsed or something altogether different. A lot was riding on her fingers, but those ten digits were up for carrying this new song.

· ❦ ·

"Monroe didn't have time to say hello, Mama. He had to meet his family for lunch—or I should say dinner. Why must it be nearly two o'clock every time when church lets out?" McKinley slapped the back of his right hand into the palm of his left to emphasize the last six words. Most of the congregation had scurried like ants from the sanctuary after they'd sung the final *amen* of the doxology. A few members gathered in groups in various corners of the sanctuary, chatting.

Paulette laughed and chucked him gently on his shoulder with her fist. "McKinley, hush your mouth. It's barely one fifteen."

"But it'll be well after two by the time y'all finish up here and we stop by the grocery store on the way home. Tell me I ain't lyin'." He stuffed his hands in his pockets and leaned against the side of the pew.

"You lyin'. We're goin' out to dinner once your dad finishes with the stewards, so no stop at the grocery store. Now, boy, be quiet and follow me so I can take off this robe and make sure those kids didn't destroy the choir room." She waited as he collected his Bible from the pew.

"Why do y'all still wear those heavy things? It's sweltering up there." Once McKinley graduated high school, the first thing he did was hang up his choir robe for good. He'd proclaimed that the next robe he wore would be a heavenly one.

"It's not that bad, and it's worth a little discomfort for the sake of uniformity. If we didn't, we'd have all manner of dress up in that choir loft, distractin' the boys even more than they are now." Paulette lowered her voice a notch and murmured, "See, that's what I'm talkin' 'bout. Look at the Turner girl over there. The robe covers all that up. Now I'm surprised at her mama. Sarah Lou should know better. Mmm-mmm. I won't have Reverend Maiden preachin' about any of my choir members."

"Mama, that *girl* you're talking about is a young woman, and at this point, she has her own mind. I should think you couldn't blame or credit her mother." McKinley trained his eyes on the scarlet carpet when they passed Ms. Sarah Lou and her daughter.

As they strolled down the aisle, his mother smiled hello at two ushers who were replacing the envelopes in the backs of the seats and collecting odds and ends members had left behind. Obviously everybody was well aware of Paulette's reticence, for no one approached them as they made their way toward the front doors of the church. She seemed to shrink once she stepped away from that oversize piano.

"I was hoping for more homemade biscuits today. Ow!" This time, the punch had some oomph to it, replacing its former jocularity.

"You think you're funny, don't you? That's all well and good until it comes time to pay for dinner."

"I've got a well-padded wallet in my own back pocket, thank you very much." McKinley pushed against the swinging door and allowed Mama to pass into the vestibule first. They turned right to head down the hall toward the large storage room where the choir stored its robes and other materials.

"But do you have the car keys?" At his crestfallen look, she laughed. "That's what I thought. I knew that would change your tune."

"Speaking of tunes, I liked that last song. I hadn't heard it before." He pressed the handle and shouldered open the heavy door, pushing back against it so she could enter the warm, musty room.

Mother wrinkled her nose and lifted the mantle over her head. "Time to get these robes dry-cleaned."

McKinley helped her shrug out of hers. "Told ya. But back to that song . . . there was something about the words. Maybe because it included Psalm 23. We had to write it down on this big poster paper in my third-grade Sunday school class, with all the *thy*s and *thou*s." He hummed a few bars as he tucked a hanger into the flowing arms of the burgundy robe and made sure the name of the church was visible on the gold stole. Then he hooked the hanger on his mother's waiting finger.

"It's called the King James Version," a gruff voice pronounced behind them. "It's probably been a long time since you read it for yourself."

Mother and son looked over their shoulders at the senior

Baldwin, standing in the doorway. McKinley waved his weathered Bible he'd tucked into his armpit. "This is the New King James, but I'm used to the NLT."

Fred wrinkled his lips. "Etta, that song was too country and western for my taste."

"What's country and western about God being our anchor in the storm?" McKinley pushed aside empty hangers so his mother could fit her robe among the others and followed his parents into the hallway.

"What's country about an electric guitar? That's more rock and roll, isn't it?"

"Exactly." Fred flicked the light switch. "I wasn't sure whether I was at a hoedown or a rock concert."

"There's a time and a place for songs like 'Come to Jesus,' even if nobody came today. But several did come when we reminded them that once we leave the altar, He alone is the anchor. Our faith. Not the church building, our family, or friends like Monroe. Not what we think faith looks like but what it is. Jesus' love surrounds us, as the song goes. All of us. And those folks pledged their life to Christ." Paulette waved her hands in the air in a hallelujah.

McKinley tried to cover his grin with his free hand, but it leaked around his fingers.

"He might like it, but I'm not talking about tickling people's ears with some feel-good tunes. What happened to the hymns and spirituals, gospel music?"

"You mean, like 'Gimme That Old-Time Religion'?" McKinley still had nightmares about sitting through church as a child while church members ten times his age groaned their way through songs.

"Yes, and stop looking like you had something bad to eat. We're throwing away our distinctive sound. It communicates our history, the brokenness of soul and spirit, and we're adding rhythm and blues and rock and roll—"

"And country and western? Our songs should communicate the faith behind it, right? Not the people singing it. Shouldn't it, Dad?"

"You mean people like Monroe George? He's not a member of our church. The music is to worship the God we're praising," Fred snapped.

McKinley shrugged. "Well, I was pleasantly surprised to see all those different faces in the church—younger, older, lighter, darker—especially my best friend's."

His father froze. "Best friend? Still, after all these years? I'd imagine you don't have that much in common."

"We have more in common than you think." McKinley reached for his mother's armload and smiled in response to the *thank you* she mouthed. "Anyway, that's a big change since I was here last. Sunday mornings tend to be our most segregated day of the week. Wouldn't God love to see us standing and singing together?"

"There's nothing wrong with holding on to our traditions."

They'd reached the double oak doors leading outside. McKinley flipped through the crisp pages of his Bible and started reading. "'But He answered and said to the one who told Him, "Who is My mother and who are My brothers?"

And He stretched out His hand toward His disciples and said, "Here are My mother and My brothers! For whoever does the will of My Father in heaven is My brother and sister and mother.""

He looked at his father. "That's from Matthew, chapter 12."

"I know the chapter and verse," Fred responded stiffly.

McKinley stared through the glass but looked past the stragglers descending the steps and walking toward the freedom the parking lot offered. All he could think about was his father and his dang traditions. He saw his mother move in his periphery.

Paulette's hand hovered over her husband's shoulder, not quite touching the dark-blue suit coat or the man it covered. "Fred, is there something else on your mind? I know we're not going to stand here in the vestibule, arguing over Scripture, the musical selections, and who I invited to church. Actually, I really hoped you'd gladly welcome somebody who's so special to your son. And I spent a lot of time on that new musical arrangement."

Fred's shoulders rose and fell, into his wife's grip and then out of it in the space of a breath. "I'm sorry, but . . ."

McKinley did a better job hiding his shock than he had masking his laughter. Dad, *apologizing*? He faced his folks.

"But what?" Paulette asked what McKinley couldn't.

"I just . . ." Fred peered through the glass, but as far as McKinley could tell, only two cars remained out front, theirs and the pastor's. "I hear what Reverend Maiden preached about, what you two are singing about with Monroe sitting right there with us. Love, forgiveness, trusting Jesus to guard my soul in the middle of the war. But sometimes my humanity just gets in the way."

His mouth opened again and clamped shut. Then his lips parted just enough for a few words to eke through. "Let's go. I'm hungry."

Chapter Ten

MCKINLEY ADDED A SCOOP of sugar to his cup and drained the rest of the French vanilla creamer. Paulette could tell the bottle was empty from the echoey clunk it made when he set it down on the counter. *That was a new bottle.* The child must be pouring it straight down his throat when she wasn't looking. She watched him slowly rotate his spoon clockwise, then counterclockwise before setting the cup in the microwave. He rested his head against the cabinet, his eyes on the coffee dripping into the pot, as the seconds ticked down to the beep. But he didn't move as his eyes slowly drifted shut.

Paulette shifted in the doorway so the floorboards could announce her presence.

McKinley immediately straightened and withdrew his cup.

"That won't keep you up tonight?" She dipped her head toward his hand.

"Nah. I laugh at this coffee. *Bwa-ha-ha-ha!*"

Paulette managed a breathy "Heh-heh-heh," but it almost hurt her insides to laugh. The afternoon had stretched like a warmed piece of chewing gum. She didn't think it would ever end.

Once the three Baldwins had changed clothes after their early dinner at the buffet, they'd gravitated to the den. Something about McKinley's return home had pulled the three back into their former habit of spending Sunday afternoons together. They'd turned on *The Bad Seed*, a 1950s-era black-and-white thriller they used to enjoy, but today, they'd only suffered through thirty minutes before Fred had begged off. He retreated to his garage office and McKinley had left to answer a call, leaving Paulette to kill more plants all by her lonesome.

"I'm just clumsy," she murmured to herself, picturing the herbs gasping for life in the pots below the sunroom window.

"What?" McKinley peered at her over his cup.

She picked at the black dirt packed under her fingernails. "Just thinking about my favorite lines from the movie. How's your coffee?"

"Good and hot, but we're out." He walked over to the trash can, depressed the pedal, and dropped in the large bottle he'd emptied a few minutes ago.

"No worries, I figured as much. We have an extra in the garage fridge. I noticed how you heated up the milk first before pouring the coffee. Nice." Paulette enjoyed one cup of strong liquid caffeine a day but drank it black. Fred preferred plain old half-and-half with a tad bit of sugar. The fancy French vanilla was all for McKinley.

"Kelsey showed me how to do that. It keeps me from cooling off my coffee with the amount of creamer I use. I'll replace the backup on my way home tomorrow since I'm planning to be here all week."

So the time together today hadn't sent him scrambling back to the hills. *Yet,* she emphasized. Paulette feigned interest in reorganizing the cookbooks to hide her relief at his visit's stay of execution, however temporary. She couldn't squelch her curiosity, however. She'd kill to have her notes right now to give her questions guardrails, but hearing his answer was worth the risk. "You said Kelsey? I'm assuming that's who called."

"Is *who* who called?"

Paulette looked up from the Church Ladies Divine Desserts cookbook entry for fresh lime pie that had snagged her attention. This recipe actually looked doable, even for an inept cook like herself. Not too many ingredients. "Who?"

McKinley frowned. "You asked me about a call I took earlier." He aimed an index finger at the page she was holding open. "Are you thinking about *cooking*? Again? You've spent more time in the kitchen this weekend than you have my whole childhood—if you don't count the years you spent when you were teaching in here."

"I wish you'd stop sayin' that, or at least sayin' it like that." Feeling like her dreams of pie had been stomped on by a pair of size twelve boots, Paulette closed the book with a slap. Fred would just have to continue managing all the meals and desserts in their household. She'd stick to what she did best: keeping the home fires burning. After slipping the book back into place and straightening the stack, she brushed her hands together. Matter settled.

"Saying what, that you're cooking more? Why is that a bad thing? It's never too late to change—until it is too late, that is." McKinley set down his empty cup beside the sink. He started opening cabinet doors, one after another. "Where do you keep the snacks in this house? They're not in their usual places."

"If it's never too late, then you shouldn't be so shocked to find me in the kitchen, wearin' an apron. Does your Kelsey like to cook?" Paulette sloshed some water in his cup and poured it out. She upended it on the plastic rack beside the sink. "As far as snacks, you know it's your daddy and me alone here now. You won't find—"

"*My* Kelsey?" McKinley was gripping the handle of the refrigerator door. He let it go, and it slowly whispered close.

Paulette balanced her bottom against the drawer by the stainless steel sink and crossed her arms. "Well . . . I mean, you know, your girlfriend. The creamer heater. Has she shared any other cookin' tips you can pass on to your mama? I imagine she misses you. It was nice of her to call this afternoon."

She listened to her rambling but couldn't seem to stop herself. Diarrhea of the mouth, her mama once called it. At least that's what Daddy told her. If Paulette hadn't had a fit of coughing, if God hadn't sent some globule of spit down her windpipe at that very moment, she probably would've kept right on talking around her foot. As it was, she managed a choked "I hope . . . *cough, cough* . . . we get to . . . *cough* . . . meet her one . . . *cough* . . . day."

McKinley crossed the kitchen and patted his mother gently on the back. "Are you okay? Need some water?"

"Uh-hmm." Paulette cleared her throat and shook her head. She took a deep breath. "No, uh, I'm fine. I just swallowed something." Unnecessary words, her nosiness, the rest of her toes, and her heel had wedged in her throat and blocked her windpipe.

"Oka-a-ay. If you say so. But to put a stop to your many questions and assumptions . . . no, Kelsey isn't *mine*. I'm not sure where you came up with that." McKinley returned to foraging around in the refrigerator.

He certainly hadn't lost his habit for letting out all the cold. Fred used to tell his son, "Take a mental picture of what's inside the refrigerator and think about it. Don't stand there with both doors wide-open. Nothing's gon' change." But she decided it wasn't worth the reminder. She'd already gotten the conversation off on the wrong foot. No need to blast the rest of her toes to smithereens by bringing up his daddy.

He gave up on the refrigerator and moved to the shelves beside the stove. He waggled a box of macaroni and cheese. "Now that's what I'm talkin' 'bout, my favorite! Do you have any plans for this?"

Paulette flicked her fingers that told him to have at it. Maybe the macaroni was what *he* had been "talkin' 'bout," but it wasn't the subject first and foremost on her mind. How could she work her way back to her questions around his love life? She bent down under the island and plucked a medium-sized pot from the shelf below. Then she walked over to fill it with water.

"I got it, Mama. The least I can do is boil the noodles. I do cook for myself, you know, when you and Dad aren't around." McKinley peeled back the lid on the box, his coffee a thing of the past.

They both relaxed in the silence settling between them as they watched the water go from a simmer to a rolling boil. After he poured the macaroni into the pot Paulette couldn't stop herself from filling, she handed him a spoon. "Here you go, Mr. Self-Sufficient."

He had the grace to smile as he accepted it. "As far as Kels is concerned, she's a good friend. Really good. I don't know what I'd have done without her the past two years since I moved to Philly. She . . . I don't know . . ." He shrugged.

Just like a man, her son. Paulette wished she had the gumption to ask, *She what?* but chose to finish the statement herself. *She twists your hair, calls you when you visit home, drives you to the airport, improves the way you make your favorite drink. Answers when you call her "Kels."* He didn't know what he'd do without her—what he used to think about his mama.

"I'm glad she's been so . . . supportive, McKinley. Does she know how you feel?"

He stirred the pasta and set down the spoon. "Yeah, I guess . . . ? I don't sit around writing notes about my love and gratitude—"

Love notes! Paulette nearly dropped the packet of hot dogs she'd dug out of the bottom of the freezer. She'd remembered how McKinley always paired the two processed foods, so she'd made a point of picking some up last month. She always wanted him to feel at home in Hickory Grove, however few and far between his visits. Did Kelsey—no, Kels—do the same for him in Philadelphia, make him feel at home?

"But she should have a pretty good idea how I feel. How long does this cook? I forgot to set the timer."

"Now, you know I don't do timers. Let's say you have about five more minutes. You can test it at that point. Throw it at the wall and see if it sticks or something. Doesn't your dad add salt to the water when he boils pasta?" She extended the shaker to him.

McKinley laughed. "For homemade, not for boxed, Mama. And I doubt elbows will cling to the wall like fully cooked spaghetti. You should really turn in your oven mitts. What would your mother say about your culinary short-comings?"

"That's not a pot for you to stir, Son. Besides, I think we can agree my mama wouldn't have the right to say a doggone thing to me about my limitations in the kitchen. You and your dad keep bringing her up lately when both of you should know better."

"Maybe because of the time you've been spending here in the kitchen wearing an apron—at least figuratively."

Paulette brushed her hands together much the way Fred did when he was ready to move on to the next thing. "Well, since you seem all set, I'm goin' to prepare my lessons for tomorrow. I have students first thing. Knowin' my home-schoolers, they'll be ten minutes late, but I need to be ready on time nonetheless." She stalked out of the room, not waiting to see if he got the message. Paulette was relatively sure it came across loud and clear.

Chapter Eleven

MONDAY

When Frederick stepped out, he hunched his shoulders against the chill in the air. Though the sun hadn't risen far enough in the pink-tinged sky to warm the earth, he could tell September was creeping to an end, taking summer with it. The tall trees leaned into the wind, as if they were trying to put up a strong defense, but the reddish edges of the leaves swirling about in eddies along the ground prophesied the coming days. Fred buttoned up his blazer as he waited for his son to gather his satchel and insulated coffee mug and step from the car. He nodded at the younger man. "Ready?"

Junior was still waking up, if the way he was dragging his feet across the gravel was any indication. Fred liked to arrive early, before anyone else; it gave him time to make the coffee in the break room and pour up a cup, then sip on it as he strolled through the empty halls. He wasn't above surveying the work of the other designers and peeking at Knox's calendar, not that he was purloining any ideas.

Fred relished playing the part of Mufasa from *The Lion King*, feeling that everything the office's overhead lights touched belonged to him. Later, he derived an inexplicable satisfaction from nodding at "late worshipers" from his drafting table as they walked by the office door he always kept open. If McKinley was going to accompany him to work this week, he'd just better hitch up his pants a little earlier in the morning and make the best of it.

Before they crunched across the forty feet to the double front doors, a car, its engine purring as it pulled into the lot, parked in one of the spaces marked for management. Frowning, Fred watched the interloper alight from his car and lock his doors. *Of course. I should've known. Like a moth to a flame . . .*

A smile sparked an alert twinkle in McKinley's formerly glazed eyes. "Monroe! He-e-y-y." He raised his mug. Coffee dripped through the open lid onto the rocks below.

The other half of M and M. Knox's apparent heir to his furniture-designing throne. Truly, Fred was hard-pressed to find something *not* to like about Monroe, but he wouldn't rest until he did, partly to ease his own conscience for the animus he held against the young man. From the talk around the office, Monroe was a fine catch; any woman would love to snag him. But he and McKinley clung to their bachelorhood like a life raft in turbulent seas swarming with whales large enough to swallow them in one gulp. Fred couldn't blame them. Lately, he felt like he was running from the Lord, too.

"Mr. Baldwin." McKinley's best friend thrust out his hand.

"Hey there, Monroe." Fred got the sense the young man was daring him to squeeze it as tightly as he had at church the day before, but Fred had to give it to him: he had a strong grip. Even Fred's papa would've had to agree.

Once, Fred had been walking with his grandfather down Hickory Grove's Main Street, and the owner of the local jot-'em-down store had stopped them to chide the elder Baldwin about his outstanding bill. After the man had gone his way, Papa's nose had scrunched up, making his forehead wrinkle from his brows to his hairline. He'd scrubbed his right hand on the side of his good Sunday pants before he'd clasped Fred by the shoulder and pinned him into place with his brown eyes.

Papa's voice always sounded grave-deep. "Frederick, you can learn somethin' by the way a man takes yo' hand. Whether he's got somethin' to hide, somethin' to say, or somethin' to prove."

"Whatcha mean, Papa? Why you shakin'? You afraid of somethin'?"

Somehow the older man had managed to keep his eyes

from overflowing. The tears that filled them had helped cool the fire that burned into his grandson's. Papa had looked the same way the night the stroke had felled Grandmama and he'd told Fred to run through the woods to use the neighbor's phone: he was facing a frightening truth head-on.

"Boy, I ain't afraid of nuthin' and nobody. But just mind what I say. The man will shake with one hand and steal yo' life wi' t'other. Listen wit' yo' eyes and yo' ears when it comes to the man. But don't trust neither one."

Fred squinted at Monroe in the parking lot of George & Company as the wind captured the rest of the memory and stole it away.

"Mr. Baldwin, I left mah proposal for the new nested-base router on your desk. I think it'll work much bettah when it comes to cabinet production. This router does all the borin', and when the wood comes off the machine, most of the hard work is done. Did you see the proposal?"

So that's it. Something to prove. Fred nodded his head at the young man who looked like Monroe but sounded so much like his father, Knox. "Yes, sure did. And I agree with you. That should save us lots of time, and we'll recoup the investment."

Monroe beamed. "I'll see what Dad has to say when he checks in later. Mom is forcin' him to take off for a few days after meetin' with a distributah at the market. They'll be at Wrightsville Beach until Wednesday night, but he should be in the office first thing Thursday. You'll probably talk to him yourself before then, if he has his way."

As far as Fred was concerned, the decision was made. No need to hear anything Knox had to say, even if he'd been in town, sitting in the office across from his own. Fred himself had taken hold of most of the decisions that affected design and production, and Knox simply signed off on them.

Junior's eyes communicated admiration. "Look at you, Roe, acting all grown-up, leaving proposals on desks and such. If you can convince my dad to use email, you'd really be doin' something."

"Why would I do that when I'm just going to print it out in order to read it anyway? Hard copies are better on these." Fred tapped the corners of his eyes. "You'll find out yourself one day." He resumed his march to the building. Time was a-wasting out there. As it was, he wouldn't be able to peek into Knox's office with Monroe around, though he still hoped to enjoy a walk through the halls and a quiet cup of coffee. No thermos for him.

The keys jingled as Fred turned the lock. "I'd ask you what you're doing here so early, but I have a good guess it has something to do with Junior here—*um-hmm*, I mean, McKinley." More and more, the longer Fred was around him, the name he wanted to call his son triumphed over the name he was supposed to call him. From the looks of it, however, his son hadn't noticed his father say it out loud. He stood back so the two friends could enter the building.

"No, sir, I've been spending more than enough tahm with this dude. I'm about to get sick of 'im. Actually, I came in this early to get a jump on some projects."

Fred caught his son's eye as he turned on the lights in the foyer. "'More than enough time'? But you just got home last Thursday."

McKinley shrugged as he glanced at Monroe. "We hung out in Philly last month."

"Yeah, man, good tahms." Monroe cleared his throat and angled his head toward the wide flight of stairs to the left of the main desk. "I'm headed up to my office. When you get a moment, come by. Still meetin' us for lunch?"

"Can't wait. Catch you later." The two bumped fists and Monroe took the floating stairs two at a time.

"You didn't mention Monroe's trip to Philadelphia." Fred wasn't sure why his heart felt stomped on, as if someone had chosen him last to play kickball. It wasn't like Junior had shared much of anything over the past nine months since he and his mother had last laid eyes on him. *You could've visited him yourself if you weren't being so muleheaded. Then you wouldn't be jealous of Monroe.*

"I didn't?" Junior mounted the stairs.

Junior knew good and well he hadn't. But Frederick wasn't going to press the issue. That wasn't his style. Maybe he'd ask Paulette later, and based on what she said, he'd lay claim to the hurt or let the matter go.

· ೞ ·

McKinley centered his sketch pad on his lap and shifted his position on the leather settee. He sat back with his arms outstretched, the fingers on his left hand twiddling his pencil.

He surveyed the foyer from his spot against the back wall and reimagined the layout, where the furniture would be placed, the new colors and accessories he envisioned.

New, large windows across the rear to allow more natural light. Green, deep-blue, and gold fabrics, paired with creamy half walls that invited more movement and conversation. A splash of orange here and there just because he wanted to. Clients browsing the latest displays in an additional showroom to the right. Distributors gathering in offices on the left. Caterers preparing food in the remodeled professional kitchen space. Mr. George presenting over lunch or dinner in the large meeting room in the back. Plants, real and artificial, sprouting from shelves, behind desks, and in the corners. Dad, patting him on the back in front of his colleagues, saying, "Job well done, Son."

McKinley couldn't remember the last time he'd dreamed of hearing—no, *expected* to hear—those words. Then it all came back to him: the minutes following his graduation, sweating under the blazing sun on the lawn of North Carolina State University . . .

"It's called a master's of architecture, Dad. I'm going into interior design."

His father had frowned. "I'd hoped you'd at least build things, since you didn't choose furniture design. I didn't pay all this money for you to learn how to make rooms look pretty . . ."

Two sets of footsteps tromping down the stairs and toward the back door woke McKinley from the nap he didn't know he was taking.

". . . acting like he's the big man on campus," a gruff voice muttered.

"But, man, you wait until Knox comes back," responded another snidely. "He'll put him in his place."

"Preferably outside. Clinton George had the right idea, lettin' the *right* people in and—"

"Keepin' the wrong ones out. And I don't mean at a no-smokin' section by the woods. The old man's prob'ly rollin' round and round in his grave right now seein' that . . ."

The back door swung open and clanged closed.

McKinley sat bolt upright, blinking slowly, trying to process the words, the voices, but his muddled brain wouldn't cooperate. He'd whispered on his cell phone until the wee hours like a teenager, and then Dad had insisted they accompany the rooster to work. If he'd remembered his father's morning routine, he might have ended last night's call early. *Nah, it was worth it,* he quickly reconsidered, *but I need to do something about what I heard.*

"What are you doing there, Junior? Are you sleeping on the job?" Dad had walked up during McKinley's half-awake state, and he stood there, his hands fisted on his hips, with his blazer thrown back.

He stands like a crime-fighting superhero. Maybe I should put him on the case. McKinley pushed himself to his feet, sending his pad to the floor with a slap. He winced as he squatted to retrieve his paper and pencil. Second on the agenda: replace that sofa. It was nice-looking, but customers certainly wouldn't find it comfortable. McKinley hoped it wasn't one of his father's designs. "I closed my eyes to picture the design we discussed this morning, and I guess I nodded off."

"You must have had a big lunch if you were sleeping so hard you didn't hear me walk up. I said your name twice. What will people think, seeing you conked out during work hours?"

McKinley knew that his father really wondered what people would think of him. Dad was always so focused on appearances. "Well, if you don't say anything else about it, I won't tell Mama you keep calling me 'Junior.' See, I wasn't as 'conked out' as you thought."

Dad pursed his lips, obviously not enjoying the feeling of the corner against his back. "Well, it's not a good look. Let's just leave it at that. Are you ready for the tour of the floor?"

"The floor" was what George & Company called the manufacturing end of the business. McKinley wasn't sure what all he'd redesign on that side of things, but he needed to explore his dad's ever-deepening involvement in G&C, what he should have set out to do last year instead of running away. For Mom's sake alone if nothing else.

"You ready? Do you need anything from the bag you left in my office?" He glanced at his watch a second time.

"No, I'll take general impressions and thoughts on this pad. Let's go."

Dad turned to lead the way across the campus, so dubbed by the employees. Trailing just behind him, McKinley raised his arms above his head and shook off the indolence that had settled on him after lunch. His clouded mind still hadn't figured out what he should do—if anything—about what he'd heard the two men say and what McKinley considered the underlying threat they presented to his father's position.

Once the sun had stretched and fully wakened, it had risen to the occasion with a power that made McKinley want to shed the blazer he'd worn for his father's sake. The grounds were lit with a golden glow that chased any hint of fall back under the shadows of the trees trimming the parking lot. The breeze was strong enough to cool his forehead . . . and carry a faint whiff of cigarettes.

"If I could, Dad, I'd get rid of that smoking area and add seating out there. Maybe something like that chair you were working on Saturday."

"Well, you can. Feel free to get to work on that." Dad used the side of his shoe to push a fallen branch off the sidewalk and into the grass. He peered up at the trees. "We need to get somebody out here to trim those. One good ice storm is all it would take, and they'll hurt somebody this winter. Just a lawsuit waiting to happen."

"Hold up. You're designing furniture, signing off on proposals for new bird's nest routing thingamajigs—"

"Nested-base routers." His father moved his hand as if to hurry McKinley's thoughts along.

"Yes, those. You're the one who commissioned me to draw up interior design plans, and now you're talking about getting trees trimmed. What's going on? The last time we talked in December—"

Dad held up the hand that had been reaching for the door to the warehouse. "You called what you were doing 'talking'? It was more like an inquisition."

That wasn't how he remembered it. "I'm only wondering how people feel about all this responsibility you're taking on."

"What do you mean?"

"I mean, are you well-liked around the office?" McKinley swatted at a fly.

Dad slid his hands into the pockets of his slacks. "Do you think I care if I'm liked, Fred Jr.? This isn't high school. Respect carries more weight than popularity."

"But what's the atmosphere here at G&C? You said yourself you're only one of five. Do you think it's hard for them taking direction from a Black man?" McKinley trusted his father to know the "them" in question.

"Isn't it always?" His father bit down on his bottom lip and looked at his feet for a moment before raising his head and meeting his son's gaze head-on. "Look, I know you're talking about Bill and Ray. I was at the top of the stairs, and I heard them spoutin' off. They're hot under the collar about having to go outside for a smoke, and it loosened their tongues—what does the Bible say? 'Out of the abundance of the heart the mouth speaks.' But that's not everybody, not even most. You'll find a rotten apple—or two or three—in every barrel."

The fly buzzed around McKinley's open mouth. Sometimes his father shocked him out of his shoes.

"Besides, I'm not *inside* G&C; I'm at the top."

His father had raised an issue that was more pressing than the attitudes in the workplace. "And again, my concern is, does Mama know the particulars about how you got there? What does Mr. George and the family think?"

"I've made it clear that I'm not going anywhere. That's what your mama needs to know. But Bill and Ray? Their butts are headed *out*. For good. They're not keeping up with the program." Dad shrugged and opened the door to the floor. They stepped inside the building, and the heavy steel door thunked to behind them.

McKinley took a deep whiff of shellac, lacquer, and fresh wood, scents that took him back to the days when he and Monroe used to sneak into the building. He watched a tall, muscular woman wearing jeans and a dark-blue crew neck T-shirt stride up to them, carrying what looked like blueprints under her arm.

"Hi, Mr. Baldwin. Is this the son you've been bragging about?"

Dad clasped McKinley's shoulder and smiled at him. "Yes, this is Fred Jr. But if you see Paulette, do me a favor and tell her I introduced him as McKinley. Son, this is our day supervisor, Ms. Lacey, one of the people I told you about that I recently hired."

"Hi, Ms. Lacey." McKinley shook her hand, thinking about his father's words: *Five Black people—four of them in manufacturing who call me, the fifth, 'Mr. Baldwin.' And one of those four I recently hired. Do you know how I feel when I hear them call me—me—Mr. Baldwin? Like we live and work on some kind of plantation, and they're in the field and I'm in the house. But I'm not the right color to work in the house."*

"Nice to meet you. Actually, it's 'Mrs.,' but call me Kim. That's what I keep telling your father. I feel old enough with all this gray in my hair."

His father laughed. "That's called wisdom. I've got some myself. Well, if you'll call me Fred, you've got a deal . . . Kim. I'll be with you in a minute to talk about those changes in scheduling that will affect the second shift. I need to show my young architect around."

"Sure thing, *Fred.*" She saluted with the thick roll of papers.

As she walked away, McKinley studied the green G&C logo emblazoned across the back of her shirt. "So you didn't answer earlier. How do you think Mr. George is going to feel about all these changes you've been making? He is your boss."

"Knox is not my boss."

A mask had settled over his father's face. McKinley wondered if he would suffocate beneath it. "Well, you do work for—"

"I work for myself."

Dad's tone brooked no argument. That was his way—honor him with silence, however oppressive, however dishonest it felt. McKinley never felt like himself during these moments. Always a baby in his mama's eyes; never a man in his father's, despite the compliments his employee had shared. What was the truth?

"I design furniture for George & Company. That's what I do. Knox and I do not have a relationship, and he doesn't tell me what to do. I'm not interested in his feelings, and he's not interested in mine. I think the business world would run more efficiently today if people left feelings out of things. I'm here to build things out of wood—to make furniture, not friends. It's called professionalism."

McKinley couldn't hold still, like he was a five-year-old sitting on the front pew, waiting for a long-winded pastor to close his Bible and the choir to sing. He certainly wasn't waving his fan in agreement in the amen corner. "But we're not automatons. Life doesn't work like an assembly line. You don't even employ one in here." He made a sweeping gesture to include the floor buzzing with activity around them.

"Dad, *people* run companies; we live in relationship to each other. You, me, Billy, Ray, *Kim*. And that means thoughts and emotions—*feelings*—are going to get in the way. As much as Mr. George obviously values your dedication and hard work, he'd welcome your input." McKinley wondered if his father avoided the guilt that probably accompanied him to the office each day by divorcing his emotions from his work.

"I don't give input. That implies I don't have any say-so, that I lack authority when that couldn't be further from the truth. I don't step off anybody's sidewalks." Dad's measured look seemed to imply that McKinley squatted on the weaker end of his mental scale. "Son, *input* is what you're giving me."

• ☙ •

Paulette's armpits felt damp, and she detested the feeling. She never broke into a sweat. When all her girlfriends were complaining about suffering the effects of their personal summer, she'd felt cool as a cucumber. And she didn't even eat cucumbers. *Chill,* she thought as she settled on a word she'd heard her students say. *That's a better way to describe Paulette Baldwin. I'm usually chill.*

She felt far from chill today though, with this eight-year-old banging her fifty-year-old Steinway with those worrisome sneakers that lit up every time they made contact. Paulette was closer to boiling over. She fanned the back of her neck, damp under her hair. Somebody had better come get this child.

But Paulette was supposed to be that somebody, the grown-up charged with that ignominious duty. Lucy Parker's mother had had the good sense to park herself in the Baldwins' driveway for forty-five blissful minutes, far from her daughter and her light-up shoes. Right this minute she was probably tapping away on the cell phone she kept glued to her fingertips even during piano recitals, leaving an indignant Paulette to count the number of times Lucy kicked at the brass pedals on her mama's upright piano as she warmed up with her arpeggios. The instrument was the only thing Bett Burdell had given her besides her thick brown hair, creamy complexion, and a legal-size envelope of dividend-paying memories.

Week after week, Paulette kept the busy little body still by gently patting Lucy's shoulder when she started swinging her sneakered feet, telling herself each time that the child was *inadvertently* striking the piano. Paulette would clench her jaw and remind herself that Lucy was just a precocious child who was worth the investment, like all young people.

Whomp!

"Enough!" Paulette had more important things to worry about today than polishing those scuff marks marring the piano's burnished finish.

Without saying a word, Lucy's fingers trailed off the keys. Even her obedience sounded discordant. And the way she cut her eyes at Paulette told the truth and put the devil to shame: the tiny musical wonder in ponytails knew exactly what she'd been doing.

"You've got to get up." Paulette gathered Lucy's books. The only child she planned to break a sweat over was her own. The girl's mama wasn't paying her enough to handle this, and her impish attitude had outpaced her God-given talent.

Lucy planted herself on the bench and crossed her arms. "I still have twenty minutes . . . Mrs. Baldwin."

Paulette noted the delay in Lucy's show of respect, for that was exactly what the child was putting on. Well, the show was over. "And you can use your remainin' time outside, writin' the notes on the last five measures, since I know you didn't practice last week and you'll try to learn the piece while you sit here like you did last week and the week before. You can sit beside your mama while you get it done. It's apparent you need some quality one-on-one time with her."

Her student's foot shifted.

"And if you touch that pedal one more time, it'll be the last thing you do in my house. Do you understand me?" Paulette didn't know what the exact consequences would be, but her tone bubbled with enough lava to convince the girl she'd encountered the right wrong one to mess with.

Lucy hopped up. "I'm going to tell my mama!"

"That's exactly what I want you to do, Lucy. Hurry along then and get to steppin'."

After showing her out and waving peremptorily to her mother, Paulette shut the door behind her with a click. Then she turned the dead bolt for good measure. Paulette huffed and brushed her bangs from her tacky forehead, already resolving to apologize for her uncharacteristic behavior before next week, assuming she'd cooled off by then.

Paulette shoved her hands in her pockets. The fingers on her right curled around the box, the item that had really sent her into a tizzy. Lucy Parker was only the flint that had set her smoldering kindling ablaze. She had to get this back into McKinley's room—more specifically, into the pocket of those distressed pants he'd been wearing the day they picked him up from the airport. And she needed to do it right now, before Fred drove him home from work. *What is that boy doing with a ring?*

You know what, she answered herself, absently stroking the velvety hump of the square-shaped jewelry box. *Say it, Etta.*

She stared over the piano, through the window in the front room. "It's an engagement ring. My son bought an engagement ring. He's getting married." Paulette whispered it, though she could've shouted it. Fred was at work, and the photographs on the nearby bookcase weren't paying her a bit of attention. None of the folks in the matching antique brass frames had spared her a thought, so focused they were on their own eight-by-ten-size world.

But Paulette's mind was fraught with speculations of its own. "What in the world, McKinley? I thought you said y'all were just friends? Why couldn't you tell me . . . *me* about this Kelsey? How can you possibly want to marry somebody I—we—haven't even met? This girl doesn't really know you if she doesn't know your family." Agitated, in need of something to do—anything other than returning the ring to its rightful place—Paulette straightened the music books and set the bench under the piano. She considered getting the bottle of Pledge and a dustcloth, but that would conjure an image of little Miss Lucy and her irksome feet.

Paulette aimed to settle her mind by shuffling through the house, fluffing a pillow here and shifting a book there. She rearranged the hand-carved wooden dogs, cats, rabbits, deer, and birds that Fred loved so much, something she did once a week. Funny how he never noticed her various arrangements. Eventually she dragged her reluctant feet back to the front room. There wasn't much mess to straighten, even with McKinley making their company a crowd again. And there wasn't too much she could do with one hand, what with the other in her pocket fiddling with that ring.

What an unusual setting—a peach sapphire on a thin, rose gold, diamond-studded double band. It had to have set him back a pretty penny; maybe that was why he hadn't taken much convincing to accept this paid assignment with George & Company. The ring was unique, like McKinley. McKinley and this mystery woman.

"You might call her 'Kels,' but I call her a stranger," she grumbled.

The soft hum of the garage door jolted Paulette back to the present. She hadn't realized she was glaring at the sapphire while the black-and-white photographs judged her silently. Paulette snapped the box closed and dashed up the front stairs as nimbly as her creaky knees could take her. With more purpose than she'd had the past thirty minutes, she went straight to the laundry room at the end of the hall. There, she inside-outed the jeans and tucked the box into the right front pocket and scooped them up, along with the small pile of underwear and T-shirts she'd collected from his room. She strewed the clothes over McKinley's floor, just as she'd found them.

"No good deed goes unpunished," she murmured.

Chapter Twelve

TUESDAY

This time, Frederick had the car all to himself, so he turned to the sports-only radio station. One of Paulette's students had just so happened to reschedule his lesson at the time the Baldwins planned to leave. A meeting between McKinley and Monroe had "popped up," and his son had stayed at the office to run some design ideas by him. Strange how Fred was the only one free to pick up Aunt Juju and Uncle Lawrence from the train station. His shoulders slumped, and his foot let up on the accelerator and the car crawled up the hill to the stop sign. The honk behind him forced Fred to turn right and pick up speed.

No telling how this four-day visit with his aunt and uncle would go. The silent protest McKinley waged was coming through loud and clear, and Etta was yet praying. That was what he hoped she was doing as she walked around, muttering under her breath; if it was anybody else, he would've slept with one eye open. When he'd entered their bedroom last night, his wife was already on her knees beside the bed, and she was still crouched there when he came out of their bathroom, dressed in his pajamas. Fred surely hoped God had an ear to their bedroom door.

Funny thing, when he was a boy, he actually thought it was Julia who had a direct line to God, that it was He who did her bidding, and not the other way around. Frederick was eight years old when the stroke had taken his grandmama, and Papa's youngest daughter immediately had pushed her feet into her mama's shoes. Not the ones with the high thick heels, reserved for special occasions, that she kept on the floor of her closet, but her cotton slippers with the dangling threads she wore around the house when she did her heavy-duty work. Even after Julia married Lawrence when she was twenty-two years old, she'd continued to stride confidently, taking care of everything the way her mother did.

"And she's stepping on everybody's toes to this very day." If anyone had been sitting in the passenger seat, he would've had to lean over the console to hear Fred's words.

Aunt Juju hadn't traveled farther than the back bedroom of her father's ramshackle farmhouse after she'd tied the knot with Lawrence. She'd told her new husband where the tools were stored and tasked him and her nephew with hammering and nailing and painting and sealing. Papa had always been too busy tending the hardwoods on the ten acres they'd managed to hold on to, to do much else on the farm perched on the tree-covered hillside. Between Fred and his uncle, they'd made short work of rehabbing the formerly drafty house that had threatened to topple off the edge of town where Papa had erected it before he'd married Fred's grandmother. If a tornado hadn't battered the wooden structure in 1984, that was probably where his childless aunt and uncle would be at this moment, instead of three hundred miles away near Lawrence's people in Virginia.

"Good thing. There's not enough prayer in the world that could've kept Etta from leaving me if they hadn't moved." Fred pushed down on the signaling arm and turned left. Ten miles to go, thirty-five miles behind him. More than fifty years and his life's work, forever impacted by his uncle Lawrence and aunt Juju. He kept his eyes on the road, but he could clearly see the day his love affair with furniture design began.

He was barely thirteen, and Fred was balancing on the two back legs of Papa's chair on the front porch. Through half-closed eyes, he was watching the last of the mourners return to their cars or walk down the long road leading to their own houses. Most were clutching foil-wrapped dishes, unashamedly carrying away more comfort than they had brought with them, as if it was their due. His grandpa hadn't been in the ground but a few hours, and life without him had looked as cold and lifeless as the branches stretching toward that steely February sky.

Fred had never had much of a father or mother to speak of. His papa had filled both those roles after his mother had left him sitting at the kitchen table in front of a bowl of dry cereal; she never returned from town with the milk she'd set out to buy. As Fred balanced precariously on those chair legs, he wondered what would keep Julia from running off with her new husband. Why would she stick around to care for her nephew, who was straddling that awkward dividing line between man- and boyhood? Papa had raised Fred with a strong, unwavering hand, but the teen couldn't imagine managing the small farm by himself, that was, if his aunt and uncle didn't foist him off on some other unsuspecting relative and sell Fred's inheritance.

The question that had lodged itself in the back of his throat finally worked its way past his chapped lips. "What I'm gon' do now?"

Through the tears eking from his nearly closed lids, he spied a tall figure tramping up the hill toward the porch, steady despite the pinecones underfoot, prickly polka dots adorning the grass. Other folks tended to stick to the dirt tract leading to the front door to avoid getting tripped up. Fred swiped at his face and laid eyes on Julia—should have known.

She walked with her shoulders back and her neck straight, as if someone were holding her up by an invisible string. "Frederick." His aunt never used the diminutive version of his name. "You'd best put that chair on all fours befo' you find yourself on the ground."

Fred paid no attention. It was time he started listening to his own mind. *Ain't I almost a man?*

"You've been sittin' here on this porch a mighty long time. You want me to make you a plate? You didn't eat."

It was so like Julia to notice, even while she'd been seeing to the folks milling about their home, refreshing cups of lemonade and refilling their servings of deviled eggs and fried chicken; helping her own elderly aunts and uncles to their feet or to a comfy spot to sit a while; stopping children from tracking dirt through the house and keeping their parents from pocketing Grandmama's collection of wooden animals that Papa had carved.

Julia gracefully suffered all the niceties and nosiness from folks who should've known better but didn't, nodding when they shared their keen observations: "He sho' looked good" and "They did him right today" and deflecting questions like "Why didn't they include yo' sister on the program?"

Fred, feeling more boy and less man despite his stubbornness, didn't respond to her offer of a plate of food. He focused instead on rocking on the four legs of the wooden ladderback chair, testing how much farther he could lean toward the wall behind him.

It turned out, it wasn't that far. Before he could catch himself, the back left leg waved the white flag and ceded to his weight. It caved inward, and the chair coughed him up onto the porch floor.

Julia didn't laugh at him sprawled there, give him an I-told-you-so twist of her lips, or weep and wail over the chair her father had constructed from their own maple trees and a dozen used nails and screws. She didn't help her nephew to his feet either.

"You should use things for the purpose they're designed. That there wasn't meant to be no rocking chair, Frederick, as you very well know. But how about you and your uncle make you one out of those pieces? That would be better than choppin' the rest up and throwin' 'em into the fire tonight. If it turns out right—which I suspect it will, knowin' my Lawrence and the blood runnin' through your own fingers— y'all could go on ahead and make three, and we'll all have a comf'table seat come next spring to watch the seasons change, before the flies get too bad. You had the right idea, just not the right means of seein' the thing through to the end."

Fred scrambled to his feet and dusted off his good pants.

"When I go in to make your plate, I'll send your uncle so y'all can get started. A leg and a wing? I'm-a have to make more eggs 'cause those greedy folks took the last. I don't like mine with vinegar anyhow."

His tumble must have knocked some sense into him because before he knew it, Uncle Lawrence had clasped him by his shoulder and was walking with him to the barn to search for tools and wood they could fashion into runners, legs, arms, and spindles. From then on, the two spent summers redesigning and repurposing old furniture they found around the house and in secondhand stores, transforming them into more useful pieces. Over time, they even sold enough to help make up the difference Fred's college scholarships hadn't.

"And that was that," Fred announced to the empty car as he drove into the depot. He'd never lost his passion for giving new life to a dead piece of wood, and it had started with that couple right there, waiting for him on the platform, who had loved on him like he was their child, not their orphaned nephew.

To think Frederick had considered for even a second asking them not to come. Maybe Junior had the right idea, but he certainly didn't have the right means of seeing a thing through to the end.

• ల •

"Are these the collards? Maybe that's what's growing over there." Paulette crouched next to the mystery vegetables growing in the back right corner of their yard, a rectangle of cleared space just beyond a cluster of maples and pines. She clicked the short nail on her index finger with her teeth, and then she spit out the dirt that was embedded in it. Nobody had reminded the novice gardener to mark the spot with the name of what she was planting back in the summer. Oh, well. She'd figure it out come October. Whatever she harvested, they'd eat. *If* she had something to harvest.

She eyed the feathery fronds poking from the ground and the darker leaves to her right. They were starting to look the same, even the lettuce, in this late-afternoon light. Paulette pointed and took a stab at naming them. "Kale. Broccoli. Maybe peppers. Those could be the radishes." Not that they even ate radishes. She had taken Google's recommendation on the types of veggies people planted that time of year, and the Home Depot expert had agreed. At least they'd look pretty sliced over the salads, a food even she couldn't burn. If she couldn't learn to grow food, how was she expected to cook it?

Cook . . . "That's right, the casserole!" Paulette checked the slim watch on her wrist and exhaled a grateful breath. She had about ten more minutes, maybe twelve. All she'd had to do was slide the chicken dish into the oven and bake it, and then remember to take it out at the appointed time. Fred had completed the legwork—cooking and dicing the chicken, boiling the pasta, sautéing the vegetables, and mixing up the ingredients—before heading to the train station. It was about time to head inside before she ruined it.

"Need some help, Mama?"

Paulette cupped her hand over her eyes and squinted into the sun at the face looming over the wire fence. The face that had captured the heart of some girl named Kelsey. "Hey, there! Home already? Where's everybody?" She plopped flat in the dirt to relax the pressure on her bent knees. They seemed to chide, *Shame on you, Etta. You should've known better.*

"I didn't go with Dad to the train station. I was hanging out at the Georges' after work, and then Monroe drove me home." He unlatched the gate and entered the enclosure.

Paulette closed her eyes as she placed both hands on her

back and stretched. She opened one lid when she felt him studying her. These Baldwin men, they just didn't intend to miss a thing. "What? Do I have some dirt on my nose?"

"Nope, no dirt. Are you all right?"

She grimaced. "I just waited a bit late in life to try my hand at gardening. It's not for the faint of heart or knees, despite what everybody says about square-foot gardening this and box gardening that. But yes, I'm fine."

Paulette wished she could tell him that her heart was hurting a tad. Or confide that she was getting tired of hearing her own lone voice echo in their rambling house. And that she was already starting to miss him, though it was only Tuesday and he wasn't even married yet, let alone back in Philadelphia. *Oh, McKinley, I wish you could tell me why there was a sapphire in the pocket of your jeans.*

He bent over and eyed the plants. Then he rubbed a leaf between two of his fingers. "Is that all? I couldn't tell if you were happy to see me just now."

"I'm always happy to see you, sweetie. It's these plants that are making me *un*happy. I'm worried I'll have to visit the farmers' market every weekend to buy fresh vegetables like I did Saturday and then pretend I grew them myself." She was tempted to throw her hands up in defeat and dig up all her hard-grown work.

"I thought maybe you were worried about Aunt Juju and Uncle Lawrence."

Paulette reached up and squeezed one of his hands. "And I think you're dreadin' their visit more than I am, mind you."

"No, it's not that. I love seeing them, and it's not like Uncle Lawrence says more than his allotted two words a day. It's . . . well, I'd hoped to keep you to myself while I was home. I was looking forward to having some time to talk."

Talk! She sucked in her breath and thrust her fingers in the soil with renewed vigor. Just as she thought, those were radishes. She forced herself to keep her voice even as her fingers nudged a bulb. "Talk? About what? We have some time now." *The casserole can wait a few more minutes.*

McKinley straightened. "I don't know . . . life. You, me, Dad. Your new interest in gardening. You *and* Dad."

"And maybe you *and* . . . ?" Her lighthearted wink belied the import of her open-ended question.

He smiled laconically. "That, too."

Paulette swallowed hard as she moved leaves aside, not sure what she was searching for, what garden maintenance was supposed to look like. What a parent's relationship with an adult child was supposed to feel like. She plucked a dead leaf and dropped it on the pile of weeds she'd pulled, hoping it wasn't a harbinger of the direction of their conversation. "So what do you want to know?"

McKinley crouched on a knee beside her. His outspread fingers sifted moist soil. He shrugged. "I say we start at the end and work backwards. How are you and Dad doing?"

He would go there. As much as she didn't want to accompany him on that particular adventure in self-exploration, she couldn't keep herself from peering into his face—not so he could read her expression, but for her to search his. "Fine. Why? Something I should know?"

McKinley's mouth opened and closed and his head tilted from one side to another. "Somehow I feel like you're hedging. Just 'fine'? Not wonderful or amazing?"

"Okay, make that wonderful and amazing," she huffed, scrambling in the dirt for her spade and clippers. With all these tools, she could appear on a gardening segment of the *Today* show, but she'd only be playing the part of an expert on TV. Truly, she couldn't tell anyone watching her what to pinch or what to keep, what was a weed and what would bear fruit. Paulette was struggling just to fit the set of clippers into its designated spot in her gardening basket, beside the spray bottle of organic insecticide. *Now, there's an oxymoron if I've ever heard one. Is there really such a thing?*

"There you go again. I'm serious, Mama. Y'all don't seem to talk much." He plucked the clippers from her and slid them in. Then he extended his free hand to help his mother to her feet.

Paulette tried not to grunt as McKinley pulled her up. She brushed off her knees and bent to retrieve the hose. As she coiled it around the hose mobile, water dropped from the bib onto his leather shoes, but he didn't seem to notice. "I told you about his schedule, McKinley."

"But that's about when he's not home. I'm talking about the lack of communication in the house when Dad *is* home. We used to laugh and talk around the table before dinner, during dinner, after dinner—in fact, you made sure I didn't run from the kitchen as soon as I finished eating so we could talk for at least another thirty minutes."

"Then you'd say, 'We've been together all day . . .'"

"And you'd point out, 'That was homeschooling. It doesn't count.'"

"'This is about spendin' time with family,'" she finished with a smile, remembering, wishing, mourning those days that she'd taken for granted.

He ducked down and peered into her face. "Yes, this is about family."

Paulette plucked at her lashes to disguise the sudden rush of tears. "McKinley, we should talk about what's goin' on with you. Your dad and I are your dad and I. Things . . . things change a bit when your child grows up and leaves home. Your only child at that." She opened the gate and tromped through the yard toward the house, pulling the cart behind her. Paulette heard him follow.

"Mom, did you say your only *child*? He left home for college years ago. I'm looking into the headlights of thirty." He fell into step beside her. The basket he held bumped her leg.

"Don't remind me, McKinley. That means—"

"That you've been married even longer. Is that what you were going to say? You two can't fall apart now that I'm not here 24-7. There's no way my presence was the mortar between the bricks."

They'd reached the liriope-bordered concrete path that twisted in one direction toward the storage house and in the other, toward the detached garage. The wheels of the cart creaked to a stop and Paulette looked into her son's intense dark-brown eyes. This time, she didn't feel like a microscopic amoeba under his lens.

"No, you're not the mortar, McKinley. We're just findin' our way. We poured a lot of ourselves into a certain someone." Even in her mind's eye, her grin was a poor facsimile of its original.

He didn't even try to fake one in return.

She studied her toenails poking through her open-toed sandals. *On second thought, I don't even dress like a real gardener. Look at me, daring a snake or a spider to bite my feet or an ankle. And these nails . . . If I can't keep them painted, the least I can do is keep them cut.*

That used to be Fred's Saturday night job, clipping Paulette's toenails. Then he'd paint them. Way back before McKinley was born, when he was still a prayer in their hearts. But then that prayer was answered, and she had a baby to snuggle and talk to. And Fred had a baby boy to carry on his dreams.

Suddenly Paulette felt she couldn't hold herself up. She leaned so heavily on the cart, she nearly toppled it over. What an effort she'd expended to keep up appearances over the past four days since McKinley's arrival. And now to hear it was all for naught: McKinley felt less reassured and more concerned because of her efforts. Paulette took a deep breath, but much like she had with her clippers, she couldn't figure out how to fit together all the pieces, not in any way that would make sense to her son. As she turned toward him, the garden behind McKinley captured her attention.

Her voice was soft as she thought about that first, harrowing day of planting. "You know, when I decided to try this whole gardening thing, I asked your daddy to help me with it. He has a way of seein' where things should go, how they should be laid out or fit together. I knew that particular gift would come in handy with this garden. But I made the mistake of bustin' into his office right when he'd had one of his so-called 'breakthroughs' with a piece, you know how that goes." She rolled her eyes at McKinley.

Yes, he was nodding along. He was well acquainted with his daddy's breakthroughs.

"So Fred either mistook my request for help as merely a suggestion or an announcement, or maybe he just plain didn't care at that particular moment, because he didn't move. Did not move, McKinley. Before I knew it, I found myself all by my lonesome diggin' a twelve-foot-long area about five inches deep . . ." Paulette stretched out her hands to help McKinley envision just how big a job it was.

"I was mad as fire, yet even more determined at this point to get it done. I had something to prove, to myself and to him." Paulette could still feel how crazy angry she was at the time, how lonesome and uncared for. Everyone living within five miles of their house was aware of how she felt about yard work and the insect life that came with it. And the folks living within a heartbeat of her knew part of the reason she hated it was because that's how her mama met her daddy—and why her mama eventually left them both. To be left to her own devices to dig out that yard!

But that's neither here nor there, she told herself, scrubbing away the thought along with the persistent grime on her palms.

"All those creepy-crawlies scurrying away from my shovel nearly melted my resolve, let me tell you, but it took the sight of a footlong earthworm to finally snag my husband's attention. Boy, did I scream!" Paulette reared back and laughed about what had scared her half to death, something that still made her back tingle when she came across one.

"What did he do?" McKinley seemed just as caught up listening to the story as she was telling it.

"Well, he explained what a good sign it was, that the earthworm told the truth about the soil. In fact, we needed more of them—you heard me when I said *we,* didn't you, McKinley? *We* my foot . . . humph." She shook her head. Fred had a way of getting in the game right at the buzzer and awarding himself MVP.

"As ugly as they were, they performed a good work by aeratin' the soil as they digested all the fungi and dirt and squirted it out of their hind parts. Their presence actually improved the soil . . ." Paulette trailed off as she wondered about the truth of her own relationships. They could all use a few earthworms to process and repurpose all that was unhealthy.

Her next words came slowly. They had to figure out where her thoughts were leading her first. "Every marriage waxes and wanes, McKinley. Your dad's and mine, it's no different. We started out with all this passion—physical and emotional."

McKinley abruptly rubbed the back of his head. He glanced at the large hydrangea bush beside them in desperate need of a pruning by someone who knew what he was doing. Its leaves still clung to the trees though its bright-white blooms had shriveled, refusing to acknowledge that summer was a thing of the past. He reached for one of the branches and plucked at the crispy petals.

"McKinley, you asked like a grown man, so I'm talkin' to you like you're one."

Her voice seemed to force him to stand still, for he dropped the dead flower and faced her, chagrined. He squared his shoulders and looked her full in the eye, Baldwin style. "I'm listening."

"Okay. Fine. I'll skip over the passion stuff. You're standin' here, a livin' and breathin' product of that passion, so you have a pretty good idea of what I'm talkin' 'bout. Just think of a young married couple as new believers who're on fire for Jesus. All they see is Him, like all your daddy and I saw was each other. The sun rose and set in Fred, in me. We were two against the world. Then came you, work, piano, furniture, other dreams, other passions. *Your* needs. Homeschooling. Disappointments. Frustrations. Things that pulled us in other directions—not necessarily apart, mind you. They just stretched us. Thin. And now—"

"Now what?" McKinley shifted from one foot to another.

And now you can see right through us. Not that Paulette could say those words to her son.

A shriek pierced the air, making them both jump a mile. Paulette slapped her forehead.

"Well, now what you're going to do is call the alarm company and convince them not to send the fire department. Tell them your mama just burned dinner to a crisp. That's all."

Chapter Thirteen

⸻ ❧❦ ⸻

"I WOULDA THOUGHT we'd had something otha than hot dogs and lettuce, Frederick. You know I don't much like processed foods. And all those leaves get in my dentures. I know your wife don't cook like our people, but after all these years, I'd imagined . . . no, I'd *hoped* for somethin' better for my only nephew and his family."

Cre-e-a-k!

"Fred Jr., is that you?"

"Shoot," McKinley hissed. It had been his every intention to hide on the stairs for another minute or two, letting his aunt Juju retch her bellyful of complaints on his father. He wasn't sure how long he could listen to her upbraid his mother, especially when it wasn't really Mama's fault that dinner had literally gone up in smoke. If only that darn floorboard hadn't gone and told on him.

"Yes, Dad, it's me. Just coming to finish up the dishes." He trudged down the stairs as if that had been his intention all along. When he turned the corner into the kitchen, he injected cheerfulness into his voice. It pained him. "Hi, Auntie. Where's Uncle Lawrence?"

The years hadn't stolen one inch of Julia's erect bearing. At the moment, she was ruling from the head of the Baldwins' table, in a white linen blouse with a purple-and-blue silk scarf draped around her shoulders and looped at the base of her neck. When they'd sat down to eat earlier, Dad had ceded his spot at the shorter, left side of the wooden rectangle to his aunt, the oldest living member of the Baldwins. He'd repositioned himself at the opposite end, which had uprooted his mother. For the next few nights, she would be relegated to one of the middle seats across from her son, basically sitting at the fold-up table like a child at Thanksgiving.

Usually Mom moved easily back and forth from her spot at the table to retrieve what everybody needed during mealtimes. She'd started serving in that capacity since Dad did most of the cooking. "I won't have any Henny Pennys in my house!" Mom had attested long ago. "I might not be able to bake the bread, but I can sho' nuff slice it and serve it."

"Frederick McKinley Baldwin Jr. Your great-aunt is sayin' something to you." Dad sounded irritated, and saying McKinley's full name was more his mother's style.

But what really bothered McKinley was his father's tone. It sounded too much like a reprimand for McKinley's twenty-seven-year-old taste. "Sir? I mean, ma'am? My mind must have wandered somewhere else. I believe I'd asked Aunt Juju about Uncle Lawrence."

"I believe you're right." From the looks of it, Aunt Juju had slurped some unsweetened lemonade.

Dad propped his chin on his fisted hands. "While your mind was doing its so-called 'wandering,' your aunt explained that traveling takes a lot out of your uncle, so he's in the bedroom."

"Where did you go, Fred Jr.? You know, when you ask a question, you need to listen for an answer. Didn't your mama teach you that?"

"Nowhere far, Aunt Juju, nowhere far." McKinley mentally kicked himself for forgetting to nail down that stair. He'd be sure to do it tonight.

"So, Fred Jr., your daddy's been sittin' here, braggin' on all your drawin's. He cain't say enough about them. When are me and yo' uncle gon' see 'em for ourselves?"

McKinley's eyes shot a question at his father. Did she say *bragging*?

"I don't know if that's quite the word I'd use. I was only describing all the hard work you've put into the project at the office. I can tell, and I appreciate it. Your mother was right to suggest I hire you for the job."

Mom. Of course. It wasn't like his father had thought to ask him. McKinley swallowed his *thank you*.

"Speaking of Paulette, where she been? It's nearly eight o'clock. She disappeared right after . . . *ahem*, dinner." Aunt Juju, obviously hard-pressed to call their meal what it was, smoothed a stray hair, not that any part of her press and curl was out of place. It looked like the straightening comb was still smoking on the stove.

"Remember, Etta has choir practice on Tuesday nights. The seniors sing on first Sunday, Juju." Even at sixty-three, Fred had never grown out of using the derivative of Julia's name, what he called her as a child. When she'd taken over raising him after his grandfather died, he stopped thinking of her as a big sister and dropped the appellation of *Aunt* in deference to her new role in his life. In true Baldwin fashion, her nickname had adhered to McKinley's lips once he was old enough to form words, something the woman had gracefully suffered, even enjoyed.

Dinner was quite another thing they'd all suffered through, with varying degrees of grace.

McKinley and Paulette had dashed into the house the minute they'd heard the alarm, but it was too late. Fred's chicken casserole was a charred block. By the plumes of smoke pouring from the oven door and filling the kitchen, they were lucky the glass dish hadn't exploded and destroyed the heating elements. McKinley thanked God he'd been able to divert the alarm company, for that would've mortified his mother, having her husband pull up to the house behind a fire truck; ruining the dinner he'd taken the time to prepare was painful enough. As it was, Mom had had to resort to cooking something she could neither destroy nor grow: a gigantic bowl of salad and homemade mustard dressing. McKinley had been pressed into service to man the grill.

"Weren't those Italian sausages delicious, Aunt Juju?" McKinley couldn't resist asking. "Mama and I thought you'd enjoy them."

Julia sucked her teeth. "Do you have a toothpick, Frederick?"

"Must be a celery seed from the dressing. Fred Jr., get Juju a toothpick. They're in the drawer by the stove."

McKinley had been idling on the perimeter of the kitchen, hoping for a way to slide from the room and the conversation and sidle back upstairs. His father's directive had hooked him, however, cutting off all means of extricating himself. He tried to keep his shoulders from sagging as he shuffled toward the drawer.

"Speaking of stoves, what in the world you gon' do with that big ol' fancy appliance you got over there, Frederick? Etta sho' don't have need for that, just like she didn't use the other one. You gon' work yourself to death, Nephew." Though Julia's laugh seemed to search far and wide, it couldn't find any humor to attach itself to. It must have sounded lonely to her own ears because she finally gave up and clamped her lips together. Her eyes continued to sparkle.

"She'll do fine, Aunt Juju. In fact, Mama's been cooking quite a bit lately. She made a big breakfast for me Saturday morning—grits, homemade biscuits, sausage. Didn't she, Dad?" McKinley extended the small plastic container of toothpicks to the older woman, but he threw down the gauntlet in his father's direction.

"Well—" Dad flattened his palms on the table.

"Cookin'? If that's what you call choppin' up lettuce, slicin' a few tomatoes, and blackenin' a dozen hot dogs . . ." She pinched a slender wooden stick from the others in the jar, her smirk informing them that wasn't what she'd call it.

"They were Italian sausages, Aunt Juju. Not hot dogs. And I grilled those. They were made of chicken and fennel."

"Fennel? Is that what got so stuck in my teeth?" Julia wedged the toothpick in between her back molars.

McKinley imagined she had more than just a few seeds stuck in her craw. "I doubt it. Like Dad said, it was probably the celery seed from that delicious homemade dressing. Didn't you like the food?" He kept his tone light, but he dared her to buck up against her own sense of propriety and say something outright negative.

"I thought they tasted pretty good. I've eaten plenty of sausages before, and I've even killed a hog and made my own. Never tried chicken sausage though. But I bet these was better for you than pork. And, Juju-bean, you'll have to get that dressin' recipe. That was some good." The quiet voice drew the three sets of eyes that were already in the kitchen. Uncle Lawrence's slight form was framed in the arched door-way between the kitchen and the den.

"Uncle Lawrence, hey. Are you feeling better?" McKinley could have kissed the man for his timely appearance and soft words.

"Wasn't no need to feel better, but I do feel rested. Thank you for asking, nephew."

"It's too bad you didn't also feel like shavin' before you walked in here. You don't look fit for comp'ny. You're sho' you're all right?" Aunt Julia frowned at her husband, concern dousing the spark of mischief in her eyes.

"Is some comp'ny comin' I didn't know about?" Uncle Lawrence stroked the white bristles along his jawline and winked at his wife.

Julia shook her head and dismissed his joke with a flick of her fingers, but she continued to give him a careful once-over. The couple had a brand of communication that only they understood. It had seared them together for nearly sixty years.

"Why don't you come have a seat." McKinley pulled out the ladder-back chair nearest Aunt Juju.

"I'm fine right where I'm standin'. Don't you worry, I'm able to find my own way when I want to." The eighty-five-year-old drew himself up to his full five feet nine inches, causing the rubber-tipped end of the mahogany cane he clutched to hover for a second a hair above the hardwood floor.

"I know, I know. I was about to spoon up some ambrosia, and I thought you'd want to sit down and have some. Anybody else care for a bowl?" McKinley hadn't intended to attack the man's pride, something his uncle wore like his brick-red suspenders and wide brown leather belt. But unlike those braces he strapped on, his confidence seemed to serve a purpose: they made up for the authority Julia did her best to sap from him. Leaving the chair right where it was, McKinley gave his uncle space to slide in when and if he so chose.

"I'll take you up on that ambrosia, but I'm gon' have a seat on the back porch. No need to waste this fine evenin' God gave us, twitterin' like birds around this table." He tap-tapped from the kitchen.

Aunt Juju leaned her head and followed Uncle Lawrence's progress through the sunroom and out onto the deck. She didn't speak until she watched him, through the side window, slowly lower himself into a lounge chair that faced the backyard.

"I think I'll do the same, Fred Jr. Your uncle prob'ly wants my company out there. Only, give me just a spoonful or two. My stomach is feelin' some kinda way after eating one of those sausages."

"Let me lend you a hand, Juju." Dad scooted back his chair and prepared to rise.

"I'm closer, Dad. You don't need to get up." McKinley believed his great-aunt's advanced years were owed a measure of respect, but he felt called to defend his mother's honor. What kind of son would he be to let anyone step on her toes in her own house, especially since she wasn't around to speak up for herself? Not that Mama would.

"I don't need help from nobody." The whir of Julia's motorized wheelchair shushed them both. Her fingers moved the joystick to reverse, and she backed up from her position at the end of the table. She skirted the chairs as she rounded its corner.

McKinley jumped back to prevent her from rolling over the top of his bare feet.

· ⌘ ·

His aunt was barely seventy when she lost her first leg and nigh on seventy-two when the doctor had to amputate her second. The same disease that took both of Juju's limbs had taken hold of Papa, and in his case, it didn't let go until a stroke claimed his life. Lots of folks in his grandfather's generation called it "sugar," but Frederick wouldn't give diabetes such an innocuous name.

Not that being a double amputee had slowed her down or sweetened her up, not even one jot. If anything, his aunt was hell on wheels. She informed anyone within earshot, "I'm better off rollin' than buried" and didn't wait to see whether or not they agreed with her. Uncle Lawrence had learned to move that shiny cane of his with a bit more vim and vigor to keep pace with Juju as she whizzed through JOANN Fabric and Craft, hunting for material and notions. In fact, they all had to work to keep up with her, to dodge her chair and her tongue, which she aimed at any and all who didn't have sense enough to pay attention.

Fred shook his head as his aunt turned up a nose to his offer to help her cross over the doorsill onto the brick pavers, but he admired the way she reversed and then pushed ahead, full speed. It took her two tries to do it. Then she maneuvered around the glass table in the middle of the deck toward the lounge chairs and sofa swing at the other end, coming within a hairbreadth of scraping some black paint off the wrought iron rail.

Noticing her mounting frustration when her leg rests kept bumping the furniture scattered about the pavers, he pointed toward the woods skirting the backyard. "See where the trees get thicker at the edge of the grass? There's a family of deer that like to bed down at night in there." When Juju turned her head in the direction he'd indicated, Fred nudged the table a tad to make room for her.

She moved back and forth until she'd situated herself beside the wicker chair Uncle Lawrence had settled in. After glowering at his feet that were propped up on the matching ottoman, she wrapped her fingers around her armrests and craned forward. "Y'all need to do somethin' 'bout those tall weeds growin' out there. Your neighbors gon' start talkin' 'bout you."

"Oh, that's Etta's project." He figured the early evening light had made it hard for her to spot the tops of the vegetables poking through the ground about half an acre away.

"Mmm-hmmm. I see why those deer are campin' out. So they can be close to what y'all callin' a garden. Etta had best build that wire fencin' higher than that, or she won't have nuthin' but a few chewed-up leaves to harvest. Of course, she might not have more'n that no way, deer or no deer."

Fred tried not to wince as his son distributed a bowl to each of them. He thanked God that Paulette was safely out of earshot, away at rehearsal. "Ye-a-a-h . . . that's Etta's baby. I have to give it to her, all the effort she puts into that garden.

You should see her—reading books on planting, talking to friends, googling. She had to keep herself from throwing the man from Home Depot into her basket and cartin' him home."

Junior slid the chair under the table. He stared at his father. "You noticed?"

Fred shrugged. "You think I wouldn't know how much time she invests in her garden? I live here, don't I?"

"You know, McKinley, there ain't nuthin' like watchin' somethin' grow that you planted yourself. God prob'ly took that seventh day to simply admire His creation, what He made from the dust of the earth." Uncle Lawrence was a man of few words, but the ones he selected were dropped just so into place, like the pieces of a jigsaw puzzle. In deference to the mama who'd married his nephew and birthed his great-nephew, he always used the name Paulette called her son, something that rubbed Juju raw.

Maybe that's why he smiles when he says it. I know this ambrosia ain't that good. Frederick nearly choked on the chuckle he tried to hide after swallowing a mouthful of the fruit salad he'd whipped up especially for his aunt's visit. Paulette didn't get along with the cherries he put in it, so he only prepared the treat on special occasions.

"Well, I don't understand it. It's not like she's gon' cook none of it. She spends every wakin' moment on that piano in some form or another. Got no time for the stove. Or you, by the looks of you sittin' there by yourself." Juju's pointed tongue flicked a piece of coconut off the corner of her upper lip. "But she wasn't raised knowin' hard work, not like you were, Frederick. Those pale hands of hers weren't intended for gettin' dirty and brown in the sunshine."

Junior stretched out on the swing to the side of the table. He propped his left leg on a cushion and used his right to push off the brick pavers and set the swing in motion. "Mama is one of the hardest-working women I know, and as far as her hands are concerned, I'd prefer they were clasped in prayer anyway. Wouldn't you say so, Dad? That's definitely something Mama invests precious time doing."

Fred's lips flattened. Junior had flown down to North Carolina with more than a set of building plans in his suitcase. He also seemed bound and determined to pit his father against his great-aunt, pushing an agenda Fred didn't want and Etta didn't need. Nothing good would come from poking the bear, especially when Juju was worn-out from a long day. And probably still hungry. The former she'd never admit, and the latter they'd never hear the end of.

Julia's spoon clattered against the porcelain bowl. "Fred Jr., why you standin' between me and yo' mama? Facts is facts. Nobody's talkin' about prayin'—unless you plan to lift up that garden out there or the food she—"

"Aunt Juju, I'm not standing between you and Mama. Why would I need to do that, considering celebrating her is the reason you and Uncle Lawrence decided to visit in the first place? We're all family here. We stand together, don't we?" Junior's eyebrows looked like fat caterpillars had crept across his brow to give each other a kiss. He gave another gentle push with his toe, and his swing moved languidly back and forth, back and forth.

What was with that boy and his infernal questions? Trying to look all wide-eyed and innocent, when he knew he was up to no good. Fred pushed his empty bowl away from him, toward the center of the table. "Yes, we're family. And nobody's standin' nowhere. Except you, Junior. I know you just made yourself comfortable, but how about you get up and take these two bowls to the kitchen. Please."

His son put down both feet, then rose and sauntered to the table. "Anything else, Dad? Aunt Juju? Uncle Lawrence?"

"Yes, light the citronella, if you don't mind. The mosquitoes found us. I'll be glad when the evenings get cool enough they don't come out. Also, check the phones and the voice mail to make sure we haven't missed a call from your mama."

"Yes, sir. Maybe if she gets home early enough, you two can go for a walk."

Frederick watched his son gather the bowls and head inside. He didn't know the last time he and Etta had taken a walk together. Maybe when they were pushing the stroller around the block right after they'd moved into the house. He'd wanted to show all his neighbors just who was living next door.

His aunt's face looked smushed. "Is somethin' wrong with Fred Jr.? Seems like he's got somethin' on his mind."

And you don't seem to like it too much, Fred guessed. "I don't think anything's wrong necessarily, Juju, but I do think he's got a mind full of something." He handed her a napkin and pointed to the right side of his chest.

She looked down at her breasts and brushed off the piece of clementine clinging to the white linen. She groused at the faint orange stain it left behind. "My bosoms just seem to reach out and catch everything I eat."

"All signs point to a woman. Love will make you say all manner of things. It'll embolden you." Uncle Lawrence dragged his spoon around the sides of his bowl, dredging up every last lick of whipped cream.

"Well, I don't like it. Got him smellin' himself. Whatchyou make of it, Frederick?"

"I think the only woman on Junior's mind is his mama. He hasn't seen her in a long time, and she's got a big birthday comin' up. He probably wants it to be special."

"Yes, there's somethin' 'bout a son and his mama." Juju swiped at a lightning bug and shook her head slowly, her tone leaking bitterness into the cool evening air. She'd never been able to have children of her own, though that didn't stop her from being freehanded with her advice to Paulette. When she opened her palm, Juju stared at the crushed remains of the bug she'd captured.

Fred nodded along, faithful to the woman who'd had a hand in raising him, not the woman who hadn't wanted to. His mama had left him at such a young age, his heart didn't remember how he'd loved her. All he could envision was dry cornflakes.

Uncle Lawrence squinted at his wife first and then his nephew. "The two of y'all sittin' there noddin' and shakin', cancelin' out each other as I see it."

"You hush, Lawrence. We know you might not have been sittin' there grinnin' like that if that man who'd kept sniffin' round me had paid me more attention. Now, put down that spoon. You done."

"To hear you tell it," Lawrence murmured. He dropped his utensil with a clank but popped the last mini marshmallow into his mouth. Then he showed all his teeth, including the gap near the back.

Frederick rolled around his aunt's recollection in his own mind. "Juju, from the story Papa told me, your would-be suitor was up to no good from the get-go. He was actin' as a front for Clinton George, the man he worked for. They knew Papa wouldn't have given a white man the time of day, especially a strange one, but you helped him get a foot in the door."

"Maybe I should give him a call and see what he's been up to. He might be feelin' lonely and want some comp'ny." Lawrence squeezed his wife's hand and smiled.

"What, you old . . . !" Julia played tug-of-war with her husband but after a few seconds, she interlaced her fingers with his.

"Sounds like he was tryin' to soften you up so the two of them could get their hands on the farm. To hear Papa tell it, it nearly worked, too. He nearly lost the whole kit and caboodle to Clinton George and his front man."

"He was 'bout white himself, with pretty, slick hair. Always wore a hat. Couldn't tell much difference. He wasn't one of us. Howard . . . Hew . . . *Hugh*. That's it! Hugh somethin' or other, I believe he called himself. Said he was from somewhere farther east. Once I heard him mention somethin' 'bout Spring Hope. Didn't Etta come from there or near'bouts?" Julia's eyes were slits, like she was staring into the past at that face, considering what she'd do if she could get her hands on the con man.

Lawrence let go her fingers and twiddled with the spoon.

Junior had reappeared on the deck without Frederick noticing. He stood there holding a long match to light the citronella candles. "Them, us. Is that your problem with Mama, that she reminds you of the man who broke your heart or 'the man' who helped steal a part of the family's farm? Speaking of, what are you going to do with the homestead?"

Fred cocked an eyebrow in his son's direction. "What's there to *do*?"

"Mama and I were talking. Dreaming really. Have you ever considered building a bed-and-breakfast on the land or, better yet, turning this place into one? Then you and Mama could tear down—"

"Tear down!" Juju's gnarled hands gripped her wheelchair. At first, she looked like she was going to rise up and out of it.

"Junior . . ." Fred lowered his head. Could Paulette honestly consider giving up their home? That boy was always starting something.

"Hear me out, Dad. Why leave it as some memorial to what you lost when you could make something better . . . together? Y'all still have more than ten acres!"

"Just who is this 'y'all'? Sounds like your mama's layin' claim to history that ain't hers." Juju snatched her arm away from her husband's gentle patting. "Stop that, Lawrence!"

He sighed and looked down at the table. Then Uncle Lawrence slid his feet off the ottoman, clamped a hand around his cane, and pushed himself to his feet. He retrieved his bowl and spoon with his free hand and headed inside. *Tap-tap, tap-tap.*

· ᥴ ·

"Good night, brother. Bless you, sister. Beautiful solo. Soundin' good. You tore it up tonight!" Paulette offered a good word to each of the members inching across the rows of the choir loft and down the risers to the sanctuary floor. Once the church had emptied, she rested her head on the piano and closed her eyes.

A few minutes passed before Paulette had the energy to sit up and stare out at the empty church. The overhead lights bounced off the stained glass. Humming a few bars of music to herself, she stood, lifted the lid on her bench seat, and dug through the sheet music stored inside. Finally she found what she was looking for: a burgundy hymnbook. The church used to keep one or two in the wooden pocket in the back of each pew or have the ushers disseminate them to the congregation. She stroked the gold lettering on its cover and asked the empty church, "Why did we ever remove these from circulation?"

She flipped page after page past one traditional song after another—"Leaning on the Everlasting Arms," "Love

Lifted Me," "Amazing Grace," "What a Friend We Have in Jesus." Finally she landed on "Because He Lives," a Frederick Baldwin–approved oldie but goodie, and wrote down the page number. *Perfect for the congregational hymn selection,* Paulette sighed, the pages flapping as the book slowly closed.

She shook her head as she stacked the rest of Sunday's sheet music on the piano stand one by one and tucked it all inside her folder. Sure, she could face tomorrow because Jesus lived, but how about her in-laws? Could she look them in the eye after serving such a disaster of a homecoming dinner? Her husband probably would be none too eager to see her either. But no matter. Paulette couldn't afford to lose another precious minute with McKinley, trying to avoid Fred's aunt Juju. *Time's a-wasting.*

She'd certainly frittered away priceless minutes during rehearsal, working and reworking the order of music. There was no point going over it again, so Paulette slogged toward the front doors to secure the locks. She might as well email the music selections to the church secretary tonight so he could print Sunday's programs.

Halfway down the aisle, Paulette spun at the sound of voices in the sanctuary. "What in the world . . . ?"

"Honey, it's only us. We remembered you had choir prac-tice tonight, so Belinda and I hid in the ladies' room until everybody was gone. We thought we could get in a visit while you were locking up. Oo-oh, I can't wait another minute until you tell us about that ring you found!" Andria grinned, her blue eyes sparkling. Her wispy blonde hair swayed against her shoulders as she danced from one sneakered foot to the other.

Belinda tugged her shirt over her joggers and smiled. "I hope you don't mind, but we came straight from the gym. You haven't returned one text since you sent that first one, telling us what you found. We got worried and just had to check on you. Is everything okay?"

Mm-hmm. Paulette could tell Andria was pleased with their shenanigans, but Belinda looked like she'd been coerced into coming along, as usual. Paulette had met Belinda in the nursing mothers' room at Mount Olive decades ago, before her friend and the rest of her family had moved their membership to a larger church across town in search of a younger pastor and a more diverse membership. That's where Belinda had met Andria and introduced her to Paulette, and the three women had formed a close-knit circle.

"Belinda, hush. She doesn't mind a bit. Now, you two come sit down." Andria wrapped her dark-amethyst–tipped fingers around Paulette's elbow and led her to a pew. She slid in first and pulled her friend in behind her. "Sit down, sit down. My husband will be lookin' for me, so we can't linger too long." Andria flipped her hair behind her ear.

Paulette, sensitive to Belinda's newly widowed status, patted the woman's knee. They both always seemed to be playing follow the leader behind Andria, the most gregarious of the three.

"So?" Andria held up her left hand and wiggled her fingers. She pointed to her third digit.

Paulette knew her friend wasn't showing off her simple gold wedding band. "So-o-o-o I haven't talked to McKinley yet. But it was most definitely an engagement ring. Nothing friendship about it, and he definitely didn't buy it to wear himself. Such a unique setting and a sapphire the color of a peach. Really special."

"Like your boy," Belinda murmured.

"Yes, like McKinley. And also like him not to say a word about it." Paulette sighed.

"You don't know anything about the girl, other than she's his hairstylist? Maybe when she comes down, she can finally help me match my new hair color." Andria brushed back her blonde bangs to show her reddish brows.

"She's not his hairstylist, just his . . ."

"Friend," Belinda finished.

"*Girl*friend," Andria amended.

"Future wife." It was time for Paulette to accept the fact that their small family was growing, what she started praying about the day she caught two-year-old McKinley kissing a little girl on the playground. "We—*I*—need to come to grips with the idea. It was bound to happen. So what, I haven't met her. He hasn't introduced me to a lot of people he sees every day. And a lot of people I have seen, I don't like. The main thing is, I just wish he'd trust us with the truth."

Again, Paulette sighed. "It sure is a pretty ring though. Maybe y'all will see it for yourselves one day soon."

"Well, I'd better get invited to the wedding!" Andria

looked put out at the prospect of having to hear about the nuptials instead of witnessing them for herself.

"Andria, hush. This isn't about you. They'll probably be in Philadelphia, wouldn't you say, Etta? I know people don't believe in traditions too much these days, but the bride and her family do still host the wedding, right?"

"Traditions," Paulette muttered, thinking about Belinda's point. "It's Fred's stranglehold on traditions that chased McKinley to Philadelphia in the first place, at least I think that was the case. Now McKinley's gonna marry some strange woman named Kelsey, and I'll never see my grandchildren!" She buried her face in her hands.

Belinda laughed, albeit gently, and rubbed her friend's back. "This girl right here already has McKinley married and her mysterious daughter-in-law pregnant."

Andria covered her mouth but couldn't keep her shoulders from shaking.

Feeling the movement beside her, Paulette glared at both of them before she chuckled herself. "I'm so glad to see y'all. Thanks for checkin' on me."

Andria wrapped an arm around Paulette and reached behind her to squeeze the left shoulder of Belinda, the other slice of their friendship sandwich. "Somebody has to drag you out of that hole you jump into from time to time. If we don't, who will?"

"Certainly not Fred. He just might toss me in, especially after tonight."

Belinda leaned in close enough her large, purple-tinged

'fro brushed Paulette's cheek. "What do you mean, especially after tonight?"

"Well, while I was havin' a heart-to-heart with my son, dinner went up in smoke—literally—right when Fred's aunt and uncle arrived."

"Ooh, not the gruesome twosome!" Andria pretended to stab herself in the heart. "You definitely needed to see us tonight!"

"You don't know the half. Uncle Lawrence is a sweetie, and Julia's not *gruesome* necessarily. Just set in her ways. It's shameful, me complainin' about her. Didn't she give up her life to raise Fred, her sister's son? He wouldn't be the man he is if it wasn't for her—"

"And you can't stand her."

"No, Andria! I love her. She's my family."

Belinda turned to sit kitty-corner in the pew, nearly face-to-face with Paulette, and their knees knocked against each other. Her small hazelnut-colored hands stilled Paulette's fingers that were busy plucking nonexistent fuzz from her pants. "And you don't like her."

"I don't like her . . . very much," she whispered, unable to help herself. "But I do love her, and I so want to like her."

Belinda hugged her close. "It's okay, Etta. Of course you do. God's not going to smite you. You can't like everybody. He knows everything that's in your heart, your sitting down and your rising up. She's your family, that's true . . ."

"And we're your sisters, the ones who love Jesus just as much as you do." Andria's red lips parted in a grin. "Sure, it's a shame you don't like her, but Belinda's right: you can't like everybody. Go on ahead and serve her and love on her even if she doesn't return the favor, but you don't have to pretend to be pals, for goodness' sake. That's why you have us.

"Try on this truth for size: Richard and I haven't been intimate in over a month. I'm tired and irritable and if I hear him say one more thing about hockey . . . girl." Her eyes rolled toward the chandeliers suspended over them. "But I still love him, and I know I'll get over myself once my hormones figure out what they're doing. He's my best friend, something menopause can't change. All true."

"Hey, I hate my mother's cooking, my children get on my nerves because they're always hovering since their father died, and my boss micromanages like the dickens. One day, I'm going to take her job because I know more and I work harder. Oh, and Andria here can't drive. She almost killed us on the way over! And just because her people are Irish doesn't mean green is her lucky color." Belinda aimed a thumb at Andria's cardigan sweater as she winked at Paulette. "So true."

"*We're* your family, despite Belinda's rudeness. Your aunt-in-law would never let y'all stay in her house when she wasn't there." Andria pressed a palm to her chest. "I would."

Belinda shook her head. "I'm sorry, babe, but I wouldn't. I don't know any Black people who'd do that. Regardless, I know you still love me and you still *like* me. Now it's your turn to step into the confessional. If I can do it, you can. I dare you."

"Yeah, girl, what's the scoop?"

"Well . . ." Paulette stared at the cross behind the pulpit.

"Well?" The other two intoned.

"Well, the truth is, I'm frustrated with my son. Why does he shut us out? Why does he make it so hard to talk to him? I gave up my life to make sure he had one, and now he won't let me in so I can see his heart, to know him as an adult the way I knew him as a child. And I'm tired of hearin' that that's natural. No, it most definitely is *not* natural, not for us. I refuse to accept that. What's natural about me havin' to snoop through his room to find out what's goin' on in his life? And yes, I admit, part of me wasn't just doin' his laundry; I was snoopin'.

"Speakin' of natural, isn't it natural for me to wish my in-laws would go back home so I can celebrate my sixtieth birthday—there, I said it—and enjoy my son's return in peace? If only I had the guts to tell them, but why do I have to tell Fred what should be obvious? We just have to see his doggone aunt and uncle every couple of months, but we let nine go by before seein' our only son! I know something happened between him and McKinley last Christmas. Something big, something more than Fred told me. I mean, I know I have piano students and Fred has the company, but that's our son, for goodness' sake. We should've made the time to work out whatever it is.

"And those students of mine . . . Lord, have mercy! I'm thinkin' of steppin' down as Mount Olive's director of music and quittin' these piano lessons. I think God is callin' me elsewhere, away from this instrument I've lived behind most of my life. Where He's callin' me, I don't know. To build a greenhouse maybe? To hike the Blue Ridge Mountains and be as physically alone as I am emotionally in my own stupid house? Not that I've told anybody about how I'm feelin'. Something McKinley and I have in common."

Paulette's chest heaved with her effort to take in much-needed oxygen. "I couldn't talk to Fred even if I wanted to. He's hidin' his own problems from me, from his son, maybe even himself. Who knows what it is—something to do with that darn company, that's for sure. He's always tryin' to prove something or workin' to make up for what he's lost or had to give up. But who is he to condemn somebody else when the log in his own eye is big enough to build a house bigger than that stupid model he pretended to give *me* for my birthday?"

Andria opened her mouth and closed it, for once out of something to say.

Belinda squeezed Paulette's hand. She whispered, "Paulette . . . ?"

Paulette nodded as she looked from one shocked face to the other. She swiped at what had been tickling her cheek. Surprised, she drew back her hand and stared at the tears on her fingers. "Should I have chosen dare?"

Chapter Fourteen

Paulette wiggled her toes carefully so as not to disturb the covers. She blinked in the weak sunlight leaking through the shutters, guessing it wasn't quite seven. Beside her, Fred shifted to a different spot in the bed. She listened to him breathe evenly, enjoying the weight of him on the memory foam. She scooted back a little and settled against his side, close enough to feel the hairs on his arms.

Lately, she'd been waking up alone. Fred shot out of bed at the first hint of light; he rarely used an alarm to wake up. When Paulette heard him brushing his teeth in the bathroom, she'd huddle in the warm depression he'd left behind in the mattress, trying to capture his scent and the memory of his body before it faded. On those mornings, she gained an inkling of how her daddy must have felt those first few months and years after Mama had abandoned their bed for good.

For a minute, she listened to the early calls of the birds as they greeted each other in the flaming-pink azalea just outside her window, announcing the arrival of a new day. *Thank You, Lord, for this gift. I don't know what You have planned for me today, but I trust You to prepare me for it. Amen.* She kept her prayers short and to the point this time of morning and focused on the hint of sunlight dusting the room. If she didn't, she'd doze off and pick up whatever dream she'd been immersed in before she blinked open her eyes.

"Mmmm." Fred stretched his right arm outside the covers. "What time is it?" His voice was still wrapped in sleep.

"Early," Paulette whispered and waited for him to swing both legs over the other side of the bed and pop up. She stiffened, bracing herself for his withdrawal.

But then he wriggled his shoulders, relaxed his arm, and tucked it under the blanket and sheet. He encircled her and drew her more tightly against him. Within seconds, he was breathing deeply again.

Suddenly she felt wide-awake, alert to every curve of his body against hers, to the shadows getting chased from the room, to the sound of the robins telling each other good morning, to the musky vanilla scent of his lotion. Yet Paulette didn't dare move. Not for the world. She burrowed into him so not even a whisper could slip in between them where the cotton threads of his T-shirt and her satin nightgown squished together, and she closed her eyes.

· ✁ ·

Fred's side of the bed was cold. Paulette could tell without reaching for him, but still she flipped onto her back and stretched her arm across their queen-size bed. When her fingers curled around the mattress's edge without encountering a six-foot-tall, man-shaped hill, she opened her eyes, disappointed but not surprised to find Fred up and out. Finding him there would've shocked her more.

She hunched her shoulders as she curled onto her right side and blinked at the small crystal clock on the dresser. *Eight thirty.* "Shoot," she grumbled. Piano lessons started in an hour. That gave her forty-five minutes to read her devotions, shower, dress, and eat and less than fifteen minutes to warm up her own fingers to prepare to demonstrate the lessons. Paulette had to prepare all parts of her mind and body for her students. *Thank You, Jesus, that today's not a Lucy day!*

She dove under both sets of pillows on the heels of that thought and groaned. "But it is a Julia day."

Thirty-eight minutes later, Paulette, dressed in a sunset-gold shirtdress and heather-gray ankle-high leggings, was perched at the bar holding a mug of black coffee in her right hand and a note from Fred in her left. She read:

Etta—Uncle L and JJ asked to tour the floor this morning and then go out "for something good to eat" (ha-ha). We'll see you at the end of the day. Check the refrigerator and set the timer.

The second hand on the wall clock ticked away the moments she spent savoring the handwritten words. Fred's rare attempt at humor didn't even sting. Not one iota. Reveling in the good news, for once celebrating her solitude, Paulette watched the steam twirl and dissipate over her cup as the refrigerator hummed to her left and the dishwasher swish-swished on the other side of the bar. Otherwise, the house was silent, save for her first contented slurp of the day.

"Ugh." Paulette's nose wrinkled. Just yesterday, her morning cup was familiar and comforting, though strong. Today, the brew bit her taste buds. She swirled the brown liquid but didn't detect any sneaky grounds that had somehow outmaneuvered the filter. Paulette considered for a mere second or two before plopping down her cup. Ignoring the splashes on the granite, she retrieved the plastic bottle of French vanilla creamer from the refrigerator. McKinley's creamer. She poured a generous amount in a clean glass and nuked it for ten seconds, heating it like Kelsey had taught him. Then she drizzled it into her coffee.

Paulette sipped the unfamiliar concoction, then leaned over the bar for the sugar tin. She considered half a teaspoon but opted to dump in the whole spoonful. After stirring it in every which direction, she tested it. "Mm-mm-mm. Amazing! First my coffee, then the world." Paulette forced herself to take languorous sips to make the experience last.

Ding-dong!

Paulette's eyes flew to the wall. Today's first student had arrived, early for her homeschooling crowd who typically reserved the afternoons for their piano lessons, between morning classes and evening sports. But Hugo tinkered on the other side of life's keyboard. She smiled when she pictured the lanky teenage boy who had a gift for composition and playing by ear. He apologized for every missed note and responded to her every direction with a "Yes, ma'am," and a "Thank you, ma'am." Yet all the apologies in the world wouldn't make up for the fact that he couldn't read a note for the life of him.

Paulette inhaled deeply and drained the last of the sugar at the bottom of her cup. Hugo was one of the few students she was going to miss.

· ᴄᴈ ·

Frederick stepped back to let his aunt and uncle enter the floor before him. The trio was assailed by the smells of unfinished oak, pine, and maple and oils and machinery as soon as they stepped inside. Dust motes danced in the sunrays streaming through the large windows around the building.

"What do I hear, Frederick?" Juju shouted.

Fred pointed to the back right corner of the thirty-thousand-square-foot factory. "Do you want earplugs?" He'd become inured to the persistent, high whine of the equipment—the sanders, planers, and saws—but it could grate on newcomers. Fred considered the sound money to his ears.

"No, I'm talkin' 'bout that." She pointed to one of the sets of speakers mounted to a high beam in the ceiling.

Fred laughed as he tuned into "You Brought the Sunshine." "Oh! That's the Clark Sisters. 'You gave me peace; you gave me grace . . .'" His head bopped.

Juju swatted his fingers holding on to her chair. "Boy, I know who's singin'. I want to know *why* they're singin' in here? This is a place of business. How do they feel about that?" She indicated the people working in various areas on the floor.

"Why you wond'rin' what they think about it? From the looks of thangs, I bet the Lord is pleased," Uncle Lawrence pronounced.

"Well, there's a difference between a Sunday and a Monday, and I'm not talkin' 'bout the spellin'. This isn't church. Not everybody likes gospel music or believes in God. What about management?"

"It's about livin' the gospel, and it seems like our nephew is doin' that. Wasn't Jesus a carpenter?"

Julia cut her eyes at her husband and snapped, "A poor one."

"Well, we're not poor, and I'm the only management you need to worry about. George & Company has been in business for nearly a century, and it's getting stronger and bigger every day thanks to me. According to Knox, we're a family, and *my* 'family' listens to gospel music when they work." Was it just yesterday that McKinley talked to him about building relationships at the office? Fred shook off the thought.

"If folks don't like it, they're free to go somewhere else. It's not a plantation; I don't own a soul working here. Now, why don't we go on over to this side and see what's goin' on?" Striving to get the derailed tour back on track, Fred gestured toward the tall woman directing a group of five people. He walked slowly down the aisle so that Uncle Lawrence could keep pace with them.

He waved at the group. "That's my new foreman who runs the first shift. She calls the lead team together at seven thirty every morning so they can review that day's needs—orders, plans, problems from the day and night before. She stays on until four, when she typically passes the baton to DJ, the second shift foreman. His group either finishes up what the early shift started or prepares for the next." He kept strolling and nodding at his employees.

Juju's mouth opened as she took in all the craftsmen handling the band saws, grinders, and planers, guiding finished cabinetry along conveyor belts, rubbing cloths over chairs, inspecting drawers, applying stains, measuring, tapping joints into place. "How many people work for George & Company now? When we were comin' up, old man Clinton had about ten men workin' in a building in his backyard. And your papa didn't have but two people workin' that tree farm of his at any given season."

Fred inhaled deeply, his shoulders trembling under the weight of this moment. He knew just how much things had changed since he was a young boy—and how much they hadn't. His gratitude warred with his frustration. "We employ more than one hundred. Some are journeymen carpenters and a few are apprentices who are learning the trade. Most have been here for years. I hope to hire more experienced people next year as we expand."

He pointed. "We're adding a bigger room to accommodate our testing of the wood, to see how it holds up in extreme temps and moisture found in the Deep South or Southwest. We want our products to withstand all types of conditions, not just the moderate climate here in the South and mid-Atlantic, areas where our sales group has focused on."

"So Knox is growin' the business?" Lawrence's question brought Fred to a halt in front of the clean room, where inspectors worked in a dust-free environment.

"*We're* taking the company in a different direction. Still doing mostly regional, custom work, but also adding boxed cabinets that can be easily assembled, installed, or replaced so we can grow in other marketplaces."

His uncle nodded as his eyes roved the warehouse.

Juju twisted around to peer into her nephew's face. "Does Knox George know it's a *we*?"

Fred started moving again. "He found out when I told him."

· ↭ ·

When McKinley was little, he'd wait for his mother's cue as they turned onto the long tree-shaded road that led to their neighborhood, situated two giant steps beyond the city limits. Then he'd let down his window, dangle his hand out of the opening, and push against the wind all the way to the top of his street, right where she had to slow down. He never won the battle against his invisible foe.

Today, McKinley felt like a winner—at least that's the way he was grinning as Monroe made that last left onto Rosewood Drive. Summer's heat had come for a last gasp, and the sun beat down on his arm. A warm breeze flowed through the shiny black Jeep Wrangler, but McKinley knew Monroe soon would have to close up shop for the season, what his friend called converting to the hardtop during the colder months. For now, McKinley enjoyed riding with his spirit as free as his hands. Until, that was, he arrived home.

Monroe pushed the button and shut down the music as they parked by the mailbox outside the Baldwins' house. Immediately they heard faint piano playing emanating from the pale-yellow Victorian.

McKinley pictured his mother at her Steinway. "*Sonata Pathétique*, second movement. Mom must have something on her mind."

"Look here, bro." Monroe's slow drawl elongated the last three letters and added a *w*.

McKinley grabbed his buddy's shoulder and shook his head. "Man, I've told you not to say it like that. Maybe you should just drop it altogether. It's not comin' natural to your South Carolina roots. You left the state, but man, the state never left you."

"Okay, how about *Mac*. Is that bettah?"

A glower replaced McKinley's grin. "Ha-ha, not funny."

Monroe turned off the ignition. He leaned forward and

draped both arms around the steering wheel. "Thawt that would get your attention. When are you gonna have that sit-down with your folks? I get the sense you're plannin' to leave a note Sunday mornin' and drive away, nevah to be seen agin."

"Roe, what are you talking about? We just laid out the plan over lunch. You were sitting right there, nodding along." McKinley stared through the windshield. A large crow swooped down and jabbed at something undetectable in the middle of the road. After a few seconds another settled beside it with a great flap of ebony wings.

"Sure, I was there, and I heard everythang you said. But why wait until Saturday? No offense, but . . ." Monroe leaned his forehead on the wheel.

"Usually, when somebody says 'no offense,' they're about to say something that rubs you the wrong way."

"You might take it that way, but I'm tryin' to look out for y'all. That's my job, ra-ight, to look out for both sides? I'm the best ma-an, yours and hers, and *mah* job is to help y'all make the best decision right now, one you can live up to. That all of us can live up to, not only now but for the rest of your lahfe. Who cares about toasts and dinners—tahm's too short for any of that, although I could tell some stories about you two."

Monroe's grim expression didn't invite McKinley to laugh, not that he felt like it. He watched the birds pecking at the tarmac and listened to the voice that sounded more and more like Knox George every day.

Monroe sat up straight and shifted, drawing and holding McKinley's attention. He idly fiddled with the leather wrapping the steering wheel. "I respect the heck out of you, ma-an, but this is not just about you. You know that. And it's not about only your dad or your mom. It's tahm for you to step up to the plate. If this is what you wont, whatchyou both wont, then now's the tahm to say so. Don't wait for some big reveal this weekend ra-ight before you drive off into the sunset, after you ruin your mom's sixtieth birthday. You're brangin' two fam'lies togethah. That's powerful, *bro-thah*."

"This isn't how I envisioned things working out. You know that, Roe. You *know* that."

"You don't have to say it more'n once for me to believe you. It's not what I believe that mattahs anyhow. You're not marryin' me, even though it may eventually feel like it." Monroe lightly cuffed McKinley's chin and chuckled.

McKinley still couldn't work up a laugh, not even a smirk. The fingers on his right hand silently played a duet in a sonata meant for one on the outside of the Jeep's door. "You know she asked me to wait, so I waited, even though I didn't want to . . . not at first. But the more I thought about it, man . . . Aunt Juju and Uncle Lawrence, they changed the ball game."

"More'n not havin' both sets of parents in town?" Monroe looked skeptical.

"More than not having both sets of parents in town. Part of me wanted to run through the streets of Hickory

Grove shouting, 'The Baldwins are coming! The Baldwins are coming!'"

"Uh, you know Paul Revere didn't actually—"

McKinley chuckled. "Yes, Roe, I know he didn't actually say those words, but you get the picture. When I heard about my great-aunt and -uncle's visit, it only made the longest trip home of my life even longer. I mean, stopping in Thomasville *and* High Point . . . come on!"

Monroe chuckled. "Dude, your aunt is a piece of work, no offense—and this tahm, I mean it. I was so glad we had lunch plans. If we'd-a had to sit across a table from those two eyes glarin' at me, there's no way I could've finished a barbecue sandwich. Well, maybe the sandwich, but not the hush puppies."

That was saying a lot, McKinley knew. His friend's appetite was legendary. "It makes sense to wait for my future in-laws to come and my aunt Juju and uncle Lawrence to leave. Less fuel for the fire. Much better."

Monroe's sigh was loud in the car's close quarters. "Bettah for who—you or your parents?"

Whom, McKinley heard his mama's voice whisper in the quiet. The music in the house had stopped.

But Monroe's commentary hadn't. He ran his fingers through his thick brown hair. "I must say, I didn't feel all that comf'table sittin' with your father in church Sunday. Talk about all eyes on me. I felt lahk a pig at a chicken factory."

McKinley cupped his hands around his mouth and belted, "'One of these things is not like the others. One of these things doesn't belong.'" The birds scattered at the raucous sound.

"Ha-ha, but that service didn't feel like an episode of *Sesame Street.*"

"That was one moment in time for you, but try feeling that way in the office every day. Talk about odd man out."

Monroe nodded slowly. "Personally, I don't think your folks will have much of a problem acceptin' that you're gettin' married until they find out who you're marryin'."

McKinley leaned his head against the leather headrest and squeezed his eyes shut. The truth still found him hiding there.

"I mean, I'm just sayin'. Bruh."

Chapter Fifteen

PAULETTE WATCHED MCKINLEY climb from Monroe's car. He didn't head inside right away but leaned on the passenger door, and the two friends continued conversing through the window. Whatever they were talking about caused her son to move his hands and arms about; his upper extremities had quite a bit to say. She gently set down the piano's fallboard to cover the keys and left the front room. By the looks of things, he and Monroe had as much to work through as she did, and they deserved privacy.

It was a shame she hadn't afforded McKinley's jeans the same right to hold close their secrets. She wouldn't be in such an unsettled state right now if she had. Paulette was wrung out from fretting over what-could-have-been and what-might-it-be in both her own relationship and in her son's. Top that off with a full day of piano lessons that was finally behind her and dinner with her in-laws that loomed ahead of her like Hickory Grove's shadowy view of the mountain peaks. No wonder she stumbled on the first step leading to the second floor.

By the time she made it to the upper landing, Paulette was nearly crawling, at least emotionally. In need of a distraction, she dragged herself to the laundry room at the end of the hall. She stored away the detergent and fabric softener and scooped out towels from the dryer. So immersed in folding and stacking them, she didn't hear McKinley enter the house until he was standing a few feet away from her.

"Hey, Mama."

"Ooh, Lord, have mercy!" Paulette dropped a large towel and clutched her chest. It took a minute to catch up to her breath, which had escaped through her open mouth. When she did, she smiled at McKinley over her shoulder and panted, "Hey there." He sounded more and more like home, but she'd better attach bells to his shoes.

"Sorry, Mama. I didn't mean to scare you. Is this how you spend your free time?"

"I had to run a couple loads earlier between classes. Your father was startin' to run out of underwear." She moved to the washing machine and reached deep into the tub to withdraw a clump of wet underclothes. After peeling off a white undershirt, she shook it and tossed it into the dryer. Pairs of underwear followed suit. Peel, shake, and toss. "Did I see you with Monroe?"

McKinley leaned against the doorjamb and crossed his arms. "Yes, we had a meeting this morning to talk about that nested something or other."

"I believe the name you're lookin' for is 'nested-base router.' Fred has been mumblin' those words more than he has my name." Paulette closed the lid of the washing machine and pressed the buttons on the dryer controls.

McKinley slapped his forehead. "Yes, that's it! I think I've blocked it out. Monroe is just as excited as Dad. He says even though it's more expensive, it will save G&C money in the long run by getting more done, faster and more efficiently."

She shrugged and responded breezily, "Well, I wouldn't know. Fred has been puttin' in such long hours at work, we don't discuss the office much when he gets home. I can tell something's on his mind, but he doesn't share much in the way of specifics. I don't know what to ask, and he obviously doesn't feel like tellin'."

McKinley gazed at her hard and long as if trying to determine whether her nonchalance was manufactured or genuine. "Then you didn't know he was buying a new building?"

"*He* was? Don't you mean Knox?"

"Yes. Dad. Not anymore though."

Paulette turned her back to McKinley, blinking away tears. More unknowns to worry about. She dug out a plastic hanger from the bin and threaded it through the neck and arms of a man's polo shirt. She hung it on a line strung across the back wall of the laundry room. "So what brought about the change in plans?" She listened for his answer over the rattling of hangers behind her.

McKinley handed her a pink nightgown. "Sounds like he and the Georges have been going back and forth for more than a year about it. Mr. George wanted to build a bigger warehouse to accommodate the production pieces, but Dad was concerned about maintaining their tradition of quality on the custom side. Then along comes Monroe with this proposal about a router that could help them increase productivity in a smaller space. Plus, they wouldn't necessarily have to hire more people but focus on training a few."

"Quality versus quantity." She hung up the nightie.

"I bet it killed Dad to admit that Monroe's idea seems the perfect compromise."

Paulette extended an empty hand. "To say a thank-you probably stuck in his craw is an understatement." She watched McKinley use his thumb and index finger to hand her a lacy yellow bra.

He acts like he's ten. How's he gon' feel hangin' up more than his mama's fancy undergarments? And just like that, the heaviness descended again. It made itself comfortable as it reattached itself around her shoulders. Forgetting herself, she blurted, "You'd better start gettin' used to this."

Immediately the satiny black pair of underwear McKinley pinched became a hot potato to his fingertips. "What are you talking about? I've been doing my own laundry since I was thirteen."

Uh-oh, you've gone and done it now, Etta. "What I mean is . . . you know, one day . . . when you get married. I'm used to babyin' you, but soon I won't be around, and you'll be takin' care of somebody else." She reached over for the panties he'd flung to the side and hung them up before working on the towels she hadn't finished folding. Her armpits dampened again. The temperature in the small room had started to rise, but she had a feeling it had nothing to do with the warmth from the dryer and everything to do with their conversation and where it could lead.

"*Soon?* What do you mean, soon you won't be around? You make it sound like you're leaving Dad. What has he done this time?" His laugh sounded nervous.

For a moment, Paulette watched the clothes tumbling about in the dryer window. When she finally spoke, her voice was low, her words slowly forthcoming. "I just know our opportunities together are fadin'. Fast." How could she share she'd found the ring without him thinking she was riffling through his things? *Because you were riffling, Etta. Technically. But if he just told me what was going on in his life, I wouldn't have to,* she reasoned, going toe-to-toe with herself.

"Ma? Come on, what's up?"

Ma. From "mother" to "mama" and now "ma," the name he knew she detested. It conjured images of milking cows and covered wagons and lean-tos and barn raisings. She couldn't even raise a pot lid properly. *Ma.* McKinley plied those two letters the way she used his full name—to get her full attention. Well, he had it. Paulette dropped the wash-cloth and faced her child-who-would-be-grown.

"Um . . . I, um, McKinley, I found your, um, the box. With the ring inside." The words barely gathered momentum before coming to a standstill.

"Ring?" His bottom lip fell open after he exhaled the word.

"I'm sorry, Son. I didn't mean to snoop. I decided to do your laundry—" she spread her hands wide to encompass the baskets of clothes in the room—"and there I was, smellin' your shirts and checkin' your pockets, doin' my usual pre-laundry canvassing. And I found—"

"The ring." McKinley sighed.

"Yes, the ring." She expelled a deep breath after sucking in some air through her nose. "It's beautiful, I have to say, even though it took me aback when I saw it. I take it, it's an engagement ring. For a girl we haven't even met." Paulette plastered a face on this hair-twisting Kelsey who had the nerve to love her son without meeting his family. Didn't young women want to know the roots of the tree these days?

· ᏋᏗ ·

McKinley worried his gulp was audible in the life-size silence between their words. It dwarfed his thoughts.

"Actually, you *have* met my fiancé. Well, she's not my fiancé yet, not formally. I do still have the ring . . . for now. She wanted to wait until everybody knew everything before we made it official." He swallowed again.

Mother knocked over a stack of towels as she stepped toward him. They tumbled off the counter and onto the floor; the room looked as confused as the expression on her face. "You make it sound like you'll be asking her soon. Does that mean she's flying in? But wait . . . we've met her? I think I would've remembered meeting your Kelsey."

McKinley held up his palms. "Whoa, Mama. Slow your roll. My Kelsey? Who's—wait, *that* Kelsey? No! No, I'm not marrying Kelsey. Haven't we covered this already? I told you, she's my friend. My best friend after . . ." He could just hear the pregnant mother of three laughing now. More than likely, her extremely protective husband wouldn't think it was that funny.

"After who?"

He'd promised he would wait, but he realized that was a promise he couldn't keep. If he wrote the answer on the lines crisscrossing his mother's palms, would that count as not telling? Probably not. But McKinley took his mama's hand, almost as if he was about to do that very thing, and drew her out of the sweltering laundry room and down the hall. He could feel her stumbling after him, so he opted for the first likely spot.

They sank slowly, side by side, on the hardwood at the top of the stairs towering over the front hall. McKinley took a moment to stare into the eyes of his first love, his mother. The woman who used to know him best but who now didn't know enough. He wished to enjoy the quiet in that moment, for he knew this precious peace wouldn't last long. Explosions had a way of ending a détente.

"Why all this lead-up, McKinley?"

"Well, Mama, maybe you should get used to hearing 'Mac,' at least while I'm in town." He squeezed her hand and watched her lips murmur the name *Mac*.

Then her eyes widened and she gasped. "*Emmie!* You're marryin' Emmeline *George*? Lord, have mercy!"

• ⁊ •

She probably had the greenest eyes in the whole George family. They stood out even in the prescription glasses she'd been forced to wear since she was six years old. Emmeline never liked them.

"Child, you're eighteen and on your way to college. It's about time you accept how God made you. Be grateful. They make you stand out. Nobody else in your family looks quite like you, let alone the rest of the hillbillies in this county. Now, put those unusual eyes on this music and play this measure again." Paulette tapped the book on the stand.

Emmie always took more than her allotted forty-five minutes even as a little girl, but Paulette never minded. The three young Georges used to come to the Baldwins' on Thursdays and spend the afternoon and early evening taking their piano lessons, playing with her son and laying waste to the kitchen. Together, the four of them—Monroe, Lacey, Emmie, and McKinley—buzzed in and out and through the house like a swarm of locusts.

Paulette had rather liked the noise and confusion, as well as the joy on McKinley's face when he was with the Georges.

With only Emmie left and her older siblings off to school and the workforce and Monroe preparing to return to college in a few weeks, the house was starting to get quiet. She'd considered homeschooling the only option for her family, but sometimes it got lonely for McKinley, an only child, and then for her, the mother of one. Playdates, park days, and classes with other students didn't replace rubbing up alongside a brother or sister all day, every day when they could. Something she and Fred couldn't give him and what his personality needed to keep him from burrowing under his bunk bed with his bugs, books, pencils, and drawing pads. Then God gave McKinley the Georges.

But what He hadn't given Paulette was the patience to deal with Emmie and her complaints—at least that was how it felt. Every week, it was something else with that girl: her height, her weight. Life as the baby of the family. Her overbearing father. Now, one of her best features—her eyes, of all things. She'd been moaning over them for two weeks.

Paulette huffed and put most of her weight on her right foot. "Emmeline George, if you don't play this measure, I'm gon' tell your mama on you!" The threat was an old joke between the two, and the young woman paid no mind. She never had.

"I'm tired of looking different from everybody else, Mrs. Baldwin. Monroe has these blue eyes you can dive into. Lacey's are hazel with these dark fleckies, like Mama's and Daddy's. I know we're not related, but yours are so beautiful, and Mac's are a deep and dark brown. When he looks at me . . ." Her voice trailed off as she studied the piano keys.

Oh, Lord. My child had better not be turnin' his eyes on Emmeline George. When could McKinley even think about looking at this child? He'd better be finding him a beautiful Black woman at NC State and hittin' the books!

Both Paulette's brows arched—she never could raise only one. She didn't really like where the conversation was going and the way it made her heart drop to her feet as they traveled there. And Paulette never could stand when Emmeline called him Mac. "When Mc*Kin*ley and I look at you, you mean?"

"Of course." The eighteen-year-old's face flushed. She played middle C, then proceeded to find the note on the lower and higher octaves on the piano.

Paulette sat down in the chair she kept nearby when she was ready to write notes at the end of a lesson. She tilted Emmeline's face toward her own. "Do you know how hard to find green eyes are? They're the absolute rarest. Green eyes actually mean your irises have a little more melanin in them, melanin and lipochrome, than say Monroe's. Just not as much as mine and *McKinley's*. Light reflects off the blue and the yellow and make what?"

"Green." Emmeline shook her head. "You make everything a homeschool lesson, don't you, Mrs. Baldwin? Poor Mac . . . *Kinley*."

"Yes, my poor son," Paulette chuckled, "and neither he, Monroe, nor your sister is more special than you, Emmie dear. The light shows the true color. The Light—" she directed an index finger toward heaven—"shows the true colors in here." She pointed to the left side of Emmeline's chest, where her heart was thumping so sadly. "And that's all that matters. Not what you look like. Don't ever forget that. 'If we walk in the light as He is in the light, we have fellowship with one another, and the blood of Jesus Christ His Son cleanses us from all sin.'"

The girl had peered up at her. "Is that what you really think, Mrs. Baldwin?"

Paulette knew that was what she was *supposed* to think and told herself to pray about it. But her guilty feelings didn't have anything to do with that day's lesson. She reached over and tapped the page on the piano stand. "How about you face forward and play the notes those beautiful eyes of yours can see in that first measure."

· Ᏽ ·

"McKinley, are you tellin' me you're marryin' Emmeline Jean George? Monroe's sister? Knox and Sarah's baby girl? The child who sat on that piano bench nearly ten years ago—" his mother aimed downstairs toward the front room—"and told me she gets the shivers when my son looks at her. *That* Emmeline?"

McKinley wrapped his fingers around hers and brought Mama's hand down to rest on his thigh. "The white girl I grew up with who's the daughter of Dad's boss. Yes, that Emmeline. None other." He covered their clasped hands with his right.

"But." She closed her lips around the word. Finally she managed to whisper, "Your dad is going to have a fit. A pure-dee fit."

He nodded. "Probably. You seem to be having a small one yourself. I'm afraid you're going to start foaming at the mouth." His eyes never left her face. McKinley wanted to witness the emotion as it sprang from her heart and planted itself on her face, before she had a chance to show him what she wanted him to see—or what she thought he wanted to see.

"But how?"

Still, he had to squint, peering into those eyes of hers Emmie admired so, wondering if those two sets of three little letters were what his mama had intended to say the first time. "How do people fall in love? How did you and Dad fall in love? I don't think there is a *how*.

"One moment there was Emmeline over here and McKinley over there." He let go of his mother's hands to hold his own pair far apart. "The next, there was an Emmeline and McKinley." He entwined his fingers. "Corny, but true."

"Well, until she's wearing a weddin' band under that gorgeous ring you plan to give her, you'd better be more like this." She pulled his hands an inch apart.

"Mama." McKinley tucked in his bottom lip.

"Emmie and Mac . . . ," Mama breathed and squeezed shut her eyes. It was as if she wanted to disappear and go where he couldn't see her.

No, he didn't know how, but he knew when. Perhaps if his mother had studied him as intently as he was studying her, she would've been able to see just how much. Somehow McKinley had to explain it, even if only a little bit, of the deep well of feeling he had for the woman who had turned his heart upside down and inside out and was about to do the same thing to his world. He had to fight past his own reserve, his own desire to constantly erect high walls to restrain the curious and retain any words that could betray his thoughts.

McKinley stared down through the stained-glass window over the front door. "Last fall about this time, Monroe brought Emmie to Philly. She was considering taking a job in the area because she wanted to get away from the family business she'd worked in her whole life in some capacity, and full-time since she'd graduated from college. 'See more of the world,' according to him. He brought her up for the weekend so we could hang out for old times' sake."

His mother's eyes had opened. She seemed to catch every word he said and hold on to it with her free hands that were slightly cupped in her lap.

"So I made a plan to show them every touristy place Philly had to offer—the Liberty Bell, Independence Mall, the Philadelphia Museum of Art . . . But before we could do that famous run up the museum's steps and jump up and down like Rocky Balboa, Monroe got a call from home about some issue his dad was having in the office, and he waved us off so he could work it through. Before we knew it, Emmeline and I had spent three hours strolling around that museum, talking, laughing . . ."

"And looking into each other's eyes," his mother murmured.

McKinley nodded. "Hers looked more hazel than green that day in the Dox Thrash exhibit. A lot like yours, in fact. Maybe it was the light, just like you said. I couldn't tell you anything else about what we saw. I just remember she was more interested in me than she was in learning about one of the inventors of Carborundum printmaking. It was one of the best weekends of my life. I was like 'How could I have missed this . . . missed *her* all those years?'"

"You didn't. She was your friend."

"I did though. Because she was my best friend's baby sister. But there she was, all grown-up, looking at me like I was all that and a bag of chips." McKinley smiled at the memory. Some of the fortifications around his heart had crumbled a bit, letting in a revealing shaft of light.

"Emmeline was barely two years out of college, McKinley. It was probably hero worship."

McKinley heard his mother's frown before he saw it, so focused was he on looking back to that day from a year ago. That first date. "Well, she's almost twenty-five now, and she never worshiped me. I was her stanky older brother's friend. Her piano teacher's son. *Her* friend who taught her how to make a goal kick nearly every time."

"The son of the Black man who can remember not being allowed through the front door of the building where he works for the white cousin of the man who barred him." Paulette stretched her legs out and balanced the heels of her feet on the third step from the second floor. She rubbed her temples. "This cannot end well."

"That's the point: I don't expect it to end." McKinley's voice was soft yet firm.

What he expected was a fight, just not on this front. He'd told himself, surely if anybody understood, it would be his mother. Maybe subconsciously, after all this time, he'd taken to heart his great-aunt's scurrilous notion that the former Miss Paulette Burdell was a white woman who'd gone and snagged herself a good Black man.

Chapter Sixteen

——— ❦ ———

IT WASN'T UNHEARD OF IN 1960 to see a Black man tend the neighbor's lawn in Norwalk, California. But it did get tongues working overtime when folks found out he wasn't just talking to the men clipping the hedgerows and watering the flowers in other yards; he employed them. He didn't merely use all the supplies in the back of the truck he drove; he owned each and every one. As a teenager, Harold Burdell had long determined he didn't want to spend his whole life working for anybody but himself—Black, white, or otherwise. The minute his busted knee got him honorably discharged from the Army, he plunked down all he had on a truck and a lawn mower and declared himself the owner and operator of Burdell's A+ Lawn Care.

And that was the "how" behind his meeting Bett.

One day, the well-bred daughter of one of Harold's customers went from peeking through the curtains at the tall, good-looking man with the burnished skin to waving hello when she "just happened" to walk outside to the mailbox while he worked. Then she learned he was Harold, the owner, and that his gently spoken words took a bit longer to say because they hailed from clear across the country, from North Carolina. A few weeks later, after insisting Harold drop the *Miss* in front of Bett, she was asking him about her mother's prickly pink wild roses he'd saved from sure death, now blooming quite beautifully in her backyard.

Over time, Bett learned that the purposeful, ready-with-a-smile man had originally joined the Army to experience something other than toiling for a dime so somebody else could make a dollar. Harold became more than a curiosity or an act of rebellion against her white father and Greek mother. He was the man she loved and would marry, despite the world's opinions on what was allowed and not allowed. Hadn't the State of California declared she could do just that, a little over a decade earlier?

But her parents couldn't have cared less what four of the seven members of California's Supreme Court had to say about anti-miscegenation laws. They refused to allow their oldest daughter to set fire to the family's booming restaurant business by marrying "outside her color."

Paulette used her thumb to trace the figures of Harold and Bett Burdell in the black-and-white photograph she was holding. They were sitting side by side on the roof of a dented olive 1957 Plymouth Fury, the car he'd purchased after selling off all his tools and his truck and letting his employees go. Harold had told his daughter the picture was taken the day he and her mother had set out for North Carolina with little more than the twinkle of hope Paulette could detect in their eyes.

McKinley had to pull Paulette to her feet after sitting for forty minutes on the hardwood floor at the top of the stairs. She'd limped behind him on numb legs and tingling feet down to the front room, where she wandered from one framed image to another, picking them up and setting them down or adjusting their tilt on the pimpernel-colored walls. The picture of her parents was one of the few tangible memories of their marriage she could put her hands on.

"According to Daddy, Bett's father—my grandfather—practically yanked out his sideburns the day she announced she was gettin' married. He asked her, 'Why did God put Blacks and whites on different continents all around the world if they were meant to marry?'"

McKinley snorted. "Did he really believe that?"

"Probably. People say even crazier things than that to justify their hatred and ignorance. From what I understand, Bett responded with something like 'But I met Harold right in our backyard. And if that was the case, you shouldn't have married Mother. She's from Greece!' Bett had the golden-touched complexion to prove it, from what I remember of her."

Paulette offered the photo to her son. "Ironically, it was your grandfather's light-brown skin that she loved most. Bett told him he reminded her of a warm piece of buttered toast."

"So essentially he was the best thing since sliced bread as far as your mother was concerned. But if that was the case, why did she leave, especially after fighting so hard to marry Grandpa in the first place?" He brought the image within a couple inches of his nose. Someone would've thought this was the first time he'd laid eyes on it, but the picture had hung in the family room for years before she'd relocated it. A bare nine-by-thirteen-inch rectangle still marked the spot there.

Just as with the photographs, Paulette had shared many of these old stories about her family with her husband and son. She could tell that now McKinley was considering them all from a different perspective, like studying a chrysanthemum from the roots up instead of focusing on its petals. She shrugged, more to buy time than to communicate a lack of opinion about his question—for she had much to say on the matter. "You know her father didn't take their marriage sittin' down. He decided to go on the offensive and crushed Daddy's business before the news could drive away his own customers. I don't even know if it would've."

"That's because you don't want to admit it. I'm surprised they didn't lose more than his lawn company," McKinley muttered.

"Well, *that's* because they left California to try to start fresh after all Daddy's customers dropped him. I don't know where they thought they would go, though, since their marriage wasn't legal everywhere at that time and barely accepted anywhere at all, whether it was legal or not. This was years before the Loving decision, you know."

She could tell McKinley remembered their past discussions about the landmark case involving Richard and Mildred Loving, a white man and a Black woman who risked imprisonment and worse to get married. *Loving v. Virginia* eventually led to the country's legalization of interracial marriage in 1967. "I remember the way Daddy once described their cross-country drive back home—"

"With your mom pretending to be a very light-skinned Black woman when a car filled with men drove them off the road—"

"Which is ironic when you think how people felt they had to pass for white to survive." Paulette sighed. They both knew her family's story backwards and forward. Its outcome was determined a lifetime ago yet continued to reverberate through the generations.

By the time Harold and Bett Burdell eventually made it back to the East Coast, she was pregnant with Paulette. The couple eked out a living up north, living hand to mouth, sometimes in secret, until Bett eventually decided the only thing she could do for them was give them up. So she left her four-year-old daughter with Harold, telling him Paulette would grow up whole with him instead of getting split in two, between her mama's world and her daddy's. Bett returned to the people she'd left behind in California.

"And to go back to the people who rejected her in the first place. How could she even consider them family?" McKinley set down the photograph and fixed his dark-chocolate eyes on his mother's.

Paulette feared he could see the pain she'd buried, so she turned toward the piano, the place where she loved to run and hide. Swallowing, she forcibly modulated her tone, only speaking loudly, yet evenly, enough to be heard over the soft chords she played with her right hand. "They're all she had, McKinley—her parents, their restaurants, that money. Most of what I know about her, my daddy told me. Of course, years later, I heard from the attorney managin' their estate. What she couldn't give me while she was livin', she gave me when she wasn't. Not that I wanted anything from Bett. Not then anyway. At least some of it went toward payin' for your college."

She'd composed herself enough to face him. "But that's why you need to listen to me, Son. You don't know what you're gettin' into. Look at my mother—"

But he was backing away from her toward the large foyer, his hands waving off her words. "Uh-uh. No. This is not 1960s North Carolina or even California. And I hope Dad won't disown me for my decision. *My* decision, Mama. Emmie and I aren't planning to run around the country looking for people to accept or support us or take us in. Times have changed."

Paulette trailed him and grabbed one of his hands. She pulled him back and forced him to sit in one of the wingback chairs that faced each other in front of the piano. "That's not what I'm sayin', McKinley. I just want you to think of the implications of marryin' this girl. Sure, we'll accept you. There's nothing *not* to accept . . ." Her heart thudded in her chest, and for a second she couldn't breathe. Who knew how the other half of her *we* would react to this news.

"Yes, times have changed; it's not the 1960s. But I've learned you can't legislate love or forgiveness. Only Jesus can do that. I was little, but I remember the stares I got when I walked beside my dad, and his skin was lighter than yours. People whisperin' and wonderin' how I came to be.

"I know North Carolina isn't Philadelphia, but your children will deal with some of the same issues, the same ignorance and bias. Don't be naive, McKinley. My own daddy kept lookin' for a love that looked more like him, but he never found it. You know how your aunt treats me, and she's my own people."

He snorted. "Your skin color wasn't your daddy's problem, and Aunt Juju isn't anybody's people, Mama."

"McKinley! Shame on you." Yet she knew he was right. Julia would criticize Jesus for letting "just anybody" touch the hem of His garment.

"It's the truth. I love Aunt Juju, and I respect her. But I'm not afraid of her."

Paulette thought the button on McKinley's pink polo shirt would fly off and hit her in the eye, the way he'd squared his shoulders and puffed out his chest at his attestation. "So you say. If color isn't the issue and you're so big and bad, why haven't you told anybody about Emmeline? Why did *I* have to come to *you* about this engagement ring?"

· ↩ ·

McKinley slumped in his chair. It was like Mama had stuck a pin in his heart and deflated it. *Why didn't I just tell them the first night I was here?* Emmeline had asked him to wait until she was in town, and then her own parents had left town, but he should have insisted. Instead, he tried to attack his family's biases to wear down their resistance and win the war from the inside out. But he was no Trojan horse.

"I'm not tellin' you who to love. Lord knows nobody told me and they tried to tell my parents. And I like Emmie—"

"What, some are your best friends are white? Isn't that how the saying goes? Hey, you can do better than that, Mama, because some of your *family* is white." He knew his tone sounded bitter, but he couldn't help it. He didn't want to help it.

"Boy, don't be funny with me. I don't appreciate it." She pulled back from him and sat straight in her chair. "I've done my best to show nothing but respect for you and your manhood, but you will honor me as your mother. None of that snide business. You know I don't play that."

Humbled, McKinley nodded at this side of his mother, who'd raised up to her full height and demanded attention. He used to see this part of her more often, the Paulette Baldwin that refused to put up with her child's mess.

"As I was sayin', I've always liked Emmeline. To be honest,

next to Monroe, she was my favorite George—even though adults aren't supposed to have favorites, so please don't ever tell her sister, Lacey. I've had some good times with that girl, right here in this room at this piano.

"Part of what makes me question your . . . engagement—" she dipped her chin and swallowed before continuing—"is your fear."

This time, it was McKinley who sat straighter. *What is she talking about?*

Mama wrapped her fingers around his wrist, keeping him from rising from his seat. "You're afraid of something, McKinley, and it can't be just how you think we'd react. Do you really think I'd reject Emmie solely because she's white? Who cares? That would be rejectin' a part of myself, my own blood, my own history. What did I used to tell you? 'I don't care who you marry, as long as she believes in Jesus, loves you, likes me, and wants to homeschool.' In. That. Order. It's still true."

It seemed McKinley heard those words about every other week from the moment he blew out those sixteen birthday candles on his cake and took a giant leap into manhood. His mama had been entreating the Lord on his future wife's behalf for decades. Now they both had a face and a name to add to those prayers.

"Yes, I do worry about you. A lot. I worry about a lot of things that don't have anything to do with who you are but how the world sees you: Will you be safe if the police stop you on the road? Do your managers regard you on equal footin' with your coworkers? How will the world treat my grandchildren? Yet how you live depends on how you live out your faith. Truly, that colors how you see the world, and that's so much more important than how the world sees you.

"I know what a good son you are, McKinley, don't get me wrong. But I wonder what kind of husband you'll be, what kind of father—'cause that 'first comes love, second comes marriage, then comes the baby in the baby carriage' ain't just a rhyme I used to sing in school. I'm stewin' over this because . . . your love for Emmeline has to be bigger than your fear of the world, your concern for what your daddy and I think or what your great-aunt is gonna say.

"You're gonna deal with a good deal more than that, and you must know that. Frankly, you make a bigger deal over her color than I do. Carin' about her complexion is like worryin' over the width of her shoulders or the size of her feet, how fast her hair grows and how tall she is. Things beyond her control and that have absolutely nothing to do with her character or her faith or how she feels about you.

"Bett's love for me and Daddy wasn't big enough. It just wasn't. She didn't have faith enough in God or her family to hold on. She said she left for our sake, but did she? So that's a teeny-weeny bit of what I'm thinkin' about." His mother held apart her index finger and thumb about a hairbreadth.

"I'm selfish enough to admit I hate to lose that part of your heart you'll be givin' to this woman—*any* woman. But the news is really startin' to sink in, and I'm overjoyed at the thought of you gettin' married. My son, *married*. And I'm gettin' a daughter! I mean, a *daughter*. Wow, finally!" Paulette sat back for a moment and stared into space.

"I just want you to keep her, McKinley. You'll have to ask God to examine your heart and mind and reveal to you what's really beatin' in that inward part. Not the stuff you won't volunteer or give me a straight answer about. The truth about yourself that's hidden deep inside, in a place even you can't see. I pray He shows you. You *and* Emmie."

McKinley concentrated on the view through the large window over the piano. At this time of year, many of the trees were shedding leaves that typically obscured the neighbor's house during the spring and summer. Now the thinned-out branches revealed the porch across the street that faced their own front door. If it wasn't for the direction of the sun that created shade and flickering shadows, he could have peered directly through the Pfeiffers' windows and witnessed whatever their family was doing inside. The idea of somebody peering through his windows, literal and figurative, made him cringe and squirm in his chair.

Unable to find a comfortable position, he stood, and his mother's fingers released their grip. His arm felt cool where they'd held him. McKinley looked down at her, gazing up so earnestly into his face; he could almost see her heart pounding there on the sleeve of her dress.

"Mama, I hear what you're sayin'. For the most part. You're imagining things that aren't there though. You know that you and Dad aren't always the easiest people to talk to. He expects me to do things his way because he considers himself this trailblazer. Dad doesn't get it when I disagree with him or when I think for myself. It's not that I'm not well versed in all he's lived through, how he's pulled himself up and made a great success of his life. I've learned a lot from him.

"Does that mean I can't live my own life, forge my own path? Yes, some white people did him and Great-Grandpa Frederick and Aunt Juju wrong. But that doesn't make every white person evil or beholden to me. You want to protect me from every hurt possible, and you want to know my every thought. You pointed out yourself that that's not realistic since I don't know everything about my own self. Maybe you're like Dad, trying to make up for what you and your family lost. Who knows?

"Mama, I can't tell you what I don't know. But neither can you. And what I do know, I might not tell you, at least not yet. But that doesn't make me afraid, just like not carrying my old Bible in my hand 24-7 doesn't make me an unbeliever. It may just mean I'm waiting for the right time."

Her forehead wrinkled.

McKinley couldn't restrain his laughter. "Okay, that was my awkward way of slippin' that in. I know you were trying to chastise me just a little bit because you didn't think I took my Bible to church on the regular. You're wrong, though. I do." He jiggled his phone. "And I study it, maybe not all day every day like you do, walking around here quoting verses every minute."

His mother seemed to hear the joke and chuckled a little as she sat there, looking up at him with moist eyes.

McKinley could tell she thought he was blowing smoke. He sighed. "What?"

"Nothing. Tryin' to listen with my heart and not my ears. Besides, I think I've said enough. We'll both have plenty more to say soon, especially when you talk to your dad about your marriage."

My marriage. McKinley ran a hand over his face. Now was the time to tell her what he knew about *her* marriage, since he'd just crowed about how unafraid he was, and it seemed like Dad was taking his sweet time not to. He opened his mouth to speak as his mother pushed herself from her seat and walked over to plant herself again before the black-and-white photographs on the bookshelf. "Mom. There's something else."

"Our children always seem to bow under the weight of their parents' expectations, don't they?" Mama picked up a framed picture of a six-month-old McKinley, decked out in a fuzzy, one-piece footed jumper with a yellow teddy bear stitched across its bib. His baby cheeks practically rested on his shoulders. "They bear the disappointments, the struggles, the hopes, and the unmet goals of all those folks who came before them. It's a lot, all our could'ves and should'ves."

"Yes, it is. When does it let up?" McKinley's voice carried a weariness that was more than physical. He was tired of listening and talking, though they both had more thoughts to share, despite her words to the contrary just a few minutes before.

"When they do." Paulette shrugged, surprisingly concise.

"What, the expectations?"

"No, the parents." She smiled. "That's the way God intended it, Son. Don't let it get you down. We're all playin' the roles we were meant to play."

McKinley couldn't think what to say.

"We talked so much about what could happen after the wedding, I don't even know what inspired you to ask her in the first place. Wait." Pink flushed her cheeks. "This isn't a shotgun wedding, is it?"

He knew she was asking if an unexpected pregnancy had prompted his proposal. "Mom, come on . . ."

"No judgment, no judgment. I just—" A faint *beep-beep-beep* of the alarm cut short her words. Mama looked over his shoulder in the direction of the back door.

"Knox might need to bring his shotgun. Your dad will probably come locked and loaded, and that man will need to defend himself."

Chapter Seventeen

FRED DIPPED the tip of his small brush in the container and slowly applied the black paint to the shingles, so as not to drop any on the linoleum floor of his office. The first row gleamed, in stark contrast to the rest of the unfinished roof covering the thirty-six-inch tall, three-story Victorian house. At this rate, it should take him about two more hours to complete that part of the project, then on to the rest of the model.

He stood back and cast an eye at the unopened cylinders on the wooden table, comparing the amount of paint to the size of his brush. He tried to calculate how much time it would take him to cover the house's wooden slats with lavender and then paint the trim goldenrod. Anybody else might just slather on the color, but that was antithetical to his methodical way of doing things: everything in order and order in everything. Even so, he should finish with plenty of time left over to let the paint dry several hours before the big reveal Friday. The *second* big reveal, which he stubbornly hoped would go better than the first.

That settled, Fred used his toe to release the brakes on the four casters. Then he wheeled the table the house sat on closer to the open sliding-glass door, the room's only window. He crouched over it and returned to layering firm, even strokes of glossy lacquer, the starry scope beyond the window a quiet backdrop.

Before he could finish the third row, he heard footsteps on the stairs leading from the garage bay to his workstation. Fred waited. Yes, those were definitely footsteps. And voices. He looked behind him to make sure the heavy black drapes he'd installed were enclosing his other project. Fred was glad he'd had the foresight to plan for such an occasion.

Knock-knock. The door rattled as it opened and Junior peeked into the room. "Dad?"

"Who else would it be?" Fred waved Junior in, relieved to see his face. He put down his brush and steeled himself for a discussion about his Victorian, for Fred no longer considered it Paulette's gift. He moved to clear the floor of crumpled paper, an empty wastebasket, and other odds and ends.

Turned out, Fred was waving *them* in, for Uncle Lawrence shuffled in behind Junior, his burnished red cane beating a familiar tattoo on the linoleum. A brilliant smile cracked the older man's face wide-open as he rested one hand atop the other on the curved derby handle. "Hi, Nephew. Caught you by surprise, huh?"

"Yes, I thought you were tired of me. Or just plain wo'-out, as Papa would say," Fred laughed. Juju should have tucked in her husband an hour ago, tops. Fred had kept the two out most of the day, and he could tell the long hours had worn out the older man, though he hadn't complained once. His aunt had taken care of that part of the conversation.

Uncle Lawrence shook his head. "No, sir, not me. I got some miles left in these old bones." He jiggled one foot and then the other to prove it. "Julia's the one. She's prob'ly snorin' by now. Carryin' on as much as she does takes a lot out of you."

The two men enjoyed the laugh and the truth buried in it.

"So is that the house I've heard so much about?" Uncle Lawrence aimed his cane in the direction of the cart.

"It looks good, Dad. I see you've added some color. It's different than . . ." By the expression on Junior's face, he seemed to be searching for a hole to jump into.

"What, different than what Etta said? It's okay. I know she talked about it. Probably told you the whole conversation, the way you two go on."

Uncle Lawrence winked at his great-nephew and snickered. "Actually, I think Paulette and McKinley been talkin' 'bout another couple you might know."

Thinking he'd heard his uncle wheeze, Fred started to inquire about his health, but then Fred felt movement behind him. He spun to his left and caught his son by the end of his T-shirt. "Hey, whatchyou doin'?"

Junior had edged between his father and the worn leather sofa pushed up against the right wall and was about a man's shoe length from the black curtain. "What's goin' on back here?"

Fred shook his head. "Uh-uh. Nope. It's not finished yet. I've already been burned by an early reveal. Don't even think about peekin' behind that curtain."

"Come on, Dad." Junior pointed to the slight bulge behind the material and took another step toward it.

Fred stepped in front of the younger man, spread his arms wide, and splayed his fingers. "I said leave it alone, Fred Jr. You and your mama have been thick as thieves, with all those wide eyes and whispering in the kitchen. You've got more business to worry about than mine by the sounds of things. Wouldn't you say so, Uncle?"

"Yep, I'd say so, Nephew." Lawrence tapped to the chair. His lips formed an O and he blew out a deep whew when he plopped down.

Fred squinted at his uncle, but again, before he could inquire about his health, Junior claimed his attention by sidling closer to the curtain. "I'm not playin' with you, boy," he growled.

His son held up his palms in surrender. "Okay, okay." He backed toward the sofa, where his great-uncle sat. "You're right. We've got things to talk about anyway."

"Uh-oh. I thought as much. Maybe I should sit down

myself." Fred took a few steps toward the tall stool across from his uncle while keeping one eye on Junior. Then he made an about-face toward the three-foot-high structure waiting patiently for him to return. "On second thought, I'd better keep my hands busy."

"Mama said it was a beautiful design."

Lawrence sat forward in his seat, bracing both hands on his cane to stabilize his position.

Basking in what he assumed was their admiration, Fred pushed open the tiny front door before pointing to the seam along the roof with his index finger. "See, I built hinges on the top and you can swing open the whole thing to see the inside. I just started painting the shingles, so I can't show you how it works now." He looked at the other men over his shoulder.

"What made you think to give my niece that? I asked you before: what's a sixty-year-old gon' do with a dollhouse?"

Fred couldn't make sense of Uncle Lawrence's quizzical expression or his question. All he knew was that he didn't hear applause from either the younger or older Baldwin. They certainly seemed less than wowed by his unique gift. "W-well," he stuttered. "It's not really a dollhouse. It's a model."

"Is this project what's been taking so much of your time? To hear Mama tell it, she didn't know what you were doing over here. Maybe orchestrating a hostile takeover of George & Company, heh-heh." Junior eased over to the Victorian and leaned down to peek through the mullioned plastic panes. His fingertip raised and lowered a window. "Impressive."

But the moment felt so much less than that to Fred.

"So you thought Paulette was gon' like it?"

That was exactly what he'd thought before she'd entered the room Saturday morning and broken the magic spell. Uncle Lawrence might have phrased his words like a question, but Fred heard the large, definitive period he'd used to punctuate them as he reclined against the cushions and balanced his cane against his knee. Was he wearied by his nephew's apparent insensitivity or the day's adventures?

Junior straightened. "I'd ask if you needed help, but I can tell you have this task well in hand."

Fred squinted at the house, considered his son's unspoken offer, and glanced at his uncle's impassive face. A trapeze artist could've crisscrossed easily from one corner of Lawrence's flattened lips to the other. Fred wheeled the cart holding the house away from the screen doors and back to the center of the room. He nodded at the supplies in the middle of the table. "Get a brush."

After he showed Junior what he was doing, he slid the canister he'd been using to an equidistant spot between them. They each took a side of the roof and commenced to painting.

"Have you thought about doing it this way, Dad? Dab a little more paint on the brush and press it down like so." Junior dipped his brush into the paint, then flattened it against the shingle. His method splayed more of the bristle against the small piece of wood.

"I see, thanks. That'll save some time without causing mess." *Glad to see some of the expensive education is paying off.*

Junior grinned and returned to work.

Fred dunked his brush in the cylinder. "So what brought you two up here to talk? Is it something to do with the renovation? I told Etta I thought it was too much."

"No, no, everything is going well with that. Why would you think it was too much?" Junior's brush sank into the can like it was filled with quicksand.

"Not too much for you in particular. Too much in general. You know, things, details, people involved. I told her I hoped you'd feel free to come to me if you had any problems." *Lord, forgive me for that. Is it a lie if I'm avoiding hurting his feelings?*

Not that Fred was successful, by the looks of it. Junior retrieved his brush. Wordlessly, he tore off a sheet of paper towel from the roll mounted on the desk and cleaned off the paint trailing down the wooden handle.

"Anyway, what are y'all doin' up here in my domain?" Fred flourished his free arm to encompass all the random chairs scattered about the eight-hundred-square-foot room. When his uncle silently absorbed his nephew's realm, he shrugged. "If I'd known I would have company . . ."

A long, rectangular, unfinished wood table sprouted from the middle of the workspace, right under the set of three low-hanging lights they'd snagged from a downtown bar that was closing. He and Paulette stored any and all extra furniture in his makeshift office; there was no rhyme or reason to its arrangement. A decrepit green leather sofa graced one wall, while boxes were stacked on the opposite side, interspersed with unused lamps, old toys of Junior's Paulette couldn't part with, a recumbent bike that no one had pedaled in a decade, and the infamous black curtain he'd hung to block off the far left corner. The unadorned glass door provided a clear view over the attached balcony railing and up into the cloudless, starlit sky. It was the one room on the property Fred refused to decorate, organize, or rearrange because usually, when he mounted those garage steps and entered that room, his thoughts and emotions swirled about in just as random a fashion.

"Ahh, this looks like a man's space. That other—" Lawrence nodded toward the main house—"is too pretty. I can get comf'table over here." He crossed his arms over his slight paunch, scooched his shoulders from side to side on the overstuffed cushion, and closed his eyes.

Fred willed himself not to make eye contact with Junior. They both knew Fred had had more of a hand than Paulette in decorating the main house, and she'd had a free hand depositing various and sundry into this office. Far be it from him—or his son—to point out those two little-known facts. He cleared his throat and cupped his left hand under his brush to prevent any drips on his floor. "You were sayin', Uncle?"

The older man didn't bother opening his eyes to look at them. "Not me. My great-nephew over there somewhere. Paulette came whisperin' to me about walkin' over here with McKinley the minute Julia turned in. I'm just as in the dark as you are, though I have my suspicions."

Junior rubbed a hand back and forth over his thigh. "Suspicions? That has a negative connotation."

"Say what you will, but Uncle Lawrence must be on the right track. You're either trying to start a fire on your jeans or drying off your hands. You see him, Uncle?"

Lawrence's chest moved up and down steadily.

"I guess he was more tired than he realized," Junior mumbled. His fingers went from rubbing to drumming.

"If I was your mama, I'd call you by all three of your names. Tell me why Etta sent you all the way over here and with reinforcements." He aimed a free thumb at Lawrence. Why he bothered to avoid saying his uncle's name, Fred didn't know; the man was out like a light.

"Okay." Junior cleared his throat. "For one, I'm moving back." His announcement plopped out of his mouth and hovered in the air between father and son. Looking as shocked to utter the words as his father was to hear them, he laid his brush across the open can.

"What did you say?" But Fred heard him all right, though he nearly dropped the paintbrush he held. He just didn't know what to do with the news, how to react.

"I said I'm—"

"Moving back. Right." Something inside of Fred wanted to grab hold of Junior and wrap him up, so excited he was to hear the news. A flight to Philadelphia took less than two hours, plus the drive to the airport, but the distance between them had grown exponentially in the last year alone. Fred tried to shush his pesky inner man, who still managed to whisper, *The differences between you don't have anything to do with mileage.*

That part of Fred refused to get stuffed into his mental closet. It was the mean side that clamored for attention when he was feeling like the odd man out during the family movies he didn't want to see. When Junior and Etta put their heads together over the math books to decipher y-intercepts and slope equations. The third wheel at the farmers' market, watching them subtly elbow each other and chuckle. The person whose room across the driveway was stuffed with his son's castoffs, not preserved books from his own childhood and one-of-a-kind treasures. Who ached for his wife a lot more than the son missed his mother. That small side of Fred kicked his heels when Etta couldn't figure out what to say to Junior on the drive home and felt more than a little dismayed to hear that he was coming back within hugging distance. To stay.

"Isn't that great news?" Junior's fingers had stilled. No more happy dancing on his denim-covered knees or dabbing paint to cover missing areas on the house. He stared at his father as if trying to read his mind.

There was no danger of that. Even Fred couldn't decipher the myriad emotions and thoughts swirling about inside. They were like a language spoken in a foreign land. He did know that he loved his son, and he would find a way to live with the tension in the heartstrings.

The brightness of Fred's grin rivaled that of the light fixture above them. Forgetting the paint-soaked brush he gripped, he clapped Junior on the shoulder. "That's great, Son! I take it your mama has already heard the news. How did this come about? Don't tell me this G&C project lured you here."

• ℰ℘ •

No, McKinley definitely couldn't tell his father that. He'd put into works his return to Hickory Grove the minute he'd formulated his plan to propose to Emmeline, the day he'd decided which engagement ring to buy, over two months ago.

He swiped at his shoulder with a damp paper towel as his father pushed the house to the corner and concealed it with the black drape, along with whatever else was back there. "Well, you might find that part even more interesting."

Dad raised an eyebrow on his way to the small bathroom connected to his office. "Oh, really? How so? I can't imagine anything more exciting than hearing my only child is moving back home. But aren't you buying a house?"

"I am, just not in Philadelphia." McKinley wadded up the useless paper and followed Dad. A quick glance behind him at the older man on the sofa told him he need not worry they'd disturbed him. Uncle Lawrence's chest was barely moving. He leaned against the doorjamb.

"Which brings me to my second announcement—the more important: I'm getting married. At least, I'm planning to get married. I haven't officially popped the question yet, though I have a pretty good idea what she's going to say."

For a minute, the only sound in the room was a faint ticking above them. McKinley broke the standoff between his father and him and looked up. A large eggshell-colored moth tangoed with one of the light bulbs. When his eyes again locked with his dad's, he felt they were suffused with more confusion than surprise.

"*Married?* So your mama was right about all that business with Kelsey. This lady friend is your fiancée? Does this mean you're *both* moving down?" The water flowing over his fingers went from black to gray to clear.

"No, not Kelsey."

"Kelsey's not moving with you? Why?"

An old cartoon flashed through McKinley's mind in which the character tried to outrun a snowball that gathered in speed and size as it careened downhill. That was how McKinley felt at that moment. Not even Sisyphus would be able to shoulder the weight and stem the questions that threatened to roll right over him and sweep him up and away. He took a breath. "I know this is big news, and I'm going to tell you everything if you'll let me. Mom was on fire for Kelsey—"

Dad shut off the faucet. "Wait. Did you say 'was'?"

Trust Dad to hang on his every word. "Yes, *was*. Just like I explained to Mama earlier, Kelsey is one of my best friends. Who's already married. And six months pregnant. And who has no intentions of leaving her husband or Philadelphia to marry me and move to the North Carolina foothills." He smiled. *Okay, one down.*

"So if not Kelsey, then who?"

"Y'all got pretty attached to a woman you've never met!

Jeez Louise!" McKinley hadn't used that particular phrase in years. He brushed his hand over the curly tops of his twists, imagining what the other architects in his firm would say, hearing his exasperation. He was known for his calm demeanor in a crisis.

His father dropped the brushes into an empty cup on the counter and checked out his uncle, who slept on behind them. He reached for a hand towel. "Forgive me for not listening with my mouth closed, but you're taking us all on quite a roller-coaster ride here. What did your mom have to say about all this business about moving back and getting married—or did she already know?"

Dad didn't know the half. Shoot, not even a quarter. McKinley took a deep breath. "There's nothing to forgive. I'm going about this all wrong. Let's start over." He backed up and walked to the double sliding doors. A breeze flowing through the open right side caused the edge of the black curtain to swish in the breeze, but the mystery hiding behind it didn't distract him this time. He'd been concealing enough secrets of his own; he couldn't afford to learn about another.

His father moved to stand beside McKinley; however, his son's profile seemed more of a phenomenon than a few billion balls of brightly burning plasma. Feeling a steady, nearly palpable pressure on his cheek, McKinley took his father's gaze head-on. "About a year ago, Monroe—"

"*Monroe!*"

McKinley's burst of laughter was so sharp and loud, for a second he thought he'd awakened Uncle Laurence. *Nope.*

He wiped the tears from the corners of his eyes. Maybe now his explanation would bring his father a measure of relief instead of consternation. "No, I'm not marrying Monroe, but you're getting warm." He chuckled again. "Let's have a seat out here."

He slid back the screen and waited for his father to follow him onto the wooden deck before pulling it closed behind them. McKinley watched Dad sit into one of the rocking chairs he'd made with Uncle Lawrence as a boy. They'd been refashioned since then but were just as sturdily built. The two men scooted them to face the driveway before McKinley retraced his story's steps.

"About a year ago, Monroe and Emmeline came to visit me in Philly. She was interviewing for a job in Cherry Hill, New Jersey."

"Right, I remember that. Knox was up in arms about his baby girl leaving the state. What does she do exactly?"

McKinley swallowed his huff of impatience. Just like his parents' generation to wander off on this type of rabbit trail as soon as the trip started. "She teaches kindergarten."

"And she had to go way up there to look for a job? There're no good schools around here where she could work? Sounds like someone else I know. Oh, that's right; you're coming back."

"Actually, *we're* coming back." McKinley peered between the branches stretching across the sky. A wispy cloud scudded over the stars. He wondered if the flapping of wings off to his left was one of the bats that tended to find a home in the garage's eaves every fall, despite his parents' best efforts to fend them off with a cinnamon-laced concoction.

"Emmie didn't get that job and eventually got hired at a private school in Maryland, but that's neither here nor there. We spent that long weekend together, the three of us at first, and during that time, something . . . something clicked between us." He risked looking at his father. He shouldn't have. The man's eyes narrowed with a suspicion that almost stopped McKinley's heart.

"What do you mean, 'the three of us at first'? And what's this *something*?"

McKinley's voice deepened. "You may remember that was during a time when G&C was negotiating some deal for their wood." He pressed on at his dad's curt nod. "Monroe kept getting called away by his dad so he could learn the business, and he insisted I show Emmie all those places we'd all planned to explore together. So I did. During that time, we had the opportunity to talk to each other, really talk. In a way we hadn't. Ever."

Dad scooted to the edge of his deck chair. His hands seemed to itch to help him get his point across. "What are you talkin' about, Fred Jr.? Y'all have most certainly talked before—I mean, you've known each other for, for . . . I don't know . . . most of your lives, I'd expect. Don't tell me you got caught up in some romantic moment and you think you're in love! Aren't you a little old for that?"

His father's emotions were tripping over themselves in their effort to see what would get expressed first and loudest.

McKinley organized his thoughts and deliberately chose what he needed to say, not what he wanted to say. "No, we didn't get 'caught up,' as you put it."

His father's shoulders slumped in relief.

"But yes, Dad, I love Emmie George. With all my heart. This isn't some fly-by-night romance or a weekend fling sparked by Monroe's visit. We see each other quite often, every chance we get. Maryland's not that far from Philly. Emmie has become my best friend, the person I want to talk to first thing in the morning and the last voice I want to hear at night. We share similar hopes and dreams, backgrounds . . . She's my life, the life I want to lead from this moment forward. I'm not going to hide my feelings, and I'm not going to keep her away, waiting for you, Mom, her parents, or anybody else to feel ready for us. Not anymore."

Dad jumped to his feet and stamped to the rail.

For a second, McKinley feared he would launch himself off the balcony, but then he came to himself. That was Frederick McKinley Sr. standing there. He would lay hands on his son to shake some sense into him before the man would think to harm himself, no matter how out of sorts he was feeling. He decided to wait for his father to steady his thoughts.

Night birds called to each other within the thick grove that grew on the right and wrapped all the way around the back, behind the garden, to the other side of the house. During the springs and summers, the Baldwins could barely see their neighbors. At the back edge of the yard, a doe tipped closer to the wire around the garden. Her ears flicked in McKinley's direction and her nose twitched for a second or two before she returned to inspecting the fence. A breeze whispered against the back of his neck but didn't quiet or cool the roiling sea within him. It was then he thought to pray, though he wasn't sure what God had to say about the matter at hand.

Finally Dad rotated clockwise toward McKinley and leaned a hip on the rail, becoming the man in the three-quarter moon that hung in the sky behind his head. His gray hair sparkled like silver threads. "Have you thought about what you and Emmeline don't share, Son? You talk about similar backgrounds, but growing up in the same small town doesn't constitute a similar background. Apples and oranges can grow in the same orchard, you know. Not all your experiences are the same—in fact, I'd venture to say most of them aren't.

"She'll never know what it's like to grow up as a Black man in the South or anywhere else, to tell you the truth. I'm sure you've dealt with your fair share of racism in Philadelphia and other places you've traveled. Probably within that architectural firm of yours. You know how it feels to have people watch you, to wonder 'what if' when you see a police officer in your rearview mirror, to work harder and longer for less. But you can't know how it feels to worry about your child, McKinley. To consider the possibilities and the impossibilities in his future because of the color of his skin. The parents of your Miss George built a life for her on the hard work of my parents and my grandparents and my great-grandparents and so on and so on. The legacy she inherited, we gave her."

McKinley dropped his head. He knew this was coming. And it wasn't that he'd never stewed over those very same thoughts more often than he cared to admit. But he knew he couldn't wallow in the questioning, the flashes of anger, the moments of fear. Those bitter roots would choke the life out of the joy and hope that both his parents had planted in him when they taught him to honor others over himself, to walk in truth, to live by his faith. To love—and forgive—the way Jesus loved and forgave.

His desire to make his father understand drove him to his feet. In his new position by Dad's side, the older man didn't look as imposing or grim; the passion in his father's eyes not cloaked by the shadows yet mirrored in his son's. They were just looking from opposite sides of the same fence.

"You and Mom taught me a lot more than history, math, or current events when you homeschooled me. Did you believe any of it, or were they just repurposed lessons from Sunday school?" McKinley paused, hoping for an answer. "I'm serious, Dad. Was that whole thing about loving my neighbor a lie?"

"Of course not, Fred Jr."

"Then I take it you meant only love the ones who look like me."

"Now, Junior—"

"But wouldn't that exclude my own mother, your wife of thirty-five years? You know, Paulette Baldwin, the woman whose father loved her mother the way I love Emmeline. Not because of what I see with these—" McKinley tapped his eyes—"but with this." He clasped both hands over the left side of his chest.

"And you see where that got him, don't you?"

"Farther than you're going to get when Mama finds out what you're really doing at G&C, which has nothing to do with buying a new router. Is that what this is about, Dad? You're worried that my marrying Emmie will finally expose the truth? You have to tell her, Dad. Because if you don't—"

His father grabbed McKinley by both shoulders, and he did shake him just as McKinley had suspected, more to jar, but not hurt, him. "You don't care that your grandfather lived from hand to mouth, raising his daughter on his own because he wasn't good enough?"

"It wasn't because my daddy wasn't good enough. No, sir. It was because *she* wasn't, God help her. At least her love wasn't enough," a voice intoned from the doorway.

The men's heads followed the words.

"Mom," McKinley breathed.

Chapter Eighteen

FRED'S ARMS DROPPED to his sides and he buried his hands deep in his pockets. He returned to staring out at the near blackness stretching beyond the upper deck.

"I couldn't keep myself from comin' over here to see how this conversation was goin'." Paulette lifted her foot over the iron track for the sliding door.

"I suppose you can say it's going . . . ," McKinley murmured.

She reached out for McKinley's hand and squeezed it. Then she stepped up to the rail and bumped her husband's arm with her shoulder. It barely moved. "Fred? How're you doin'?"

He nodded once. "Peachy."

Fred's response conjured images of their family trip to Arizona when McKinley was fourteen years old. They'd splurged on a guided tour of the Sonoran Desert to experience the wildflowers that bloomed there in March and April every year. Cool, dry, prickly, beautiful, wild . . . just how Paulette would describe her husband at that moment as her eyes traced his profile from his slightly receding hairline, over his lined brow, across the bump in his nose, to the full lips she hadn't felt on hers since . . . could it be Saturday? She adored every inch of his inscrutable face.

Paulette sighed. "I take it McKinley shared his news."

Fred cut his eyes at her before going back to his moonlit tour of the backyard. "Which news would that be exactly? He dropped more than one bomb tonight."

Paulette glanced at McKinley, who shrugged, palms up and fingers splayed to signify surrender, before heading back inside his father's office. She leaned against the rail, her arms crossed, hoping that one of the many thoughts imprisoned inside her husband's mind would somehow find a key to free itself.

"I suppose you think this is all okay. That boy can do no wrong with you." Each syllable was dredged in resignation, spoken low in Fred's throat.

"I'd venture to say not much about this situation is *okay*—but no, I don't think he's doing anything wrong. If that makes any sense." Surely he didn't think she'd been party to McKinley's plans and had collaborated to keep Fred in the dark. To keep them both in the dark. She wondered if the Georges knew what was going on.

Wrong. Paulette had to mull that word over. Did Fred mean legally, morally, spiritually? If so, she'd have to enter an emphatic "Not guilty, Your Honor," on each count. As parents, they'd done right by McKinley, taught him how to think for himself, to be a strong, mighty man of valor. Like father, like son. Where was the wrong in his decision, even if they disagreed with it—if *Fred* disagreed?

Paulette moved things around in her mind, and dang if she couldn't find anything to grumble about regarding Emmeline George. While the pews at Valley Grace and Mount Olive might look different on Sunday morning, the God they worshiped was one and the same. He even looked the same, according to her Bible, despite the golden-haired portrait that might hang in the front of Emmie's church and the Afro-sporting version in McKinley's. Paulette's only real gripe was how her son had come to share his news, not the news itself.

But Fred was shaking his head. He obviously wanted no part of it, wrong or right. "I don't see how you can think you're taking the high road, let him—"

"Whoa there, cowboy. Time to dismount. McKinley is way past *lettin'* and *allowin'*. We both have to learn to respect his decisions. Weren't you the one intimatin' that very thing last Thursday, when it came to goin' to Thomasville? This is probably harder for me than it is for you. Even before you virtually pushed him out the door last year, you'd let him go."

"I know you're not standing here talkin' 'bout some photograph! This decision will affect the rest of his life, not your all-important Christmas distribution list."

Paulette had been engaged in a long-term game of tug-of-war with God, constantly giving Him her bitterness and frustration and taking it back. Now she wrenched it from His hand and dropped it straight in Fred's lap. "And you think I don't know that his life equals our life? His wife will be my daughter-in-law, the mother of our grandchildren. The future of our family, which is much bigger than the feelings you inherited from your dear papa or your all-important, overbearing aunt."

"Are you minimizing what my family went through? What they sacrificed for me? Papa and Juju gave me everything, not just my *feelings*, as you put it. Not all of us were left independently wealthy!"

"Independently wealthy? No, you didn't say that to me!" Paulette stepped closer to Fred, the only person who needed to hear every word she'd never said. "You called me wealthy because of what some person I've never met stuffed into a manilla envelope? That was blood money, and it didn't atone for being abandoned by my mother after gettin' dragged from one small, dusty town to another while my parents looked for acceptance and four walls to call home. I was broke, Frederick—broke and broken, not wealthy. I didn't have love or money, just a piano."

She swallowed. "Until I had a family of my own. And that's when I found everything I could have ever wanted. Because of love, Frederick. Not hate."

· ↝ ·

Fred squinted, trying to see something either deep inside or far beyond either of them. He murmured, "Love for McKinley maybe. Not for me."

The breeze picked up in strength, sending leaves skittering across the concrete drive below. An owl hooted somewhere deep in the trees. Half an acre away, the lights in the neighbors' upstairs window winked out.

Paulette shook her head and pushed away from the rail. She took a step toward the door leading inside.

"What, you want to make sure your son knows he has at least one parent on his side?" Fred's laugh lacked humor.

She reached for the screen. "I can see there's no talkin' to you. As usual."

"*As usual?* When was the last time you tried to really talk to me?" Fred didn't bother with keeping his voice low this time. He threw his words like a lasso, partly hoping he could pull his wife to him. The other part of him didn't know what he'd do if he could draw her back. Did he really want to hear what she had to say?

The pain in his words apprehended her, not the words themselves. Paulette froze a few feet away from him and thrust her fingers into her hair. "When? *When?* When I could find you, that's when. When you seemed to be listenin', that's when. When you could bother with something more than George & Company business and that resentment toward anybody with a nose and hair straighter than yours, that's when."

"Is that what you think? That I have an ought against every person with lighter skin than mine? You must not think that much of me, Etta."

"I don't know what I think, Fred. You're always complainin' about 'the man' this and 'the man' that. And you'd deny your own son the love of his life because of the color of her skin."

Sighing, Fred rubbed his temples and squeezed closed his eyes. "Not because of her skin color. Because of her last name."

"Aren't they the same?"

"Maybe I'm not the one with the problem." He smirked. "You are."

All the oomph appeared to leave Paulette. She seemed to lack the strength to raise her eyes. "Maybe I am. Maybe I'm that small a person that I envy their struggle, my father's and my son's. Daddy did his best to keep Mama. He held on to her with everything in him for as long as he could and gave up everything he had to do it. Shoot, to *not* do it. And now McKinley is followin' right along in his grandfather's footsteps, fightin' like the dickens for their love. But I do believe, in the end, my boy will have a different story to tell."

Paulette pressed the back of her hand to her mouth and finally managed to face Fred. "Tell me: would you fight for me?"

He watched her swallow a sob as the tears streamed down her face. Though he ached to hold her, he knew somehow she'd reject his comfort. Fred's voice rumbled up from his throat. "I feel like I fight you every day."

"I didn't say fight me. I said fight *for* me. For us. Like our marriage was something worth havin'."

He said nothing, hoping she was finished.

But she wasn't. Paulette choked out, her voice thick, "Do you love me in spite of my color and what it reminds you of?"

He stared at his wife's precious face, as pale as the moon, then studied the backs of his wrinkled hands. He flipped them over and counted the lines in his palm, barely discernible in the light.

"Fred, do you?"

He'd never experienced such a bone weariness and made the mistake of letting it speak for him. "Isn't that better than because of it?"

· ᘓ ·

Ah, Dad! I think she would have preferred "regardless." McKinley collapsed against the table that was used as a desk–slash–workspace–slash–lunch counter. His hip knocked over the sealed canister of paint, and it rolled off the side and onto the floor with a bang.

The clatter drew his father's attention toward the screen door. His mother walked to the left, swiping at her eyes. McKinley stooped down and retrieved the can he'd knocked over and set it upright. Though it had to be obvious to them that he'd been eavesdropping, he didn't care. He would've had to be deaf not to have heard their . . . discussion. Even now, their heated murmuring made him think of the spit and sizzle of an overflowing pot on a gas flame.

Uncle Lawrence deserved an Oscar for his portrayal of "Man Sleeping on the Sofa," but McKinley figured he might as well get up at this point. The fireworks were fizzling out. They'd better be, for the good of all involved. No need to rouse Aunt Juju and bring her into the fray, worsening matters. McKinley hated to think what would happen should she notice her husband's absence and come looking for him.

"Uncle? Uncle Lawrence? You can get up now. We can just leave as quietly as we came. Those two won't notice a thing." McKinley rounded the table. "Hey."

But the older man didn't stir.

McKinley gently laid his hand on his uncle's shoulder. At his touch, Uncle Lawrence slumped to his right. At first, McKinley stared and his breath caught in his throat when he realized that his uncle wasn't pretending to sleep; he was unconscious. Then McKinley came to himself and sprinted for the screen door separating the room from the balcony. He pushed both his hands against the mesh and yelled for his parents.

Both Paulette and Fred stood stock-still. Even the anger in their voices seemed to hang in midair for a second before shattering and falling into millions of forgotten, harmless pieces around the couple as he choked out, "Mom! Dad!" a second time and beckoned to them.

His father must have detected McKinley's desperation, for he set his mother aside—the movement gentler than his words sounded a moment before. He was the first one to dash toward the sliding-glass door and across the threshold. Fred's loafers caught on the heels of McKinley's Vans as the two men beat it back to Lawrence's side. Despite their long strides, Paulette was only a step or two behind them.

McKinley knelt by his uncle, who had collapsed against the cushions of the sofa, his head tilted toward his left shoulder. The edge of his chin touched his chest and his mouth was slightly ajar. McKinley pressed two fingers of his right hand to his great-uncle's wrist while the thumb on his left tapped out three numbers on his cell phone. He felt a soft hand grasp his shoulder and he met his mother's eyes.

She leaned in close and panted, "What is it? What happened?"

McKinley shook his head. Only God knew. He'd been too focused on the adults wrangling on the balcony to pay much attention to an uncle he'd assumed was carrying out an elaborate pretense to give his parents privacy. He hadn't noticed if Uncle Lawrence had struggled for air or motioned for help.

Dad put his head to his uncle's chest. Then he carefully wrapped his arms around the man and guided him down to the sofa and wedged a pillow under his head. The motion pulled Uncle Lawrence's hand free from McKinley's.

"Oh, Fred." His mother sounded like she'd lost all hope.

Finally a nasal voice identified himself on the other end of the line and asked McKinley, "What's your emergency?"

He wanted to shout, "Why do you sound like I'm calling to order a pizza? Don't you know a man is dying over here!"

But he filled his chest with air, let it out on a count of five, and injected a measure of calm authority into his voice.

"Yes, this is 87 Rosewood Drive, Hickory Grove. My eighty-five-year-old uncle isn't breathing. We need an ambulance. Right away."

Chapter Nineteen

Paulette touched the side of the mug. Hot but not sizzling. She removed it from the microwave and poured coffee over the heated cream and sugar, stirred it, and took a slow slurp. Her eyes fluttered closed and she asked her cup, *Where have you been all my life?*

Approaching footsteps forced open her lids. Fred, freshly showered, yet looking like he could use the caffeinated jolt more than she could. She padded around the counter in her slipper-clad feet and met him by the refrigerator. "Here. Merry Christmas."

He considered the unexpected gift.

Paulette took one of his hands and set the mug into his palm. "Don't worry. There's only cream and sugar in it. It's safe."

Fred murmured, "Thank you" directly into the cup as he tilted it slightly and took a sip. He slid onto a stool at the bar and stared into the brown liquid as if the steam whispered the answers to life's biggest questions.

Perhaps they did. Paulette plucked at a hangnail, just as unsure what to do with herself. It was barely nine, and the day stretched ahead, full of unknowns. She'd canceled her afternoon lessons and texted her hairstylist about changing her precelebration shampoo and blow-dry. Nobody felt like partying at this point, least of all the birthday girl.

She looked around the kitchen as the silence grew deep enough to drown in. Brew more coffee? Ease out of the room? Call the hospital . . . again? Paulette was afraid that if she went with door number three, the charge nurse would stop responding. Another quick glance at the clock minding the two of them pointed out that Lawrence had been admitted little more than eight hours ago. Everyone on his hospital floor already knew all the Baldwins by name, and the new shift had just clocked in. As it was, Julia was probably gearing up for the fit she was going to give them when she arrived. The hospital didn't need another family member pestering them.

Aunt Juju. She'd shocked them all with her calm response last night when Paulette had burst into the guest room and roused her from sleep. After listening to the news of Lawrence's collapse, she had thrown back the covers, lifted herself into her chair, and wheeled into the adjoining bathroom. Only Julia's trembling hands betrayed her inner turmoil as she manipulated the controls.

Thinking about Julia reminded Paulette that she was supposed to make tea for the older woman to take with her. She filled the stainless steel kettle with water and lit the gas, thinking about how they'd all huddled together outside the double doors in the emergency room and awaited word on Lawrence. After Reverend Maiden's arrival had turned their quartet into a quintet, he'd enjoined them to have "a word of prayer," so they'd laid hands on Julia in loving support.

But really, the grim-faced matriarch was the true pillar holding up the family. A stunned McKinley couldn't believe he'd missed any SOS from his uncle while a guilt-racked Paulette agonized over both her failure to uninvite her in-laws and her desire to send them packing. In her mind, the stress of the trip could have caused his collapse, but if they'd never come, Uncle Lawrence might have died without their quick action. Either way, she was in the wrong.

All their stoicism and hand-wringing left little room for Fred, but her husband had squeezed himself smack-dab into the middle of things. He'd planted himself at his uncle's side the minute the staff found him a bed and insisted McKinley and the pastor take the "womenfolks" home to rest. Fred had come home thirty minutes earlier to shower, change, pick up Julia, and return to the hospital.

Always on the outside looking in. Paulette curled and uncurled her fingers and took a deep breath. Now wasn't the time; the man had heavier weights to bear than his wife's low self-esteem when it came to her position in the family. "When I checked on your aunt, she was nearly dressed, so she should be out any moment. Want something solid to go with that coffee? I could nuke you a sausage-egg-and-cheese biscuit."

"No thank you. I couldn't eat a thing. This coffee hit the spot." When he set down his cup, it sounded as empty as his voice. "But Juju might want breakfast."

Weeee!

Paulette turned off the flame under the kettle. "No, she doesn't. Lack of appetite runs in your family. I'm the only one who snacks from stress. Notice that open box of Frosted Flakes."

Paulette riffled through a blue- and yellow-striped jar holding an assortment of teas. She discarded one bag after another. "I put the kettle on for Aunt Julia to make her a to-go cup. Think she'll mind drinkin' something fruity? I know she's more a peppermint type of gal."

"I'm sure whatever you make will be fine." Fred's slurred words sounded muffled.

Well, that makes one of us. "So what did the doctors . . . ?"

Paulette had settled on a flavor and turned to find her husband's face buried in his crossed arms on the bar top. Quietly she dropped the bag of herbal tea in a thermos, submerged it in boiling water, and screwed on the cap. She didn't bother with cream, honey, sugar, or lemon; Aunt Julia drank her tea like she delivered her words: plainly and unadorned.

When she padded around the counter to go check on the woman's status, Paulette couldn't keep her hand from rubbing Fred's back.

"Mom?"

McKinley was standing at the base of the stairs. Pointing to Fred, she held her finger to her lips and motioned for her son to follow her on to the family room. "What are you doin' awake? I didn't hear you come down."

He shrugged. "I finally hammered down the creaky board on the stairs last night. It was messing up my ninja skills." McKinley bent over to hug her tightly. "Good morning, by the way. How'd you sleep? You're looking as bleary-eyed as I feel."

Paulette brushed at the hair that had escaped her scrunchie. "Not as bright-eyed and bushy-tailed as I'd like, but I'm doin'. I'm just relieved to hear your great-uncle is doin' better. He should be comin' home tomorrow at the latest. Maybe even by tonight, according to the nurse I talked to earlier. Your father fell asleep before he could tell me more."

McKinley threw his head back and expelled a breath. "Thank God. What is syncope anyway? Googling it gives too much information."

"Basically, your uncle lost consciousness due to some interruption in blood flow to his brain." She set a hand on his arm and left it there. "Yes, put that way it sounds way too serious, doesn't it? In someone your age, without a preexistin' condition, a doctor might attribute it to dehydration or overexertion and call it a day. No need for the fancy ambulance ride like your great-uncle took last night. Shoot, you know my friend Belinda? She gets light-headed from standin' up too quickly."

Paulette glanced around her and lowered her voice even more. "But Uncle Lawrence is over eighty, and we all know he wasn't standin' up at the time. Quite the opposite. And haven't you noticed how tired he's seemed since he got here?"

McKinley nodded. "I thought Aunt Juju was just wearing him out."

"There is that." Truth dried out the humor in her chuckle. "Plus, all the 'excitement'—" Paulette's raised eyebrows emphasized the word—"couldn't have helped last night. I think the doctor is runnin' a few tests like an EKG, some blood work, and I don't know what all, to make sure there's nothing else goin' on. It could be as simple as high blood pressure or low blood sugar or as complicated as a stroke."

She squeezed McKinley's upper arm. "All that information might hurt as much as it helps, but it all comes down to one thing—we need to pray, not worry."

He snorted. "Are you taking your own advice?"

"That would be a no, but don't tell anybody. Selfishly, I keep askin' myself why this happened on my watch. The in-law–slash–outlaw struggle. Your father's people would have a conniption if something happened to their oldest-livin' relative while they were here!"

"Mama . . ."

Paulette shook her head. "I don't need a pep talk. This isn't about me. I know your great-aunt will kick some medical butt as soon as she gets to the hospital, and we'll have more answers soon enough. Speakin' of, let me go check on Julia. Dad is drivin' her back to the hospital as soon as she's ready."

"Well, then, let's go, because I'm ready!"

Paulette jumped. Her nerves were a mess, and obviously, so was her hearing.

Julia rounded the corner from the hallway leading from the guest room. She greeted them both with a nod.

"Hi, Aunt Julia. I made your tea."

"That was *your* tea that you insisted on makin' for me. I told you I didn't want nuthin'." Julia motored closer, her lips pushed out as if they'd gotten stuck whistling.

Paulette stepped back to protect her uncovered toes from Julia's wheels.

McKinley stayed put, forcing his great-aunt to come to a halt. He leaned down and kissed the older woman on her lined cheek. "Hey, auntie. Mmm, you smell good."

Julia had the nerve to contort her pursed lips into a smile after nearly mowing down McKinley's mama. Leave it to her son to put out the fire on the dragon's tongue.

"Thank you, baby. Now, let me get by so I can go. Oh." Julia wrapped her long fingers around McKinley's and brought him in even closer, as if she meant her words for him alone. Her purple-tinted mouth nearly touched his ear, though her whisper was audible enough for any stage aside. "I talked to your uncle, Fred Jr., and he wants you to bring by that new fiancée of yours. It would do him a world of good to meet her, and I want to see the young lady who had the nerve to take your heart without my permission. Why didn't you tell me?" She thunked him on his forehead.

When McKinley straightened up, he looked like he'd seen a ghost, and there was nothing holy about it. "Uh . . ."

Julia squinted up at Paulette. "I thought so. Your mama ain't happy about you gettin' married. She's tryin' to keep you all to herself. Paulette, you've gotta let the boy grow up sometime, make his own decisions! You kept him all tucked up under your wings, you don't know how to act when he's ready to fly by himself. Stop shelterin' him!"

It was entirely too early in the morning for this nonsense. Julia had never been a proponent of anything Paulette-related, and it wasn't until McKinley had graduated with honors from college that Fred's aunt had conceded that *maybe* Paulette hadn't messed up her nephew's education or his life. And now the woman was implying she was the one against him getting married instead of her precious Frederick. Paulette had half a mind to . . .

McKinley reached over with his free arm and covered his aunt's hand with his. "Auntie, don't worry. Mama is the reason I'm ready to commit to Emmie in the first place. She's shown me what it means to really love somebody outside of myself and my own expectations, beyond how they treat me. It's that 1 Corinthians 13 hopes, believes, and endures all things kinda love. Now we'd better go wake Dad so y'all can get goin'. From what I understand, *somebody's* tea is cooling on the counter."

Paulette blinked at her son for a second, so proud she

could eat him up. But she didn't know where she'd stuff him; she felt so full to the brim she couldn't speak.

"Emmie?" Julia looked from one face to the other. "Now where have I heard that name before?"

Suddenly motivated, Paulette patted the arm of Julia's chair. Lord knew she wasn't ready to open up that can of worms at this early hour of the morning. She could just imagine Julia showing out at the hospital, skyrocketing Lawrence's blood pressure, causing him to have another fainting spell. Or worse. "Aunt Julia, we'd best get a move on. Your husband will be lookin' for you, and at this rate, you're goin' to miss the doctor's rounds. You know they come early."

"Not if they know what I know," Julia grumbled.

· ᴄ⁄ɔ ·

Fred punched *A3* and watched the individual-size bag of pretzels drop to the bottom of the vending machine. He pushed back the heavy glass and his fingers scrambled for the packet. Then he held still, needing to work out the timing in his head. *Three . . . two . . . one.* Fred snatched back his hand and let the door bang shut. He stood and looked around, a bit embarrassed but grateful he'd escaped unscathed. One of those doors had caught his fingers as a child, and he still winced at the thought of it.

Fred tore open the bag with his teeth and plucked and ate the whole ones, leaving the broken pieces behind. Crunching, he strolled back to room 467. Fred paused at the door and peeked through the glass. He smiled and decided to wait a minute for the lovebirds to stop smooching. She could be crusty, but his aunt loved herself some Uncle Lawrence. He considered for a moment. *Imperfect, like the pretzels you left in the bag.*

When he saw a familiar figure in a white coat striding down the hall, Fred poured the rest of the bag into his mouth and chewed quickly as he backed through the door. "Knock, knock! Cut it out, you two. We have company."

"You wish you had it like this," Uncle Lawrence chuckled, cradling his wife's hand.

That I do, Uncle. That I do. Fred flattened the empty bag into a tiny square and did his best to make his eyes smile. "I'm glad you're feeling better."

"Won't never feelin' bad," the patient snapped.

"Now don't get all snippy, Lawrence. You're lookin' good, is all."

Tap-tap. The door opened and a head of short and curly gray hair peeked in. The doctor widened the opening and entered the room, flanked by two young men in rumpled, pale-blue scrubs. "Hey, there! We have a full house this morning!"

"Mornin'. I see you brought some company with ya this time." Lawrence waved from the bed. "Did they come to help me pack? I'm ready to get out of here. We came to Hickory Grove to spend some time with my niece and nephew, not to get stabbed and measured."

"Of course you didn't, Mr. Mason. I understand, and we're going to do our best to get you out of here as soon—and as healthily—as possible." The white-coated physician washed and dried her hands at the sink, then offered an "air shake" to Fred first, who was standing nearest the door, and then Julia. "I'm Dr. Gerhardt, the cardiovascular specialist on the floor today. I hope y'all don't mind me bringing a couple of interns with me."

She had a kind face, but Fred could tell the woman didn't care what they minded. He nodded to the two she had in tow before addressing her. "Hello, Dr. Gerhardt. I'm Frederick Baldwin, Lawrence Mason's nephew. That's my aunt Julia Mason, my uncle's wife."

Juju nodded curtly as she moved around to the other side of the bed. The stouter intern with the beard fell against his partner when her wheelchair plowed into his knee.

The doctor pressed her stethoscope to Uncle Lawrence's chest. "How's everybody today?"

"The question is, how is my husband? It don't matter how we're doin'." She sat tall in her chair.

Dr. Gerhardt draped her stethoscope around her neck and took another instrument from her coat pocket. "Actually, it does. How y'all feel impacts my patient's health and ultimately his ongoing care. And also, I'm just a naturally curious, pretty amiable sort of person, and I genuinely want to know. So. How are you?" She gathered the folds of her jacket and glanced around the room, a pleasant expression softening the wrinkles around her eyes and mouth.

Watch out now! I know she didn't just put Julia Mason in her place. Fred had to admire Dr. Gerhardt's boldness and hoped her skills backed it up. He spoke over the outraged harrumph from his aunt's side of the small room. "Doing fine, Doctor. Doing fine. We're worried about my uncle, of course. Tired from a short night of sleep, but doing fine. Thanks for asking."

"Since we're givin' health updates, you mind tellin' us about my husband? It's nearly noon, and you've kept us waitin' on you and your entourage to get here."

Fred hid his chuckle. Juju might just crank up her chair to its highest speed and take these doctors out if they weren't careful.

"Well, we could've enjoyed a pleasant conversation if I'd come earlier, but I decided to reorganize our rounds this morning to give his tests and blood work time to come in. Thought that would make for a more productive visit, and I hope that was all right." Dr. Gerhardt's lively eyes touched on all the folks in the room. They seemed to twinkle a little more brightly when they landed on Julia.

"Once we reviewed everything, it seems they confirm—" she flipped up his chart—"that Mr. Mason here suffered from a syncopal episode last night."

"So he fainted?" Fred's eyebrows furrowed.

"Not exactly," the taller, yet unnamed intern interjected. "Lawrence—"

"Mr. Mason," Dr. Gerhardt murmured firmly from her spot by the head of the bed.

"Um-hum, my apologies." He shrugged. "H-he just reminds me of my grandfather."

"Well, he's not your grandfather. And shame on him for allowin' you to call him by his first name. I'm sure your grand*mother* told you 'bout respectin' your elders." Juju obviously was in no mood to be placated.

"Y-yes, ma'am, of course not. I mean, of course." The young doctor struggled to continue. "Well, Mr. Mason was dehydrated, which is why we've been giving him fluids through this IV, and his heart rhythm is abnormal."

Dr. Gerhardt wiggled her hand from side to side. "*Somewhat* abnormal. But that might've been a singular event. Do you have a history of high blood pressure? I only ask because—"

"Because we're Black. Well, no, he don't. And he's not diabetic or overweight and he can't stand watermelon." Juju crossed her arms. "I get tired of doctors makin' assumptions about Black people, of us gettin' 'less-than' type of care. Folks actin' too familiar like this one here—" she cut an eye at the offensive intern—"like we all 'meemaws' and 'pawpaws.' You see what I'm talkin' 'bout, Frederick? You hear about this happenin' all the time."

"Excuse me, Mrs. Mason. If you'll let me finish, I was going to say I only ask because his systolic and diastolic numbers were elevated when he was brought in. But that could be because he fainted and I'm sure the ambulance ride was fairly exciting. I'm coming into this blind, as he's not my regular patient. Just trying to paint a more complete picture so we can best treat him."

She waggled her brows. "By the way, I might be white,

but I much prefer watermelon over quinoa, and I called my grandparents Pop and M'dear, before either of us makes any more erroneous assumptions."

Both Fred and Lawrence looked at Julia. She clamped her lips shut.

The physician jotted notes in the chart. "So no history of high blood pressure. Then what about low-pressure readings? That's also a common cause. There's no word yet from your primary care physician back in Virginia, but maybe he'll shed some light when we do hear from him. In the meantime, we're going to schedule an electrocardiogram and a stress test for tomorrow morning, and if they look good, we can send you home later in the afternoon. Maybe after you get a good lunch on us. Once we discharge you, you'll have to take it easy and keep an eye out until you see your physician. But first things first, we'll see what we can rule out or determine here."

"All I hear is the sound of money flappin' out that window. I thought all he did was faint." Juju's eyes narrowed.

"Well, technically, that's what syncope is, a temporary loss of consciousness. Mr. Mason's episode lasted . . . hmmm, let's say a little longer than most. At least more than I'm comfortable with. Which could mean it's heart related. Now, don't be alarmed. Cardiac syncope is common and treatable, as long as it's monitored. But I don't like throwing around terms and suppositions. Let's just make sure."

Dr. Gerhardt's words and tone sounded final, like she was ready to rally the troops and head for the door, but she merely shifted to her other foot and propped the metal chart on her hip. "Any questions, Mr. Mason? Mrs. Mason? Mr. Baldwin?"

Fred, nonplussed by her demeanor, knew he should ask a question somewhere, but for the life of him, he couldn't pluck one from the air. Paulette would just have to fuss about it later. *That is, if she's still talking to me.* All he could think to offer was "Please, call me Fred."

"Well, I have a question. This has never happened before. Could it be somethin' he ate? We had these strange-tastin' sausages Tuesday night, seasoned with somethin' called fennel, I believe. Got it all between my teeth."

"Aunt Julia, I know you're not suggesting Uncle Lawrence fainted because of the chicken sausages my wife served you." Fred felt an unfamiliar tightening in his chest, in the area around his heart. Somehow it didn't feel physical.

Dr. Gerhardt laughed. "No, Mrs. Mason, chicken sausage would not cause your husband to lose consciousness."

"But it has to have *somethin'* to do with this visit." Juju shook her head at Fred. "I've never felt truly comfortable with your—"

Uncle Lawrence patted her hand. "Shhh, Julia. Enough of that. If anybody is uncomfortable durin' our visit, it's my niece, Paulette. Bein' here has helped me feel better than I have in months."

He turned to the doctor. "I haven't told my wife some thangs, Dr. Gerhardt, but I s'pose I need to come clean before you start runnin' tests I don't need. This isn't the first time I've had one of these syn . . . syn . . ."

"Syncopal episodes?" Fred scooted closer in his chair.

"Yes, one of those. My doctor at home recommends a pacemaker."

"What!" Aunt Julia almost exploded from her wheelchair.

Fred noticed the intern nearest his aunt hold out his hands as if to steady her, but he didn't look brave enough to touch her. *I bet she doesn't seem like any grandmother he's ever known.*

"Now, Julia, that's why I didn't tell you. You'd be in that office gettin' all excited and makin' all kinds of noise. I can handle this."

"Like you handled yourself right into unconsciousness last night?"

"Mrs. Mason," Dr. Gerhardt began.

"I'm lookin' after my husband."

"And I'm looking after my patient, which supersedes your relationship with him while he's under my care." She stepped to the bed and picked up Uncle Lawrence's wrist. The physician pressed two fingers to his wrist and studied her watch for sixty seconds.

"My professional opinion? You both need to calm down, although by the rate of his pulse, Mr. Mason is calm. Extremely calm. I'd say bradycardia sounds about right."

"Mm-hmm. That's the word my doctor used." He nodded his head vigorously.

Meanwhile, Fred was shaking his head. "Uncle Lawrence, I can't believe you."

"Now don't you get started, Nephew. My doctor and I've been talkin' 'bout it, but I'm goin' on ninety years old in a minute or two. A pacemaker? That sounds like puttin' in a lot of time and money to restore a used car."

"Mr. Mason, did you talk about a temporary, external device?" Dr. Gerhardt's face radiated a mixture of expertise and concern. She proceeded to calmly walk her patient through various complications and alternatives he obviously hadn't considered.

Thirty minutes later, Dr. Gerhardt's calm mien had settled the atmosphere in the room. Even Juju sat still, her fingers interlaced with her husband's. The couple had both decided the cardiologist's office should set up an appointment with his primary care in Virginia the following week.

She glanced at her watch before encircling the whole room with her smiling blue eyes. "Okay, I guess my work here is done. For now. I have children at home to see to once I finish with my two here at the hospital." The doctor aimed a thumb at the sheepish-looking interns, who had mumbled all of two words after Julia had worked them over.

Uncle Lawrence chuckled. "Thank you. You've been a blessin'."

"Indeed. I'll walk y'all out." Fred nodded at the bearded blond doctor beside him. He hadn't expected as much from him as he had from the other intern. *Your grandfather? Really, brother? You should've known better,* he silently chastised as he clapped the doctor on the back.

After he accompanied the group to the door, Fred finally came up with two questions that would make him look good to Paulette. Patiently, Dr. Gerhardt answered them as the younger physicians left them to converse at the nurses' station. He firmly shook her hand. "Thanks again. I think we all feel better now." Behind him, the telephone beside the bed rang. He heard his uncle pick it up.

Dr. Gerhardt's cool fingertips belied the warmth of her blue eyes. She lifted up the gold chain around her neck and revealed a simple cross that dangled for a moment before she dropped it behind her collar. "I can't take any of the credit, Fred. Enjoy your aunt and uncle. If Mrs. Mason has her say, they'll both be with you at least another couple decades. She seems to have more fires to burn." The doctor winked at him. She didn't bother speaking to the interns as she walked away, seemingly trusting them to fall in step behind her. Fred returned to his uncle's bedside.

The older man placed the receiver in its cradle and slapped his hands together, a habit he'd passed on to his nephew. "Guess what?"

"What? Or should I ask who?" Fred pointed to the phone.

"That was McKinley. I told him I'm gon' be here another night, so he's gon' bring that girl of his tomorrow. Then I can see what all the commotion is about."

Juju wiggled her shoulders from side to side and clapped.

Chapter Twenty

⁂

"HEY, THERE, MR. BALDWIN!"

Fred threw a hand up in greeting but didn't stop pushing his hand truck long enough to see who had spoken to him. Fred had gone to the floor to work on a project with Curtis, one of their journeyman carpenters, and he didn't have many hours to do it. Which was why running smack into his day-shift supervisor was the last thing he'd wanted to do.

She, too, was none-too-thrilled about their surprise encounter. "Ouch! Hey!"

"Hey, there . . . I'm so sorry. I was in a rush to get to the back. I didn't see you." Fred set down the hand truck. He hoped his chagrin was enough to bandage the situation as he peered around the large brown box he was pushing. He'd swiped the cardboard packaging a few days ago from G&C's storage room in case Etta saw him coming and going at the house with it.

"Oh, it's you, Mr. Bald . . . Fred. I couldn't see you behind that thing." Kim rubbed her hip.

He stepped from around the dolly to check on her. "Forgive me, Kim. I truly hate I ran into you like that. You won't call OSHA on me, will you? Are you okay?"

She waved him off. "I'm fine, fine. I've been hit by bigger pieces of furniture—which I'm assuming is under there. Do you need any help?" Kim ran her finger down the page on the clipboard that was never far from her. "I don't remember any special shipments or deliveries scheduled for today."

Fred returned to the helm. "Well, it's a special project I'm working on that I enlisted Curtis to help me with. You won't see it on there." He nodded at her clipboard. "But I need to use the small room in the back. Is it free? Curtis said he had some time this afternoon."

"It's your company. If you have time, he has time." Kim stepped back and extended her right arm with a flourish so he could move by.

It's my company. What would Knox think, hearing her say that? Obviously Fred had sold the new supervisor on that idea when he'd brought her on, even without seeing his name emblazoned on the outside of the building or on her biweekly paycheck. He strengthened his grip on the handle of the two-wheeler.

"You know what? Better yet, let me clear a path ahead of you to prevent another run-in if you don't mind. Just follow me, but don't run over my heels, please." Kim smiled and led the way.

• ❧ •

Paulette struck the first chords as if they were marked *f* for forte before playing the next few measures pianissimo, so softly the piano seemed to be quietly mourning. At the last, she crooned, "'If I should die, and my soul be lost, nobody's fault but mine.'"

"Mama, why are you in here singing that old spiritual?" McKinley stood in the wide doorway of the front room, hand in hand with Emmie. He shifted from one foot to the other.

"What's wrong with you, Mac?" Emmie elbowed him gently. She shook her head at him before walking over to the piano. "Hi, Mrs. Baldwin. That sounded lovely . . . but sad. Are you okay? Did something happen to your uncle?"

Paulette scooted around on the piano seat. "No, baby, nothing's happened to Uncle Lawrence." She patted Emmeline's hand resting on her shoulder. "What, you don't like my choice of music, McKinley?"

"It's not that I don't like it. I only thought you were into more up-to-date songs. That one sounds like you're working in the fields somewhere, hoping to overcome." He rubbed the back of his head.

A ball of disappointment rolled around in the pit of Paulette's stomach. Somewhere she had failed him. For so long, she had encouraged him to keep his eyes forward, and she wondered how many opportunities he'd missed to learn from his past. "I am workin' in the fields, Son—the mission fields. Been there my whole life and will be there until I die. There's a lot to be learned from music like this."

"You sound like Dad."

Paulette thought about it, and then she remembered the discussion she, Fred, and her son had engaged in after church. "Now that I think about it, McKinley, your father had a point. Old doesn't make it out-of-date. We don't have to get rid of it because we were singin' it before you were born."

"But that was written forever ago!"

"Boy, do you know how long forever is? Eternity past to eternity future. God has been listenin' to us sing for thousands of years and never tires of it. What gives you the right to come in here and say my way of doin' things is passé?"

"And actually, Mac, that song wasn't written forever ago." Emmeline encircled his waist with her arm.

Paulette wanted to shout for joy as she waited for the young woman to finish what she was saying. There was hope for him yet.

"Led Zeppelin sang this in the late seventies. I wouldn't call that ancient history. You didn't sing it the way they did, Mrs. Baldwin, but it did sound pretty. I like your interpretation."

"I sounded *pretty*? My, my *interpretation*!" she spluttered. Paulette's exasperation with the two people in front of her drove her to her feet. That was another thing Fred had right: this girl was clueless about the history of her future fiancé's people, their music and its meaning and its impact. But then so was McKinley. Paulette was sure their ignorance didn't stop there.

"That song was originally written and sung by Blind Willie Johnson back in 1927. So yes, I guess that was probably 'forever ago' in your opinion. Not quite in the fields, but we were close enough to still remember the sorrow and the injustice of it. Johnson was a gospel and blues artist who played something called a slide guitar. Go and look it up, *Junior*. You'll see he's singin' about deep spiritual matters like salvation, the struggles of faith, and the fear of his soul being lost if he didn't get it right. Comin' to grips with his own responsibility and not blamin' other folks. You won't pay for somebody else's sin, but nobody's goin' to pay for yours either."

Paulette shook her head. "Emmeline, I appreciate the compliment, and no shame on you. Or you either, McKinley. I take the blame for what you do or don't know. But don't ever act like your family or your history embarrasses you, or pretend that the past has nothing to do with the right here and now."

She waggled her finger back and forth between them. "You two are together right now because of all the people who came before you. Their faith, their music, their marchin', their dyin'. Even their givin' up. Don't let it define you or limit you, but don't turn a blind ear and eye to it, either of you. I'm mainly speakin' to the son I gave birth to right now, but I pray you both take these words of mine to heart. The words and the lyrics, while you're at it.

"Now," Paulette huffed, feeling spent but knowing she had more to say, "where is your father, McKinley? Have you heard from him?"

He swallowed. "At George & Company. He came home while you were taking a nap and grabbed some things from the office. I think he said he would meet us at the hospital later this afternoon. Emmie and I were about to grab some lunch with Monroe."

Paulette checked the time on her wristwatch: 1:30. "Okay, would you two mind droppin' me at G&C? God willing, I'll be able to catch a ride with your dad to the hospital. I hope you don't mind if I play a little Mahalia Jackson on the way."

· ᙍ ·

Fred strapped on his goggles as he waited for Curtis. He'd chosen his favorite type of hardwood to work with. Maple. Its smooth, reddish-brown finish would look beautiful with the dark stain he'd chosen, the color that closely mirrored the mahogany sofa Etta had admired in High Point. Would she even remember that day and their fun chat about that chair? Did sixty-three-year-olds actually flirt with their wives? Fred couldn't believe that only a week had passed since they'd strolled through the furniture market after picking up McKinley.

He reached down into the box and picked up the pieces, setting them on the worktable one by one. Carefully, so as not to get a splinter, he ran his hand over each of the curved legs and measured them against each other to make sure they were even. They still needed sanding and smoothing, something he hoped the journeyman carpenter would help him do. This particular wood had enough grain in it to keep things interesting but not too much to distract from his design. Fred tapped a leg against the palm of his left hand, relishing the sound it made. Maple was sturdy enough to withstand the wear and tear of life in the kitchen.

Life in the kitchen, something he hoped to convince Etta to believe existed. What he considered one of the best birthday gifts he could offer her. "Etta is going to love it," he murmured to himself. *Well, I hope she loves it,* he amended, thinking about the miniature Victorian drying by the glass doors in his home office. He'd been wrong about that, too. But that was because it was what he wanted. He could admit that now in the cold light of day.

Fred stood back and considered all the different parts of the chair that needed to be smoothed and sanded, drilled, stained, and fit together. It was an elegant design, but not elaborate or fancy—timeless. Like Etta. He could imagine it sitting at the end of the table and a matching one for him facing it. Or perhaps they wouldn't position it at the table; he could put it in the sunroom near those herbs of hers, and she could sit in it as she watered or pruned them or whatever she did to keep them halfway living.

After studying the back to the chair, he set it down and thought about the seat. The cushion for that would need to be upholstered, another skill he didn't have. He'd already ordered a velvety fabric with a slightly nubby texture, but it was on back order. It wouldn't get here in time for her birthday, but that didn't matter. He wouldn't rush it, this piece of kitchen furniture.

That's what he was going to call it. This chair would be part of the Etta Collection, George & Company's newest foray into the design world. Inspired by the woman who inspired him. *More like beat me up.*

He'd been sweating over the idea for months, but it wasn't until early yesterday that the style and form of this introduction to the collection had struck Fred. It came to him in a dream and caused him to oversleep. When he'd awakened, he was curled around the very woman he'd been dreaming about.

A hand on his shoulder jarred him from his mental meanderings. He twisted to look over his shoulder. "Kim? Hey, I thought you were Curtis."

"Nope, and I'm sorry to say there's not going to be a Curtis. Not today. He had an emergency and had to leave early. Is there something I can help you with? You seemed a million miles away just now."

Fred sighed. There was no way he would get this piece even close to finished without Curtis's expert assistance. While his own design skills were top-notch, he was no professional carpenter. Fred could operate a handsaw to cut straight lines and hammer a few nails; he could put together a kit like the model house and add a few personal details. But people like his grandfather, Uncle Lawrence, and even Curtis had the gift for bringing pieces of wood to life with a few tools and transforming a design into a long-lasting member of the family.

"Seriously, Fred. I know what I'm doing when it comes to wood; I'm not only good at pointing my finger and managing people." Kim edged closer to the pile of maple on the worktable. She seemed to be waiting for an answer.

Fred looked from her to the wood. Then *birthday* flashed in bright neon-red lights in his head. What choice did he have? His wife's birthday was Saturday. Technically, that was about thirty-two hours away.

He clapped his hands together. "Okay. Where do we start?"

· ↢ ·

The tires crunched over the loose gravel as McKinley drove his rental onto the lot of George & Company. He pulled within a few feet of the front door and put the Pacifica in park. The early afternoon sun glinted off the windows of the building.

Before McKinley or Emmeline could say "hi" or "bye," Paulette reached for her sweater, looped the strap of her leather purse over her shoulder, and opened the back door. "I'm going in. You say you're meetin' Monroe for lunch?"

"Yes, ma'am, a late one. In fact, we're just swapping out passengers. When you asked for a ride, I texted him about meeting here. He'll hop in and—there he is now."

Paulette's door swung open wide. She grasped the hand that was proffered and allowed it to draw her from the car. "Thank you kindly, young man," she joked.

Monroe said nothing. He climbed in and shut the door with a decisive click.

Paulette shrugged. Since she had a right to hold her peace, she couldn't lay claim to Monroe's. She leaned into Emmeline's open window. "If my ride doesn't work out, McKinley, you can pick me up when you drop off your passenger in the back."

"Your ride. Is that what you're calling Dad these days?" McKinley grimaced.

"It is what it is, baby." *And sometimes it is what it ain't supposed to be.* Paulette waved at the couple in the front seat. She didn't wait for them to pull away before heading for the front door.

"Oh, Mrs. Baldwin! Mr. Baldwin wasn't upstairs. He must be on the floor."

She looked back at Monroe, whose face lacked its usual animation. "No worries, but thank you. I'll wait for him in his office. Maybe I'll check out some of those mysterious designs of his that are claiming so much of his time."

Paulette entered the shadowy recesses of the foyer and greeted the receptionist seated behind the large front desk. "Okay to go up?" Without waiting for the young man manning the phone to answer, she moved toward the stairs in the rear. *They really do need to open up this area and let in some natural light. I wonder what McKinley has planned.*

The fluorescent lights on the second floor hummed above her as she passed rooms that branched off the carpeted hallway. Paulette smiled at familiar faces gathered around the coffee maker in the glass-fronted break room and nearly stopped to chat with people she hadn't seen in months. Instead, she wiggled her fingers and pointed toward Fred's office, wordlessly acknowledging them while trying to say, *"I'd love to talk, but I have to go."*

Her husband's door was near the end of the hall and on the right, directly across from Knox's large corner office that looked toward the hills out front. She was surprised to find Fred's door partly open, for her husband typically closed it when he left. He used to go so far as to lock it when he stepped away from his desk, but Paulette convinced him that could arouse suspicion.

Maybe that means Fred's in there! Paulette paused in the hallway and smoothed her hair. Then she raised her fist to knock for propriety's sake, but before her knuckles struck the wood, she heard a deep voice inside intone, "They took mah business. Now they wont to take mah daughtah?"

Paulette stepped back and glanced behind her. No, this was Fred's office. She could've sworn she'd heard someone inside.

"Ah be doggone if Ah'm gon' take this lyin' down," continued the voice.

She flung open the door, fist still held high. "Knox? Yes, that is you!"

The door banged against the stopper with such force it swung back and bumped Paulette on the shoulder. The George & Company owner jumped to his feet behind the desk bearing the solid walnut nameplate with *Frederick M. Baldwin* etched on its brass cover.

She looked around the room but didn't see her husband sitting at his drafting table on the chair she'd given him. "What are you doing in Fred's office, sittin' at his desk? Are you okay?"

Knox's chest heaved as his eyes traveled from Paulette's raised fingers to her face and back again.

Paulette lowered her hand and adjusted the purse strap on her shoulder. Something must have happened to his wife or oldest child to cause him to look and act this way. "You're scarin' me, Knox. Did somethin' happen to Sarah or Lacey? I just saw Emmeline and Monroe, if that puts your mind at ease."

"Ah'm nevah gon' be at ease, not with you Baldwins around." He wiped his mouth and chin with his hand. His hair stood out in salt-and-pepper spikes, and perspiration dotted his high forehead and upper lip.

Paulette had never seen the man appear so disheveled and out of sorts. Normally he wore freshly pressed, designer dress shirts opened at the collar and tucked into dark-colored slacks. He gelled his silver-streaked hair and brushed it back from his brow until it touched the base of his neck. It was hard to see Emmeline in Knox, the carefree young woman whose curls always worked free of their ponytail holders and who dressed in low-slung loose jeans in various colors and V-necked T-shirts. She probably wore a variation of that wardrobe to kindergarten.

Could this really be about the wedding? Paulette pushed the door gently this time until it shut with a click and walked closer to Fred's desk. No need for the rest of the building to get an earful. She took a deep breath. "Knox, calm down and tell me what's goin' on. I hope you're not worried about havin' another Baldwin underfoot with McKinley movin' back home."

The man studied her through narrowed eyes. He took a shaky breath and then another before smoothing a hand over his hair from his crown to his nape until it looked more kempt. Knox seemed to be gathering the pieces of himself he'd let go before company showed herself. "Paw-lette, you know 'bout your son and my Emmeline." As usual, his words trip-trapped across his tongue in a slow, roundabout fashion.

"Your Emmeline and my *McKinley*, yes. Is McKinley the 'they' you referred to who wants to take your daughter?" Paulette purposely said his name twice to drive it home to Knox.

"You must be as upset as we are, me and Emmeline's mama. This mixin' of families."

As if they were eggs and flour in a pound cake! "To tell you the truth, I wasn't as upset as I'm gettin' now. And obviously not for the same reasons." She felt steam building in her ears, but she tried to turn down the heating element that controlled the temperature of her words.

"Well, maybe you can help me figure out how to tell my children about losin' their fam'ly business. Just gave it away to somebody tryin' to get back at all of us for somethin' we didn't have nuthin' to do with?" He turned to gaze out the windows.

"Who's gettin' back at you, Knox? I have no idea how I'm supposed to help you do anything. Obviously something is goin' on between you and Fred, and it affects my son and possibly Emmeline. What if either of them had walked through that door and found you behind this desk, talkin' about stealin' your daughter and your business? As much as Fred has done to make George & Company a success! You'd best believe he wouldn't be standin' here, discussin' your choice of words. You sound like a stranger to me right now." Actually, he sounded more like the person Fred believed he'd always been. She studied Fred's desk for clues.

"We've watched our children grow togethah, and then to have your husband treat me this way. It's unacceptable. That's the only way Ah can describe it. Un-ac-cep-ta-ble." The last five syllables strolled from his mouth at such a low decibel, they were probably meant for his own ears, not anyone else's.

Least of all Paulette's.

"Knox, you're actin' like our families haven't known each other since Monroe and McKinley were in elementary school. That means you can call people by the name their mama gave them and trust I'll know who you're talkin' about. McKinley, Sarah, Frederick . . . Pick one and use it, and stop this 'my wife' and 'your son' and 'our children' nonsense. That's what I find unacceptable. And let's not forget 'they,' the word that got you in hot water in the first place."

"*Ah'm* in hot wa-tuh? How dare you, Paw-lette! Just because Fred thanks he's runnin' the comp'ny the George fam'ly started several lifetimes ago don't mean he can take ovah my fam'ly or the rest of my life. Could he really believe Ah wouldn't do somethin' 'bout it?" His words bounced off the glass but didn't pick up speed.

Paulette shook her head, trying and failing to clear it. She stalked closer to the desk. "You're talkin' in circles, Knox, but you're not sayin' a word of sense. What I do know is I'm not goin' to stand here and talk to your back, and if that's what you had in mind, you'd best think again. I need to see your lips movin' so I can better understand you. And say it plain."

Knox buried his hands up to his wrists in his pant pockets and hung his head. After nearly a minute, he pivoted counter-clockwise and glared at Paulette. Now his rock-hard face looked more angry than distraught. Knox's chest rose and fell like he'd just run a marathon.

Paulette was feeling some kind of way herself. For some reason, she was afraid, not of Knox, because she feared no man. It was the unknown that frightened her. She felt like she was standing at the edge of a great precipice, peeking over. Something was rumbling at the bottom, something porten-tous and life-threatening. Taking a giant step would lead to certain death—but of what, of whom? Paulette tried to steel her resolve, to brace herself for a hard landing.

"Let's calm down, Knox, before either of us says some-thing we—"

"Don't talk t' me like Ah'm a child," Knox growled. He picked up one of the large sheets of paper Fred had scattered about his desk. "This is still my comp'ny, no mattah what the contract says. Shoulda known bettah than to let a Baldwin get his toe in the door. Ah tell you, my people was right. Letcha get a foot in the door, and look what happens." He flung the page and it fluttered to the floor.

Paulette staggered back a step as if Knox had slapped her. Truly, he had, and his harsh words had left an indelible mark on her heart. "Wh-what did you just say to me?"

"W-e-ll . . ." Knox gave out and suddenly shrank half his size. "What Ah meant was . . ."

"Never mind. I don't need you to tell me what you meant because you said it. That's what happens when you squeeze a sponge." This time, she was the one who turned her back on him, but only for a second. Then she gave him a hard and steady look, as if she could see right into his heart and mind.

"You regret ever lettin' us in the door, huh, Knox? 'Us' as in Black people? If that's what you say to my face, I wonder what words you use when you're behind closed doors? How *dare* you, after sittin' at my kitchen table. Trustin' us with your children. Callin' us friends, no less, and laughin' in my face. For years! Worse, sittin' up in church and probably singin' in the choir. And all the while, you're wearin' a mask.

"I 'suppowse' you think it's okay to call us employees but not good enough to call us in-laws, Knox George? I 'suppowse' it was fine for your children to play with ours as lowng as there was no mixin' of fam'lies?" Paulette did her best imitation of the Knox she used to know.

She stretched out her arm toward him so he could see it clearly. "Am I not white enough for you to call family? Well,

God sees your hypocrisy. You can't say you love Him but hate Fred and me at the same time."

Knox pinched the bridge of his nose and squeezed shut his eyes. "Nobody hates you, Paw-lette."

"That's Mrs. Baldwin to you. To you and your wife, since I imagine you speak for her, too." Her words were as stiff as his laundered shirt. She used the arm of her sweater to dry the beads of perspiration from her forehead and then tossed it on the chair in front of the desk.

He opened his eyes and held her stare. "That was out of line, what Ah said."

"Out of line? Is that what you call it?"

"Ah'm feelin' the same way Fred is."

She held up her hand. "Don't even try to stuff your feet in my husband's shoes. I mean it. How do you think he's gonna feel when I tell him about this conversation, about findin' you sittin' here in *his* office, mind you, mournin' the day you ever hired him?"

"He's gon' feel just fine, *Mrs. Baldwin.*"

His smirk was the warning signal at a train crossroads, alerting her that something more was coming. Paulette took a step back, knowing deep down she didn't want to know what it was.

"Fred knows my feelin's exactly 'cause Ah been told him a long time ago. And it's not 'cause he's Black. My folks warned me not to trust a *Baldwin.* Tell me somethin'. What would you do if somebody—and Ah don't give a whit whether he's Black, green, purple, or wha-ite—came into your house and stole your life's work from unda your nose? Ah'm not the only one wearin' a mask."

"What are you talkin' about?"

"Your husband. Two years ago, the market was down, and we was losin' more and more money. He knew we was 'bout to go unda, and he swooped in to save the day." Knox waved his hands in the air beside his head and sang the last words. The afternoon sun glinted off his rings; sparkles danced on the walls.

"He gave us a pile of money. A pile. Just what we needed to get ovah the hump, and we ain't nevah looked back since. Said we didn't need to pay it back 'cause he loved the business as much as we Georges did. He considered it an investment. An investment, he said, due to his long hist'ry with the business. Hist'ry my left foot."

A pile of money. But where would Fred get that kind of money? Paulette squinted at Knox, but not because the light streaming through the large window was too bright. She was having a hard time seeing the whole truth and nothing but.

"That was blood money, you know. Repayment for how his fam'ly was treated a long time ago. Not by me though, nevah by me. He took ovah, little by little. Runnin' thangs. Makin' decisions behind the scenes at first, now all out in the open. And Ah cain't do nuthin' 'bout it due to that agreement. He has me by the . . . *ahem*. Excuse me, ma'am."

"Are you sayin' . . . ?"

"The name ovah the door might say George & Comp'ny, but you might as well spell George *B-a-l-d-dubyah-ah-n*. This business is more yours than mine, if you look at the piece of papah with my name on it. And now your son is tryna take my baby girl. Y'all wont the whole pie, not just a slice of it. Well, Sarah and Ah won't have it. We. Won't. Have. It." Knox pounded the desk with each word. The nameplate rattled and fell flat and a pencil rolled onto the floor. "And neithah will Monroe and Emmeline, once they know the whole truth."

Paulette couldn't keep herself from trembling. It started from her head and worked its way down to her legs. To still her hands, she placed them on the desk and used them to bear her weight when she leaned forward. "Knox, are you tellin' me that we . . . my husband . . . own George & Company?"

"That's as close to the truth as Ah can take ya, Mrs. Baldwin. You gon' have to go the rest of the way by yourself."

Chapter Twenty-One

FRED BUFFED THE WOODEN LEG, sending wood dust flying into the air. He'd already smoothed the other three legs, and this was the last one. After he turned off the finishing sander and set it down, Fred held it aloft. "What do you think?"

Kim took it. She ran her hand up one side of the maple and down the other. "Nice, but I'd use this two-twenty grit sandpaper on everything. You want it dust free so the stain will apply evenly."

He sighed but knew she was right; there was no rushing perfection or skipping steps. Fred took the sandpaper and rubbed the piece vigorously in the direction of the grain to make sure it was completely smooth. Out of the corner of his eye, he saw Kim lift one of the other chair legs from the table.

They scrubbed and abraded and smoothed quietly together, until finally Fred held up the part he'd started with. He watched her set down her leg and the ultra-fine grit paper and take the piece from him. She turned it over and over and slid her hand over it, testing the rounded edges. From her expression, he could tell what Kim was going to say, even with the goggles over her eyes. "Perfect, isn't it?"

Kim beamed, obviously proud to be part of the process of creating. "As anything can be that God didn't craft Himself. That's going to be one fine chair there, Fred. The maple, it's almost too beautiful in its natural state to stain it. You can see the truth of the wood. Who bored the holes?"

"Curtis. This piece was part of another demo I was designing, and then I got the idea for this chair for Etta. I'd hoped Curtis and I could complete the work together, but now I'm glad he had to leave. I mean, I didn't want him to have a family emergency. You know—"

Kim's touch on his shoulder was featherlight. "His car tag had expired, Fred. That's all. That was the emergency."

"Heh-heh. Okay. Anyway, wait until I get the upholsterers to affix the cushion." He could picture it, how it would look in their kitchen. How Paulette would look enthroned on it at the table, smiling. Something he hadn't seen her do in too long.

"Ooh, go 'head, now! What color?"

"In the orange family. That's McKinley's favorite color.

Our son." In his mind's eye, Fred rotated to the left side of their table and imagined Junior sitting there beside Emmeline.

"McKinley? I thought you always called him Junior."

Fred shrugged. "About time I started givin' a man his due. It'll take me some time to get used to it." He aligned the legs, arms, seat, and back of the chair on the worktable, separating the pieces they'd already smoothed with the grit paper from the others.

Kim stepped up beside him and retrieved her abrasive. "It looks wide enough for two."

"But it's just the right size for one person to get good and comfortable in, right?" Fred ran his palm over the seat. "That was my idea for a good piece of kitchen furniture. Folks like to hang out in the kitchen, no matter how many rooms you've got in the house that are meant for gathering. So you should have the chairs that invite you to stay and sit and enjoy the food and the conversation, without sacrificing a practical and comfortable design. If necessary, two people could sit here— small people, sure—but it's not quite big enough to call it a bench. It'll fit at the shorter sides of the rectangular table."

"Or use one on each side of a square one. And large families could place a couple on each of the longer sides of a longer table." Her eyes danced as they looked off in the distance. She seemed to be committing the design to memory. "Ingenious."

"Paulette's gotta love it. Our customers will, too, when we add this to our catalog as part of the 'Etta Collection.'

Only thing, the birthday girl won't get it Saturday because thanks to you, it won't be finished." Fred shook his head and frowned at his shift supervisor.

"What? Hey!"

He laughed. "Only because your eye for detail and perfection is even sharper than mine. But of course, I'm the one who hired you." Fred pretended to pat himself on the back.

Kim glowed. "I guess so."

They stood there for a minute, both sets of eyes on the table. Then Fred tapped his watch face with his index finger. "I guess we might as well stow these somewhere and resume after the weekend. I need to head to the hospital soon to check on my uncle. Talk to Etta. I'll be off tomorrow."

"That's right. Celebratin' the big day." Kim smiled, but her eyes moved to look over her boss's shoulder.

"Yes, and bringing home Uncle Lawrence . . . What?" He turned around. "What's Paulette doing here?"

· ఌ ·

"Your mom seemed pretty resigned, wouldn't you say? Like she was this soldier going off to war." Emmeline twirled the bendy straw in her glass of iced tea. Condensation pooled on the outside and dripped onto the table.

"Yeah. Curious minds wont to know. What's goin' on?" Monroe's cheek was stuffed with a bite of his buffalo chicken salad sandwich.

"Come on now, man. Feel free to finish chewing before you ask me a question. Are you going on thirty or three?"

McKinley balled up his napkin and dropped it on his empty plate. He checked out the people who'd also chosen to dine outside on the circular tables around them. It was warm enough a bee had come out of hiding and was buzzing around the planter.

"Sassafras is a nice chain to add to downtown Hickory Grove. When did it open? I thought I'd have to give up this kind of food by movin' home," McKinley gushed.

Emmeline gave a cursory look at the other diners before her eyes returned to their origination point. "Nice try, Mac. What's going on with your folks? How're they taking the news?" Her index finger pointed at him first and then at herself.

Monroe took another enormous bite as he nodded along, his eyes trained unwaveringly on McKinley.

The hostess had seated the three on the side of the building at one of the umbrella-covered wrought iron tables. McKinley reclined in his chair and looked beyond Emmie at a truck rumbling by on the two-lane street bisecting the town. A group of women clutching bags emblazoned with the consignment store's insignia chattered in front of the menu mounted on Sassafras's front window. The server led a couple to the table to the right of them and explained the specials of the day.

Monroe slurped his Coke and eyed his friend through nearly shut lids. "Well?"

How McKinley wanted to avoid this discussion, especially in front of Monroe, whose mood that day was as mercurial as the weather forecast. But then he pictured his father stalking across the driveway toward his office, taking all his emotions, thoughts, and plans with him—and leaving his wife and son behind. His fingertips traced the light-blue veins on the back of Emmeline's hand. "Well, I wouldn't describe my folks as thrilled."

"What! Why? Your mama loves me." Monroe's salad-stuffed croissant was halfway to his mouth. He dropped it with a splat on his plate, sending sweet potato fries flying to the table.

"Yeah, and she still does. But she probably wouldn't want me to marry you either."

Emmeline's brows furrowed and she set down her glass. "Either? Your mom doesn't want you to marry me?"

"That's not what I said."

"That's exactly what you said, Mac."

"I'd have to agree, bruh."

McKinley frowned at Monroe, who frowned right back at him. This wasn't the time for his friend to finally get the pronunciation right. "I don't need your input right now, Roe."

"Remember that thing I said the othah day in the car about you marryin' me, too? I meant it. Every word." Monroe picked up his sandwich and took a more reasonably sized bite. He chewed, never breaking eye contact.

McKinley sighed and stared at the toes of his Nikes through the holes in the table for a few seconds. He would have to adjust to Monroe in the role of protective brother-in-law. "I didn't mean 'either,' not in that sense. One of the first things Mom said when she found out about us was something like, 'Oh, Emmeline has always been my favorite George.'"

"Hey!" *Splat* went Monroe's sandwich again. He retrieved a fry and popped it into his mouth.

"Sorry, Monroe, although remember, I'm still not marrying you. And yuck, for eating the ones touching the table. As far as her last words were, Emmeline, they were more like, 'Oh, wow! My son will get a wife, which means I'll get a daughter.'" McKinley smiled and held his hands in front of him to show he wasn't hiding anything. "See? It's all good."

Emmeline smirked. "Not quite all. So you're sayin' she was happy about you marrying me specifically or the idea of you getting married in general? There's a big difference. And you do know that you haven't mentioned your father in this conversation, Mac."

And he hadn't planned to, although he realized it would be foolish for him to think he'd get away with that, now that Monroe was playing worse cop to Emmie's bad cop. McKinley needed to pull his head out of the sand, shake it from his ears, and face reality.

"Yes, sweetie, there's a difference. But I know Mama, and she doesn't split hairs. She meant *you*. Most specifically." He lifted her hand and pressed his lips to her palm. "She can't possibly love you as much as I do, but she does love you for me. No worries."

Moisture suffused Emmeline's eyes and she cupped his jawline with the hand he'd kissed until Monroe cleared his throat.

The couple pointed their chins in his direction.

"I'll give you an 'awww, how cute.' That happy moment fully deserves all that attention and more, and I truly hate to interrupt . . ."

To McKinley, Monroe's sarcastic tone belied the sincerity of his words.

". . . but you still haven't said a word about Mr. Baldwin. And from what I remember, he conducts the Baldwin train. What did he have to say about the pendin'-as-yet-unofficial nuptials—unless I'm missin' a diamond ring somewhere?"

Emmeline snatched back her left hand and glared at McKinley as if she'd been the target of an elaborate ruse. "That's right! Stop tryin' to sweet-talk me; it's distracting. So your mom is kinda on board, but what about Mr. Baldwin?" She sat back in her chair and crossed her arms, as if to prevent McKinley from wooing her away from her main objective.

Fool me once, shame on me. Fool me twice, shame on you, huh? McKinley cut his eyes at Monroe, who shrugged and smiled back snidely. "I'm going to be honest with you, Em."

"*Always* be honest with me, Mac. Always. I don't care what it is." She looked serious.

"Yeah," Monroe seconded.

"Shut up, Roe," McKinley ordered.

"Hush, Monroe," Emmeline told her brother at the same time.

"My father's going to need some time to adjust to our relationship. That's the plain fact. We've discussed his feelings about race. They come from a real place, real experiences."

"But what about his faith, Mac? That's real, too, isn't it?" Emmeline's expression communicated confusion, not judgment.

McKinley shifted in his seat. "Yeah, sure. His faith is real. As real as mine is, and no doubt, his has been tried more than my faith has. But he's been through some things, Emmie, at the hands of white people—"

"Some whaht people," Monroe interjected.

"Okay, *some* white people." McKinley nodded. "But that's easy for you to make that distinction. It's like me telling a mother who's lost her baby to a drunk driver that a daily glass of wine is good for you. Sure, Jesus can turn the other cheek, but Dad's not God. His record of wrongs is a mile long and grow-ing. Reverend Maiden teaches them about loving everybody the same way I'm assuming your pastor does, but they probably hear 'in spite of,' not 'because of' a little more than you do.

"You see, my great-grandfather had to lie in a ditch for four hours, waiting for the Klan to stop hunting for a Black man to hang. Any Black man. Grandpapa had to work three times as many years as other white men in the county to save up to buy his land—and then one of your ancestors stole half of it and used Grandpapa's lumber to build your own family's wealth. My dad ate in the back of restaurants like this one and was taught to hold his head down and step off sidewalks if he knew what was best for him. And don't get me started on what my mother's family went through.

"Now, before you think that was a long time ago, picture me, your future husband—" McKinley aimed a finger at

Emmeline first and then at Monroe—"and your best friend, sitting by himself in his eighth-grade co-op class. That was because one of the other homeschool parents told their son not to sit next to a n—" His throat caught on the ugliness of the word and the pain of the memory. "And if I ask you to name your top ten favorite authors or musicians, do any of them look like me?"

Slow down, McKinley. Don't let your words run away from you. His words and the emotions they engendered. He used the moment to take a sip of his iced tea and evaluate his captive audience. They both seemed like they were keeping up.

Their server approached the table. She leaned on the scrolled edge of the fourth seat, empty except for Emmeline's purse and Monroe's blazer. McKinley stared at the lime-green fingernail polish on the tips of her pale fingers that tapped against the back of the chair.

"Hi! Can I get y'all anything else? We've got a delicious pecan pie in the back, made fresh jus' this mornin'." Cady, or so the name tag read on her chest, tucked a strand of long brown hair behind her ear as her head swiveled from Emmeline to her big brother. It never stopped to see who was sitting between them.

Emmeline's return smile seemed to fight for life as she glanced up at the fortysomething woman and answered in a thick, husky voice, "No thank you."

"We're done," McKinley added curtly.

Cady oozed more sweetness in Monroe's direction. "Want me to bring ya the check?"

He looked at McKinley, who'd offered to treat them to lunch. At McKinley's nod, Monroe responded, "Yes, please."

Cady's shoulders danced and she winked at Monroe. "Sure thang, honeybun."

McKinley watched her strut from one table to the next before entering the back door of Sassafras. "I'm the one and only child of two one and onlies, but my experience and their experiences aren't singular. And I'm sad to say they're not over either. I work as hard to get noticed and promoted—heck, just respected alone—as my dad did to get his foot in the door at George & Company.

"So my parents are concerned about us. I'm sure down deep, they're happier for us than they can say. They love me, they adore you—and I'm talking about you, Emmeline, not you, Monroe. They can't wait to meet their grandkids one day. But I'd say their attitude is more like cautious optimism."

McKinley sighed. "You know, Dad is carrying some heavy baggage and he's dealing with some stuff that's going on with Mom, with work . . ."

"I'll say." Monroe wiped his mouth with his napkin.

Both McKinley's and Emmeline's heads turned his way. This time, neither one shushed him.

"I hear what you're sayin', McKinley. And I feel for everything your dad and his fam'ly have endured, but that doesn't make ra-ight wrong, and wrong ra-ight." His eyes were hard aquamarines in his face.

McKinley squinted at him and he sat taller in his seat.

"I don't think your dad's attitude about your relationship

with my sister comes from how his grandfathah was treated. I think it's based on how your dad is treating my fam'ly."

Emmeline looked from one man to the other and back again. "Monroe, what's wrong? What are you talkin' about?"

"I get it, what your fam'ly has gone through. But y'all haven't cornered the market on pain and sufferin'. And it seems to me your dad is causin' his fair share." Monroe turned his back to Emmeline and leaned forward in his seat toward McKinley. He jabbed the table with the tip of an index finger. "I know somethin' more is going on. My dad won't tell me, but I can tell. And sittin' here, listenin' to you make excuses for him . . . There's more to this than meets the eye, and you know it."

McKinley leaped to his feet with such force his heavy iron chair fell over onto its back. "If I didn't know better, I'd say you were calling me a liar. Me and my father."

Monroe took his time pushing back his seat and tucking his hands in his pockets. "And if I didn't know bettah, I'd say you were takin' me for a fool, just like your fathah took my dad."

Chapter Twenty-Two

THE WHEELS OF THE MERCEDES straddled the grass sprouting in the middle of the meandering dirt road. Branches leaned in, brushing the car's finish as it navigated the twists and turns through the woods. Fred barely noticed what sounded like wooden fingers scratching at the roof, for his ears craned for any utterance from his wife. Paulette had seemed stuck in time from the moment she'd clicked on her seat belt and ordered, "Drive."

So he had. To virtually nowhere first, then to a destination that took shape as the fog dissipated from his mind. His wife had shocked him, showing up on George & Company's floor like that. It had been years since she'd visited him at work, let alone at the production building. When he walked up to her, he noticed the salt streaks on her cheeks that cut a trail from the corners of her flat eyes to her chin. What had happened? Did she come for help, for support and comfort? Or was she there to chuck him headfirst into the penalty box . . . again?

But he couldn't get close enough to ask her; her icy demeanor had rebuffed him. It had silently shouted, *"Stay back!"* and he couldn't bring himself to shout over the noise of the machines. Fred didn't want to risk drawing even more attention than they had. Already he could feel several pairs of eyes on his back as he'd hurried her out, his hand hovering a hairbreadth from the middle of her back. He thought he saw a few dots of perspiration on her otherwise-pristine pink blouse, right between her shoulder blades, but Fred shook off the incongruous image that didn't fit with his picture of his wife.

"Oh!" Fred braked hard and the car jerked forward. A light-brown rabbit bounded across the road, its tail barely escaping the tires. "Whew. I think Papa would've torn me up if I'd hit that rabbit. You shouldn't kill something you can't eat." He glanced over at Paulette, hoping to elicit a smile, a twitch, a glance at the memory.

She barely blinked. "From what you've told me about your upstanding grandfather, he would've been upset about a lot of things. A smushed rabbit is the least of it."

Fred's breath caught. Her voice was so raspy. She sounded broken. His mouth opened and his throat worked, but not a word formed. Fear choked off the questions he wanted to ask, an emotion that was somewhat foreign to him. The other night was the closest he'd come to this sense of dread, how he'd felt when he'd laid his uncle down on the sofa and searched his body for signs of life. His hands shaking slightly, Fred pressed the gas pedal and put the car in motion, albeit a little more slowly.

The road seemed more like a wide, rutted path in spots as it wound uphill. Fred had expended less and less effort to maintain it over the years, and the oaks, maples, pines, and wild berry bushes had reclaimed much of the Baldwins' ten-acre property, including the two-mile-long means of accessing the cleared space in the middle of it. The car had to dip and duck under and around overhanging rocks, for they seemed to cut straight through the hillside at times. To his right, past Paulette's sculpted profile, the sun glistened off a sliver of blue that peeked through the red, orange, yellow, and green overgrowth. Most days, that shallow stream napped lazily in the sun; during a torrent, it overflowed its banks and threatened to take the road with it as it rushed toward the gully lining the main road.

Finally, after the "speed bump," what Fred called the natural hump in the road that helped block some of the water, he veered right into a large cleared area, sprinkled with stumps, fruit trees, weeds, and wildflowers. These three acres surrounded the house—or what was once the house—where Julia and Lawrence had put the finishing touches on their nephew. Now it was not much more than a tumbledown stack of rotting lumber leaning on each other for support.

The way was less bumpy as Fred drove the Mercedes around and parked in front of the four steps that led to what had been the front porch before it had collapsed upon itself.

He switched off the ignition, pocketed the keys, and sat for a moment in the stillness. In his periphery, Fred saw Paulette pull the handle on the door, but he held his peace as she stepped from the car. The car shook when she slammed the door. *Maybe I should give her a minute to herself,* he decided, more out of self-preservation than thoughtfulness, and he closed his eyes.

But that wasn't her plan. Suddenly his door was wrenched open, and Fred nearly tumbled onto the moss-covered ground. He caught himself by grabbing on to the steering wheel.

"Get out, Frederick." Paulette glared at her husband like she could eat him up—after carving him into tiny pieces and covering him with hot sauce.

Something inside him welled up, and he wasn't sure if it was outrage, pride, or a natural urge to defend himself. Fred filled his chest with air and blew it out through slightly parted lips on a slow count of ten. Then he got out and hitched up his pants by his belt loops. Fred stood there in the bright headlights of her eyes, within the vee the open door created. "Okay, here I am. Out of the car."

Paulette burst into tears. And by the look on her face, she was just as horrified as he, just as helpless to stem the flow.

Fred moved toward her, out of the shelter of the door, but her stumbling feet took her on a zigzag path away from him down the slope from the house. He kicked aside pinecones as he trotted after her. Grabbing her by her shoulders, he forced Paulette to turn toward him. "Etta, Etta, please."

She buried her face in her hands and continued to sob.

"Etta, come on. Let me—"

"Let you *what*? Let you what?" Nose dripping, cheeks covered with tears, Paulette dared him with her red eyes to finish.

"You have to let me explain! Is this about Kim, my day-shift supervisor?"

"What are you talkin' about?" Her voice cracked.

"When you walked in and saw us talking on the floor, I had a feeling you suspected something between us. Paulette, you have to know I would never, *ever* touch another woman. I'd never cheat on you."

"You thought seein' you talkin' to another woman would upset me? Either you must think you're pretty hot stuff or I'm extremely unsure of myself. No, Fred, I would never think you've been unfaithful. Not like that."

"Not like what?"

"Maybe you should be worryin' about how God sees you, Frederick."

At those words, Fred's thoughts stuttered. He struggled to form coherent syllables and phrases. Frankly, he didn't know what to do, and so he couldn't find a way to respond.

"I thought so. You know you're wrong. And even you can't make excuses for it now."

He couldn't look full on into Paulette's face, standing

there with the sun an orange-and-yellow fireball behind her. His lids lowered over his pupils. Maybe if he tried, he could see what evil she believed lurked inside and reason through her accusation. "What does that mean—'even you'?"

Paulette's shoulders drooped. "I said exactly what I meant. Even you can't come up with a valid reason for what you've done, what you've been doin' for years." Her chest rose and fell and her eyes no longer focused on him. "For years."

All at once, relief washed over him like a wave. He didn't have to hide from her anymore. "You know about George & Company."

"Yes, Fred. I know. I confronted Knox in your office, and he told me. You used our investments from the money my mother left me and basically blackmailed him into handin' over the reins to G&C. Do you feel better now?" Paulette could have been talking to the pile of bushes squatting to the left of the house.

He crossed his arms. "In some ways, yes."

"I bet you do. I admit you were right: Knox is carryin' the same hatred as Clinton George. He's done a good job at pretendin', until his back was pushed to the wall. But your need for revenge . . . How could you lie to me, Fred? And your son?"

She finally faced him, as if she hadn't found the answers she was looking for in the wildlife. "How is the way you feel any different than the way Knox feels? Your grandfather is dead and gone. He's gone on to his reward and you're not doin' him any good, carryin' on this legacy of bitterness."

It wasn't Fred's work that had kept him away from her. His conscience had driven him away. The guilt had been eating at him for months, starting the moment he gave Knox and Sarah the money to save G&C. What he was doing had stolen the joy of creation and design, and the more successful the company became, the more he hated himself.

That same guilt robbed Fred of the words to explain it away. He stood there, opening and closing his mouth, starting and discarding one explanation after another. Fred felt cold inside despite the heat from the sun beating down on the grass.

"Say something, Fred! Convince me that I shouldn't walk back down that long road and find a way to leave you, leave us—or whatever it is you left behind when you ran after your past. Your past and your greed and your need for revenge. Were you ever really with me?"

"How can you ask me that? We've been married for more than thirty years."

"My dad used to wonder the same thing. 'Was she ever really mine?' That's what he'd ask himself." Paulette spoke quietly to herself, as if he'd said nothing. Maybe she didn't think he had.

"Etta—"

"I think Bett loved that lifestyle her family's money provided her more than she loved my daddy and me." She stared at Fred in wonder, like she was seeing him for the first time. "And you took Bett's payoff to fund your own payback. Tell me, was our marriage real or just part of your need to spit in somebody's face and prove something to Julia?"

The truth of his feelings for her finally freed his tongue. "No, Etta, no. I adore you. I was only trying to take care of you. Then all of this came between us, and I didn't know how to explain it . . . to either of you. And it put me on the outside looking in at the both of you. How could I honor both the family that had given me everything and the family I wanted to give everything?"

"By lovin' us. Hate is never the right choice. I pity Knox. He's a ridiculous man who's too foolish to know he's really lyin' to himself. But you, Fred? Not you. And here I was, thinkin' it was me, that I had done something." Paulette's words built momentum and energized her feet. As she paced the yard, she slipped on the pinecones and fallen leaves.

Fred swished through the high grass behind her. "My family is the most important thing to me. I never wanted to make you feel abandoned or less than, Etta. I don't hate anyone. I was just trying to do right by you."

She spun. "But how about doin' right by yourself!"

Fred slipped and fell to his knee at her sudden stop. When he looked down at the ground, he felt like he was looking into a mirror and another man was staring up at him.

"Oh, you're hurt? Well, that makes two of us." But she sounded cold, as if she wanted to inflict pain, not convey her own.

He winced at the twinge in his knee and brushed at the grass stain. His fingers came away bloody.

Paulette gasped. Her eyes grew wide over the fingers cupping her mouth. "Fred! I'm sorry. I didn't mean it."

"Actually, I think you did." He pressed his mouth to his hand and tasted the metallic tang.

"No, no, I didn't, Fred. As heartbroken as I feel, I never want to hurt you. I know too well what that feels like." Fresh tears gushed down her face. Paulette tenderly reached for his hand and replaced his lips with hers.

This . . . this was the Etta he knew, his wife of thirty-five years kissing away the blood on his hand. Still looking much like the young woman who'd nearly been mown down that spring afternoon she'd finished her senior music project at the College of William & Mary. Not only didn't Paulette like to count her steps, but in those days she'd rarely watched them.

He could still see her now, dashing across Jamestown Road from Ewell Hall to meet a friend at the Art Museums of Colonial Williamsburg. He'd been looking out the window of the bus he was riding on, wondering if the white lady in the knee-length denim skirt was going to stop. When the city bus screeched to a halt, he'd realized the answer was no.

The last passenger, Fred had hopped down the steps along with the driver to check on the coed, all the while wondering what he could possibly say to the strange woman who didn't have the sense to know she couldn't outrun a city bus. Though he was prepared to stand up for the man driving the vehicle, he wasn't looking forward to bringing down all of Williamsburg on their heads. But the fault was hers nonetheless. Something she admitted immediately, much to his shock.

"Oh, I'm so sorry! I hope no one was hurt!" Paulette had risen on her tiptoes to look over his head into the bus, obviously not caring a whit about the sheet music littering the road and scattering to the four winds.

Once the driver had realized she was all right, he'd returned to his post behind the wheel, determined to complete his route. Yet something about her face . . . Fred couldn't pull himself away. He'd decided to finish his historical tour later, and he waved the driver on.

"Don't worry about it. The bus is empty. He was driving it in for repairs after dropping me off. Are you okay?" He scanned her for injuries.

"Oh, my, your head!" She dug through her bag, but all she could seem to find were music books, composition papers, and pencils. "Paulette, really?" she'd murmured to herself. Seemingly giving up, she'd whisked off the sweatshirt she wore over a sleeveless, formfitting tee, and used its arm to dab at the bloody knot on his forehead.

Fred didn't even know how he'd banged it. All he knew was his entire body came to life when she touched him. The cars that blew their horns and drove around the two of them still standing in the street didn't find this revelatory, however. He guided her over to the sidewalk.

"I'm fine, thank you." Fred had clasped her hand and stayed her ministrations. "If you're sure you're okay?" He let her go and made a move toward the bus stop.

Paulette shifted from one sandal-covered foot to the other—later, he learned she was praying—and responded with a demure smile, "Yes, but I wouldn't mind some help collectin' my music."

For the life of Fred, he couldn't understand what she'd want with him, and he was struggling to get past his grandfather's warning to "never be alone with a white woman." But he'd taken one more look into her hazel eyes, and he'd decided he didn't care what Papa had to say. They weren't even alone, not there on Jamestown Road, and he was willing to help her do anything she needed to do or go anywhere she wanted to go. It wasn't until they were strolling away from the museum and the friend awaiting her that he'd learned that her family's heritage was just as complex—and half as Black—as his. But by then, it no longer mattered to him.

But he knew it mattered now. The onslaught of her tears and rage had beaten him down. They couldn't keep doing this, standing there in front of his grandfather's teardown, with his hand to her lips. It hurt too much to be this close to her physically when she felt so far from him in every other way. "Paulette, I don't know what to do or say to make this better."

She must have thought the same, for she withdrew in slow increments. It seemed the last thing she wanted but the only thing she knew to do.

His fingers brushed the inside of her upper arm. "Please wait."

Fred hurried to the trunk of the car and lifted out the heavy, striped blanket Paulette made him keep there for emergencies, along with the extra food and water and the first aid kit. It was a part of their life in the foothills. When Fred held up the blanket and waved for her to follow him, he felt her hesitation. But then she trudged up the hill toward him.

For such a time as this.

· ᥩ ·

"I can't believe we left my brother." Emmeline's cheeks were aflame as she huffed down the street.

"Well, he was the one who got me kicked out. His newfound waitress friend Cady wasn't about to throw his sorry butt out the door, that's for sure." McKinley lengthened his stride to keep up with her, nearly running just ahead of him. Her anger had lit a fire in her feet and her golden-red hair fluttered like flames behind her.

"What was wrong with him? I can't believe he'd attack you like that." She glanced back at him over her shoulder but didn't slow down.

McKinley rubbed his jaw. He was pretty sure it was bruised. "I'm the one who threw the first punch."

She stopped in the middle of a sidewalk square. "Trying to defend me because I was defending you." She studied his face. "You'll be fine. My kindergarteners have worse boo-boos." Apparently satisfied, Emmeline resumed heading pell-mell toward the car.

McKinley caught her hand.

"Mac . . ."

"No, Emmie. You're walking like a wild woman, trying to

put some distance between us. Whatever is going on between our parents—and between Monroe and me—is not going to take us down with it. We will not be a casualty of this war. You feel me?" He wrapped his arm around her waist and tried to bring her closer.

She stiffened at first. Then Emmeline relaxed against him and rested her brow on his chest though her arms remained at her side. "What's goin' on, Mac? Monroe leveled some pretty serious allegations against you and your family."

He spoke into her hair. "I'd rather not have this conversation on the main street of Hickory Grove."

She reared back her head and peered up at him. "Well, I'd rather not have this conversation at all."

"Touché." McKinley swallowed. "I don't know everything. But I have a pretty good idea this has something to do with a large sum of money. Specifically, my mother's."

"Your mother's money?" Emmeline's mouth was smushed against his soft cotton polo, muffling her voice.

"Last year, right before Christmas, I decided to work in my dad's office over the garage. I was looking through his desk for one of those special drawing pencils he has, you know the ones with the—"

She nipped his skin showing through his unbuttoned collar and pulled away.

"Oopf, okay. Yeah, back to the subject. I came across some paperwork from the bank. There was quite a big number involved. Blow-your-mind kinda money."

Emmie squinted up at him.

A man walking his dog grumbled under his breath and threw them a curious look as he edged around them.

"Sorry, sir!" Emmeline called before concentrating on McKinley. "What are you talking about, Mac? Is your dad involved in something illegal?"

He snorted. "Straitlaced Fred? Not hardly. But I guess he's renounced that title. It has to do with Mama's money."

Emmeline laughed. She resumed walking toward the car at a more leisurely pace. Their conversation seemed to have doused her fire.

He fell into step beside her. "What's so funny?"

"What you said, about your mother coming from money."

McKinley dropped her hand and stayed where he was. "Why is that so hard to believe?"

She spun and cocked her head at him. "I know you're not going there, McKinley Baldwin. You've never told me a thing about your mama being wealthy, so this isn't about race, if that's what you're thinking. Goodness, is this always going to be a thing between us?"

McKinley tucked his bottom lip under his top teeth and brushed his hand over the top of his twists. She was right. Not everything was about race. He was wrong to expect the worst. What was it he'd professed to his mother, that their love was straight from 1 Corinthians? Theirs was a "bears all things, believes all things, hopes all things, endures all things" kind of love. He needed to act like it.

"You're right, Emmie. After dealin' with that waitress back at Sassafras, I'm feeling somewhat sensitive."

"Yes, I noticed. She surely didn't expect you to pay for the check after ignoring you the whole time."

"Yeah, plus my best friend treated me like persona non grata." She put her weight on her right hip. "I forgive you."

"It doesn't look like you forgive me."

"It didn't sound like you asked for it. But looks and sounds can be deceiving, I know." Emmeline didn't move, but she seemed more receptive. "So what about your mother and this money? And my family's business? There's a lot I don't know, but here we are talking about marriage."

"There are no ifs, ands, or buts about that." McKinley caught up to her and unfolded her arms. Then he ran his hands from her shoulders over her arms and interlocked his fingers with hers. She held them but maintained her position a foot away from him. He squeezed his eyes shut, and when he opened them, he started talking.

"Long story short, my grandmother was extremely wealthy. The money came from some restaurant chain her family owned out West. When *her* parents died, they left it all to her because she ran everything—probably out of guilt for giving up her husband and only child. And then when my grandmother died, she in turn left everything to my mom. The attorney eventually handled the sale of the restaurants and gave her an envelope with a check in it as well as the deed to the house in California."

By this time Emmeline's mouth was wide enough for the Pacifica to park in. McKinley freed one of his hands to lift her lower lip.

She opened it again and asked, "But I thought . . . well, I don't know what I thought. So what does this money have to do with me?"

"That's where last Christmas comes in. I asked Dad about this bank statement that showed this huge debit. I was worried that he was doing something . . . if not illegal, at least something he shouldn't be with it. Mama had never mentioned anything, so I knew she couldn't have known." McKinley was getting tired of talking and thinking, and he still needed to process what had happened with Monroe back at Sassafras. He was quite certain, however, this wasn't the time to give up the ghost, not if he wanted to remain on sure footing with Emmeline.

"And then he told me he was 'investing' in George & Company." He shook his head, thinking back. "That's what he called taking her money. We went back and forth that day, because what he was doing went against everything he'd ever taught me, all I knew about Frederick Baldwin Sr. I accused him of deceiving Mom and he gave me some song and dance about the situation being more a 'surprise' than a deception.

"But I couldn't be a part of it. He wasn't telling me the whole story behind what he was doing, and a little voice told me Mom wouldn't agree. Or at least not agree with how or why he was doing it. To avoid coming between them, I got the heck out of Dodge. Mama would've been able to read my face and know something wasn't right."

The breeze had picked up and blown thick, sun-burnished strands across Emmeline's face. "And you didn't come back until now. Why?"

"You know why. For you. With you." He brushed away her hair and kissed her cheek. "And to make sure my dad came clean because I couldn't propose to you with this secret between us."

"And all I thought Mrs. Baldwin got from her mother was that dang piano that gave me so much grief every week," Emmeline mused, mostly to herself.

"Ha-ha. That piano gave us *all* some grief, including her."

"But that still doesn't fully explain why Monroe was so angry. If it was only an investment, however secret, why did Monroe accuse you of lying? If your dad is keeping something from your mom, that sounds like a Baldwin family problem, not a George family problem."

He couldn't answer, but he had to wonder himself. They were all confused and had taken it out on each other. He and Emmeline stood there lost in their own thoughts as cars passed back and forth on the two-lane road. The dog walker who had passed them a few minutes earlier returned from the opposite direction carrying a large brown bag speckled with grease spots. The aroma of fried chicken greeted their noses as he approached.

"Y'all good?" he asked, slowing down a bit.

McKinley smiled and nodded. After the man had moved a few squares away, McKinley chuckled a little. "Gotta love Southerners." Then he rubbed his jawline again. "Some of 'em anyway."

Emmeline sighed and pulled her bemused boyfriend toward the Pacifica, parallel parked a couple spaces ahead.

A teenager climbed from the passenger seat of a minivan parked behind them and started sliding coins into the meter. An older woman shut the driver's door and locked the car.

"I can't believe you punched Monroe and that I left my only brother flat on his bottom beside the table." She looked back in the direction of the restaurant. "If this situation wasn't so serious, it would be funny. The shock on his face!"

"Maybe we should go back?"

Emmeline moved closer to him and touched his cheek. "It *is* turnin' purple. I think we should give him another minute. Give you both another minute. Do you have any more change?"

He considered her a moment, and then he dug into his pockets.

Chapter Twenty-Three

———————— ❦ ————————

PAULETTE LOCKED HER ARMS around her knees. From where they sat at the highest point of the Baldwin property, she could distinguish the variegated hues of the evergreens scattered among the reds and golds. Another time, she would've been enjoying the arrival of fall. Right now, she felt like she was fighting for her life.

"For goodness' sake, Etta! The Lord knows I wouldn't take money from the company! That's what you thought?" Fred had stretched out his injured leg, and he leaned on the bent knee of the other one as he plucked the scales of a pinecone. "I put all our money *into* the company. To save it. That's why I worked so hard, to make sure those new ideas I had didn't fail and that George & Company didn't take us down with it. Paulette, don't you trust me?"

She closed her eyes. Of course she did, but that wasn't worth a plug nickel. "Do you actually think stealing from us is better than embezzling from G&C? Not only did you risk our family's livelihood, you risked our marriage to carry out a vendetta."

She shook her head in disbelief that her normally astute husband had gotten it so wrong. He had the nerve to think he was in the right, that he'd been misunderstood. The victim. Again, he was truly in the minority, because she'd bet no one else would agree with him, not even his aunt and uncle, who thought the sun rose and set over his slightly balding head.

"How am I risking our livelihood when you never touch that money? If you hadn't talked to Knox, you'd never have known."

She couldn't look at him. Even if she had, she didn't think she'd recognize this man who'd made off with the voice of her husband. "Do you realize how you sound? You're basically saying you would've kept lying to me."

"That's not what I'm saying, Paulette. You're turning my words into stumbling blocks and using them to trip me up."

"That's your conscience. How can you reconcile all this with your faith in God?"

"That's a question you need to ask Knox, not me. My faith is sure. I serve a just God."

"Yes, you do, and He says He will repay. What does McKinley have to s—?"

"McKinley is gone, Etta. We're still here. And we're the foundation. The basis of our family unit. It's not just about him."

She tried to get up from the blanket, but it required too much effort for a woman with creaky knees knocking on the door of sixty. Before she could clamber to her feet, he'd taken hold of the arm closest to her and wouldn't let go. His eyes pinned her to the spot.

"I've felt on my own for years. You invest all your affection and time in that boy. Y'all can communicate without sayin' a word and I get left out of the whole conversation. By the time I made this decision, I was already on my own. Why would I need your two cents at that point, telling me what to do?"

"Maybe because I'm your *wife*. We're supposed to be in this together."

"You've felt more like his mother than my wife."

Now that did hurt. She yanked her arm from his grasp and stared above her. Streaks of orange and yellow stretched from one end of the sky to the other. A hawk circled overhead. That rabbit might have cheated death for the last time.

Tears eked from the corners of her eyes and trailed into her earlobes. Paulette let them fall and pool there. "Do you know how much I love you?" Her quietly spoken words drifted on the slight breeze that was cool enough to remind her winter was but months away.

Fred buried his head in his arms. "You sound like you're reading one of McKinley's children's books." His voice was weary.

She shook her head a little and smiled wryly. "But I'm not asking you to guess like that father hare who was trying to get his son to bed. I'm asking you if you know. Do you?"

Fred rose up. "Is that a trick question? I'm not sure what you expect me to say."

Of course he didn't know. He didn't want to admit it. Love wasn't something a person could quantify, but she had to try. Numbers seemed like the only thing he could understand. She uprooted a patch of dandelions trying to disguise themselves as grass while Fred sat as still as the pile of wood that used to be a home. "I've loved you more . . . more than that money I never thought about. More than myself. More than the past. Who cares about what happened on that side of the dirt? I've got too many cares in the here and now."

"Well, I'm not you, Etta. And if I don't do something today about what was done to my family yesterday, what kind of man would I be?"

"The man of faith I married."

"I can be that man and still want justice." Fred turned toward his grandfather's ramshackle house. A squirrel ducked under the long beam blocking the door. Vines poked through the crumbling brick chimney. Darkness and shadows reigned behind the broken windows where sunshine once danced. Moss threaded with ivy crawled around the left side of the house and across the yard. Papa never could get much grass to grow in the shade of the chestnut trees, their limbs now shedding green and yellow-tinged leaves.

When he reached for a canoe-shaped frond and plucked

at it, Paulette's hands covered his. After a moment, he tilted his head in her direction.

"I get it, Fred. I never wanted y'all to feel like I did after Bett walked out on us, how forgotten I felt when she sent me that piano. As if a thing could replace a mother's love. I wonder if I took up studying music just to prove something to myself, that I'd gotten over Mama leavin' me.

"But I'm tired of provin' I'm worthy of givin' and receivin' love. Daddy spent more time with his girlfriends and his regrets. Thinkin' if he'd done this differently or that instead . . . If he had, I wouldn't have ever existed, a thought that never came to him. I worried so much about our son. He could never go through what I did."

"You're convicting yourself of the very crime you accuse me of—you loved something more than us. Except you chose your fear and resentment. And McKinley."

Paulette gasped. Her heart broke to pieces and all of her poured out. She sobbed into her hands, alone beside him.

· ☙ ·

Fred let her cry. His throat felt like it was filled with gravel, dry and rough.

"In all that strivin' I forgot about you, didn't I? I left it up to you to assume how precious you are to me, Frederick. Talk about injustice. I'm sorry, Frederick." She dropped her hands. "You're my very life."

Silently he dried her cheeks with his hand as he absorbed her sorrow. Then he scooted over, centimeter by centimeter on the coarse blanket until his gabardine-clad thigh pressed against her bare one. His arm encircled her incrementally.

Instead of moving away, Paulette leaned into him and turned up her face to his, her eyes full of questions.

Tentatively, he tilted his head down and his lips reached for hers. At first, he only tasted salt, but then the sweetness that he remembered struck his tongue. Her hands were like the leaves that drifted to the ground around them—featherlight, landing where they would—but then they found purpose and she suddenly, intentionally, gripped his shoulders. At long last, she wrapped her arms around his neck and pulled him down to her and they lay together on the blanket. His lips stopped searching and questioning, for they knew her. This was Paulette, his wife.

She shifted against him and Fred lifted his head. His deep-brown eyes didn't want to let go of hers, but he didn't want to make her uncomfortable by holding on too long.

Paulette's eyes started to overflow again. "No," she murmured.

Fred pulled back.

She pressed herself against him and whispered against his mouth, "I was talking to my tears, and they wouldn't listen. Please, don't go."

"Etta . . ." He thrust his fingers into her thick dark hair and somehow brought her closer. "I love you so much. More than I can say."

"I know. I know."

Chapter Twenty-Four

"That was Dad." McKinley pressed the red circle on his iPhone. He tried to recapture the feeling of his go-to spot, when he propped against the wall under his bunk bed. It had been over a decade since he'd been able to sit up straight, yet he felt secure, peaceful, and sure of his next steps there. Not exactly what he was feeling at the moment behind the wheel of his rental car, his eyes closed against the sun bouncing off the hospital windows.

"What did he want?"

He opened one eye and looked at Emmeline sitting in the passenger seat. "He was letting me know he's upstairs in my great-uncle's hospital room."

"Oh, okay." She looked out the window. "Have you heard anything from Monroe? I was hoping he'd call last night, but he didn't."

"No, at least not yet."

She toyed with the control for the window, making it go up and down. "I feel like I'm hopping from one fire to another."

McKinley shut both his eyes, looking for his happy place. He needed to prepare himself for the visit ahead.

"Mac?"

"Yeah . . . ," he breathed.

"Are you still glad you told them we were coming?"

He sighed and sat up straight. "Not the 'her' part of them. I know we'll lift Uncle Lawrence's spirits, but Aunt Juju? Talk about fire." He unclipped his seat belt. "But you know what? I should've told everybody a week ago. A month ago. Shoot, the first minute! This would've all been behind us at this point."

Emmeline stared through the windshield, the light turning her auburn hair gold in spots. "I hated my mom not knowing, not being able to tell her what was going on." When she faced him, her lips curved a little in that self-deprecating way she had. "Maybe I'm just looking for her approval."

His fingers searched and found hers. He just couldn't keep himself from touching her, especially now that his love had come out of hiding. "No. Sounds like a good mother-daughter thing. My mother could tell something was up, but she didn't know exactly what. To be fair, I didn't make it easy for her. I was trying to keep more than my love life from her. She dropped hints like crazy, asking me about you the whole time I've been here."

"Me!" Emmeline's free hand seemed to hold her heart in place. "But she didn't even know about me. And you hadn't been home more than a minute before the cat clawed its way out the proverbial bag."

"That's because she knows her son. Too well. According to her, she picked up on changes in my attitude." He winked at her. "Apparently, loving you has changed the way I walk and talk." McKinley leaned over the console that blocked them to kiss her tenderly.

She let go of his hand and cradled his face with both of hers, keeping him close to her for a minute before she withdrew slightly and rested her forehead against his. When she sat back and opened her eyes, Emmeline gasped.

McKinley whirled to his left. An elderly man whose beard rivaled Santa Claus stood at the edge of the car's hood, mouthing something at them. McKinley reached for the door handle.

"Mac! Wait!" Emmeline's hand scrambled to hold on to his.

"Excuse me? What did you say?" The edge in McKinley's voice could have honed a razor.

The stranger pointed a finger so crooked that it took aim at the entire car. "I said, you young people today, kissin' and carryin' on in public. Shameful! Gals walkin' round here, half-nekkid, showin' off parts only they husbands should see. It ain't right. And if yo' mama and daddy won't tell ya, I will." He stalked off.

McKinley stood there, one leg still in the car and one out, watching the outraged stranger move farther and farther away. Well, *that* wasn't what he'd expected. He heard the Pacifica's passenger door slam and he turned from the retreating man's figure to share a chuckle with Emmeline. Her flashing eyes killed his laughter.

"Tell me, Mac. What did you think he was saying? Why did you hop out of the car like that?"

McKinley put his other foot on the ground and closed the car door. "Come on, Emmie. You know why. You thought the same thing. I'm glad he was just a crotchety, old-fashioned dude who hates public displays of affection."

"Okay, that was this time. But what about next time? What will you do if someone says something out of turn about our relationship? Treats you like the server did at Sassafras or how you suspect your aunt will treat me? Tell me what exactly. Are you going to punch him like you punched my brother? Knock 'em flat on his rump?" She gripped his chin.

He winced because that spot was still sore. His eyes narrowed as if he could picture exactly what he would do. "First of all, make that *when* and not *if*. And I don't know, Emmie. Improvise, I guess. Ask him if he needs help with something. Tell my family what I think of them."

"So you plan to confront everyone who acts like he has

a problem? That can get kinda tiring, don't you think? And lonely. Being that helpful, I mean."

McKinley gently peeled away her fingers but held on to them. "Emmie, you don't understand."

"What don't I understand, Mac? That we might run into a lot of stares, some hatred and ignorance, people who just want to 'help' us in one way or another? Believe me, I understand. But we can't go through life on the defensive with everyone else and keep the peace between us. How's that going to work? We're going to have to consciously see our love for each other and for others through our lens of faith. No matter what.

"Can you do that—be McKinley and let me be Emmeline, or is our race going to come first every time like it did with our own parents? We need to decide before we run through the gauntlet upstairs. See, I'm willing to give it all up for you. I've done that—I've chosen love. What about you, McKinley? Have you chosen love?"

McKinley dug the heels of his hands into his eyes. He felt cold and hot all at once when she stepped away from him and the sun struck his body, unhindered.

Neither moved, although the world continued to shift and change around them. A group clutching pink balloons, bags stuffed with colorful paper, and an empty car seat walked toward the hospital's front doors. An ambulance, sirens blaring, zoomed around the circular drive toward the emergency entrance. The crosswalk sign beeped, and people in scrubs and white coats passed each other in both directions.

McKinley's chest expanded and retracted and he extended his hand for her to shake. "Hi, I'm McKinley, but the love of my life calls me Mac. And you?"

She shook it. "You can call me Emmie. Nice to love you."

He loosely draped his arm around her shoulder and brought her closer to his side. They rested against the side of the door, but he still felt a distance between them. "Look, it's been a long day. Can we just chalk it up to that?"

"It's only one o'clock, Mac." But she laid her head on his shoulder.

He inhaled the jasmine scent of her shampoo, savored the silkiness of her hair against his cheek. "My day started yesterday, Emmie . . ." His voice petered out as he envisioned the three people waiting for them in room 467. "And it's not over yet."

"I take it you're referring to this visit." She wrapped her arms around his waist.

It only took him a second to relax against her, to tighten his hold. Emmie never seemed to care about who might be watching or pointing . . . or frowning. She didn't keep her love for him at arm's length, something his parents did more as the decades passed. Actually, McKinley had had to get used to her lack of reserve, her demonstrativeness. He wondered, would they still be strolling hand in hand at ninety years old or would the cares of the world have beaten them down by then and driven a wedge between them?

"'Perfect love casts out fear,' you know." Her whisper tickled his neck.

She can always read my mind. "I know. It's just that my parents aren't quite like your parents, accepting and supporting us, no matter what."

"Ha!"

The pigeons pecking the ground near them flapped their wings and hovered for a second before settling down.

Calmer, she asked, "Remember when I told you about their last-minute business trip?"

McKinley drew back his head to squint at her. "Yeah . . . ?"

"Well, it wasn't just about work. I told you I couldn't keep our relationship from them any longer, but what I didn't tell you is that our conversation didn't go as smoothly as I thought it would. They had to go to the beach to recover or hide out or . . . something. Maybe that's what my dad was so upset about, and Monroe had it all wrong."

He twisted so he could look at her full on, again putting distance between them. "You think he's upset about losing his baby girl?"

Emmeline's expressive face shouted, *"Not on your life."* "I'm afraid that when it comes to the Georges, business is one thing; family is another."

"Why didn't you tell me? What do you want to do?"

"Put on that engagement ring you'd better give me. Live my life. Pray for them and give them space to come around. Because it doesn't matter, Mac. What other people think, how they feel about us, even if they're the people closest to us. We know we love each other. We're doing the right thing. Their problems aren't our problems. All of that. It's time we make our own traditions—that's what you told me, Mac. And I believed you. I *believe* you, present tense, not past."

The rubber sole of her pink Converse high-tops made a scratching sound on the concrete as Emmeline edged her left foot closer to his. "But what about you, do you still believe?"

McKinley looked down at the ground. He'd given her those shoes for her twenty-fifth birthday. His right foot bumped up against hers.

· ☙ ·

Paulette quick-stepped to the elevator doors, but they *shushed* together just before she got there. She sighed and pushed the up arrow and watched the numbers change over the other elevators. Her mouth formed an O when familiar voices behind her caught her attention.

"Mom, I thought you were already upstairs!" McKinley let go of Emmeline's hand to hug her.

Guilty as charged. She and Fred had stayed out until the wee hours before creeping into the house like rebellious teenagers. When he woke this morning, Paulette wasn't ready for more talking—or anything else. So she'd feigned sleep and let him and Julia leave for the hospital ahead of her. McKinley had probably assumed his parents had driven in together because Paulette had closeted herself in her room, listening as he'd dressed, eaten, and eventually headed out, ostensibly to pick up Emmeline. Once she was completely alone, she cried, prayed, and cried some more. And made herself some of McKinley's yummy coffee. One day, she'd have to hunt down that Kelsey in Philadelphia and hug her.

"So, Mom, have you been upstairs already?"

"I should've been, but no, I'm just getting here." Paulette held up a disposable coffee cup and a white plastic bag. "I thought your dad and your great-aunt might need some sustenance."

Actually, what she'd done for the past hour was tramp around the hospital's atrium and practice her arguments, much as a prizefighter shadowboxed in his corner of the ring before he heard the bell. But she couldn't tell her son that, especially in front of Emmeline. That beautiful young woman—*Who am I kidding? Girl*—had exuded this excited, yet resolute air from the moment she'd hugged Paulette and murmured, "Hello, Mrs. Baldwin," back at the house. How could she, a soon-to-be sixty-year-old woman, have to work up the gumption to face her own husband and a couple she could outrun if she had to?

The elevator to the right dinged and the doors whispered open. The three of them stepped in. Paulette pushed the button marked *4* and the two sides closed. "Y'all good?"

McKinley played with Emmeline's fingers. "Yes, we're good. They won't know what hit 'em."

The way her son was looking at his fiancée. That was how Fred had looked at her last night. Paulette felt her cheeks grow hot, and her heart swelled—before it plummeted. Maybe that was the problem. Did the Baldwin men get caught up in what they saw, not by what they couldn't see?

If McKinley considered Emmeline the golden goose, he'd better muster up the courage to wrestle the giant for her. Would Fred fight for her, or had they experienced a passionate moment in time?

"What's wrong, Mrs. Baldwin?"

She waved her hand at her future daughter-in-law. "Everything, dear . . . and nothing at all."

"In other words, don't worry about it, Emmie. She's not going to divulge her secrets. It's not her way." McKinley shook his head at his mother.

"You know me too well." The elevator's bell chimed and the doors retracted. Paulette stepped out of the five-by-six-foot box onto the tile floor. "Want me to go ahead as we talked about and break the ice?"

McKinley shrugged. "Do you have an ice pick in your purse? Then we might as well go together—unless you don't want to be caught sleeping with the enemy."

Too late for that. Paulette blinked away the tears and the thought and pretended to chuckle, although McKinley sounded like he was only partly joking. The three fell into step, their faces grim as they wove through the bevy of quiet activity. They dodged the nutritionist pushing a large cart filled with lunch trays, then had to walk single file to avoid a team of doctors striding three-deep down the middle of the hallway. Nurses chatted at the station and other staffers moved in and out of rooms. Paulette tried not to invade anyone's privacy by peeking around any partially open door they passed, but she had to fight the urge to go sit a while with a few elderly patients she couldn't help but notice lying alone, oxygen tubes in their noses and blinds closed over their windows.

At room 467, she paused and took a deep breath. Uncle Lawrence's was one door that was completely shut. Probably Julia's doing. She wasn't the kind to welcome the uninvited. A firm male hand on Paulette's shoulder propelled her into the room after she pressed on the handle and pushed open the door. But then she discovered there was no need for all the mental and emotional preparation, all the silent prayer during the trek from the elevator. The bed was empty.

But the room wasn't.

· ⁊ ·

Fred looked up from his cell phone as the three entered. His breath caught. *I'd forgotten how lovely she is. My sixty-year-old bride.* "Hey, there."

"Hey," Paulette answered softly, her cheeks rosy. Her shoulders sagged as she took in the rumpled white sheets and smushed pillow.

"Don't worry. They'll be back soon." Fred slid his phone into the pocket of his long-sleeved button-down shirt and walked around the end of the bed. He stopped just shy of Paulette and searched her hazel eyes for a flicker of life—their marriage just couldn't be dead to her, not after yesterday. Unsure of what he'd detected, he took a halting step and leaned in to kiss her cheek, hoping all the while she wouldn't rebuff him.

Paulette turned her head and touched her slightly open mouth to his, only for a second before pulling back. Her eyes seemed to be asking him, *Now what?*

Fred knew what he wanted but not exactly what to do about it, so he decided he'd better keep talking before he made a complete fool of himself. He caressed Paulette's cheek and stepped back. "I don't know if you forgot, but Uncle Lawrence had to do a stress test. If he passes, they should release him later today. Juju accompanied them to make sure the technicians didn't mess up. Frankly, I think her input will motivate the technicians to pass him with flying colors, no matter what the result."

His son's laugh was deep and bounced off the walls of the small, private room. "Of course, she did. Well, that gives us time to take a bite out of the elephant, so to speak. Emmeline, Dad . . . here we are."

Fred smiled. "So we are."

Junior moved up to stand beside Paulette, drawing Emmeline with him. The young lady seemed as befuddled about the next steps as Fred himself felt.

He extended his hand to Emmeline just as she stepped forward with arms slightly outstretched. His eyes widened; then he stepped into her embrace and awkwardly patted her back.

"Hi, Mr. Baldwin. It's really good to see you."

Suddenly he was transported to his backyard, scooping up a young Emmeline, who'd somehow bent the wheel of his son's bicycle—Junior's brand-new neon-green mountain bike he and Etta had given him for his tenth birthday. Apparently, the child just had to test-drive it even though she didn't know how to steer and pedal simultaneously, and had summarily crashed into the thickest, sturdiest oak tree on their property. Having heard the boys yelling at a different decibel than usual, Fred had run out back and found Emmeline sprawled at the base of the unharmed tree under the damaged bike, with its front wheel still wobbling as it tried to spin.

Emmeline had stared up at him through a tangle of bangs sticking to her forehead and immediately stopped screaming, as if she trusted him to make it better. She'd wiped her nose with her forearm and said those same words: "Hi, Mr. Baldwin. It's really good to see you."

Just like that day in his backyard, Fred analyzed the situation in the hospital room. Though it didn't involve an expensive bike and a bloody knee this time, the same question came to mind: *How much is this going to cost me?*

And from deep inside, he heard a hushed *Everything*.

Fred found it wasn't as hard as he thought it would be to smile at the girl. "I'm happy for you. Really." He squeezed Emmeline's hand more sincerely than he'd embraced her. "Welcome to the family."

Then he held up a finger in front of the younger couple and lightly clasped Paulette's arm. He pulled her aside and leaned in to her ear. "I was hoping we could have some time together before I left."

At her hesitation, he shook his head briskly. "No, no. To talk. Only to talk. I was doing some thinking. With your birthday tomorrow and their health issues, why don't I arrange to have Juju and Uncle Lawrence return to Virginia in the morning? I've already talked to his cousin."

The door opened. From behind them, Juju boomed, "Who do we have here? Fred Jr., boy, glad to see you!" Her chair sped to the right as an orderly pushed her husband toward the bed. "Now, Lawrence, don't mind none of us. You get you some rest. I can see they already sent somebody up here to check you out, but they gon' see soon enough that nobody's made a decision yet. Move 'em in, move 'em out, always rushin' folks. We gon' take our time. Paulette, I see you finally made it."

"Yes, Aunt Julia, I'm here." Paulette sounded like she was singing an old refrain as she stepped away from Fred.

He swallowed his disappointment and moved to pull back the sheets for Uncle Lawrence.

Paulette leaned down and kissed the woman's brow, causing her plastic bag to crinkle and its contents to shift and roll about. "Nobody's kickin' you out. And I promise we'll leave if we start disturbing Uncle Lawrence." She nodded at the beleaguered-looking aide as he pushed the chair from the room. "Thank you so much, sir."

Juju pointed at Emmeline. "That's one thing I agree with, so you better hear me, miss: nobody's kickin' us out. That means you or some other representative will hafta come back here once we hear from that know-it-all doctor. Until then, you can go somewhere. We'll see *you* later." She wheeled herself around the other side of the room and smoothed the covers over her husband.

Paulette moved closer to the bed and squeezed Uncle Lawrence's shoulder. He patted her hand.

Is Etta giving them all this attention because she doesn't want to be close to me? Fred followed his wife's movements hungrily.

"Go on now. We'll call you when we need you." Julia waved her hand peremptorily in Emmeline's direction.

Fred squashed his selfish thoughts, realizing there were more pressing matters at hand than his lonely, hurt feelings—"matters" like Emmeline, who looked from McKinley to Paulette to Fred himself.

She opened her mouth.

"Oh! Juju, this isn't who you think it is." Fred waved his hands.

"Aunt Juju. Uncle Lawrence." McKinley reached for Emmeline's hand. "I should clear up the confusion. This is who I promised to bring up to meet you. She doesn't work for the hospital; Emmie's with me. I hope one day you'll consider her one of us. Just like Dad does."

Chapter Twenty-Five

———————— ❧⟨❦⟩ ————————

A FLY COULD'VE MADE a comfortable home in Aunt Juju's gaping mouth. After a few seconds, his uncle used two fingers to raise her bottom jaw and kept them there. His kind smile coated the others in the room, but his outstretched right hand was meant to touch Emmeline only. "Hello there. My great-nephew's had plenty good to say 'bout you."

McKinley nudged his fiancée-to-be forward.

Emmeline's green eyes sparkled as she sidled up to the patient and he enveloped her small hand within his. After a beat, when she seemed to realize he had no plans of letting go, she perched on the edge of his bed. "You'll have to fill me in, Mr. Mason, and I'll tell you what's true and what's not."

McKinley thought his aunt would explode. He was grateful

for his great-uncle's staying hand that kept the pin in the grenade.

"So tell me 'bout yourself." Uncle Lawrence freed his wife's jaw and wrapped both his hands around Emmeline's.

She glanced back at McKinley. Sensing her silent entreaty, he moved behind her so she could rest against him. "Well, as Mac probably told you, I'm Emmie, the youngest of the three George children."

"*Emmeline!* I knew I'd heard that name before," Aunt Juju hissed. Her lips moved silently as if she was telling a story for her ears only.

Mom cut her eyes at Dad, who seemed incapable of uttering a word. "I was wonderin' when you'd remember because you've met her people, Aunt Julia: Knox and Sarah George, who own George & Company."

His mother seemed to look pointedly at his father before continuing, "Surely you remember seein' her runnin' through my house. You probably even told her to sit down more than once. Our little Emmeline is all grown-up now, with an emphasis on *our.*"

To McKinley's ears, his mother's laugh sounded forced. He silently thanked her for the effort she made and read the *you're welcome* in her barely perceptible nod. Mom set down her coffee and the plastic bag in the chair beside the bed and withdrew packs of peanut butter crackers, two oranges, popcorn, some beef jerky, and a small pack of Hershey's Kisses, one of his father's favorite treats. He hadn't seen Dad enjoy them in a long time.

"And you're tellin' me that *this* is—"

"The future Mrs. Emmeline George Baldwin. Yes, Aunt Juju." He kissed the top of his fiancée's head.

His great-aunt shook her head back and forth, exhibiting either disbelief or outright rejection. Uncle Lawrence's hand inched across the sheet in her direction, but she snatched back her fingers and braced her elbows on the arms of her chair. "Well, I'll be a—"

"Julia." His father didn't move, but his voice traveled across the room without having to raise it one decibel.

McKinley remembered that voice. It was the one that kept him from dashing into the street after his soccer ball; that used to caution him he'd best watch his tone and append a *sir* after an insolent-sounding *yes*; that told him something one more time without actually telling him one more time. At that moment, McKinley gladly welcomed the sound that once warned him his day of reckoning was coming.

"I don't know why you speakin' my name like that, Frederick. He's the one needs a good talkin'-to." She pointed at her great-nephew. "What are you thinkin', Fred Jr.? And just who is this *Mac*?" She sniffed after she said the name.

"You're looking at him, Aunt Juju, the very one you call Fred Jr. and who my mama named McKinley." Part of him wished he could snatch the words out of the air, but it was too late. They had exploded like a sneeze and sprayed the unwitting ears of everyone in the room. He rested his hand on Emmie's shoulder, steadying himself for whatever else she had to say.

He watched her settle against the back of her chair. Yet he had a feeling she was merely getting comfortable, not relaxing—a big difference when it came to Aunt Juju. The woman had plenty of words clamoring for attention on her tongue, and more than likely she was taking her time deciding which one to extract and show off.

"What gave you the idea to shorten my great-nephew's name?"

As McKinley weighed whether to address her tone or her words, he felt Emmeline shift against him. Her pulse quickened beneath his fingertips. Before she could respond, he shrugged, his mouth forming an upside-down U, and responded, "I don't know. I did, I suppose. I think it's cute. Just as special as Fred Jr."

Beside him, Mom gasped. She seemed to ready herself to jump into the fray, but McKinley caught her eye and shook his head. She cleared her throat and stepped back a little.

"But that's not your name, at least not the name your mama gave you. Here you go at twenty-seven years old, lettin' some girl use a derivative of your name.

"Em-me-linne," Julia sneered, making the three-syllable name sound like four, "that woman over there carried Fred Jr. for nine months, sweated through a whole day's worth of labor, and nearly died for him. You can ask her."

That was the first time Aunt Juju had ever given his mama that much credit. It was almost funny. Almost.

Dad retrieved the bag of candy and opened it. Then he unwrapped a Hershey's Kiss and popped it into his mouth.

His fingers crushed the silver foil. "I don't know if I'd call it a derivative necessarily, Aunt Juju. And technically, didn't my mama—your sister—give me my name? Paulette allowed me to pass it along so our son here could be a 'Junior.' And since it's his, I suppose he can shorten it, change it, or certainly give it away to whomever he pleases."

Julia smoothed out nonexistent wrinkles on her blue polyester skirt and shifted her position in her chair. "Even to the one who tried to steal it? All I know is I never heard not one of us breathe the name *Mac*."

Dad shrugged. "With all due respect, you have now, and you'd better get used to it. I suspect *Mac's* future wife will use it quite often. Aunt Ju-li-a."

· ↝ ·

"Did the doctor say when we would hear the results from the stress test and blood work? It's gettin' late." Paulette opened the bag of cheddar popcorn she'd packed and sidled over to the far left corner of the room. She hadn't planned to eat any of the snacks she'd brought, but she was out of something to occupy her mouth. If it was full, it was less likely to get her in trouble. *Lord, guard my tongue.*

From her spot, Paulette figured she could watch what was going on but not get caught in the fray. It also put her a little closer to her husband, whose eyes followed her every movement.

"Fred, are you hungry? I see you watchin' that popcorn like a hawk. Paulette, why didn't you offer your husband somethin' to eat?" Julia obviously didn't miss much, even with one eye on the younger couple chatting in such a lively fashion with Lawrence.

I wonder, does her head spin all the way around or only in my direction? "Fred, are you hungry? Want to share this bag of popcorn?"

"That's not real food," Julia groused. "He probably needs—"

"Thank you, Etta. I'd love some." Fred scooted back to her on the wheeled stool he'd borrowed from the nurses' station. He winked at Paulette when his lips brushed her fingertips.

She blushed as he crunched on the kernels.

"Child, you havin' hot flashes over there?"

Paulette leaned around Fred to see her in-law. "No, Aunt Julia, I'm fine. It's feelin' close in here." She handed Fred the bag and whispered, "Here you go. I'm going to see what the lovebirds are talkin' about with your uncle. Feel free to make your family's travel arrangements any time you get good and ready."

"Emmeline. That's a pretty name." Uncle Lawrence still cupped one of the young woman's hands in both of his. He looked more spirited than he had since arriving in Hickory Grove. Hard to believe it was a mere three days ago.

"Why, thank you, Uncle Lawrence." Emmeline smiled at him. "It's a family name."

"He's not your uncle yet, so don't you get too familiar over there," Julia grumbled. "'Bout as bad as that doctor yesterday callin' Lawrence his grandpa. Black men aren't everybody's uncle."

"He did not call him Grandpa. He said Uncle Lawrence reminded him of his grandfather. Big difference," Fred snickered. "And I believe my uncle invited Emmeline to call him by that name. She's going to be using it soon enough, so you, dear Aunt, might want to think of something for her to call you before she comes up with something on her own."

Mentally, Paulette rolled her eyes at the sheer stubborn persnicketiness of the older woman, who persisted in having her way as well as everybody else's. She strained to keep a placid expression on her face and swallow her irritation, but she was running out of cheeks to turn. "Aunt Julia, maybe you're hungry. Would you care for some peanut butter crackers? There's some fruit over there, too."

"What I'd care for is some real food, not crackers. And you know I got sugar, so I can't eat just anything."

"Sugar?" Emmeline's face wore a question mark.

McKinley leaned over her shoulder and explained in a low voice that carried to everyone else, "Diabetes."

"That's why I brought some beef jerky. It's a good snack for someone with your condition. Lots of protein, so it's filling, and it tastes good, too. Great for traveling on the train. Want me to get it for you?"

"Fine. Anything to keep you from whipping out some of those sausages you might be hidin' in yo' purse." Julia laughed, as if the rest of the room could be fooled into thinking her snide comment was meant to be humorous.

Fred slowly rose from his stool. "Juju, I thought it was pretty kind and considerate of my wife to bring you something to eat. I sho' nuff didn't think of it. It would do you and the rest of us a world of good if you kept your blood sugar at the right levels."

Julia pursed her lips and looked the other way.

"Well, I think I'm going to stretch my legs and see if I can get some information from the nurses at the station." Fred patted Paulette's shoulder and left the room.

Uncle Lawrence adjusted his position on the bed. "So you say that's a family name?"

Paulette wondered if the older gentleman was committing all this information to memory to write it down in a family journal somewhere, since he couldn't possibly be flirting with that young girl, as pretty as she was. She took up residence on the stool her husband had abandoned and rolled around to the end of the bed. There, she parked herself in the middle, where she could watch Uncle Lawrence's interaction with the young couple.

"Yes, sir. My grandmother on my father's side."

Paulette had to give it to Emmeline. That child knew how to love others well.

"Oh, so the same side of the family what tried to take all my daddy's land. Is that what you sayin'?"

"Excuse me, Mrs. Mason?"

And long-suffering, too. Paulette sighed.

Julia smirked. "You tryin' to sweet-talk your way into your *uncle's* Social Security check? 'Cause that's 'bout all we got to offer, other than that broken-down house and ten acres of trees and grass our family had to scrabble to hold on to."

"Julia." Paulette's voice was so quiet it screamed for attention. "Emmeline is about to be callin' me Mama or something close to it, which makes me a happy woman. And it means I won't let you punish her for something her long-ago cousin did. Yes, it was wrong, but it's also wrong for you to hold her color against her the way you've held mine against me."

"I knew you'd defend her. Like sticks with like." Julia puffed up like a male peacock, parading her opinions instead of feathers. Her eyes slid to McKinley. "You know they say a man marries his mama. I guess you're provin' the truth of it."

"Oh, Aunt Julia!" McKinley sounded more disappointed than offended.

Paulette shook her head, feeling nothing but pity for the woman. "Unlike your nephew, Emmeline doesn't have to steal *anything* from anybody in this room because she apparently has all she ever wanted in this boy right here, the one you yourself said I nearly died to bring into the world. You will not denigrate her because her color means what it shouldn't mean to anybody else, includin' you."

"I . . . You . . . Did you call Fred a thief?" For once, Julia's words seemed to have escaped her.

"Now, Juju-bean, settle down. Settle down. This ain't you." Uncle Lawrence finally released Emmeline to stroke his wife's fingers, curled up in a fist on the side of his bed. "You know better. What's gotten into you? Emmeline don't have nuthin' to do with all that. Stop causin' all this trouble in here." The sizzle in his eyes had gone flat.

It always amazed Paulette, the good Lawrence perceived in Julia. He used love as a strong pair of corrective lenses that helped him see his wife's heart more clearly than Paulette ever could or wanted to. What she regarded as bitterness, he understood to be pain; when Julia struck out at the world, he considered it her means of defending her own. He could laugh at his wife when Paulette wanted to pummel her and pray over her prone body. But the strain of loving the woman was draining his life's blood.

Knowing she'd let her temper get the best of her and him, Paulette moved to the side of his bed. She tapped Emmeline and nudged her out of the way. "Uncle, are we tirin' you out? We'll leave so you can get some rest. Once we hear from the doctor, we'll come back. That sound okay? We'll see you at the house anyway, and you can use this time with . . . your wife." Her lips refused to form the word *aunt*.

McKinley took Emmeline's hand, and the two backed toward the door.

But the elderly man had some words stored up from all his years of quietness. "You know, there's nuthin' wrong with seeing color. Nuthin' a'tall. I'd think either somethin' was wrong with your eyes or you were lyin' if you didn't. How else would I enjoy the changin' of the seasons or the dark brown in my honeybun's eyes if I couldn't appreciate differences like that?

"But thinking 'less than' or 'more than'? Other? Despisin' somebody else or yourself because of the particular hue of your skin? That's somethin' else altogether." He slowly turned his ashen face from side to side on the pillow.

"Julia, remember how you used some fadin' cream when we was first married? You thought you'd look better if yo' skin was lighter. Just won't happy until you could be somethin' you won't. I used to tell her, 'Julia, unless you gon' stand naked outside in the sun and scare off the birds, you gon' go to heaven or hell the color God made you, and then it sho' won't matter!'"

Aunt Julia spluttered, "Now, Lawrence, no need to—"

"Hush now, hush now. We all done some silly things in our life, things we regret. Y'all shoulda seen how I used to slick back my hair with this pomade I bought. Remember how he'd come by the house Saturday nights, knowin' folks was gettin' ready for church? That stuff smelled like antifreeze but won't good enough for my car, let alone my hair. Nearly took out ev'ry strand on my head." He patted his smooth and shiny pate.

"A man hit my car one night when I was 'bout yo' age, Paulette. To' it to pieces and left me stranded 'side the road. When he drove off, I could see him laughin'. And you know what? He looked like that sweet young girl over there my great-nephew's holdin' on to. After that, I had to walk down that dirt road from our house to the main street—y'all know all 'bout that road—for a whole month 'cause a so-called friend didn't wont to mess up his new wheels pickin' me up for work. And he was the shade of you, McKinley.

"But what sense would it make for me to hold their sins against you? Or even to keep holdin' it against them, when they both could be dead and gone? How you gon' pay back what you didn't borrow? I refuse to spend my God-given time rectifyin' old problems when the day's gon' give me a whole heap of to-dos to handle, especially since He also gave me this woman here who's more than a handful, let me tell you. And she the brownest thang in the room."

Julia's lips flattened as she glared at her husband. "Old man, you're talkin' out yo' head."

"This here might not forget—" Lawrence tapped his temple with his index finger—"what this can forgive." He pointed to his chest. Then he propped himself up on his elbow and looked past McKinley and Emmeline on his left. "I say let the pain stay buried and enjoy the life walkin' and talkin' on this side of the dirt. What say you, nephew?"

Paulette nearly felt a whoosh of wind by the way they all whirled toward the hospital door and discovered an unsmiling Fred holding it open. Glory be, he'd brought the doctor.

· ⁊ ·

"Well, that went . . . um . . ." Paulette stopped in the driveway that curved under the hospital awning and squinted into the late-afternoon sun. The words she seemed to search for were like the puffy white cumulus clouds hovering in the Carolina-blue sky: they appeared within reach but were impossible to grasp.

Fred waited to see if she would complete her thoughts. He was struggling himself and had nothing to offer.

"We could compare that visit to a tetanus shot. It hurt going in, and we'll be sore tomorrow." Paulette glanced back at him. "But it had to be done." She shivered a little and rubbed her arms, bare from her elbows down. The day had cooled as the sun had traveled toward the western edge of the horizon. Paulette stepped out from under the hospital's awning and peered into the parking lot, her hand shading her eyes.

"I suppose that's one way to put it." Fred didn't quite know how to navigate the path forward with his wife after last night. Dealing with his uncle's collapse had distracted them from their anger and hurt feelings, but not even their time together had dispelled them. Not completely. It had only softened the sharper edges. For him, the acrimony was suspended over them, like those low-hanging clouds holding her attention. It might take another storm for it to break.

He expelled a breath. This wasn't the time, however, to address it. "We should get the car. The nurse will arrive with Uncle Lawrence and Juju at any moment."

"How about one of us waits here while the other gets the car? That way, if they come down, they won't be wondering if we ran off, never to be seen again."

Junior—*McKinley, doggone it*—and a shell-shocked Emmeline had sprinted for the door the minute the doctor had shown up to discuss the results of the stress test and the conditions of Uncle Lawrence's release. Fred wondered about the differences in their family dynamics, if white folks expressed their feelings the same way. If those two had any sense, they'd hightail it out of town.

Fred remembered the way Paulette was last night, when they, too, had found a way to leave their world behind, at least for a time. Something about his face must have revealed his thoughts because Paulette inched away from him. She hugged herself around the middle and stared off into the distance. Silence set up shop between them as cars pulled in and out of the parking lot. The light at the corner changed from green to amber to red.

"So . . . rock, paper, scissors?"

Fred started. "I'm sorry, what?"

She balanced her right fist in her other palm. "Rock, paper, scissors . . . to see who gets to drive."

Who gets to drive . . . Fred snorted. When McKinley was a toddler, he made car trips an ordeal. He'd talk their ears off and request one thing after another—books, food, hand-holding, all manner of attention. Even a shorter thirty-minute jaunt felt like a cross-country ride. He and Paulette used to compete to see who would "get to drive"; the passenger had to entertain McKinley while the person behind the wheel focused on the road and sat in relative peace.

He covered both her hands with his. "No need, Etta. You can drive. She's my aunt."

"Doesn't that make her my family, too?" A light breeze picked up a long tendril that trailed across the bridge of her nose and stuck to her cinnamon-colored lip gloss.

Fred couldn't help himself. He hooked his finger around it and tucked it back behind her ear. It felt like his hand smoothed down the right side of her thick hair on its own accord. He kissed her and felt her lips cling to his, even when he murmured against them, "Your family, my burden."

She rested her brow on his chest. "Do you see me as your burden, too? And this relationship of McKinley's—is this one more thing you have to bear?"

"Etta, I—"

Suddenly the hospital's automatic sliding doors parted, and two wheelchairs emerged side by side. A hospital staff member, sweat trickling down her temples, pushed the one holding a grinning, refreshed Uncle Lawrence. Juju zoomed up beside her nephew, a small carryall balanced across her thighs.

"There you are! But where's the car? Y'all standin' out here chattin', and we ready to go! Your uncle needs to get home and rest. Come on now!"

"That's just what we were doin', Aunt Julia."

Somehow Paulette could always dredge up some kindness for the woman. She dug into Fred's right front pocket, grabbed his keys, and without a second look, darted across the road that separated the hospital from the lot as a pickup truck zoomed in.

"Etta!" Fred reached for his wife, but it was too late.

Chapter Twenty-Six

Something stirred him, a sound that broke the oppressive quiet of the house. McKinley usually found respite in his bottom bunk, but it wasn't the oasis it was before, even at this early hour. Not from the silence that had invaded the house. The sun had just awakened from its night's rest, and weak, pink-tinged arms of light barely stretched across his room to his bed. They never made it to his pillow, where he huddled in the shadows.

But what was that? McKinley craned his head from under the wood slats above him. He threw back the covers and swung his legs toward the floor. When he saw his sock-covered toes, he remembered sprawling across the bed in his jeans and pull-over around two in the morning after getting home from the hospital. Still tired, the noise drew him from his room into the hall to investigate. At first, the only sound was the creak of his own feet on the vintage hardwood. And then . . . there it was, the far-off noise that had called to his subconscious ear. *Chink.*

At the top of the stairs, he heard it again. *Chink. Chink.* It seemed to emanate from somewhere outside their walls. McKinley padded down the stairs in his fuzzy socks, the green- and red-striped pair his mother had stuffed into his hand-embroidered Christmas stocking last year. He must have dropped them in his room when he'd skedaddled to Philadelphia immediately after the holiday. Knowing her, she'd washed them and stowed them in the drawer with the rest of the odds and ends he'd left behind. But he couldn't think about that now.

Chink. Chink. Chink. McKinley froze and looked up. It was louder, but not close. Then he moved to another step and—"Shoot!"—landed on the protruding nail. If only he'd done a better job with that hammer. He unhooked his sock and mourned the hole the snag left behind. *Chink.*

He continued down the back stairs. At the bottom he turned the corner and entered the kitchen. The stove burners were cold, the coffeepot empty. *Chink* went the sound, closer now and sharper in the sunroom. McKinley peered through the condensation on the windows, a problem his parents had never addressed in their twenty-five-year history in the house. New windows. Dad had avowed they'd ruin the integrity of their turn-of-the-century Victorian. Mama argued they'd improve the integrity of their heating and cooling bill. Every winter, his father won the battle and his mother prayed about the war.

Chink. There. McKinley threw open the French door and was at the top of the steps before he heard his mother's voice in his head. *"Don't let bugs in the house."* He secured the door, then descended to the sidewalk and cut through the dewy grass to the end of the backyard. His socks and the bare spot on his sole were soaked by the time he reached his mother's garden. McKinley poked his fingers through the metal squares and pressed his forehead to the wire fencing, mindless of the imprint they'd make on his skin.

"Dad, stop. What are you doing?" Somehow he managed to speak over the clump of anger wedged in the back of his throat.

Chink. The light, early morning air must not have been strong enough to carry his aggrieved voice because his father never stopped chopping. Feathery fronds, orange and purple root vegetables, clods of earth . . . the carnage stretched from end to end of the garden his mother had worked so hard to grow. Ironically, her efforts had borne fruit. In the yard, at least. As McKinley watched, his father destroyed every green thing in the seventy-two-square-foot space in under an hour.

· ∽ ·

Fred took a brush to his nails but didn't think he'd ever get the dirt from under them. His shower had barely helped.

He held up his fingers to the vanity lights above the mirror and figured he'd have to get used to the grains of black embedded at their tips. Fred turned off the faucet and moved to the closet. Though he avoided looking at Paulette's half, he couldn't help but wade through her perfume that hung in the air. Once dressed, he trudged to the kitchen to prepare breakfast. That way, when his aunt and uncle were packed and ready, they could get a move on. They were getting on that train with Uncle Lawrence's cousin; Fred was making sure of that. His heart couldn't take any more.

He pulled out eggs, half-and-half, and 2 percent milk from the refrigerator, then moved to the pantry to retrieve all-purpose flour, vanilla extract, cinnamon, and brown sugar. Fred went through the recipe he kept stored in his brain and checked off the ingredients for the French toast casserole his aunt loved. He might as well send her off in style. *All sugared up despite her sugar.*

Fred had whisked the eggs and poured both kinds of milk before the familiar whir heralded the motorized approach of his aunt. He measured out a tablespoon of vanilla extract and added it to the mixture. "Morning, Juju." Fred hadn't come across much good in it, so he chose not to lie and called the moment what it was.

"Good morning, Nephew. Finally usin' that fancy stove?"

Fred's hands stilled on the cabinet door, and his eyes closed. When he was able to speak again, he couldn't keep his words from vibrating with a mixture of sadness and what felt suspiciously like rage. "Please don't say that ever again, not if you want to be welcomed in my house." He didn't move again until he heard the wheelchair fade into the distance.

An hour later, Fred set the table for three. As much as his spirit could have used a good talking-to by his uncle, there was no way he could stomach a meal, let alone a full conversation, with the woman who'd treated Paulette like an outlaw. And he'd allowed it, thinking it was his way of honoring his elders and all that his people had endured. What it had taken to show him the truth of how he'd dishonored his wife! And Julia's lack of remorse made it so much worse. Fred would have to trust Junior to be the man at the head of the table while he prepared his heart for the drive to the station.

Before he could return to his room, he heard the tapping of Uncle Lawrence's cane. Since Fred could tell he was unaccompanied, he leaned against a chair to wait for him.

"Hey there, Nephew. Whatcha know good?" The light in Uncle Lawrence's smile was dim. His gnarly fingers gripped the younger man's shoulder.

Fred reached up with his right hand and laid it atop his uncle's. His eyes welled as he whispered, more to himself than to his attentive listener, "How am I supposed to let her go?"

· ᥱᏉ ·

If McKinley was being honest with himself, he'd left his skills behind on his intramural soccer field. He balanced his toe on the ball and stood there panting, with a fist on each hip, staring across the backyard.

But it wasn't only his lack of skill that prevented him from dribbling effectively. His feet kept missing the ball because he couldn't keep his eyes trained on it. They kept straying to the outskirts of the yard. To the garden—or what his dad had left of it. McKinley crouched over the ball and caught his breath as falling acorns pummeled the back of his neck.

Finally he pushed himself erect, and stiffly, he launched the ball into the detached garage with a firm kick. It crashed into the front wheels of a pair of bicycles and they landed all a-tangle on the concrete. McKinley dragged himself over and set his parents' bicycles aright. After kicking their stands into place, he considered the stairs leading up to his dad's office. There'd be few family-oriented memories there.

McKinley took the steps two at a time. At first, he was surprised to find the door unlocked but then concluded, *Nothing left to hide.* But the minute he stepped inside, the model home greeted him. Immediately he rewound time, back to helping his father paint his mother's gift. The argument between his parents. How Mom looked when they bent over his great-uncle. Their ensuing trip to the hospital. Her run-in with the truck.

He stomped over to the house, so tall on the metal table, it nearly blocked the window behind it. He only intended to touch the replica, to feel the wood under his hands, but as he reached it, he tripped over the trash can filled with crumpled paper, and his hand caught the rolling stand's edge. The locked wheels prevented it from moving, but his weight tipped the small cart and sent the three-story Victorian crashing to the floor. McKinley knelt there on the splinters, in the middle of the purple shards of wood, plastic windows, and glossy black shingles.

And that's where Monroe and Emmeline found him.

"Mac!" She ran over, leaving her brother behind in the doorway. She squatted beside McKinley and rubbed his back. "Baby . . . what happened?"

"The house . . . I broke it." He picked up one chunk of wood after another.

"Dude, we all can see that." Monroe's tone was dry. Footsteps crunched toward the mess.

McKinley peered up into his best friend's face. He tried not to focus on the puffy black-and-blue streaks marring the pale skin encircling Monroe's left eye.

Emmeline reached under his elbow and helped him to his feet. She winced and spun the sapphire around on her finger. "I hope I didn't poke you. I've gotta get used to wearin' this thing." She kissed him.

Monroe grimly extended his hand. "You know, bruh, it may not look like it . . . but it's all good."

McKinley dropped a small pile of broken shingles into the open palm of his future brother-in-law. "You think? Tell my dad that."

· ↭ ·

Fred usually didn't drive with his window down because he didn't want the dust to coat his precious leather. Today was different. In fact, he realized he preferred the cool, natural breeze blowing in his face. It cleared some of the cobwebs in his mind, though it did nothing to ease the pain. When he drove into the lot, he circled to the back instead and parked. He draped his arm across the window frame and tapped on the outside of his door while staring up at the building.

He'd spent a lot of time at George & Company. Too much, by all intents and purposes. It had taken everything from him. How different his answers would be, if only he could rewind time! He could still see Etta's face, so earnest, so beautiful.

"What would you give up, if it meant savin' your family?"

Fred closed his eyes and lay back on the headrest. "Everything," he murmured.

"I mean it. Would you walk away from G&C for McKinley? For me?"

Last Saturday, her question had stunned him and made him trip over his words. Not today. "Yes . . . yes."

"I mean it, Fred. Let it go . . ."

"I will. I am." Fred imagined bars crisscrossing the large tinted window of his office.

"Everything you do is about makin' up for what you didn't have, what your family lost . . . You spend each waking minute thinkin' about how to prove your worth at that company, a company that once rejected your grandfather."

"You mean that stole from my grandfather," Fred whispered, repeating the words he'd told Paulette. "But as wrong as that was, I was the one guilty of lying to you, Etta. Looks like we all get to reap the consequences, so much I brought on myself."

Fred climbed from the car and walked over to the smoking area. Despite the chilly breeze, the fetid odor of cigarettes lingered in the air. He figured the smell emanated from the blue barrel squatting at the edge of the clearing, where the smokers tossed their butts at the end of their break. When Fred peeked into it, he saw it was about half-full. He didn't much care anymore, about the smell or the smokers. They weren't his problem anymore. He squinted up at his second-floor office. Sitting at his drafting table in that chair of Etta's would feel like another cancerous animal eating away at his soul.

"I only want you to hold on to us, not the wrongs that've been done to you . . . Workin' there does nothing but drive a wedge between us, all of us, and within yourself. You can't enjoy your life's work the way you keep holdin' on to the past. But what about our future? Your son's future?"

Plumb out of answers, real and imagined, Fred propped his right foot on a stump and balanced an elbow on his knee. With his back to the building, he stared into the copse that abutted the smoking area. The maples and oaks sprinkled among the pines seemed to glow, vibrant with fiery reds and golds even though all those colors signified impending death and decay.

"Fred?"

The voice jolted him away from all his morbid thoughts. He swung around. "Kim? Wh-what are you doing here on a Saturday afternoon?"

She shrugged. "My husband took the kids to a game, so

I thought I'd come here and put the finishing touches on a project."

Shame on him. Aside from the interview, he never took the time to ask his shift supervisor about her family. Her life hadn't mattered to him outside of what she contributed to his precious furniture production schedule.

Yet Kim's gaze was the one reflecting pity and concern. "How are you?"

Alone. But he didn't say it. Fred didn't have the heart to tell the woman the truth, especially since she had opened hers so genuinely to him, a man she barely knew and who hadn't taken the time to know her.

She must have sensed his fruitless search for the right words and put him out of his misery. "You know how people talk, especially around here, and I thought you might need something to lift your spirits. Maybe it'll give you something to look forward to, whenever you're ready to come back to work. Seriously, you won't be disappointed—I mean, I hope you won't be. Would you mind . . . ?" She pointed toward the second building. "I was cleaning up after myself, and when I went to the dumpster, I saw you over here. It won't take but a minute."

Fred stood upright. "You were on the floor?"

"Yep. I come here on the weekends sometimes. I hope that's okay."

Any other time, Fred probably would have had something to say. It wasn't the best practice, allowing employees free rein of the property outside normal work hours. But focusing on the world's idea of "best practices" was why he was sitting here by his lonesome. Without his wife. It was about time he chose the best part when it came to spiritual things.

"Sure, Kim. As far as I'm concerned, have at it. Going forward, you'll have to take it up with the new management."

Fred motioned for Kim to lead the way, and they started walking toward the factory. It was weird not seeing other cars in the lot. More and more, he felt like he was needed elsewhere.

"New management? You're stepping down?" Her eyebrows furrowed.

"It's about time. In fact, it's past time. For many reasons. But you're going to love the three I'm thinking about handing things off to. I'll still be around drawing stuff."

Kim said nothing.

Fred's thoughts settled down in the silence that rested between them as they walked to the floor. He cocked an eye toward the sky, knowing that the breeze would turn soon enough and bring snow along with it. He wondered how cold it would feel when he was alone in a drafty house of his own creation.

At the door, Kim turned to him, her expression hopeful. "Ready?"

He nodded, wishing he could muster up a smile in return, or at least adopt a more pleasant expression. But it just wasn't in him. Fred propped open the heavy door and let her lead the way. It was strange, the quietness there. He'd loved the noise and busyness of furniture making. Missing the music, he looked up to the rafters.

"I know. But there's also something almost worshipful about the silence, too." Kim seemed to read his mind. "When I'm here by myself, I can pray and talk to the Lord. Tell Him all about it, as my mama used to say. Nobody's asking me for anything, so I can do what I want." She chuckled, her eyes wide. "Oh, I don't mean you."

Fred did smile then. Grace received, grace given. "No offense taken. It makes sense. So where're we going?" Out of habit, he slapped his hands together.

"Right this way!" Kim bopped down the main walkway toward the back. She clicked on lights as she went.

They passed idle machines, empty rooms, and clean saws. Fred was a stickler for leaving the floor sparkling and ready for Monday's work and his employees followed suit. He was so busy checking out the workstations he didn't realize where they were going until he was there.

"Oh!" Fred cried.

Kim's hand flew out as if to steady him, but then she withdrew it and let him alone. Fred unglued his feet and advanced toward the "project" she had felt called to finish that day, in time for him to see it.

The chair, the special piece of kitchen furniture that would introduce the Etta Collection. All its parts fit together perfectly. The cherry stain glowed in the soft shaft of light falling upon it. Fred tipped closer, scared to touch it at first. Then he barely grazed its arms, legs, and slightly curved feet with the palm of his hand. He touched each spindle on the backrest and the dowels where each part fit into the chair. The truth of the maple shone through, fashioned by hand into a design that would've honored his wife and their marriage.

If only he had.

"Fred, what do you think?"

He half turned toward Kim, unwilling to completely take his eyes and hands off this precious gift. He stroked one of its smooth arms. "It's beautiful. Etta would love this."

Kim shuffled up beside him. Her hand was soft on his bicep. "Then why don't you take it to her, Fred. Show her the heart you put into this chair, your heart for her. Your marriage might seem dead to you, but I believe you've sown some good seeds among the tares."

· ❧ ·

Paulette couldn't believe she'd found a room in Montford, a historic neighborhood on the outskirts of Asheville. Such a beautiful town. At this time of year, its proximity to the Biltmore estate kept innkeepers hopping and bed-and-breakfasts full. Speaking of breakfast . . .

Paulette prayed, then stuck the dainty tines of her fork into the creamy edges of the baked egg in front of her. She'd managed to grip the steering wheel with one hand and the fingertips of the other but knew she couldn't wield a knife and fork. Paulette shifted her left arm, hoping to find a comfortable position for her cast, and plucked an end off her peach scone. As tasty as it was, her appetite refused to cooperate.

"Would you like some orange juice, ma'am?"

A soft voice and a crystal carafe snagged Paulette's attention. She wondered if her smile looked like one. "No, but more coffee would be lovely. With sugar and French vanilla creamer please."

"Sure thing." The woman looked at the barely touched tureen. "Not to your liking? I could prepare you something else. Some oatmeal? An omelet?"

"Oh no! No! I'm just getting used to my new limitations." Paulette held up her left arm, still sore and a little itchy. "Once I get another eight ounces of coffee, everything will be fine. I'm sorry; your name escapes me."

"Sabeth. I'm the chef and my husband runs the house." She nodded at the cast. "What happened?"

What happened? What hadn't happened? "I had a fight with a Ford pickup, and it won. Handily."

The chef's blonde eyebrows nearly disappeared in her brown roots.

"No, it's nothing that serious. I ran out in front of a car without looking, and here you go." Paulette wiggled her arm carefully.

"Feels like you got hit by a truck?" Sabeth covered her mouth. "Too soon?"

Paulette surprised herself by chuckling. "Actually, I do. Leaving your husband on your sixtieth trip around the sun will do that to you. Happy birthday to me."

Chapter Twenty-Seven

Fred had no idea where to find his wife, but he determined to do just that. Yesterday he started with Hickory Grove. Now he was driving around Rutherford County with a piece of kitchen furniture poking through the leather in his back seat. *It's probably not real leather anyway, so stop thinking about your car, Fred.* Which was easier for him to say than do.

Where should I start?

Paulette had seemed icy cold the entire time the two of them waited for McKinley to pick up his aunt and uncle and during their stint in the emergency room. She had refused to let Fred touch her. Really, he'd been afraid to, gauging the frozen look on her face. After the doctor had set her arm and released her, she'd Ubered home, which was nothing less than ridiculous. Her driver had merely followed him to his own front door. She'd taken an hour to pack their biggest suitcase, told him he could set fire to her piano, and left her house keys in the basket and her wedding rings in his palm. Then she was gone.

But where? Sad to say, McKinley hadn't heard from her either. Maybe he and his fiancée would learn a lesson or two from his father's mistakes, on what love between a man and a woman does and does not look like. Or better yet, his son would learn to listen to what his Father could teach him about it.

Hickory Grove wasn't but so big, and Fred spent hours driving in and out of every hotel and motel he saw. He'd even checked with a few local bed-and-breakfasts. Since Paulette very well could have driven out of town as fast and as far as she could get, Fred had expanded the scope of his search. Just as she had refused to ride back to the house with him when she was discharged, he refused to return to his house without Etta. The longer he drove, however, he all but left hope behind . . . until he glanced in his rearview mirror and his eyes settled on the chair.

His hope sat on four legs—and some pointy parts which threatened to rip a hole in his back seat.

Unable to stop himself, the thorough, methodical part of Fred coaxed him to drive into a gas station and retrieve the blanket he kept in the trunk. He'd tuck it around the legs and feet as protection. It would only take a second, and it would reduce his distractions and settle his mind, at least on that front. Yet, when he popped the trunk, he found there was no blanket. It was empty except for the emergency snack bag and tool kit.

Now Fred's frenzied inner man had to get the blanket back. Though he didn't know where his wife was, he did know where to find one of the last things that had touched her. He couldn't lose it. Fred refused to believe that the wind or a wild animal had made off with it. It had to be there. *Papa's house.*

It took him twelve minutes to get to the dirt road on the right, marked by bunches of Eastern bluestars. More than two feet tall, they were already donning their brilliant-yellow autumn wardrobe. Fred paid little attention to the wildlife as he began his slow ascent to the land that had set his life-changing events in motion so many years and family members ago.

Evening had set upon him, and he could barely detect the strip of water through the tree cover that would soon enough be as threadbare as the sweater he used to wear to school. His grandfather had poured every spare dime into the land to provide for his family; seeing the house in such a state of disrepair tore at him. Of its own accord, Fred's foot let off the gas. As much as he wanted the blanket, he dreaded the moment when he crossed the road hump and made the left to approach the old homestead.

· ☙ ·

Paulette was perched on the top step of the tumbledown porch, the striped blanket wrapped around her legs. She squinted as the incoming headlights spanned the yard and a car traveled like a boat on stormy seas toward the house. Finally it took the last big dip and jostled into place behind hers, in front of the house. Paulette cradled her left arm close to her side and slid her stack of sticky notes partly under her left thigh. Her heart beat a slow, heavy rhythm in her chest as her answered prayer climbed from his Mercedes.

Fred froze with his right foot in the car and a hand on the frame of his window. The *ding-ding-ding* seemed to stir him, and he opened the rear door. Grunting, he worked to unload something from his back seat before shutting both doors with his hip. Fred cast a long shadow on the ground as he lumbered in front of the headlights and set his armload down. Then he trudged toward her. The boards on the bottom step creaked and caved in under his foot as he balanced on one elbow and bent toward her.

"Happy belated birthday."

Paulette laid her good hand on his cheek, and when he stretched toward her, she met him halfway. "You came for me," she whispered against his mouth.

The lights on the car clicked off, and they rested their foreheads against each other. Paulette wondered if Bett had wanted her own husband to fight for her, if she'd waited for him by those roses growing in her family's backyard. Did Daddy need love to look more like his idea of it instead of what it was? Did their relationship need more sunlight in those early rainy days of marriage? In the end, neither of them was able to bury all they'd ever known, thought, or believed about themselves, not even for Paulette, and let something new and true grow in its stead.

Fred reached across Paulette's lap and withdrew the stack of notes. He lifted one after another. "Still layin' out your steps?"

Paulette shrugged. "A little bit. Tryin' to figure out what I'd say when I saw you."

He smiled. "*When*. So you knew I was coming?"

"I prayed you would. And look what God did. He gave me a private party." She kissed him again.

He sat on the step below her. "I have to say this is much better." He peeled off the top square and handed it to her. "Yes."

She read it and crumpled it. "You'd do that for me?"

Fred shrugged. "No, I *did* that. For us. But are you sure you won't mind all my clutter in the guest room?"

"It's not like it'll be used anytime soon." Her look was long and unblinking.

He riffled through the notes and pulled one from the middle. "I guess that takes care of this one and yes, they're back in Virginia."

Paulette let out a slow breath as she accepted the square. "How's Uncle Lawrence?"

"Better, now that he can get fussed at on his own turf. Juju is fine, too—not that you wrote down that question."

She studied her palm.

Fred lifted her chin with his fingertip. "I'm sorry I didn't shelter you like a husband is supposed to, Etta. I felt like I owed them for what they did for me when I was a boy."

"Owed them for what was freely given? I'm sure even Julia wouldn't consider your relationship recompense."

"That sounds like a fancy word for payback—like taking G&C from the Georges?"

She cleared her throat. "Seems to me you love that company as much as you hate it."

The crickets played a background concerto as he gazed into the sky. The stars twinkled at them.

"But you have to let it go, Fred."

"G&C? I told you yes. I'm going to ask Junior—"

She clutched his hand and spoke to his profile. "I'm talkin' 'bout the hate. We can remember . . . we *have to* remember what once was to see how far we've come and to motivate us to keep goin'. When Moses and Joshua and even Peter spoke to the people, they pointed to the past to remind them of God's power and faithfulness, not of Pharaoh's evil. They wanted to encourage Israel, not incite them to exact vengeance. We can't hold on to the pain. Not if we're gonna heal and do better."

He turned away from the stars and scooted back to face her. "What about you, Etta? Are you still holding on to the pain?"

She smoothed the small curls on the back of his head. "Don't worry, Fred. I'm not tryin' to resurrect old hurts between us. We have plenty to look forward to—good and bad—in the days ahead. God willin'. Speakin' of, you take care of that piano like I told you?"

"I couldn't bring myself to do it. But I have to tell you,

your garden didn't make it." He moved to squeeze in close beside her on the porch. When she unwrapped the blanket to drape it around both of them, he took the end and stuffed it under his left leg and her right.

Paulette snuggled in close to his side and stared into the yard. "We all knew its days were numbered the moment I planted it. I see you brought me something to make up for it."

"Consider it my birthday gift to you. Kim helped me put it all together."

"Oh . . . is that the day I walked in on your big affair?" She pinched him lightly.

"Not funny, Mrs. Baldwin. You're looking at Hickory Grove's version of the big chair. It might not look like the world's largest Duncan Phyfe model in Thomasville, but I think it's much better."

She ran her thumb around his jawline. He kissed it. "Well, I heard that Lyndon B. Johnson sat in that chair, as well as governors and beauty queens. How can that little ol' thing over there compete with that?"

"For one thing, I used wood from one of the maple trees Papa grew in this very dirt." He laughed at her surprise. "That chair is the real deal, not some tourist attraction people use for photo ops. It's not too big or too small, and it'll make for a great Christmas picture, especially once we get the seat finished. Nobody's going to have to help you clamber up into it, and it will hold both of us perfectly if you let me hold you. It's the first member of my kitchen furniture, part of the Etta Collection."

"Oh, is that right? Kitchen furniture, huh. Just what a chef like me needs." Her tone was wry.

"It's exactly what you need. That chair is going to grace our kitchen. And even when I'm not sitting in it with you, you can watch me working at that not-so-fancy stove of ours."

Gingerly, Fred lifted her injured arm and slipped her wedding rings on her third finger as far as they would go. His hand grazed her breast as he drew her in closer and nuzzled her hair. "What good is the past if we can't take everything we've learned from it and build something beautiful and long-lasting, Etta?"

She kissed the bridge of his nose. "You do have a way with woods, Frederick Baldwin."

Discover more great fiction by Robin W. Pearson

Chapter One

"YOU KNOW TROUBLE AIN'T CATCHIN'." Ruby Tagle's dark eyes flicked in her granddaughter's direction. "Nobody's gon' sneeze and give it to you or your Theodore."

"Did you hear your grandmother, Maxine?" Vivienne Owens stood on her toes and stretched to retrieve a small jar from the kitchen cabinet. It skittered away to the far end of the shelf.

"Yes, ma'am, I heard Mama Ruby, but I never said I thought trouble was contagious." Maxine smiled a little as she hopped down from the stool. She reached up and set the glass container on the counter. At five-six, Maxine had her mother by three inches, by her estimation, the only way she outmatched her.

"Yes, Vivienne, the girl never said she thought trouble was contagious." Roy Tagle opened the pimientos with a *pop!* and handed them to his sister.

Mother arched an eyebrow at her younger brother. "I don't need none of y'all to tell me what she said. My ears are workin' just fine. You see, I listen like a mama, not an uncle." She spooned sweet peppers into the bowl in front of her. "Now, Maxine, you've been havin' these crazy dreams for weeks now, ever since you set that appointment with Theodore's pastor. You just need to sit down somewhere."

In other words, calm down.

But Maxine couldn't calm down. She'd met Theodore in September, right after he'd relocated from New Orleans to Mount Laurel. Only God's hand could've directed him to that North Carolina crossroads of Eastern and Lexington-style barbecue. He proposed on a chilly December night at the end of a cooking class led by Manna, the Tagles' catering company. As Ruby pulled out the mini chocolate soufflé with a joyful "Voilà!" that sounded more like deep South than South of France, Teddy had dropped to one knee, to no one's shock but Maxine's. He'd toasted her with a crystal flute filled with semisweet chocolate topped off with a one-carat diamond. Now, six weeks later, sporting her emerald-cut ring, she was in her mother's kitchen, dizzy from her whirlwind romance and its effect on her life, a life it had taken her thirteen years to rebuild and only a *yes* to blast to smithereens. Again.

"It's not that simple, Mother. I can't just tell my heart to obey and expect it to fall into line."

"But you can control that mind of yours. Think on the truth, and stop runnin' around here like Chicken Little. The sky isn't fallin' on you just because your friends separated. What happened to them isn't gonna happen to you and Theodore. Isn't that right?" Vivienne looked to Mama Ruby as she stirred the potato salad, using one pink-gloved hand to hold on to the bowl.

Ruby nodded.

"I didn't say it was, Mother." To mask the shiver snaking through her, Maxine moved her shoulders to the gospel beat of the Jackson Southernaires, crooning from the Bluetooth speaker. She wished she could blame her chill on the clouds cloaking the pale-blue sky, but she knew it had nothing to do with the twenty-degree temperatures, unusual for North Carolina. The three women had been going back and forth for over an hour, since Maxine had shown up on her mother's doorstep holding her box of silk chrysanthemums.

"The thought breaks my heart, that Evelyn didn't talk to me about what she was going through. I thought she was spending the summer helping her grandmother, not running away from her husband."

Mother's spoon clanked against the side of the bowl. "Then I take it you've told her all about what *you're* going through."

Maxine swallowed a lump in her throat that felt the size of Pilot Mountain and stepped a little closer to the flames flickering brightly in the fireplace behind her. She fiddled with the ribs of her gray corduroy skirt. "I'm only saying I can imagine what Evelyn went through. Pregnant, her heart in broken pieces. Trying to avoid the whispers, pointing fingers, the dissection of her problems, the gossip from church folk. Did you know she's having a little girl?"

Though they weren't blood kin, Maxine and Evelyn Lester had considered each other family since middle school, after Evelyn had shown up at the Tagles' farm looking to buy butter beans more than half their lifetimes ago. Thing was, Evelyn's grandmother had dispatched her there with an empty bushel basket but without two nickels to rub together. Ruby simply pointed Evelyn to a spot on the porch beside her own granddaughter, and Maxine and Evelyn bonded as they shelled butter beans for the next few hours. Maxine already called herself "Auntie" to the baby Evelyn carried.

Her mother frowned and shook her head, dislodging a strand from her silver-streaked bun. "Is that what this is about? *Her* baby girl?" She aimed a gloved finger at her daughter. "If so, you need to keep in mind that it didn't have anything to do with you. Baby or no baby. Besides, her marriage is fine now. Just fine. What I'm asking myself is how you two can know so little about each other, considerin' you're best friends and all."

Vivienne returned her attention to the bowl, but Maxine figured her mother's murmuring had little to do with the potato salad.

The chair creaked as Mama Ruby propped an ample hip on the stool Maxine had abandoned. "Goodness gracious, Maxine Amelia, you don't know your end from your beginnin'. You ain't even married yet. You might not think trouble is catchin', but you're already signin' yourself up for divorce care and your weddin' is months away." Her grandma pointed to the wireless speaker. "And, Roy, turn down that music. Cain't even hear my own thoughts let alone help this child here with hers."

Uncle Roy obeyed.

Mother scooped out a teaspoonful of the creamy mixture and turned to Maxine. "Here, taste this for me. What does it need?"

"Mmm. Nothing."

Her mother nodded in response and sprinkled kosher salt over the bowl and swirled it around with her mixing spoon. She used a fresh spoon to offer Uncle Roy a sample. When he nodded, Mother finished off the potato salad with paprika and covered the sixteen-inch melamine bowl with plastic wrap.

Maxine pursed her lips and stifled a sigh, wondering why her mother made such a show of asking her opinion. "Like I said, it's just sad. For them, not me. I'm too nervous about starting a marriage to fret over ending one."

"That's because you have some sense. Getting married is nothing to sniff at." Uncle Roy squeezed Maxine's shoulder. "Viv, I'll take that to the pantry fridge and start moving the rest to the truck." He hefted the pumpkin-colored dish to shoulder level and left the room.

Mama Ruby wrapped an arm around Maxine. "First things first, don't listen to your uncle. He hasn't met the right woman yet who makes him want to set another place at the table. And next, don't let your mind play tricks on you, awake or asleep. Their problems are not your problems. Stop thinkin' of this pastor as a one-man judge and jury. From what I hear, Atwater is good people."

Her grandma was squishy in all the right places. Accepting the comfort of her embrace and her words, Maxine planted a quick kiss between the wrinkles on her velvety cheek. Then she opened the long, rectangular box on the quartz countertop and lifted out one flower after another, setting the counter ablaze with purple, cranberry, and orange blooms.

But she didn't miss Mother rolling her eyes heavenward.

Mama Ruby must not have missed it either, for she chuckled and pointed at her daughter. "Amen, Vivienne! This child here needs to look to the hills and trust God's authority and care, not just her husband's—" she spared Maxine a side eye—"that is, her *future* husband. Trusting Him has kept me and Lerenzo married. And it keeps Manna in business."

That's easy to say when y'all run your catering business while holding hands. I'm just trying to keep a fiancé. Maxine snipped the stems and leaves and arranged the artificial flowers in the olive cut-glass vase. "All I know is, these seven sessions with the pastor are going to feel like a long, drawn-out game of *Truth or Consequences.*"

Mother huffed as she scrubbed her work space. "Maxine, you can't be nobody but yourself. Everybody else is taken. Focus on your Theodore and the life you're planning with him. Guilt is the rust on the sword, let me tell you. It's been thirteen years, and you need to be done with all this."

Done with all this. Really Maxine didn't think she'd ever be done with "this," the burden she'd been toting around half her life. It had grown heavier since adding the weight of her engagement ring. Sunlight danced through the picture window overlooking the backyard, and she tilted her face toward it, hoping the warmth would seep through her skin and fill the cracks only she knew existed. But still, her finger shook as she twirled a cinnamon ringlet and looped it around an earlobe. Thirteen years had passed, but it felt like yesterday.

"I don't know what you're tuckin' in your heart's back pocket, but I should tell you John and I talked about it." Mother squinted at Maxine before she shrugged as if giving up. She strode from the sun-splashed kitchen, throwing over her shoulder, "I know you're thirty years old, and you don't need his permission, but you have your daddy's blessing, whatever you decide, whenever you decide."

A Note from the Author

MARK TWAIN said, "Truth is stranger than fiction," which is why I planted seeds of truth all along the road leading to the fictional town of Hickory Grove, North Carolina. My husband and our children, our parents, *their* parents, and so on have paved the way for this novel, and my characters get to "walk out" their very real stories of love and loss. While current events and our not-so-distant past could make us bitter, I believe our faith in the one true God should make us all better.

Acknowledgments

LIKE LOVE, gratefulness is a many-splendored thing. To God be all the glory, praise, and honor.

Recently, a young*er* mom stood surrounded by all her little people, nine years old and younger, and she asked Hubby, "What age do you think is harder—little ones or teens?"

"Neither," he responded promptly.

I know what—or rather, *who*—he was picturing: our adult "children."

Actually, when you're trying to do it right and righteously, all ages are hard to parent, especially those "children" who've technically outgrown that title. That's true whether you're raising one or one hundred and one. With little ones, you can declare, "So let it be written. So let it be done," at will, like Rameses in *The Ten Commandments*. (That's probably my favorite line, honestly.) But then your peeps grow up, and you do, too.

So this is my heartfelt, appreciative hug for you, the real-life Paulettes, Fredericks, and even McKinleys—family members trying to navigate that difficult world of loving and leaving while still holding on. My two sets of parents set the bar. Between them, they represent more than one hundred years of marriage and decades of parenting as they reared Eddie and me along with our dear sisters, Atondra, Starlyn, and Carla. Every day our parents show us what "in sickness and in health" and "'til death do us part" really mean. Of course, I'm forever grateful for our seven heartbeats, Nicholas, Katherine, Benjamin, Faith, Hillary Grace, Hallie, and August, who keep threatening to fly the coop—or to never leave. (I'm not sure which would be harder.) You've walked alongside me and even carried me from time to time, which isn't the easiest thing to do because I'm as stubborn as Fred, as nosy as Etta, and I've gained a few pounds in quarantine. Thank you for serving as my resources and early readers and for not destroying the house when I ignored you in those last, hairy weeks when I typed nonstop.

And speaking of resources . . . thank you, Christie Dragan, for loving this story from the beginning, for plopping yourself right there in the midst of the Baldwins and seeing your face in their family portrait. Where would I be without your eagle eye and your tasty compliment sandwiches? One day soon, we'll have to make time for another sleepover and eat heavenly cake and spanakopita in our matching red pajamas. Belinda Bullard and Andria Gaskins, my character Paulette didn't get your green thumb or your cooking skills, but she did get a pair of do-or-die friends because of you and your unique way of telling it like it is. Christie Benton, Liz Barnes, and Deb Brown, your prayers got me through many a sleepless night. Jamie Collins, your expertise gave me the wherewithal to put Thomasville on the map for my readers. It was a hoot building my story around my love of furniture.

Yet there'd be no furniture-designing Baldwins without people like Cynthia Ruchti, who's a wealth of wit and wisdom. Her "heartfelt counsel . . . is as sweet as perfume and incense" (Proverbs 27:9). The warm welcome of Tyndale's Karen Watson, Jan Stob, Elizabeth Jackson, Isabella Graunke, Wendie Connors, and my other extended publishing family can teach Southerners a thing or two about hospitality. My editor, Kathy Olson, gently yet expertly shaped this story and made it fit for sharing with the world. Lindsey Bergsma, you turned what I wasn't sure I wanted in a cover into everything the Baldwins and I could ask for. To writers like Beth K. Vogt, Lisa R. Howeler, and Jayna Breigh and enthusiastic readers such as Patrice Doten and Micheal James, who inspire me to keep at this calling, I offer a heartfelt thank-you.

First, last, and most of all, thank You, God. As one of my favorite characters, Granny B, might say, "This book liked ta killed me." It took nearly everything I had to write it, from the title to the author's note and everything in between. But the Lord did a great thing: He said He would finish the work He began, and He fulfills that promise every day, when I don't see the how or the what. The why and the who are always clear: to shed some light on our relationships, stories, and history—some bitter, some sweet—and glorify my Father in heaven. That is my constant prayer. Blessings!

About the Author

AWARD-WINNING AUTHOR Robin W. Pearson's writing sprouts from her Southern roots. While sitting in her grandmothers' kitchens, she learned what happens if you sweep someone's feet, how to make corn bread taste like pound cake, and the all-purpose uses of Vaseline. She also learned about the power of God and how His grace led her grandmothers to care for their large families after their husbands were long gone, a grace that has endured through the generations. Robin's family's faith and superstitions, life lessons, and life's longings inspired her to write about God's love for us and how this love affects our relationships with others. In her Christy Award–winning debut novel, *A Long Time Comin'*, Robin weaves a family drama rich in Southern flavor that a starred review from *Publishers Weekly* called "enjoyable and uncomfortable, but also funny and persistent in the way that only family can be." Her second novel, *'Til I Want No More*, also earned a starred review from *Publishers Weekly*, which said, "Pearson's excellent characters and plotting capture the complexity and beauty of family, the difficulty of rectifying mistakes, and the healing that comes from honesty."

While her family history gave her the stories to tell, her professional experiences gave her the skills to tell them effectively. Armed with her degree from Wake Forest University, she has corrected grammar up and down the East Coast in her career as an editor and writer that started with Houghton Mifflin Company more than twenty-five years ago. Since then she has freelanced with magazines, parenting journals, textbooks, and homeschooling resources.

At the heart of it all abides her love of God and the family He's given her. It's her focus as a wife and homeschooling mother of seven. It's what she writes about on her blog, *Mommy, Concentrated*, where she shares her adventures in faith, family, and freelancing. And it's the source and subject of her fiction—in her novels, in the new characters currently living and breathing on her computer screen, and in the stories waiting to be told about her belief in Jesus Christ and the experiences at her own kitchen sink.

Follow Robin at robinwpearson.com.

Discussion Questions

1. Paulette tells Fred that only God knows what we need to hold on to and what we should set free. What are each of the characters holding on to? How successful are they at letting go? Is there anything in your life you're holding on to or something you've been able to let go of?

2. McKinley feels that even though his parents "knew him first," they don't "know him best." Can you relate to this sentiment? What factors might play into parents not knowing their children best? Who knows you best?

3. You may be familiar with Proverbs 27:17: "As iron sharpens iron, so a friend sharpens a friend." How does this play out in Paulette's friendship with Andria and Belinda? How about McKinley and Monroe?

4. Fred struggles to reconcile the injustice his grandfather experienced with his own present reality. What kind of emotional or spiritual legacy did you receive from your parents or grandparents? What parts of it do you want to pass on, and what parts do you want to change?

5. Paulette accuses Fred of choosing his past over her, focusing on his need for revenge rather than on their life together. How is your past controlling you in ways that aren't healthy?

6. Fred wants to honor both his family of origin and the family he is building with his wife. What makes this hard for him?

7. Julia's husband is the only person in the book who somehow sees the good in her, despite her prickly exterior. Is this an accurate representation of the idea that love is blind? Have you seen this dynamic in anyone you know? What are its benefits and drawbacks?

8. Paulette and Fred each accuse the other of not making their marriage the priority it should have been—and eventually they realize they're both guilty of this. Why is it easier to see our weaknesses reflected in someone else than to see them in ourselves?

9. The Baldwin family's church, like many, struggles to find the right balance between welcoming new people and new styles of worship and holding on to beloved

traditions. Should a church change and adapt to fit the times? Why or why not? What's important to you when it comes to choosing a church? Do you prefer a more traditional service or a contemporary one?

10. Paulette tells her son, "Every marriage waxes and wanes, McKinley. Your dad's and mine, it's no different." Is there truth in this? Have you seen evidence in your own marriage or in relationships you've observed? What are some of the high and low seasons of a marriage?

11. Paulette wonders what a parent's relationship with an adult child is supposed to feel like. How did your relationship with your parents change when you became an adult? Are the changes good or bad or some of each?

12. After Paulette's accident, Fred finally speaks up for himself and his family to his aunt. Is it too little, too late? Or is it never too late to start to be more honest in our relationships?

13. The story touches on interracial marriage, which was illegal in many parts of the US until the 1967 Supreme Court case *Loving v. Virginia*. Paulette observes, "I've learned you can't legislate love or forgiveness. . . . I remember the stares I got when I walked beside my dad, and his skin was lighter than yours. People whisperin' and wonderin' how I came to be." In what ways have things improved since Paulette's childhood in the 1960s? What more still needs to change?

14. What had to die in the Baldwins' lives so their marriage
    and family could live? Consider your own thoughts,
    attitudes, and ways of communication. Is there
    anything old that needs to be renewed by the Holy
    Spirit? (See Ephesians 4:22-24.)

TYNDALE HOUSE PUBLISHERS IS CRAZY4FICTION!

Fiction that entertains and inspires

Get to know us! Become a member of the Crazy4Fiction community. Whether you read our blog, like us on Facebook, follow us on Twitter, or receive our e-newsletter, you're sure to get the latest news on the best in Christian fiction. You might even win something along the way!

JOIN IN THE FUN TODAY.

 crazy4fiction.com

 Crazy4Fiction

 crazy4fiction

 @Crazy4Fiction

CP0021

By purchasing this book from Tyndale, you have

helped us meet the spiritual and physical needs of

people all around the world.

Tyndale | Trusted. For Life.

CP1704